Dryad

The Narun – Book One

G. M. Worboys

Published by G. M. Worboys
Website: gmworboys.com

Print Edition 1.1 (January-2014)
First published Nov-2012

ISBN 978-0-9874583-0-8

Cover image and design by G. M. Worboys

For my Mum and Dad. I would have loved to be able to show this to you.

"You have shown me a strange image, and they are strange prisoners."

Glaucon to Socrates, Book VII of The Republic by Plato (translated by Benjamin Jowett).

Contents

Prologue

Last Weekend

The sunlight shone through their hair in blond halos and their laughter sparkled through the air with the sound of pure joy. He took a deep breath. The breeze blowing lightly off the lake was fresh and clean and just slightly cool, a refreshing contrast to the warmth of the sun. He wished he could somehow preserve this perfect moment.

"Dad!"

John blinked and realised that his daughter was looking at him. She was sitting on her mother's knee, leaning back against her, and watching him with wide enthusiasm. He smiled back. "Yes, beautiful?"

"Why are you staring at us?"

"Look around you, Ellie. There is no more beautiful sight to be had anywhere in the world. I would be a fool to be looking anywhere else but at the two of you."

Ellie stared at him for a few moments, then her eyes flickered to the side. She shook her head, but grinned and chuckled, as if answering some unheard question.

"What did Asha say to you?" John heard Samantha ask. He wished she wouldn't encourage their daughter in her imaginary friend, he didn't think it could be good for Ellie.

"She said Dad was sweet."

"And you shook your head?" John queried in mock horror. He started to crawl forward on his hands and knees.

Ellie squealed in delight and laughed loudly. "You're not sweet,

Dad, you're silly!"

"We need an adjudicator," John complained. He was now sitting up against his wife and daughter on the grass. He reached forward and brushed Ellie's hair back from her face, she pretended to push him away. John moved his hand up to Samantha's hair and brushed it lightly away from her neck and the side of her face, then he leaned in and kissed her warm lips. "What does our adjudicator say?" he asked softly.

Ellie pushed at his chest. "No fair," she told him. There was a pause and then she said, "Asha says you're inf-" she paused again, "in-flu-enc-ing ... the judge." It really did sound like someone was giving her lessons. Maybe they were letting her watch too much television.

John sat back and tried to look serious. "You're right. We must let the judge remain impartial. What do you say, Your Honour," he asked Samantha, "am I silly or sweet?"

Samantha put on a serious expression, she had trouble holding it, and looked back and forth between John and Ellie. Finally she declared, "I find the defendant guilty of being sssss – both!"

"Mum!" Ellie cried and hit Samantha gently on the arm. "That's cheating."

"I agree," joined in John. "I demand a retrial. Unfair I say, unfair."

Ellie stopped and stared at her father, as if puzzled by the idea that he should be complaining about her mother's declaration. Finally she said, "You can be silly *and* sweet." She said this cautiously, trying out the idea.

John nodded. "You're right, I could be."

"Not only could be," Samantha put in, "but you have been found guilty already. It only remains to pass sentence. What does the court say?" she asked of Ellie.

Ellie considered this seriously.

"Please ma'am," John asked of his daughter, "don't make the sentence too hard on this old man, I have a wife and daughter to fend for."

Ellie laughed at him and pushed him back as he leaned in toward her. She looked to the side and then back at John and her mother, the smile widening on her face. She reached up, and Samantha lowered her head so that Ellie could whisper in her ear.

Samantha smiled back at her daughter and then tried, again with limited success, to put a serious expression on her face. "The court has spoken."

"Oh no, Your Honour," John wailed softly and grovelled on the grass in front of them. Ellie laughed loudly.

"The court has spoken," Samantha repeated. "You are hereby sentenced to life—"

"Oh no," John wailed again. "Woe is me. Please be merciful."

Ellie continued to laugh at his antics.

Samantha finished, "to a lifetime of being silly and sweet to your wife and daughter."

John sat up quickly. "You mean more of this?"

Ellie nodded.

Samantha looked at her watch. "In another half-an-hour you are to be taken from this lake to commence your sentence."

"Can't I start now?" John asked.

Ellie's laughter rang out, and the sound was music to John's ears.

Seeing

1. Grief

John had wandered the house for days, he'd lost count of how many. He hadn't eaten since Ellie's funeral. He drank water from the shower when he took another, scalding hot, to try and drive away the empty cold that was gnawing at his soul. The daze of days progressed with little to interrupt his misery. Some unknown time ago the telephone had rung, trying to intrude on his desolation, it now lay in pieces below a gash in the wall where he'd smashed it.

At random intervals, like shuffling down the unlit hallway on this rainy winter night, the pain would come crashing down with renewed vehemence in sudden, overwhelming surges. Heavy, rolling waves that smashed through his being, that drove him to the ground and opened the hole deep inside his chest. A void that tried to suck the last of his self into oblivion ... but oblivion refused to come. There was only the pain.

Another wave of grief hit and his body curled up even more tightly on the cold floor. His mind writhed, trying to find some way to cope with the impossible devastation. He sucked a gasping, desperate breath of air down past the void, a breath that enabled him to give voice to his suffering. An inhuman howl escaped his throat and fought out against the roar of the heavy rainstorm that was pounding against the house. There were no words to express his grief, just this raw sound. And again, the fight for a breath and the release. And again.

Beyond all reason the pain intensified further, he felt sure his bones would break under the pressure. So much pain his mind could barely remember its cause. The pain and grief had become their own entity, feeding on him and on themselves. Lights flickered behind his eyes, and a raw deafening noise rose inside his head, a noise that surpassed even the thunder, an ever rising crescendo.

There was a wrenching sensation as something gave way. He felt, and thought he heard, a tearing and then a final resonating crunch. Physical pain joined his emotional torment. His arms raised up from his chest and wrapped themselves around his head where he imagined he could feel a large open wound gaping inside.

Something did break. Deep within his mind something gave way and his senses reeled. Sounds, scents and touch sensations bombarded his mind and left him gasping, dizzy and confused. Images flashed before his eyes – their faces staring back at him – and then everything went blank as he lost consciousness.

He was aware again. He sensed that time had passed but had no idea how much. The sound of the rain had gone, even the light had changed. The clouds had dispersed and bright moonlight flooded the hallway from a window above the front door. He could feel a strange new sensation, very much like physical cold, in the centre of his head. It was as if someone had dropped an ice-block inside his brain. It had that odd intensity where it becomes difficult to be certain whether it was very hot or very cold.

His mind was almost clear for the first time in days. He could feel the wooden floor, hard and cold against his side. His body was still in a tight foetal curl, still expecting the next wave of pain.

"Will he die?" A gentle woman's voice spoke from nearby.

"Probably not," answered another woman, this one sounding older, caring but less gentle.

"He's quiet again now, the keening has stopped. It's been days. Surely he can't survive much more."

"His body will probably rebel soon and force him to take better care – or his mind will break. There is nothing we can do, even if we wanted."

He listened to these voices. They were speaking as though they believed he could not hear them. He wondered if he cared enough to lift his head and find out who they were, and decided that he didn't. He should have been alone in the house, but if some busy-bodies wanted to watch his grief they could help themselves.

More time passed. The pain was still there, the void was still there, but he could feel that he was no longer incapacitated, not for the moment. The muscles of his back and shoulders complained as he slowly relaxed out of the foetal curl. He pushed himself into a sitting position. Leaning on one arm, he peered curiously along the moonlit hallway toward the stairs where he had heard the voices.

"He's looking at us," said the gentle voice. A slender young woman, perhaps just a girl from her small size, was sitting on the lower steps looking at him.

"He cannot see us." A woman, older in appearance but still very small, glanced at him and then watched the girl beside her. Her eyes softened with concern. "Don't get involved. It serves no good purpose to try and care for these creatures."

"Wh ..." he tried to speak but his throat was dry and very sore. He reached out towards the women on the stairs. The girl gasped and grabbed at her companion's hand.

"It's all right. Coincidence. He can't really see us," said the older woman, although she sounded less certain now.

He looked down at himself, trying to make sense of what he was hearing from these women. His body was shaking. Staring down at the floor he slowly pushed himself up until he was standing. Swaying, he put one hand against the wall to hold himself still. If the women wanted to ignore him ... that suited him just fine.

He made his way unsteadily to the kitchen and poured himself a glass of water from the tap. It soothed his throat enough that he was able to try and speak again.

"Fuck." The swearword came out in a barely audible croak. It was somehow satisfying so he tried a few more.

With that sense of achievement he stumbled to the wall and flicked on the light, blinking in the sudden brightness. Remembering the women in the hallway, he flicked on that light too and peered back toward the steps. There was no one there. He went to the back door, turned on the outside floodlights, and looked out. No one. Just the untidy lawn, wet and glistening after the rain, and then the huge trees of the forest in which the house was ensconced; their long, pale trunks stretched so far that their distant branches appeared to grasp at the moon.

He could still feel that cold place in the centre of his head. He remembered the earlier sensation of something in his head breaking, as if something in his mind had given way to the pressure. Maybe he had cracked. There must be some reason why they use that word. That was certainly what it had felt like, and now he could feel a cold breeze blowing in through the cracks. He laughed to himself, now he was not just hearing voices but seeing the vocalists. He found himself undisturbed by the idea.

"If that's the case, there's nothing to be lost in getting a wee bit drunk."

In the kitchen, in a high cupboard, he found an almost full bottle of whisky and sat down at the table to drink it. Anyone looking at him would think he had been drinking for days, but he had not touched a drop – until now. There was an empty drinking glass already on the table, he couldn't remember what he'd used it for. He reached for it and filled it with whiskey. The first few mouthfuls were very painful against his tortured throat, but such pain meant little to him and soon the glass was empty.

He was not used to drinking much at a time, with that and no food for days, the straight whiskey hit him hard. He had swallowed the second glass full before the first had time to register, but much of the third was spilled as his coordination left him. Some urge to move made him try to stand, but he tripped over his own chair and fell to the floor. The glass and whiskey bottle followed him to the hard tiles with a crash that he did not hear.

* * *

Someone was banging. Banging! John groaned. He heard a voice calling but didn't register what it said. He groaned again and tried to move. His face came away from the cold tiles of the floor with a sucking sound. He was on his kitchen floor, almost stuck to it by his own vomit, now drying cold and sticky. He was shivering with the cold.

He put his hand down to try and push himself up, and swore as a flash of pain spiked into his palm. He could see that his hand was pressing on broken glass, blood was spilling from the wound, but it still took him long moments to react.

With exaggerated care he avoided more of the broken glass and pushed himself to his feet. It was then that he heard the back door open and a voice calling to him, "John?" It was his friend Jason Manton.

"H..." John tried to call, but his voice was stuck too.

Jason came to the door of the kitchen and stared in with horror. The table was askew, a chair was turned over, and vomit and spilt whiskey splashed the floor and made the air foetid. John was stooped over, visibly shaking, his dark hair pointing every which way. All this was bad enough, but standing out from the rest was the bright blood, wet and shining on the front of John's shirt, all down his right arm, and dripping into a pool on the floor.

"What have you done?" Jason asked. He started to walk forward but John held up his hand to stop him. John saw that it was dripping blood and put it down. He held up his left hand instead.

"Watch out ..." John managed to croak, and pointed to the broken glass on the floor. He stepped around the most obvious shards of glass and went to the sink. He did his best to wash his face and hands, and drank a few mouthfuls of water from the tap. As he did he realised the import of Jason's question.

"It's okay. I cut my hand on glass just now, that's all. It's not ... you know, slit wrists or anything." John's voice was not much more than a creaky whisper.

Jason backed out into the hall, holding his arm over the lower part of his face and breathing through his shirt sleeve. The smell of vomit was not something he coped with very well, especially such a short time after breakfast.

"Sit outside for a few minutes, Jason. I'll be there shortly."

Not about to argue, Jason escaped out the back door to the fresh air.

John did what he could to clean-up quickly, had a brief shower, slapped some plasters on the cut on his palm, and then made coffee. With two large mugs in hand, he took a deep breath and walked out to Jason, pretending that he cared whether the world still existed.

"Sorry Jason, you really shouldn't have had to see all that." John handed Jason his coffee and then sat on the other wooden bench of the garden-setting.

"John ..." Jason tried, but couldn't find the words. "You look like shit!" he finally managed.

"Well *sorry*, but if you'd waited at the front door like any normal visitor I could have had that cleaned up," John said.

"I don't mean that," Jason said, nodding at the house. "I mean *this.*" He gestured at John like something the dog had left on the floor. "You're pale and so thin I almost didn't recognise you. You have great black bags under your very red eyes, and your phone has been off the hook for a week."

John mumbled something about it being broken, not off the hook.

"Look, John, I know this has got to be hard. It was bad enough when Samantha died, but now that Ellie is gone too ... I don't know what to say that won't sound trite or pointless or completely and totally inadequate, but ... I look at you and I cringe. You look like you're going to add to the tragedy, and I don't want that. We've been friends for a long time, but I have no idea what to do. ... Do you need a shrink? One of those counselling groups? ... Something?"

John closed his eyes, shaking his head. "There really is nothing," he whispered. The quiet of the forest setting allowed Jason to hear the words, and the layers of meaning beneath them.

John and Jason were good friends, but they had never developed the sort of intimacy that could have prepared them for this situation. Jason was trying his best, but John couldn't bring himself to care.

"I also dropped by to ask you over to dinner one night this coming week," Jason said later, as John walked him to the car. "Any night you like, just give us a call earlier in the day. I think Liz wants to make sure you're eating okay, and by the look of you she was right to worry."

"Thanks. I'll call you," John replied in a non-committal tone.

Jason looked at John over the car, his face full of concern. "Do call. You can't lock yourself away here. Come out and see that there are still people that care about you, John."

John just nodded.

After Jason left, John went back to sit at the garden-setting behind the house and stared into the forest. There seemed no reason to do anything but sit there.

A while later he sat forward in surprise. A woman's face was staring at him from around a tree on the edge of the lawn. He blinked and looked again, but the face was gone. He remembered the young woman from last night. He tried to remember if he had seen her before or after he got drunk. Before. That wasn't really a good thing though, was it?

It was the following Friday that John made his first visit to the Manton household since he had lost his family. Another depressing first in a world that was full of them. John remembered when he and Samantha had started counting happy firsts as a married couple: their first trip to the beach, their first dinner guests, their first motel room.

John took a deep breath and opened the car door. He got out of the car just as Jason opened the front door of his house. A black and white bundle of fur squeezed past Jason and raced in a blur down the path to John.

"Badger, you prick of a dog," Jason called, "come back here!"

The border collie leapt up at John enthusiastically and then bounded around the car looking for others. John knelt down and grabbed him as he came around the car for his second circuit. "It's just me, Badger," he whispered roughly to the wriggling dog. He got an enthusiastic lick across the face and then the dog was back off up the path to the front door where Jason stood with a worried look on his face.

"Sorry about that," said Jason, as John came up the path.

John just gave him a wry smile and handed over a bottle of wine he'd brought as his contribution to the meal. Badger had always been the main attraction here for Ellie. A house that was otherwise full of adult things and adult conversation that held little interest for her on their once regular visits here. But Badger made up for all, and his enthusiastic greeting had always been one of the highlights.

In the kitchen Liz, a small dark-haired woman, finished drying her hands, came over and looked up at John with sad grey eyes. "I'm glad you came," she said, and then gave him a hug.

John returned the hug, responding a little tentatively.

"Something sure smells good," he said, trying to ease the tension a little.

"It's just a casserole," she replied with a deprecating wave, "I thought something wholesome was best for a man not taking proper care of himself."

Putting on his best Texan drawl, which was not all that good, John responded, "Why thank you ma'am, that sure is considerate of you."

She smiled and patted his arm absently, "You and Jason go and talk work or whatever, dinner will be ready in about half an hour."

"Yes ma'am." He smiled in return.

John and Jason were graphic artists. They worked for an advertising firm belonging to one of Jason's cousins. The company had become quite large, but for reasons of its own continued to operate from the same small town in which it had started, only the premises had grown. Both John and Jason were talented, but it was in working together that they had produced the most impressive results. Jason's enthusiasm and flair, and John's deep concentration and technical expertise, combined to produce results that neither could have managed on their own. As a partnership they had become important to the company, becoming known to most of their colleagues and their clients as *the Js* – no one remembered who started it.

Dinner conversation was stilted to begin with but eventually worked around to experiences in the city when John and Jason had shared house. John was only two years older than Jason, although anyone just meeting them would probably guess closer to five, and tonight maybe ten or more. Most of the stories had been told before, but the familiarity was comfortable, something safe, and a reminder to John that not everything from his past was gone.

As John was leaving Liz handed him some plastic containers, a large meal in each. "Freeze these when you get home," she said, "and you can pull them out when you need them."

John thanked her, and then thanked them both for a good evening and drove off.

Each had dreaded all the things that may have gone wrong this evening, but it had gone well, and so each breathed a sigh of relief. It was a significant milestone passed.

At home that night John offered a prayer, not to any god, but to the memory of Samantha. Through tears he prayed, "I cannot believe the years that still lie ahead of me, the years we should have had together. Please, help me to get through this, Sam."

* * *

It was Monday morning and John was sitting at his desk across the open-plan office from Jason. John tried to concentrate on the work in front of him. The *Js* were known for their talent, but it was talent that John had trouble finding this morning.

He looked down and was surprised at the face staring back up from the paper. It was the young woman from the other night. His absent doodling on the pad had produced her image in greater detail than he'd remembered noticing at the time. Fine but clear and strongly delineated features, long flowing hair reaching past her shoulders. Colours were missing from his pencil rendering, but he remembered those eyes, an unusual pale green, looking at him with a gentle caring expression. He wondered how he could possibly have seen her eyes so clearly in that moonlit hallway. Her expression was not one of pity, and not the self-conscious flinching he saw when he walked past people in the office. This was an expression that said much more than John was willing to hear right now. And this was not the face he wanted to see! He snatched up the page, tore it roughly from the pad, screwed it up and threw it into the bin.

He turned to the window. The office was high enough to look over the other buildings, out over the fields to the beginnings of the mountains and the forest where they lived. They had loved this place. They had agreed that moving here was the best thing they could have done: a good job in a small town, and a beautiful house outside it, immersed in the natural world. They had considered themselves so lucky. He pulled his gaze bitterly back to the blank paper in front of him. Where had their luck gone?

The afternoon was almost gone when John finished the work he'd been given. It may not have been inspired, but he thought it would be adequate. It was still a little early but he packed up and left anyway, without a backward glance at the others in the office. Jason watched him go, the others pretended not to.

John drove out past the lake as usual, eventually turning off the main road onto the gravel road that wound up into the hills and through the forest to their home, just his home now. A few times along the drive he saw movement in the trees, but that was not unusual, there was lots of wildlife around here. It was one of the things they'd loved about their home.

He parked in the garage under one end of the two-storey house, and walked around the back. He sat at the garden-setting rather than going inside. He was waiting. He was sure the pain would come for him again after so many hours away. He could feel it there in his chest: a numbness, a dormant cold and black void. How long until it woke again and the vacuum tried once more to consume him? He could feel it was coming, so he waited.

He could also feel that cold spot in his head, it had not gone. It was something he was always aware of now, but it had ceased to be so distracting, and it was no longer causing the painful headaches that he had experienced for the first few days.

Movement from the forest made him look up in surprise. It was her! She walked slowly toward him through the edge of the forest. The late afternoon sun cast streaks of light and shadow that flickered over and apparently *through* her. She couldn't be real. She cast no shadow of her own and at times John caught glimpses of the forest through her body. Another slow couple of steps onto the lawn and the scene clarified, leaving John uncertain of what he'd just witnessed.

"Hello," he said.

She froze for a few seconds and then looked carefully behind her. When she turned back her expression was wary, her stance changing as if she were preparing to run.

"Who are you?" he asked, wondering if she could hear him properly.

She stepped carefully backwards to the forest edge, her hand reaching back and touching a tree. She seemed to gain comfort and reassurance from its solid trunk. "You can see me?" her soft voice asked, an incredulous half-question half-statement. It was obvious that he had.

John stared at her, uncertain how to reply. It was certainly the young woman from the other night, there was no mistaking that gentle voice despite the additional timbre of fear. He nodded, that seemed a safe response.

"How?" she asked, speaking even more softly in her fear. "You've not seen me before."

John leaned forward on his seat. "You were here the other night, over a week ago. You and another. I saw you then."

"Yes ... yes ... we were here. But you don't see us. You *can't* see us." She stared back at him. "You've never spoken to me before, even before that."

"You've been here before that?" John was surprised. She was not

16

a person you were likely to forget meeting. Her small stature, her incredible, finely built beauty, and those large pale eyes almost glowing in the late afternoon sunlight.

"I live here," she said simply.

John smiled at her. "This is our house. It has been for years now. I'm sure we'd have remembered meeting you before now, it's not that big a place." It had been meant as a joke, but the now inappropriate pronouns brought back his sense of loss and threatened to shake his fragile equilibrium. Her reaction surprised him back to attention.

"My trees were destroyed to clear space for this house!" She was angry now. "It's my home that those machines invaded and vandalised, and my peace they disturbed for the months it took to build this ... this ... this intrusion." She looked about in frustration, obviously wishing she could have found some stronger, more vehement, expression.

She appeared to be larger. To John she now appeared a more usual adult size, matching the obvious maturity of her build and face. She had taken her hand from the tree and walked a few steps toward him. Belatedly realising how bold she had become, she stopped and folded her arms.

"I'm ..." John hesitated, not sure how to finish. "I don't understand. Did your family own this land before the house was built?"

Her eyes flashed and John prepared himself for another onslaught.

"Own? Of course, humans always think they *own* things! You never imagine that it is possible to live in the world without *owning* it." Tears had come. Some mix of sadness, anger and despair came over her, her chest heaving with the passion of her words.

Then she sighed and appeared to shrink slightly. "I'm sorry," she said. "I didn't come here to argue with you. You shouldn't be able to hear me, let alone see me. It's so frustrating to have never been able to communicate with those that destroy our world. To get the chance at last ..." she stopped, unable to find the words.

John felt lost. He gestured to the other bench, "Won't you sit?"

She looked at him, unsure of what to do or say next. Finally she shrugged and moved to the other bench. As she sat down she shrank still further until she was once again the size of a young girl, her legs swinging. She appeared to take some reassurance from the fact that there was a substantial wooden table between them.

At first John just stared at her. He had seen her shrink! He couldn't deny it this time. Realising that he was staring, John moved his gaze down to his hands on the table. He sat there trying to think and the silence stretched between them as the evening got darker.

An explanation occurred to him and his shoulders slumped. He lifted his hands to either side of his head and massaged the areas just above his ears with his finger tips, as if he could somehow reach in and warm that cold spot inside. Finally, still staring down at the table, he said, "Is my mind really so far gone? I guess this is not that much different to thinking I can see Napoleon or believing that I can hear the voice of Jesus. I've always been creative, it only makes sense that my madness should be creative too." Another thought occurred to him and he smiled to himself. "At least I've got taste, Napoleon was never going to win any beauty contests."

"What are you talking about?" she snapped at him. For a figment of his imagination she sure had a short temper.

He looked up and saw that she was still sitting there. He put his hands down and looked at them again and said, "I don't want to be rude or anything ... but little of what you said made much sense to me."

He paused before continuing, "I felt my mind ... break ... I think ... the other night when I first saw you. I don't think ... you can't be ... real ... can you?" He looked up and saw her watching him across the table. He looked back down at his hands, "Well?" he asked.

After some moments she said, "I've just been accused of not existing, of being some *thing* generated by your overactive imagination. I'm not sure there is an appropriate response."

He looked up again and she was smiling at him.

Almost in spite of himself he grinned back at her. "I guess it is pretty silly to ask an imaginary friend if she's real, isn't it?"

Her expression changed, now uncertain or apprehensive.

"What?" he asked.

"Did you know then? About my being Ellie's friend?"

John looked incredulous and then a slow realisation dawned. "So that's where you came from. It's not my imagination at all, it was Ellie's!" He considered this for a bit. "I'm not sure that that makes it any better." He looked up again to see her watching him with a look too much like the pity he saw on the faces of others. "Don't you start! I don't need some figment of my imagination feeling sorry for me too."

More time passed and he realised it was getting dark and he was cold. Despite the dark, his imagination kept the woman clearly visible across the table from him. "I'm going in," he said. He sat forward ready to get up. "Did you want to come inside? Get warm? Have something to eat? Something to drink?" He was not sure of the correct etiquette when talking with imaginary friends, but he figured you couldn't go too far wrong by at least being polite.

She hesitated and then said, "I'll come in and talk with you, if that's okay, but I don't eat or drink, not in the sense you mean."

Ignoring yet another statement that he did not understand, John stood and walked to the door. It refused to let him in until he remembered that he had not unlocked it since coming home. Flicking on the outside floodlights he looked back and it seemed that at first he could see right through her to the garden-setting. He blinked and his vision cleared.

He walked into the kitchen and poured himself a large whiskey. He looked at her standing in the doorway between the kitchen and the hallway and held up the bottle. "You sure?" he asked. She shook her head so he put the bottle away before grabbing a couple of ice cubes to drop in with his ample serving.

"You should be eating more, and not drinking so much," she said.

He gave her a look and then pulled a chair out and sat down. He gestured to the chair nearest her and the hallway. She seemed nervous. She approached the chair and grasped the back awkwardly and with great concentration. The kitchen chairs were a cheap set with vinyl coverings over the back and seat. The chair slid back noisily, as if she had difficulty moving it.

"Some physical interactions can be difficult for my people" she said in explanation.

"Your people," John mused. "Who are your people? For that matter, who are you? Do you have a name?"

"Asha," she said simply.

John nodded, he remembered now, Ellie and her friend Asha.

"My people, we call ourselves aaranya. I guess you would

19

probably translate that to forest-born or tree-folk. We are narun, as in, I am narun and you are human. But asking me to describe the narun would be like asking some small town resident to describe humans. There are many variations, races I guess you could call them.

"Possibly the closest description you would have to a being like myself is a dryad, a tree nymph. Other narun might be considered naiads and nereids. Whatever." She smiled as she continued, "Of course we are not all female. I was told that that was the only aspect your legends were ever interested in. It suggests a certain lack of awareness of the world, don't you think?"

"So you live in a tree?" John asked, grasping the first part that he could understand, unable to keep the cynicism from his voice.

"Not in the sense you seem to mean, and not in a single tree." She made a face, not happy with how this was going but unsure how to make it clear.

"I am not a material being. I do exist, just not in the same way that you do. Our bodies are not made of flesh and bone like yours. Our bodies are made of prana." Seeing the blank expression on John's face she elaborated, "Prana is the life-force – the breath of life. Prana is not the soul, that is a spiritual thing. Prana is of the physical world, just not in the same solid material sense as your body."

Asha paused, trying to work out whether she was making sense. Wondering how to describe her own existence and the life of her people in terms that a human could understand. Wondering whether there was any point in trying.

"All living things are infused with prana, it is what gives them life. Your own human body is really two bodies sharing the same space: a praanin body laid over and through your flesh-and-blood body – the two work together, one reliant on the other. Narun are simply a different form of life, one that is made of only prana, needing no other material existence. If the real you, your praanin body, were able to step out from your physical body you would seem to be much like us." She pulled a face as if there were unpleasant associations with that thought. Asha looked at John's expression and decided she had said enough about prana.

"Our bodies are not fixed in form or size. I can merge with the

20

essence, the prana, of a living tree and I can become part of the tree for a time. That is how my people, the aaranya, live in the forest. The trees are our home, the meaning and purpose of our lives." She sighed. She could tell from the expression on his face that John was still not accepting this, he was trying to be politely attentive, but that was all.

"Look," she said, exasperated. "I came to see if you were managing. You were in trouble for a while and I was concerned. My time with Ellie was very special, and through her I came to care for you too, that's all. I just wanted to make sure you were going to be okay."

There was a pause before she continued very quietly, "I miss Ellie too."

Before John realised what was happening she got up and left. He walked quickly to the still open back door and looked out, but she was gone.

2. Time

For several afternoons after work John sat at the back of his house, staring into the forest wondering if Asha would appear again. Days passed and he saw no more of her.

Neither the library nor the Internet were much help. The Greek myths, and the paintings and statuary of dryads and nymphs, all depicted naked – or almost naked – nubile young women. John had no idea how old she might be, but she had definitely not been naked, he would have remembered that.

On Saturday morning it occurred to him to discover what Ellie had left concerning her friend Asha. Closed up since he had slammed the door on his return from the hospital, Ellie's room had a stale musty smell, but beneath that it was Ellie. The familiar toys on and around her bed, her favourite images on the wall, her favourite books waiting on the shelves. Overwhelmed he backed out of the room and closed the door, all thoughts of Asha and trees had gone.

Over the next few weeks John immersed himself in work and while at home he steeled himself to the task of packing away the signs that a family still lived there. First he attacked the attic, that stuff was probably on its way to the tip anyway. Then the living areas, somehow none of it was so important nor personal any more. His dreams were filled with the faces of his family, his nightmares with their deaths.

There was a lapse of another week where time at home was spent drunk and trying hard not to think about what was missing from his life. Again it was Jason that drew him back into the world. John was not ready yet to accept that life went on, but it wasn't in his nature to give up.

It must have been two months after Ellie's funeral that Samantha's parents came to visit. Her family never got along with John, they had never approved of the *city kid* that their daughter had chosen to marry. In the last few years their visits with Ellie had started to add some warmth to the relationship, but after Samantha and Ellie's death all that was gone. Their deaths must have been John's fault, there was no one else left to blame.

"Do you mind if I look through her things?" asked Sissy, Samantha's mother. "Perhaps choose a keepsake or two?"

"Sure," said John, "help yourself." And he didn't mind, not really. Samantha had had a good relationship with her mother, as far as John was concerned Sissy could have anything she wanted. Not that she was likely to take much. Even when her husband, Adam, went through things with her, they did not take much away. They were not greedy people.

When they'd first arrived Sissy had been appalled at how much John had packed away. To her it was a betrayal to not have Samantha and Ellie's photos and favourite things on display in every room, as if John needed reminding of what he had lost. He didn't know how to explain that in order to get up and function every day he needed to put away those things that would make him lose himself again, wallowing in the pain of his loss. In the end he didn't even try.

A four day visit proved to be more than enough time for all of them. On the last day of their visit they were having an early lunch, Sissy and Adam would head back to their own country town after they'd eaten.

"Any other houses up this road?" asked Adam.

"Not that I know of. The road degrades into not much more than a track a bit further up, and then wanders off into the forest and fades," John answered. "What, you looking to move here?"

Adam didn't look amused by the jest. "Just wonderin' about that blue van that's been around. It actually came in here at one point, you were upstairs with Sissy, and then it left in a hurry when it realised someone was here."

"Probably just someone gotten lost, happens a lot in summer."

Adam grunted, not impressed. "Just odd, that's all. Don't like odd."

John watched Sissy bring a cold barbecued chicken in from the kitchen. She put it on a plate on the table and started to break it into pieces for lunch. John had the strangest feeling that he could sense something about the carcass, something like a warm breeze blowing through that cold crack in his head.

He got up and went over to take a closer look. There, in the depths of the chest cavity, it felt to John as if it were alive. "Just a minute, Sissy," he said, and slid the plate across in front of him. He broke open the chest cavity, pulled the strongly seasoned stuffing out of the way, and an unpleasant smell rose from the interior.

"Erk, that's not good," came the response from Sissy. "That shop must have had this one sitting around for a while before we got there." She grabbed the plate to take it back to the kitchen, and then stopped and looked at John. "How'd you smell that from over there?"

"I didn't smell it, I saw it ... felt it," muttered John, more to himself than to Sissy.

Sissy gave him an odd look and shrugged her shoulders. "Well, that was going to be lunch. There's not much else in the fridge." She called over to Adam, "What's it going to be, peanut butter sandwiches or pick up something on our way?"

After lunch Sissy and Adam insisted on helping to tidy up, and then John saw them out to their car. From inside the car Sissy asked, "You've no family left of your own? No parents, no brothers or sisters?"

"No," answered John, "no one."

Sissy shook her head and gave him a look with more compassion than he'd ever seen from her.

"Well, thanks for the grub," came Adam's voice from behind the wheel, and the car moved off. There were no calls of "see you" or "take care". John thought there was a good chance he'd never see them again.

John thought about Sissy's question as the sound of the car disappeared down the gravel road. As far as he knew he was the last of the line. The only uncle he knew about had died many years ago without ever marrying. His mother had died before he finished high school, and his father was gone before John had finished university.

No, as far as he knew the Caldor name, or at least this particular line of it, ended with himself. Perhaps that was just as well, it wasn't a line that had had much luck.

* * *

After Samantha's parents had gone, John dismantled all the little shrines that Sissy had erected around the house. The following weekend he at last gained the strength to open Samantha's closet and pack up her things. Her clothes went in suitcases and boxes to go to charity. Her jewellery and few personal keep-sakes he wrapped and packed carefully into a sturdy crate that he moved to the attic. He could not bear to part with them, but nor could he bear to keep them where they would remind him that Samantha was not coming back to treasure them. That night he drank very heavily again, passing out in the en-suite bathroom.

A few weeks later the university called and came to reclaim the computer equipment that Samantha had used for her research work. They called again a week after that asking if they could have her research notes and journals. The computer discs meant little to John so he let them go through what was left of Sam's half of the office and take what they wanted. Samantha and John had shared the spare bedroom as an office area, continuing to work together in the same room just as they had at university. With Samantha gone John had taken to working on the kitchen table, unable to achieve anything in the now desolate area he had once shared with Sam.

More weeks passed and Samantha's assets became legally his. When Ellie was born John had started a life insurance policy and Samantha had insisted that she should have one too. The money from that came through and proved to be enough to pay off their small mortgage. He poured himself a large whiskey and one for Samantha too. Paying off the house was an event they should have looked forward to as a family. It should have been a time for celebration. John drank both whiskeys and most of the rest of the bottle. Practice was improving his tolerance and he passed out without throwing up.

Spring arrived and settled in around him. That cold spot in his head was warmer now, as if the breeze blowing through the crack had warmed up with the weather. John found himself more aware of the flowers growing beside the road and in the clearings of the forest near his house. He seemed to feel the burgeoning exhilaration of all the living things around him. He thought there may be a good reason for his hyper-awareness of spring this year. Ellie had been a spring child. The twenty-fifth was her birthday, it fell on a Sunday this year.

On the preceding Friday John was called into his boss's office. "Got an odd request for you, John. You up for a visitor or two on Sunday?" Stan's balding and portly but well dressed figure sat leaning back in his chair behind his large desk, his expression a mix of curiosity and concern.

John stared at him, his head had been full of little else but the coming Sunday and he wondered who else could possibly have remembered that it should have been his daughter's birthday. "I suppose so. I'll be home anyway," he replied, not wanting to commit further until he understood.

"We've got this odd bird flying in from America, one of those rich eccentric types with his fingers in a bit of everything. His secretary didn't or couldn't elaborate on the details, but apparently this Stephenson specifically wants to meet you. Sunday was the only day he could make available in his busy schedule. Do you mind?"

John shrugged. He'd been planning to get very drunk and depressed, not necessarily in that order, he supposed those plans could be delayed until Sunday night. "No, I guess that's okay."

So it was that on Sunday morning he had little time to dwell on his daughter's birthday. He made a rush clean-up in the main areas that he thought the guests may need to see. Stan and Jason were there by eight in the morning, in theory it was to discuss Stephenson and his companies, but in practise there was not much they could talk about, they simply had no idea why he was coming.

An ostentatious black limousine with very dark windows arrived a bit after ten o'clock. The back door opened and a huge man stepped out. At first John thought this tall, thick-set man with sparse red hair may have been a bodyguard, but the man strode boldly across to the three of them and announced himself in a deep voice.

"Hi there, sorry I'm late. I'm Waldron Stephenson but most people just call me Walt." He reached out and shook Stan's hand.

Introductions were made. Stephenson was loud, but friendly and polite. John hoped their meeting would stay polite, he didn't fancy an argument with this mountain of a man. Stephenson's suit looked tailor-made, but the man inside it looked like he should be wielding an axe or a sledgehammer rather than a pen.

Another figure stepped out of the back of the limousine. This was a slight figure dressed in baggy jeans and baggy windcheater with the hood pulled up over his head. His face was only barely visible. Cables reached from a ubiquitous music player on his belt up under the hood. The figure looked in their direction and the cold spot in John's head felt like it was twisting and suddenly chilled to ice. John tried not to react to the very uncomfortable sensation.

"My son Jamie," Stephenson said loudly. "A typical teenager, he's always got his head buried in that music machine." He looked at John. "Do you mind if he wanders around while we talk? It'll do him good to get some fresh air."

Stephenson had already waved his son on, so any response from John was redundant.

The four adults went inside and John served coffee and cream biscuits he'd bought for the occasion. They sat in the lounge room looking through the large windows out across the back lawn to the forest beyond.

"A beautiful spot you've got here, John," said Stephenson. "Some of my companies are involved in forests, well, forestry mostly, not that you'd want to cut all this down." He chuckled to himself.

Conversation continued with Stephenson mentioning more of the businesses he owned or controlled. John and Jason attempted to play tag team with intelligent responses and probing questions relating to Stephenson's conversation. More than an hour passed this way but every time they tried to extract some specific detail from Stephenson the conversation would move off in some different direction. John was getting the distinct impression that Stephenson was toying with them, but he had no idea why, surely the man had better things to do.

There was the sound of a car horn and Stephenson rose from his seat. "That sounds like my son is back at the car and getting impatient. I feel this has been a very productive morning, gentlemen. I'd like to thank you for your time."

With little more said, the big man returned to the car. It turned around ponderously and then drove off. The three men remaining stood in the front yard and looked at each other. Finally John asked, "Do either of you know what just happened?"

"Beats me," answered Jason. "You're the boss, Stan, understanding clients is your job."

Stan stared down the driveway and thought for a while. "He was here to see what sort of people we were, and to see how far we would go to accommodate him. If it turns out that he liked what he found then in a few months we might start to see some business from his companies."

"You're making that up," accused Jason. "You've no idea either, admit it."

Stan laughed. "You're right. No idea."

"But it sounded good," said John.

"Brown-nose," teased Jason.

Stan and Jason went home a while later and John had the afternoon to himself. Thinking about the odd meeting, and the discomfort from the cold spot in his head, managed to distract him for a while, but the significance of the day soon claimed his attention again. He turned out to have been right: there was still plenty of time left to get depressed and very very drunk.

* * *

Months passed. There was nothing from any of Stephenson's companies, apparently they had failed the test or whatever it had been.

John met more depressing firsts and passed them: some with drink and some with distraction. Less and less mail arrived that was addressed to Samantha. He finally got around to clearing all the school preparations that they had made for Ellie, and closing the tiny bank account they had started in her name. Life without a family was starting to take form.

Christmas day arrived and he spent most of it with Jason and Liz and some cousins of theirs that they'd invited to spend the holiday period. John was grateful for the distraction although, as usual, he found there were still plenty of hours in the day to be depressed. Jason also invited him for many other days over the holiday period. Some of the invitations John accepted and some he rejected in favour of staying home to see if his sorrows could still swim. He sometimes wondered if he was becoming an alcoholic, but most of the time he figured he'd worry about that later.

* * *

Another weekend, a Sunday afternoon. It was late summer and the holiday season was long over. John took a deep breath and once again opened the door to Ellie's bedroom. It had been months, surely he could manage it now. He went to the window, drew back the curtains and opened up, letting in some of the warm summer air. Taking another deep breath, John pulled down a suitcase from the top of the wardrobe and started to carefully fold and pack her tiny clothes. More for charity. Her toys went into cardboard boxes. Despite the temptation to keep some of her favourites, he forced himself to pack them all to be sent away.

From under Ellie's bed he pulled out some books and large pads of paper, drawings and favourite stories of Ellie's that Samantha had collected together. He passed quickly through the children's books and placed them in a box ready for charity – smiling at some, remembering Ellie's reactions, but still unable to consider keeping them. The pads he spent more time with, watching the gradual progression of her drawings as Ellie matured. It was still too early to tell whether she had inherited his skills with the pencil or her mother's fist full of thumbs.

It took him a few minutes to notice the extra figure in some of her drawings, and then it dawned on him that this was probably Asha. Not that he had forgotten her, he often thought about his brief time with Ellie's imaginary friend. Flicking through it was obvious, if you were looking for her, that Asha was in many of the drawings, even if only as a space between Ellie and her mother or father. John wondered at his own reinvention of this imaginary figure.

"Ellie couldn't always see me clearly in the last few months, but we could still speak," came Asha's gentle voice from the windowsill. "Even those few children that see us, only ever see us clearly when they are very young. We start to fade as they get older."

John was not startled. It was almost as though he knew she would be there. He supposed he did, since she was his imaginary friend now. He looked up at her small figure sitting in the open window, she was looking down at the drawings as he went through them.

"You've been gone," he said with a sad smile.

"For a while." She smiled back. "I returned a few weeks ago. You

29

seemed to be getting on with things so I thought it best to leave you be. But ... when I saw you in here today ... I wanted to see Ellie's things one last time, to remember the pretty little girl that gave me so much joy. A child is such a special gift." Her eyes glistened with tears.

"You had become a large part of her life these last few years," John told her, lifting the evidence of Ellie's drawings.

"Things can be so simple to a young child. They don't question what their senses and their mind tells them. It takes time for them to build the barriers of an adult. That freedom allows them to exper- ience and enjoy the world around them in a way that adults rarely know. Children are rare among my people so we have a tendency to become more involved with human children than we probably should." She smiled at John, "I hope you can forgive my inter- ference."

"Ellie had such little time in this world, how could I ever begrudge anyone that helped to fill her short life?" John dropped his head, tears dripping onto the pages.

A sensation, a warm presence, it took a moment for John to recognise it as a touch on the back of his hand. John looked up and saw that Asha had come down from the windowsill and placed her hand over his. He looked into her pale eyes, watering with tears and soft with gentle compassion. Her other hand reached up and touched his cheek, another warm breath, so soft and intimate.

"Oh, John," she said softly. "I didn't mean to make this any harder than it already is."

He dropped his face into his hands and howled out the sadness of his loss.

Later, as his shaking slowed and his breath became less jagged, he felt the warmth of Asha's arm across his shoulders and a glancing warmth like a kiss to the top of his head.

Night had fallen before John felt that he had recovered enough composure to move. Asha felt him stir and moved away as he prepared to stand. He made his way into the hall and turned the light on there, reluctant to turn the light on in Ellie's bedroom.

"Would you like to come downstairs?" John asked. "I promise to be better company than I was this afternoon." He tried to smile.

"Sure." Asha returned his smile and her small figure followed him into the hall.

Downstairs John poured himself a large whiskey and ice and invited Asha into the lounge room. He sat in one lounge chair, Asha curled her legs under her in another. The chair looked much too large for her.

John looked around and realised that his clean up over the months had made this once warm and welcoming room rather sparse and cold. In daylight it was better, the large windows seemed to bring the lawn and forest into the house in a way that made it feel more alive, part of the natural world. It was that natural warmth that Samantha had fallen in love with when they first found the house.

"The claim of better company could have been an exaggeration," he said with a half smile.

Asha gave him a direct look. "You've been making progress, it seems to me."

"Yes ... I guess so. Suicide has not seemed like something I'd do, not intentionally, if that makes any sort of sense. And not for any religious reasons or belief that it is wrong, it's just not me – it wasn't us. And, if you don't suicide, it doesn't leave room for much else except progress.

"They say things like "time is a great healer" and "time heals all wounds", but I don't think either of those things are true. I think time is more realistic than that. Time heals those things that can be healed, the rest it covers over or erodes away.

"I'm currently going through a stage of erosion: exhaust the ability to grieve; give away the reminders to charity; wash away reactions with alcohol." He took a large gulp of his whiskey.

"Next come the stages of deposition. I saw it with my father after my mother passed away. He never got over it, he just found things to fill in the cracks. I'm sure, if he'd lived long enough, that eventually time would have given him all the detritus of living that he needed to paper over the pain and make it bearable. It's what time does, you just have to live through it."

He smiled at her, this time with more feeling. "Not sure when I turned philosopher."

She smiled back. There was silence for a time before she asked, "Both your parents are dead?"

"Yes. Cancer took my mother, she was quite a bit younger than my father. My parents had been very dedicated to each other. It was hard to tell whether my father's heart attack was physically due, or whether it was his way out of a life he no longer wanted once my mother was gone." John paused and took a sip of his drink. "Your parents?" he asked in return.

"My father still lives, but he moved north. My mother is gone ... years ago now."

John pondered this in silence for a while.

"I'm glad you came back," he said. "When you left that other night I didn't know what to do. I wasn't sure whether I had upset you. I know I probably didn't react very well to what you were telling me. My natural reaction is to be cynical, it's the curse of this brave new world – well, human world."

"So you do believe that I'm real, now?" she asked, her expression hopeful.

He looked at her for a long moment before deciding that honesty was probably the only practical policy with an imaginary friend. "While you're here in front of me I have no choice but to believe you are real, but once you go it all gets pretty doubtful again." He shrugged and smiled. "You're here now, so let's assume you exist."

She gave him a cheeky smile. "I'll try to look as solid as I can." She shrank in size and did indeed seem to be more solid, more intense, in some way he couldn't really define.

John stared at her with confused thoughts. He'd seen her change which both confirmed and denied her as a possibility. Now she sat here, an obviously mature woman but the size of a young girl of perhaps only five or six years old, much the same age that Ellie had been. She was smaller now than he had ever seen her before.

Asha must have guessed at some of his confusion and expanded her size close to that of an adult human, she no longer appeared so out of place in the chair.

John continued to stare for a few moments, then gave an uncertain laugh. "Very good." He drew himself together, took another swallow of his drink, and tried to come up with a sensible question.

"You seem to know about humans, and you already know all about me. Can you tell me more about your people?"

Asha looked at him, trying to decide what, if anything, to say.

"I thought about this after our last conversation. The explanations that you want I just don't have. The aaranya are not a scientific race, though some of our elders do develop a certain ... natural philosophy, I think you'd call it. I think you'd like old Milla, he asks too many questions too." She smiled at John. "I can tell you what little I know or have been told by others, but I can't explain how or why it works, it just does. We tend to accept what is."

John nodded encouragement for her to continue.

"We learn most of what we need from our community and our elders, things like language and our affinity for nature, the rest we accumulate through the years. Some of us, living near humans, accumulate more than others."

"Are you immortal?" he asked.

"No, but most of us do live a long time compared to humans: two or three hundred years. We have no particular age at which we become old and die, it's more environmental. We are closely bound to our homes and to each other."

"So how old are you?" he asked, curious.

She grinned at him. "There are some questions you don't ask a female, even one of us.

"If you are going to keep asking questions it could take a while. You really should eat, before you drink any more," she said, indicating his now empty glass.

"Yes, ma'am." He grinned back and they made their way to the kitchen.

He pulled a frozen lasagne out of its wrappings and started it heating in the microwave. "It could be just as well you don't eat," he said, "the fare in this kitchen is none too grand."

As he got himself another drink he asked, "If it's not too personal, you know, like the age thing," he grinned at her, "how do you sustain yourself if you don't eat? I imagine you must need something."

"It really is built into humans to want to know the how and why, isn't it," she said, partly amused and partly exasperated.

She thought about her answer for a while before starting. "The life of the trees sustain us. Our relationship with our home is a symbiosis. The life of the trees helps to nourish us and to give us a sense of place and presence. In return we help to focus their life forces to resist disease and divert the more destructive behaviour of animals – except humans.

"It's a complex relationship: we cannot stop all disease, it is part of life; we cannot divert all animals, they are part of the balance. The trees can generally manage without us, but they have a harder time without our influence there to help maintain a good balance. We can live for a long time away from our trees and may sometimes even develop bonds in a new forest, but usually we prefer our own homes. As we get older the bonds to our home grow stronger."

Hoping that he was not being too annoying, John asked, "Last time you described yourself as a being made of life energy, I still don't know how to interpret that. You look real and solid, except for the disconcerting tendency to change size."

Asha looked at him with frustration. "I don't know how much more I can add. None of the all-too-human descriptions of energy and life-force are truly complete. Are you made of tangible matter? Yes, but there's more to you than that. Are you an animal? Yes, but that's not all. Do you have a spirit? Many believe you do. You are human and that explains what you are.

"I am narun and that explains what I am. We don't have a fixed form, but we have difficulty functioning in other forms so most of us naturally assume a human-like appearance – we prefer to say that humans have a narun-like appearance," this last she added with a smile. "We tend to prefer a size smaller than most adult humans, which I guess gives us yet another affinity with your children.

"Interaction with life systems – forests, rivers and lakes – are natural to us. They are necessary to our continued existence. But inanimate objects, particularly objects of human manufacture, seem ... too heavy and blank, the sensation is hard to describe. I can't explain all this, I just know that it is. ... We are what we are."

A "bing" from the microwave indicated that the lasagne was ready and John got up to get it. "Am I the only adult human that can see you?" he asked.

"I asked a few of my people about that while I was away. Apparently it has happened before, it is just very rare. Some primitive tribes of humans would starve themselves and smoke various hallucinogens, some combinations of which would change their mental states enough to see us for a short time.

"Apparently the change can also occur as the result of physical or mental trauma, which I guess ..." she stopped, not wanting to state the obvious. "But John ..." she stopped again, the last words soft and hesitant.

Catching the tone of her voice he put down his fork and looked up at her. "What?"

"The change isn't always permanent," she finished.

"Oh." He wasn't sure how to react to that.

"The fact that you can still see me now, after these months that have passed, is apparently a good sign," she said. "Assuming you still want to see me."

"I do," said John. It was very true, more true than Asha probably realised or John really wanted to admit. He supposed that you probably shouldn't cling to imaginary constructs, but that didn't change what he wanted.

Rather than follow that potentially awkward thread, the conversation moved on to what John had done around the house and then tentatively to memories of Ellie and Samantha. John found this reminiscence was less painful now, perhaps because time had laid down its first layers of insulation, or perhaps because he was sharing with someone that had loved them as he had.

It was late when Asha said she should go.

"Please don't stay away," John asked. "I've enjoyed tonight."

Asha just nodded, a bit distracted perhaps, and left. John didn't hear the door open or close so he got up and looked down the hall, but she wasn't there.

That night, as he lay in bed trying to go to sleep, he thought about the evening he had spent with Asha. He could feel that cold spot in his head again now. It had felt quite warm and comfortable, almost normal, for most of the evening. That it had remained quiescent had helped him to avoid returning to the question of whether she really existed. He had been able to treat everything she said as if it were possible, as if she were possible. It was easy to do while she was sitting there talking to him. Here on his own the crack in his head felt chilled and his doubts assailed him.

3. Senses

The working week passed and she did not reappear. He took to leaving the back door open when he went inside, trying to make it obvious that he wanted her to come in and talk. He was worried that she had once again decided to stay away from him and he didn't want that. He didn't really know what he wanted from her, but he knew that he was not ready for her to leave. If she was imaginary then he sincerely hoped his imagination was up to keeping her around a bit longer.

Early Saturday morning he carried a coffee out the back and sat down to watch the forest. He had only been there for a few minutes when she walked out from the trees and across the lawn toward him. The morning sun slanted in through the forest, the flickering sunlight and shadows from the trees passed over and through her, much as they had the first time he saw her out here.

She smiled as she approached and he realised that she had arrived almost as tall as he. He wondered if this was a concession to him, to try and put him at ease. It was not working. He was struck dumb by her beauty and by her impossibility, her partial transparency and her lack of shadow so apparent in this setting. He realised he was staring at her and tried to put a more casual, less astounded, expression on his face.

"Good morning," he said.

She smiled in return. "Good morning."

"Is there anything I can get you?" John asked. "It's strange to have a guest and not offer at least some hospitality."

"Nothing, thanks," Asha replied, sitting on the bench opposite. She looked across the lawn at the forest, so many luminous greens in the bright morning sunlight. "Beautiful isn't it."

"Yes. It was the setting almost as much as the house that drew us here. We felt they were a perfect match, and a perfect place for our escape from the city. It was what we wanted even when we didn't know what it was we wanted." John paused, remembering their first conversation. "I'm sorry, I was forgetting what was done to your trees to build this place. I didn't mean to be insensitive."

Asha glanced at John and shook her head. "I think my first lecture probably said more than you needed to hear. We are not an unrealistic people. Our life requires a certain level of realism, fatalism. You have to accept that death is part of life if you want to maintain a balance in the forest. My great fear was – and still is really – that your house would be the first of many, that greater swaths of our forest were about to be destroyed by some new period of development.

"But that hasn't happened and the house and road don't feel like the intrusion they once were. Enough time has passed that they have become part of the landscape again. I am not saying I would welcome more such houses, only that we accept that such things will happen. As houses go this one could have been much worse." Asha said the last with an apologetic smile. She could not in all honesty suggest that she would prefer this house to the trees that it had replaced.

"John, I was thinking," Asha said, leading up to something momentous. "The other night I was trying to tell you about who I was, who my people are, but words only go so far. If you really want to know who we are then I think you should come with me into the forest and try to see it as we see it. Today is going to be a beautiful day. Please, share it with me ... in *my* home." Asha pointed into the trees.

John stared across the table in wonder and then out into the forest. "I'd love to," he said at last. "Thank you."

He threw the last of his coffee onto the lawn and said with a grin, "I'll be back in a minute," and walked quickly inside, trying not to run. He put on his hiking boots and filled a canteen with water. He considered a jacket in case of a cool change, then remembered that she had said it was going to be a beautiful day. He blocked off a negative thought about accepting weather predictions from imaginary friends and walked to the back door. She was waiting for him at the forest edge and he rushed across the lawn to join her.

At first she followed a familiar path, heading north and then east, and then she stepped off through the undergrowth saying, "We don't have to go far, I just want to get us into the real forest, away from all disturbance."

He couldn't tell whether the trees and scrub moved out of her way or whether it was simply the agile way that she moved. The silence and smooth grace of her movement were at odds with the speed she maintained through the growth, it was obvious that she had to remind herself to slow down and wait for the flat-footed human to stumble his noisy way after her.

For the first time John took note of her clothing. He had the distinct impression this was something of a different style to what she wore the first times he met her, if only he could remember the details. Today she wore a simple summer dress that fitted her form closely, flaring from the narrow waist and stopping just above her knees. The material was coloured with striations of various browns passing through a mottled background of creams and pale yellows that complemented her long light brown hair, natural highlights glowing as she walked through patches of sunshine.

After stumbling yet again, John concluded that he should probably spend more time looking at where he was walking and less time looking at Asha. He had an uncomfortable feeling that he was paying too much attention to Asha in ways that were not right. It felt too soon to experience such feelings about another woman, disloyal to Samantha. The fact that Asha was kind and caring did not mean she would welcome such feelings. And to top it all off there was something a little ... sick, about lusting after an imaginary friend. He fell over.

Picking himself up and brushing off the leaf-litter, he concluded he should spend more time concentrating on where he was walking and less time thinking stupid and inappropriate thoughts. He looked up, Asha was looking back at him with a question in her eyes. "I'm okay," he said. "Just not as good at this as you are."

"Just a bit further," she said.

A few minutes later they entered a natural thinning of the trees, not quite a clearing, just a place where trees had not fully reclaimed the space once used by a now fallen companion. At some point in the past a large tree had fallen over, the trunk was now the only part that had not merged back with the forest floor. Another large tree, this one still very much alive, rose not far from where the fallen tree must once have grown.

Asha jumped lightly onto the fallen tree trunk and then sat cross-legged on its crest. "Sit up here," she told John, patting the trunk in front of her.

With considerably less grace he pulled himself onto the trunk and sat down, legs draped to one side. Still panting from his exertions, he opened his canteen and took a long swallow of water.

When John had recovered his breath Asha said softly, "Close your eyes and open your ears and as many other senses as you can, everything but your eyes. Hear the forest. Smell the forest. Feel the air and the sun. Try to sense the life around you. Let it touch you."

John wondered if he was in for some new-age crystal stroking or something, but closed his eyes and tried to do as she asked.

"Now just wait like that for a while," Asha said. "Give your senses time to awaken."

So John sat. At first his mind was busy with the usual distractions: an itchy nose; something uncomfortable under his leg; a bug flying past; wanting to open his eyes and analyse his surroundings; wanting to see what Asha was doing. Slowly he settled enough that the news from his other senses began to report in. He could feel the sunlight, there was a patch on his right shoulder warmer than the rest, and he could feel the touch of an intermittent breeze cooling the sweat on his face. Sounds began to register: birds calling in the distance; a faint rustle of movement in the leaf matter below him; and a faint susurrus that took him a long time to identify – it was the combined sound of the leaves and branches of the trees all around him, like a whisper of ancient secrets.

When he eventually noticed the smells he was surprised. He had expected the musty smell of the leaf-litter, that was familiar from all his forest walks, but there was also a faint sweet smell of a flower he thought he should recognise ... and he could tell there were many more smells carried by the breeze but he had not the skills to distinguish them.

He was feeling rather proud of all he had managed to sense, and was wondering whether it would be okay to speak now, when he found something more. It felt as if that crack in the centre of his head had opened up and was absorbing details from the world around him. He could not describe the sensation properly, but it seemed that he could sense the forest, that he could feel the individual presence of each tree. He could feel the trunk on which he was sitting and sense how far it extended either way and he could sense something of it in the grass and mulch either side. Most powerful of all, he could feel the presence of Asha in front of him, the sensation was so powerful that it was almost as if he could see her.

"There," she said quietly. "You do feel it, don't you? I can tell you can. I can feel your senses reaching out."

He opened his eyes and the sensation, whatever it had been, dropped away. He felt somehow reduced from what he had been just moments ago, as though he had lost something important the moment his eyes opened. "I felt ... something," he said. "I don't know what it was."

"It was life!" Asha said, excited. "That is what you were sensing. Since you can see me I thought you must be able to sense all life. We call it vedana, it's one of the five senses. Sight, hearing, smell, touch and vedana – the sense of life. Apparently it's also linked up with the other senses in some way, but you'd have to ask Milla about that."

"Taste," said John absently, "you missed taste."

"We don't eat, John, we have no sense of taste."

John nodded still trying to catch up, to take it all in, still trying to understand the sensations he had felt. "I felt you in front of me, almost as if I could see you. Your presence stood out from everything else."

"That's prana, John, the life energy I was trying to describe. Narun are made of concentrated prana so we stand out from the other life. Humans, too, stand out from simpler life forms, but not as strongly as narun. If you think of vedana like sight then the narun always look like they're standing under a brighter light."

"And this tree trunk?" John asked. "If this is a dead tree, why did I sense it as a life?"

"Because it *is* alive! It is no longer a tree but it is very much alive.

40

Termites, borers, ants, centipedes, beetles, fungus, moss and lichens. It is a complex system of life. The trunk and the ground beneath it and beside it, perhaps even more complex than the tree it once was.

"When something like a tree dies its prana dissipates and leaves the nadis, the channels and spaces where life once flowed, empty. There is a lot of simple life in the world searching for such spaces. They move in and rearrange things to their own liking and eventually a whole new life is formed – in this case that of the tree trunk, the ex-tree. It is so much more than just a collection of bugs and simple plants. It is a system, a balance and, as you felt for yourself, a presence of its own.

"As time passes this new life will run its course and the space it leaves behind will be taken up by the earth itself and eventually pass on to new trees. You may not have noticed but the soil itself is alive. Its presence is spread over such a large area that it is less distinct, but it is actually much larger than anything else here."

John put his hands down and felt the rough surface of the tree trunk, trying to remember the sensations he had felt before. He tried to imagine the life at work beneath his fingers, and tried to work out his own place in this scheme. He was not sure he could really take it in. Finally he looked up. Asha was smiling at him, obviously very happy that he appeared to be accepting what she was showing him. He smiled back at her. "Wow," he said. "I am really not sure that it has all gotten through yet but ... wow."

"Having seen that much, maybe you're ready for this," Asha said as she stood up in a single smooth movement. She ran along the trunk to what had been the base of the tree and sprang lightly across to the large tree that was still growing, a distance of almost twenty feet. She leant against the tree, a very relaxed stance, casually affectionate. "Don't panic. What you are about to see is normal, natural," she said.

As he watched, her skin and clothing changed texture and colour and she appeared to melt into the trunk. For a moment it looked like the tree had reached out to embrace her, and then she was gone. His jaw dropped. She had told him that she did this, but to see it happen, and for it to look so natural and easy ... he was speechless.

Something made him look up. He thought he saw some of the

leaves high in the branches tremble and something fell. A minute later and Asha emerged from the base of the tree. It was almost as if she were walking out from a waterfall: the bark dried off her clothes and skin and left her as she had entered. One hand stayed merged for a moment longer in a last tender caress.

She picked up what had dropped from the tree and brought it too him, jumping lightly onto the tree trunk again, presenting him a small cluster of blossoms. She sat, again cross-legged on the trunk, watching him.

John remembered to close his mouth. "I'm not sure I was ready for that," he admitted finally. He tried to thread a stem of the blossoms into the button hole on his shirt pocket but ended up dropping them into the pocket instead, hoping they would not crush.

Asha laughed. "It's me. It's what I am. You weren't going to accept it from the words, now you've seen it: ready or not." She beamed at him.

It was obvious that Asha was happier out here. She was more relaxed and more confident, and she was ready to believe that John would now be able to accept that everything she had shown him was real. John smiled at her, he couldn't help it. Asha was beautiful before, but out here, happy in her own world, her home, she was breathtaking, heartbreaking ... and, if anything, more unbelievable than ever.

Still trying to accept what he had seen, John held out his hand for hers. "May I?" he asked.

With a partly pretended coyness Asha put her right hand in his. It looked as he expected, slender and delicate like the rest of her. Her skin felt warm, soft and gentle – everything he expected of her hand, a woman's hand. He moved his thumb over the skin of the back of her hand, it felt ... like skin. There was nothing to hint at what he had seen her do.

A few moments more and he thought he felt something else, like a vibration almost beyond the sensitivity of his own skin. He covered her hand, clasping it gently between both of his. Could he be imagining this sensation as an explanation for what he had seen? A rather pointless question, since he was not sure that Asha was real at all. He turned her hand over and stroked it, as if looking for flaws.

The vibration was there! Faint but also intense, like nerves quivering in anticipation.

"You are doing it again," said Asha. "Reaching with your senses. Believe it, John, that is my essence you are touching." She drew her hand back from his grasp, but slowly. "But such a direct touch is considered ... personal." She blushed.

John stared down at his hands, not quite registering Asha's embarrassment. "I just ..." he started, but didn't know how to finish.

"It's okay," she said gently. "I know it's a lot to take in. We could have talked all week and I would not have convinced you, but here in the forest the reality is hard to resist. Isn't it?"

John looked up into her gentle eyes, his own filling with tears he could not explain. He wanted to believe her, there was little he had ever wanted more, but a lifetime of scepticism, years of cynical comment, were fighting against the evidence of his own eyes. He had felt his mind break, he could still feel the crack, and to a cynic that was so much easier to believe.

"Come on," she said, jumping lightly off the trunk and reaching back for his hand. "Come and talk to my trees."

Rather than try to find the words, John allowed himself to be drawn off the trunk and led to the tree she had merged with before.

"Feel it," she said.

He ran his hands lightly over the bark and then let them rest gently.

"Close your eyes and sense it," she said.

He did as she asked, and after a few moments he did start to sense some of what he had experienced earlier. A presence. This close it was more than that, almost like feeling a faint breeze against his fingers and palms. It had none of the intensity he had felt from Asha's hand, but it was still difficult to deny.

"That's it. That's the tree," Asha said. "That is the same stuff that I am made of, prana. All I do is become part of the flow." With that Asha merged. John was standing so much closer this time that it all seemed to happen in slow motion. Her body sank into the tree at the same time that the texture and colour of the bark came out to encompass her. Again it appeared to John as if the tree embraced her just as she accepted the tree. In the last moments as she disappeared, a smile still glowing on her face, she did seem to become part of a flow that moved up and into the trunk.

A few moments later just her torso emerged out of the tree trunk a few feet higher. "See?" she said. "It's real. I'm real. Being only partly merged takes more effort," she said and slowly slid down the tree to become fully emerged on the ground. "It's something we only do to show off." She grinned.

"Come on," she called, her voice full of anticipation. She led him through the forest and introduced him to more trees.

"Do they have names?" he asked.

She laughed. "No. Plants are not thinking creatures, there is no sense of self, just life. I have heard that some of the more eccentric aaranya name their trees and even offer explanations of individual personalities. For most of us though, we don't need that sense of identity, we just take pleasure from the sharing of life."

"And what about shrubs, grass ... weeds?"

"They have life force too, just less of it. Mostly grass and under-growth are part of the soil, they don't have much of a presence of their own. Larger shrubs usually have a distinct presence, but being so small we cannot completely merge, they don't have room for us."

"You talk about the life of the soil, can you merge with that as you do with trees?" John asked. Aware that this sense of curiosity was related to his sense of scepticism, he was not sure if asking questions was a good idea or not.

"No, not really. Not even with that fallen tree trunk back there. Not just that it wouldn't feel right, but the flows are in some way incompatible. While I am merged with a living tree I can tell a lot about the soil from the sensations of the roots but I can't merge directly."

They wandered on slowly, Asha pointing out particular plants, at times hushing conversation so they would not scare some creature scrambling through the undergrowth. Several times they stopped at particular trees and Asha would converse with them in her own way. John would try to sense each of these, with varying levels of success. Asha seemed pleased by his attempts and jubilant at his successes. After a while John's scepticism was pushed aside as he allowed himself to be immersed in the experience; managing to lose himself in the sheer joy that Asha felt for the life around her, enjoying the forest through her happiness.

It came as a surprise to him when they emerged from the forest onto his back lawn and he could see that the sun was low in the west, peering through the trees creating beautiful dapples of light.

"I'm sorry," said Asha, apparently also surprised by the time. "You've missed lunch, I just didn't think—"

"It's fine. Really. I didn't notice either. I had a wonderful day." John looked towards the back door. "Are you going to come in?"

Asha hesitated, not wanting to spoil the day and not sure how best to make sure that didn't happen. "No, I'd better go. I had a wonderful day too, I really enjoyed sharing it with you."

Neither seemed sure what to do or say next, they just looked at each other. Eventually Asha smiled, touched John's arm briefly, and seemed to almost float back into the forest. In moments she was gone and John stood there alone, staring into the trees trying to gain some last glimpse.

Most nights John continued to dream of the family he no longer had. On good nights he would see Samantha playing with Ellie in the living room or out on the back lawn. On bad nights he would imagine the accident that had taken them from him and wake up screaming. This Saturday night, a good night, Asha appeared in his dreams, playing games with Ellie while Samantha looked on, and it seemed the most natural thing in the world.

* * *

Asha did not appear the next day, Sunday. John wished he had thought to ask when he could see her next. He filled his day with catching up on housework and getting ready for the working week – the time his cynical, sceptical mind insisted on calling his *real* life.

Monday kept real life to the fore. An important client insisted on having an in-person presentation and it was John's turn to do it. Truth be known, John probably owed Jason for a great many such presentations over the last months. Late home, he hoped that Asha had not waited around for him, and he wondered at his inclination to notify her of his plans.

Tuesday was more relaxed but come five o'clock Jason suggested they stop off at the local pub, for some reason it called itself a tavern, for a beer. Monday had reminded John of how much Jason had covered for him so a sense of guilt drove him to accept, even though it wasn't what he wanted. He didn't finish the thought as to why he'd rather go home.

"So," started Jason, "you've been keeping to yourself."

John shrugged. "I've not been much good for company."

"You seem to have come a long way since ... you know, since then," said Jason.

"I've had my moments, even since then," John admitted. "But mostly I'm getting along okay. How's Liz?" he asked, hoping for a change of subject.

"Really great." A change of subject was good for Jason too apparently. "We're pregnant!" A worried expression passed over Jason's face when he realised how this might affect John, but it was out now.

"Pregnant. Wow," said John with an attempt at enthusiasm. "That's really great news. Well, great for Liz, I'm not sure how you're gonna look in a maternity dress."

Jason laughed. "Well, you know, we are supposed to be in this together."

"Yeah, I can just imagine you cheering Liz on from out in the waiting room."

The two friends fell into an easy banter, their relationship worked much better when they kept the conversation light. In the past such meetings might have gone on quite late, but Jason wanted to get home to Liz and John encouraged him.

"Time to be the conscientious husband, Jason." He smiled and fell into his fake Texan accent, "Pardner, you can't keep the little woman waitin' at home alone."

It had been a hot day, summer was still winding down, and it was still light when John got home, but there was no sign of Asha. John heated a frozen dinner and then spent some time looking over papers and drawings for work. He was still feeling restless when he went to bed and it turned out to be a bad night. He woke from a nightmare in which Asha had been standing between a screaming Ellie and some horror that stayed just out of sight.

* * *

Wednesday turned out to be a cooler, overcast day with patches of drizzly rain. Later in the afternoon it turned into a slow but steady rain although it was still not particularly cold. No one suggested drinks after work, everyone wanted to get inside out of the weather, so John made it home at a more usual hour. The rain had started to get quite heavy as he pulled in but he ignored it and went around the back to see if he could see Asha. He wondered how she managed in the rain.

He stood on the lawn for a few minutes, getting soaked through as he watched for her. He was about to turn and go in when he saw her. She was dancing! She laughed when she saw him and danced out of the trees and onto the lawn, arms raised, leaping face first into the rain.

"Isn't it glorious," she called. "It's been too long."

John could only agree that it was glorious, that *she* was glorious. For some reason he thought that she would not get wet in the rain, but here she was soaked through and still revelling in it. Her light brown hair, now dark with the wet, was plastered to her head and shoulders. Her clothes were soaked and clinging to her form in ways that John could not help noticing. Asha seemed oblivious to the effect she was having on him.

"When it has been a long time since the last good rain the forest seems to celebrate, everything opens up to lap at the water." Asha laughed and stuck out her tongue to lap at the raindrops. She spun around and leapt to a tree on the edge of the lawn and then sprang back to the lawn again, laughing all the while.

John felt the urge to run forward and hold her, to try and dance with her, but he could never match her grace nor her agility, so instead he just watched and marvelled. He couldn't get any wetter than he was already, so there was no rush to get in doors.

Sometime later Asha seemed to notice his intense gaze and become self-conscious. "This must seem a little strange to you, I guess."

"It doesn't seem strange when you do it," John said truthfully. He turned to go inside before he risked being accused, rightly, of staring. He unlocked the door and stepped in, crossing to the laundry to grab a towel and to kick off his saturated shoes and peel off his socks. When he looked up Asha was standing in the doorway totally dry.

"Getting wet and staying wet are sort of optional to us," Asha said in response to his astonishment.

"That's got to be convenient," he replied, wringing out his socks into the laundry sink to highlight his meaning.

"Can you stay a while?" he asked.

She nodded.

"Give me a couple of minutes to get dry and I will be right back down. Make yourself comfortable – wherever you like."

A rushed hot shower and a dry tracksuit later, John found Asha in the lounge room sitting on the floor with her feet tucked under her, looking through a photo album that he had left on the coffee table at some point. "I hope you don't mind?" she asked.

"That's fine," he replied and was surprised to find it was. He checked that there was nothing he could get for her and went to pour himself a whiskey. He hadn't stopped drinking, but at least the servings had become more moderate. When he came back into the lounge room, and settled in the chair across from her, Asha seemed pensive.

"There is something that I've wanted to ask, but I don't know how." Asha hesitated, looked across at him and continued, "You don't have to answer, but I was wondering what actually happened. All I ever really knew was that Samantha and Ellie never came home."

"Oh." John froze.

"It's all right," said Asha. "Let it go. I don't really have to know."

"No, it's okay," John said eventually. I can do this, he thought to himself.

"It was an accident. Just a stupid, oh-so-common, car accident. Samantha had to go to the city, to visit the university to meet with someone or something. It was the sort of trip she did every couple of weeks at least."

Asha nodded at this, she knew about Samantha's working from home, doing something for a university in the city. The university had loaned her much of the computer equipment necessary to do the work. The work and equipment allowed Samantha to stay home most of the time, to be with Ellie while she continued her studies.

"No one really knows exactly what happened. Driving too fast perhaps, she did like to drive fast, or distracted by something crossing the road. It could have been anything. Whatever it was, Samantha took a bend in the road badly and the car went off the embankment and rolled." John paused. "I was told that Samantha

48

was killed instantly ... in her coffin she looked almost serene."

John took a big mouthful of his drink, swallowed hard and then looked down at the floor. "Another motorist apparently saw the car on its roof and called the police. Ellie was alive when they got to her, and they rushed her to a hospital in the city." Another drink. "She was terribly injured, her tiny body a mass of bruising and apparently the inside was worse."

A deep breath before continuing. "For two weeks she fought her injuries. She was unconscious all that time, but you could almost see her tiny body struggling back. I watched her every step of the way, unable to help. What good is a father if he can't help his little girl?" John stopped for a minute, clutching at his drink, struggling not to lose control.

"Things were starting to look up. The doctors started to make positive noises as though she was going to make it after all, but ... suddenly she was gone."

John had stopped, but Asha could see that there was something more he wanted to say. They waited in silence, John breathing heavily.

"I was only away for half-an-hour or so. There were some stupid papers to be signed or something, I can barely remember. I just know that she was alive and beautiful when I left, looking like she could wake up at any moment ... but when I returned ... the doctors and nurses were standing over her. I knew the moment I saw them there, standing so still. Her body was still beautiful but ... she was gone. My Ellie was gone." John covered his face with his hands, taking deep breaths. He finally managed to finish. "The doctors say it was a burst blood vessel or something ... I didn't really listen to their explanations, it didn't matter. All that mattered was gone."

They sat there in silence for some time, each lost in their own thoughts. John was surprised to discover that he was still rational. The hole was there, the pain was there, but he was able to face it now. He didn't know if he had grown stronger or if time had eroded his capability for grief. He missed his family as much as ever, but he was no longer totally consumed by his grief.

Asha turned another page in the photo album and asked John about the images. With this they moved on to happier memories and the tension that had built as John had described the accident slowly eased.

For dinner John heated up another microwave meal and Asha noted that he really should take better care of himself. "Yes ma'am, I'll start tomorrow," was his glib, accented, response.

After dinner, conversation turned to some of the other things that John wanted to know. Asha explained that water and prana had some special affinity. All narun could merge with water or could choose to be wet by it or not.

"Nothing else really sticks to us," she explained. "I mean we don't get dirty or dusty or anything, but water is different, it's part of life. Water is a special thing for all narun. Large collections of water – lakes, rivers, and oceans – are huge life systems, and such places are often inhabited by narun, the samudraka and jalaja." Seeing John's blank expression she explained, "You'd call them nereids and naiads, but any narun can live in the water. We can exist in the water as a separate being or merge as part of the life of the water. When we get out we can stay wet or let it run off, as you saw this afternoon."

John just nodded, some of this was too strange to really take in, but he decided to ignore those parts he didn't understand.

"I hope this is not too personal or anything," John said, he had found himself thinking of Asha's wet clothes in the rain, "but I was wondering about your clothes." He noticed that today she was wearing a sleeved tunic, coming to around mid-thigh, and long shorts – were they called "plus-fours" or something? He thought it was probably something like this that she wore the first times that he saw her. "Where do you get your clothes?"

"Oh. ... No, it's not too personal. Clothes are purely fashion for us. They serve no other purpose, it's not like we need them to stay warm or anything. The material is part of us – sort of. We create it as part of selecting our form but once created it does feel separate. I imagine it feels much like clothing does to you, although we probably don't have the same variety of textures however much we try." To demonstrate Asha concentrated and the sleeves of her tunic seemed to fade away. She concentrated again and they returned.

"The younger people tend to experiment quite a lot, often influenced by human fashions. Some try to be different, as a protest against following the lead of humans, and at times some new fashion of our own will become popular, but humans do seem very good at finding new variations.

"There have been periods in our past where we were mostly naked, but they were before my time. These days there is a sense of modesty among most of our people and clothing is considered the decent way to be seen – although that could be another fashion that has rubbed off from humans. As we get older most of us find a few styles we like and stick with those, it's just easier."

To try and take his mind off the ease with which Asha had undressed her arms, John asked her how many of her people lived nearby.

"Not many, I'm considered something of a recluse these days. My stand is further to the north."

"Stand?"

"That's what we call our communities. There are a couple of stands in the depth of the forest to the north but otherwise, this far out, you only see the occasional young aaranya or sometimes an odd yaayaavara wandering past." In response to yet another puzzled look she explained, "The yaayaavara are nomads, not quite aaranya, tree-folk, and not quite naiad or anything else. They can be a very strange people.

"There are very few narun of any sort these days, it was not always so." Asha paused as if lost in less than pleasant thoughts. "Still, despite our lack of numbers, it is not that uncommon to see one or other of our kind wandering past. The youth of most communities tend to spend a lot of time exploring the world – it's how we get to learn about you lot," she finished with a smile.

It was late and Asha said she should go.

"When can I see you again?" John asked, wishing he could sound more casual and not so needy.

Asha looked at him thoughtfully for a few moments before answering, "Let's do something you want this Saturday."

John looked at her blankly.

"You know: last Saturday we explored my forest, next Saturday we should explore a place you love."

"Oh," John said. "I don't get out much these days ..."

Asha laughed. "Think about it, see what you come up with." They'd been walking down the hallway toward the back door. She touched his arm lightly and then simply disappeared through the door as if it was not there.

John stood stunned for a moment then opened the door quickly, in the moonlight he could see Asha on the far side of the lawn. He called after her, "You know I could have opened it for you!" She laughed as she disappeared into the forest. John turned back to look at his back door, a solid timber construction. He supposed the timber explained it. Mentally adding more questions to his list he went to bed and dreamed, good dreams, of Asha in her forest.

4. Reflection

John waited impatiently for the week to finish. He spent a lot of his time racking his brain for ideas, trying to think of places that he could take Asha that she might actually like to see. It was difficult. In recent years all his favourite places had been places to spend with Samantha and Ellie. Down near the lake had been common excursions that they'd all enjoyed, but that had too many memories still too close. Before they had moved here John had always been a city boy. There were lots of places he could show her in the city, but he doubted if she'd like any of them very much – and it was too far.

It was sometime Friday morning that John burst out laughing and attracted stares from others in the open plan office. It had just occurred to him that he was like a man preparing for a date, and he'd imagined trying to take her to the movies. The whole thing was so ludicrous that he had trouble controlling the outburst. Asha was an imaginary friend! His thoughts about her must come close to some weird sort of incest, or like kissing a mirror, or something ... and it was not yet a year since his family had died. The whole thing really was absurd. He probably was as crazy as those watching him from across the office thought.

Saturday morning, as he showered, John finally decided that it would either be the beach or Piper's lookout. Both were within a reasonable drive, and both seemed like something that Asha might enjoy. It was the best that a city-lad could come up with.

He was in the kitchen cleaning up after breakfast, such as it was, when he heard a light rap on the back door. He went down the hall and opened it to find Asha looking slightly nervous on the other side.

He grinned in welcome. "I didn't think doors were that much of an obstacle to you?"

"Going out is one thing, but I thought it might be more polite to knock to come back in," she said, "now that you know I exist." The last was added with a smile.

John gave an extravagant bow to welcome her inside. Falling to his atrocious Texan accent he said, "Won't you come in ma'am, we don't stand on ceremony here." As she came through the door he gave her a curious look, something had just occurred to him. In his normal voice he asked, "So you came and went pretty much as you pleased ... before?"

She laughed. "You make it sound sordid. I had no malign motives."

"It's okay, I just wondered. You are welcome you know, whenever you want. Is it just this door or can you walk through anything?"

"It's the wood," she replied. "The varnish makes it a bit uncomfortable but that doesn't go very deep."

"So is that like what happens when you merge with a tree?"

"No." Asha paused, trying to think of a simple explanation. "With the door there is no life in the wood any more. To me it feels to be made mostly of the spaces where life once existed, the empty nadis. I simply pass through those spaces like water passing through a sieve. In a living tree there are no spaces, the nadis are filled with the prana of the tree. With a living tree I merge my own essence, my own prana, with that of the tree and for a while we become ... more than joined, intertwined, almost one being. It's almost like mixing two fluids, except that my essence remains my own and I can separate myself from the tree when I want."

John stared at the door for a few moments trying to absorb this information, he rubbed the surface absently. Asha was quite surprised when he didn't spring another series of questions at her, he just turned and nodded at her as he swung the door gently closed.

"No more questions?" she asked.

John shook his head. "I think you've been practising, that almost made sense to me."

They smiled at each other, uncertain how to continue.

"Did you have plans for us today?" Asha asked.

"I wondered if you wanted to go to a beach? It's not that far by car." He looked at her carefully, trying to judge her reaction.

"That would be lovely, John. It's been a dozen years or more since I last saw the coast."

Asha's reaction seemed reserved, so John queried, "Are you sure? I don't want to push you into anything you don't want to do."

"I'm sure, John, just nervous about the car trip I suppose. I've never ridden inside a car."

"Oh ... I hadn't thought of that. Well, we can soon fix that."

John was enthusiastic now. He picked up his wallet and keys and they went out to the garage. When he opened the passenger door for Asha she went to sit down and then screwed up her face.

"What?" he asked.

"The material, it feels wrong to me. It'd be okay, I'd manage, but if it's possible I'd prefer some wool or cotton or something natural if we're going to be in here for a while."

"No problem," said John, relieved that it was something simple. He returned in a few minutes with a woollen blanket that met with Asha's approval, and he wrapped it over the seat and used a couple of large clips from the office to hold it together at the back.

Asha sat on the improvised cover and smiled in reassurance. "That's much better, thanks."

John took mostly smaller roads south to the coast. It made for a more interesting drive and meant that there was less traffic – the large trucks on the main roads made Asha flinch when they got close. For much of the trip Asha was enthralled by the speed, and by the constantly changing scenery, but each time they approached some road-kill she would get distressed and have John slow down so she could look carefully, trying to be certain the animals were truly dead. For most there was little room for doubt.

In one place, they were already most of the way to the coast, Asha asked him to pull over. They got out of the car and Asha went across to a small group of trees growing inside a paddock. John looked around, wondering if there was anyone to worry about him trespassing, finally he shrugged and climbed through the fence to follow her.

"I've been here before," she said, "years ago."

"What were you doing down this way?"

"It was in my youth, we all get restless in our youth. I chose to come south away from the main forests and ..." Asha paused, thinking back. "Anyway, I decided to come south. I spent a few years exploring along the coast. I remember this place. I stayed around here for a while. I remember it took me weeks to get this far, it's amazing to have made it here in less than a morning's travel.

"I remember these trees," she said. Her hands ran over the bark and merged slightly.

A heat shimmer was rising from the mostly bare paddock that surrounded the trees. On the far side of the paddock was a line of trees that marked the path of a small creek. Cicadas called to each other and a pair of crows cawed as they flew over. To John it felt like he was standing in a painting, he thought he should be wearing a hat and probably sitting on a horse in order to complete the scene, he chuckled at the thought.

Asha looked her question at him. "It's just so rural," John responded. "I grew up in the city, a place like this seems almost alien to me. Sure I've lived out of the city for a few years now, but I still haven't gotten used to all this. What I see here I know mostly from television and paintings. It feels strange, like I don't really belong."

"I know what you mean," Asha said. "I remember similar feelings when I was travelling through here on my own. I grew up in the forest and, compared to this, a forest is quite a crowded place, like I imagine a city must be. This ... it's not empty, but it's open and that is very different, for both of us."

Eventually they returned to the car and continued on. John parked near the beach he was looking for, Jason had showed it to him some years ago. It was not as well known as some beaches, so it was usually not too crowded, but this hot Saturday made it unlikely that they'd have it to themselves.

They walked down the sandy path, shaded on either side by the low scrub that grew on the dunes. Asha suddenly laughed and danced ahead, small spurts of sand thrown up by her feet as she ran. John ran after her.

They burst out from the path and onto the steep slope of the beach. Asha ran lightly ahead, John's steps were slower and awkward in the deep, soft sand. He called out that she was cheating, but that only made him laugh and slowed him down. He finally caught up to her on the firm, wet sand just above the line left by the waves. Asha was still laughing as she danced further down, kicking at the water as another wave reached its zenith. John decided that this had been a good idea after all, Asha was obviously enjoying herself.

As the wave receded John saw that Asha's footsteps were being left in the sand, more shallow than his own but still definitely there. "You leave footprints," he said, it came out almost like an accusation.

Asha looked down. "So do you," she answered, pointing to the prints behind him.

"But ..." John stopped, trying to work out what seemed wrong. "If you're not made of solid material like me, how can you have any weight to leave footprints? What's gravity going to pull on?"

Asha shrugged. "I've no idea, John. I don't know how gravity works, but none of us have ever fallen off the world as far as I know."

John looked at her in frustration for a few seconds and then laughed. "I'm sorry, you're right. I've no idea how gravity works either. It just seemed odd." John thought of his father-in-law, they had something in common after all, neither of them liked odd.

"I am *real*, John," Asha said seriously, sensing the underlying reason for John's question. She stepped closer to him and looked into his eyes. "I'm *not* a ghost or a spirit. I'm made of prana. It's real. It exists." She reached forward and touched his arm, "I exist." Another wave rushed in and boiled around their feet and she bent down and flicked water up at his face with a grin, trying to lighten the mood again. "Now are you going to get that shirt off and come in for a swim?"

John took a few steps up the beach, threw his towel on the ground and began to take off his shirt. It was only then that he noticed the group of people further along, some of them were watching him. He put his head down quickly not wanting to return their gaze, swearing under his breath. Since other people could not see Asha, he wondered just what they had seen and perhaps heard.

"Bugger it!" he exclaimed to himself, throwing his shirt down on top of his towel. "Why should I care." He turned and looked out,

Asha had already gone out far enough that she was swimming rather than standing. He ran down through the water as far as he could and then dived forward to swim out after her. "It seems we had an audience," he called to her as he drew near.

"Yes, I did wonder about them," she answered. "I guess I shouldn't draw attention to myself."

"I wasn't thinking about you, I was wondering if they thought *I* had gone crazy."

"And who said chivalry was dead?" She laughed and flicked more water at him before disappearing beneath the surface. John dived under and tried to look around but caught only a flicker of movement and then she had disappeared.

A short time later John was forced to surface and draw breath. They were well out past the breaking of the shallow waves. He bobbed there looking around for her. He felt some strange sensation nearby and then in front of him the water drew itself up into a head and shoulders. It took him a moment to recognise Asha's smiling visage in the clear substance of the water. He put his hand forward tentatively. A watery hand appeared and wetly touched his before it all collapsed into the water, and then Asha's usual form emerged again laughing.

"That's not easy to do," she said, "but it was worth it to see your expression."

"What did you do?" he asked, his surprise making him more abrupt than he intended.

"When I merge with the water I'm able to exert some limited control over it," Asha explained. "It's easier in the still water of a lake, out here in the ocean things move around a lot and that makes it harder." Seeing John's bemused expression she laughed and said, "I'm sorry, John, I'm showing off. It's not really fair when you haven't even accepted that I exist yet."

John just shook his head, he couldn't think of a good response.

Back on the beach he laid out the towel and then realised he had not brought one for Asha.

"I know you don't need a towel to dry yourself," he said, "but if you'd like to sit ..." He pointed to his towel.

"Chivalrous indeed." She smiled at him. "But there's no need, you use it. The sand doesn't stick to me so it doesn't matter where I sit."

It was a big enough towel that they could probably have shared it, but she didn't question his reservation in this regard.

"So you don't have to worry about sand getting caught in awkward, embarrassing and often painful places?" he asked.

Asha shook her head.

"Some people have all the luck." John settled on the towel to dry and Asha sat cross legged nearby. "Do you tan?" he asked.

"Not due to the sun, but I can change my skin tone if I want." With that Asha concentrated and her skin became much darker.

John didn't think it really suited her but wasn't sure he should say so. He shook his head, as if in disbelief, and she seemed to understand and reverted to her normal appearance.

"That's a talent a lot of human women would kill for," he commented. "Change your tan to match your outfit, all without worrying about skin cancer."

They sat for a while in silence and watched the small waves climb up the beach. Eventually Asha asked, "Have you experimented with your vedana since last weekend?"

John shook his head.

"You should you know. Get used to it so you learn to understand what it tells you. Like the other senses it can take time and practise to really get the most out of it. It's like not being able to appreciate different types of music until you learn how to listen properly."

"All right," said John, sitting up straighter. "What do you recommend?"

"Just close your eyes and feel it, John. You are sitting in front of the biggest presence of life on the planet: the ocean. It extends right around the globe, it's all connected and it's all alive. It's diffuse, like the soil, but it is undeniably and unimaginably huge. Just feel it."

John closed his eyes and tried to relax. He could hear the waves and feel the slight sputtering breeze. He could feel the sun beating down on him and realised he was getting very hot. There was a slight murmur of human conversation coming up the beach and there were the ever present flies. One crawled into the corner of his eye and he waved it away distracted. There was the constant briny smell of the ocean, he could even taste the salt and feel its stickiness in the air. He could hear the waves ... he could smell the salt ... he could feel the breeze ... he could feel how tired his muscles felt from the unusual amount of exercise … his head started to nod into a doze and he jerked upright, laughing.

"Sorry, Asha, I was getting a bit too relaxed."

Asha smiled. "The more you try the easier it will come."

John closed his eyes again, this time concentrating rather than relaxing. The waves were there, but now he could also hear birds, some far down the beach and a few in the trees behind him. The briny smell of the ocean was there, but under it was also the smell of rotting vegetation; some seaweed along the beach and something sweeter, some small animal or bird dead amongst it. He could feel the sand and the heat … and then he could feel Asha sitting next him, she felt closer this way and he was tempted to look to see if she had moved. That usually cold crack in the centre of his head felt distinctly warm.

He tried to reach out further, beyond Asha. It was like trying to look past a bright light into the darkness behind it. And then he felt it. Or rather he was swamped by it, overwhelmed by it. She was right, it was unimaginably huge! He had been trying to look for something specific, something tangible and distinct, but this was too big for that. It felt like he had almost fallen into it, as if he had been stretching out over the edge of a cliff to see how far down it was, and over extended. He drew back with a gasp and opened his eyes. Even with his eyes open he could still feel it. He wondered how he could possibly have missed it before. Asha was watching him with a very happy smile, she knew what he had felt.

"Wow," he said at last. "That's big."

Asha laughed. "When I first came down here I was astounded. I slept on the beach for a month before I finally began to accept it. On land most things are individual presences, it makes them … oh, I don't know, distinct, comprehensible, something. But the sea is something else. … I've often tried to imagine what it must be like to live in it."

Her tone had turned wistful and John wondered at the dissatisfaction that this might imply.

The day was getting hotter and more people were turning up. John and Asha went for another swim and then agreed it was time to go home.

The journey home was fairly quiet, each lost in their own

thoughts. When John pulled up at the garage Asha got out too.

"I did enjoy today, very much," she said. "The beach especially, but the car ride too, it was something new, something I'd never thought I would experience. Thank you, John."

"You're not coming inside?" he asked, feeling a little pathetic about the pleading tone he heard creeping into his voice.

"No ... I'm feeling a bit weary, sort of drawn out by everything. I think I need some time at home, if you know what I mean." She touched his arm in reassurance. "There's nothing wrong, I just need to rest. I'll see you next weekend." With that she headed off into the trees and was gone before John could come up with a response.

John put the car away and let himself into the house. As he sat down with a drink he realised that he, too, was tired. It had been a long week, a long day and he was not used to swimming so much. His tired body led him quickly to sleep that night. It was a night without dreams, unusual for John since the accident.

* * *

The following Saturday morning John was sitting outside, early, drinking his coffee and waiting. The morning was still cool but the day promised to be very hot. Asha appeared and walked gracefully across the lawn to sit opposite John.

"Good morning," she said.

"Good morning. It's going to be a hot one they said on the TV."

"Yes, very hot. Everything in the forest is rushing through its morning routine ready to switch off for the afternoon. Even the lizards and snakes don't like it getting this hot." She looked across at John. "It's probably going to be too hot to have you wandering around the forest, I think we should stay here."

"I guess that's best," John agreed, then smiled at her. "As long as I get to spend the day with you anyway."

Asha blushed but smiled in return.

"I've been meaning to ask," John continued, "why do I usually see you on Saturday or Sunday? Somehow I can't imagine the days of the week have much meaning to the forest."

"Oh ... I just thought it was better. When I spent time with Ellie I learned that you were often busy through the week, we didn't see much of you. So I just assumed it was best to leave you alone during the week."

"There's no need to stay away – unless you need to go to sleep early like Ellie did. I don't end up doing much during most week nights, so if you felt like talking, it'd be good to see you ... any time."

Asha looked coyly down for a moment before quietly saying, "I'll try not to make a nuisance of myself."

John just laughed. "Not much chance of that."

They chatted outside for a while with John eventually trying to make sense of human government for Asha.

Asha tried to summarise, "So a few people stick their hands up and everyone else votes to pick which of them get to make the rules for the next few years."

"Yes, but even the new people voted in have to obey the previously defined rules, at least until they can change them by formal and very long-winded procedures."

"So how does anything get done?"

"I may be excessively cynical, but I would say that not a lot does get done. It's one of the things that protects the country against bad government. It takes so long for changes to be made that there is only so much damage that can be done at a time. It keeps things stable and predictable. If government happened too quickly, if changes could be made too fast, then the country might see big changes after almost every election and the economy, and everything else, would suffer. The way things are run now it's often difficult to tell whether the election changed anything at all."

"That's just silly," Asha accused.

"Not really. People, well humans anyway, can be an emotional lot and inclined to over reaction, and to being misled by people with other agendas. Something bad happens and the immediate reaction can lead to really poor decisions. The inertia of government helps to rein in hurried decisions and limit the damage. It doesn't always work, even with such constraints we still get ill-advised wars declared. Innocent people get harmed and everyone's rights are abused as a result of such hurried government. And, because government is slow, it can take many years to recover from such badly chosen paths. But, even for all that, the system seems to work more often than not."

John stood up. "I need a drink of water. It's getting hot out here now, do you mind if we move inside to talk?"

Asha followed John into the house and he closed up to try and keep out the worst of the heat. John had his drink of water in the kitchen and then they walked through to the lounge room. On the wall on the left hung a large mirror. Something made John look into it as they walked past and he stopped, staring.

Asha paused too. "What?"

He didn't answer straight away. He reached out tentatively and placed his hands on her shoulders, gently turning her to face the mirror. "You're not there," he said finally.

"Oh, the mirror. No, they don't work for us. It's one of the few things I really envy of your material existence, the ability to see your own reflection."

John continued to stare at the mirror until Asha patted his hand still resting on her shoulder. "Come on, let's sit down. I didn't pick you as a vain person, enough with the mirror already."

He mentally shook himself and smiled at her, slowly and deliberately turning away from the disturbing lack of image in the mirror. In his head he went back over Asha's last few sentences and finally, much too late, he laughed. "No, I've never been that vain." They sat down across the coffee table from each other before another thought made it through his dazed mind. "You've never seen yourself?" he asked.

"Not my face, no," Asha answered. "As a girl I tried various experiments with water, I could wet my face and hair and then pick out a sort of reflection of the water but it didn't really show very much."

"I can fix that," he said with a grin. He stood back up. "Wait there."

He was back in a few minutes with a large pad and some pencils. He flicked over a few used pages until he came to a blank space and sat back to look at her.

Asha blushed and looked nervous. "You're serious? You want to draw me?"

"Sure," he said.

"So what do you want me to do? Do I have to sit anywhere special?" She laughed. "I don't know how to be drawn. Tell me when you want to start and I'll try to sit still and shut up."

This time John laughed. "I've already started," he said. "You don't need to sit still or pose or anything, that's not how I work."

In disbelief Asha sat forward to try and see his pad. John turned it so that she could see the outline of a head and shoulders taking shape on the page. "I thought artists were all temperamental people that refused to let anyone see their unfinished work and demanded complete obedience from their models."

"Maybe real artists are like that," John said in self-deprecation, "but I'm not that sort of artist. I'm a graphic artist and our work is done under constant review, so you learn not to be too precious about it. To be honest, if you wanted this done properly, you should get Jason to draw it. I'm technically very good, but Jason's work has that something extra that you want from real art."

"With the slight difficulty that he can't see me," Asha reminded him.

"There is that, I guess," John agreed, "so you'll just have to make do with me."

As he sketched they got to talking about movies and television. Asha had seen many children's shows with Ellie, and seen many other movies and television shows while visiting people's houses when she was exploring in her youth. "It's amazing how many people leave their television blaring while they're off doing something else, some even leave them running all night," she said. "In a lot of places it was almost as if they'd set things up especially for me.

"But I've never read a book," she sighed in disappointment. "That's something I've always wanted to be able to do."

John looked up from his pad. "I don't want to be ... indelicate, but can you read?"

"Not really ... I can recognise the occasional word and some human sign posts, but I can't really read. Not many of us can. Milla can, I think." She gave John a sad smile. "What little I've learned was learned with Ellie, I was sort of hoping to keep learning as she did."

John nodded. "Perhaps I should have kept some of her books."

"I doubt if that would be enough." Asha sat forward. "The day has gotten on and you claim not to be precious of your work – so show me." She grinned.

John smiled and added a couple of light touches before turning the pad around for her to look at, his eyes intent on her expression, trying to read her reaction to the drawing.

Asha sat back and stared at the drawing. "That's me?" she asked at last.

"It's not as good as I would like to be able to do," John said, "but if I showed it to anyone that knew you they would recognise it as your face, yes."

Asha sat forward again, looking intently.

"Of course it's not exactly what you'd see if you could look in a mirror," John explained.

Asha looked away from the drawing to look at John's face, "What do you mean?"

"Well for one thing this drawing has no colour and so it does no justice to your complexion or your eyes. For another thing, a face is not truly symmetrical. When you look in a mirror you see a mirror image of your face, this drawing is not mirrored. Come and see what I mean." John carried the drawing to the mirror and showed Asha what it looked like.

Asha's eyes darted back and forth between the drawing and the mirror several times before she nodded. "I see ... that is, I can't really see the lack of symmetry, but I can see that there is a difference."

They sat back down and John continued, "The third thing is that a reflection is alive, a moving image, whereas this drawing is static. For that reason alone a drawing like this one will never be able to give you the same impression as a reflection. If I gave Jason this drawing there is a chance he would be able to imbue it with a sense of life and movement that I never seem to catch."

"You're very critical of your work," Asha said.

"Just realistic, I know where my talents lie. It's one of the reasons why Jason and I work so well together."

"But the drawing still looks like me?" she asked.

"Oh yes, no doubt, this is a technically good drawing of your face."

"So I'm pretty?" she asked.

John laughed. "You're way beyond pretty, Asha." Asha blushed and John looked a bit embarrassed by his open declaration. "Well you are," he added finally as if there had been some argument.

John took the drawing and sat it on the mantelpiece while he went to prepare something for dinner and to pour himself a whiskey

– he figured he had earned it.

They chatted some more into the evening and then Asha said she had better go. "Thank you very much for drawing me," she added. "It really is quite something to see yourself for the first time," she looked across at the mantelpiece and smiled, "and not too disappointing."

"If you like that you should see the real thing." He had to consciously stop himself from putting his hand out to touch her face.

That night John's dreams started well but turned strange with his drawing of Asha morphing into a distorted version of Edvard Munch's famous painting, "The Scream", and then Ellie's face emerged, also screaming, as a pale almost skeletal image from the murky blue background of the painting. John woke wet with sweat and quivering with an unrecognised fear. It took a long time to get back to sleep.

* * *

Saturday night's strange, almost psychedelic, nightmare turned out to be the start of a series. Each night there was another strange nightmare, and another long time getting back to sleep.

On Tuesday more of John's real life intruded when his boss, Stan, called him and Jason into his office. Another potential new client – not as big as Stephenson would have been, but big enough to put themselves out for – they needed to get a proposal ready by Friday. John and Jason spent much of the day discussing the job, continuing over lunch. The work spilled over into Wednesday and Thursday, and when the office was closing up Thursday night they still had work to discuss, so Jason said he would be around at John's in a little while with some takeaway food.

John got home and tidied up a bit. After five nights of badly disrupted sleep he was feeling quite haggard, but he knew that he and Jason had to make some progress for this new job. An hour or so later Jason arrived and parked out front. He carried in some Chinese takeaway and they got down to it, eating and discussing ideas and sketching out thoughts on their pads. A while later they had both settled down with their own thoughts, quietly sketching and thinking at opposite ends of the kitchen table.

"Oh," came Asha's surprised gasp from the kitchen doorway. "I'm sorry, John, I had no idea there was someone else here."

"It's okay," said John. "This is my friend Jason." He said it as an introduction, not thinking about what he was doing or saying.

Jason looked up at John. "What?"

John was still trying to get his mind to catch up, looking back and forth between Jason at the other end of the table and Asha in the doorway.

"I'll go," said Asha.

"No wait," John called.

Jason looked around at the doorway, seeing nothing he looked back at John with a puzzled expression.

"See you Saturday," Asha said, and was gone.

John called after her and got up, rushing to the back door, but when he looked out there was no sign of her. He walked slowly back to the kitchen and sat back down at the table.

"What was that all about?" Jason asked.

John stared at him with no idea what he was going to say. He replayed the events trying to find some explanation for what Jason had seen ... and not seen.

"Are you okay?" Jason asked.

"Must have been daydreaming," John said. "One of the hazards of spending too much time home alone is starting to talk to yourself," he continued with a smile, trying to make a joke of it.

Jason looked at him strangely. "Not just at home either," he said quietly.

John looked back in surprise.

"A couple of Saturdays ago Liz saw you at the beach having fun with someone ... except there was no one else there as far as she could tell. She came back quite upset about it, worried about you, but we agreed to let it go. John, is there something going on?"

"You want to know if I've flipped my lid?" John asked.

Jason just looked at him.

John put his elbows on the table and started rubbing the sides of his head as if trying to reach that cold spot, the crack, that he could still feel in the centre of his head.

"You're going to make bald spots if you continue doing that too," commented Jason. When John looked up Jason explained, "That rubbing the sides of your head, that's something I've noticed you doing for months now. Do you get headaches or something? Is this something more than what happened to Samantha and Ellie?"

"Can I get you a drink?" John asked.

"No, I can't stay much longer. I don't like to leave Liz alone too late. John, is there something going on? Do you need help? Can we help? Talk to me."

John looked over the table at Jason and had to stop himself from rubbing his head again. What could he say? Sure, Jason, I've been falling in love with my imaginary friend, but I don't want any help because I don't want to stop her visiting. That didn't sound like a promising start to the conversation. He decided that little bits of partial truth may be enough.

"Yes, I have been getting headaches – since that day you found me in the kitchen actually." John watched Jason cringe over that one. Yes, that was a way to persuade him to back off a bit. "As for some occasional ... anomalous behaviour, well, at the moment I just put that down to too much time alone. Got to practice talking or my voice might stop working." He tried to chuckle with that last sentence to lighten Jason's mood.

But Jason was not in the mood to be jollied. "This is serious, John. If you're getting headaches and behaving strangely then maybe there's something wrong. Maybe you ought to see someone about it. I don't want to worry you, but I've read about brain tumours affecting the way people behave."

Uh-huh, thought John, he followed this line of thought because he had run along it himself – better a mortal brain tumour than insanity. Well, there was something in that, wasn't there? "Perhaps you're right," he agreed. "Maybe I should see someone. I'll look around and see who I can find."

Jason seemed mollified by John's capitulation and began to pack up, saying it was time he got back to Liz.

John saw Jason off, came inside and cleaned away the remains of the Chinese food. Then he poured himself a whiskey and sat back on the kitchen chair to think over what had happened. It was obvious that Jason had neither seen nor heard Asha. She had spoken clearly and the lights were all on when she was standing there in the doorway, but still Jason had not perceived her. Asha had told him that others did not see her, but why couldn't they hear her? Where was the sense in that?

She had become so real to him over the last few weeks. So real he even had a drawing of her in his pad. He flicked back a few pages to make sure she was still there. But Jason had not seen her, and he had not heard her. It was one thing to kid himself when he was on his own, but it was quite another to have her absence from reality confirmed so directly. Maybe Jason really was right, maybe it was time that John sought professional help.

* * *

On Saturday morning John took his coffee outside and sat at his garden-setting waiting for her. The sun was hidden behind clouds and the morning was cooler, as if autumn was not far away. His thoughts were disjointed. He was looking forward to seeing Asha, but he was also concerned where this was taking him. Thursday seemed to have proved that Asha was merely an imaginary friend, no more real than any child's. How healthy could it be for him to be sitting here longing for a visit from his imaginary friend?

As she appeared through the trees John's doubts were once again pushed aside by her presence. Graceful as always, she had once again assumed a size compatible with his own. They smiled at each other, each caught in their relief at seeing the other.

"I thought you may not want to see me after my intrusion the other night," Asha said.

John waved it away, he didn't want to think of Thursday night and the doubts it had raised. "I said to let yourself in whenever you wanted, it was my mistake that made it embarrassing. Don't worry about it." He paused before continuing, "I sort of presumed we were walking into the forest today, I've even packed a small lunch to take with me. Is that what you want to do?"

"I was hoping you'd want to come out," Asha said. "I thought we might visit my friend Nona, She's the one you saw – that first night."

"Sure, I'd love to," said John, which wasn't entirely true. Not that he was worried about meeting a friend of Asha's, but he was reluctant to share his time with her. "I'm ready to head out whenever you like," he said. Cursing himself for sounding like an over-eager schoolboy, he continued, "but if you'd rather sit for a while ... ?"

"No, let's start," she said, apparently pleased at his enthusiasm.

They quickly fell into a similar rhythm to previous excursions with John following Asha's lead as she wandered through the trees. It made John think of someone introducing a stranger to a room full of friends. He grinned and wondered what her friends made of him.

Perhaps an hour later Asha gestured for John to walk quietly as they entered a small clearing. A few feet away sat the older woman that John had seen that first night – the night his mind broke, his sceptical self intruded briefly before he pushed it away.

She was sitting at the base of a tree with one arm held out in front of her. On the ground around her, on her arm, on her shoulders, and even on her head were small grey birds, all busy chirruping to each other – and to the woman? – and flitting back and forth with their tails bobbing up and down as if they had too much energy to contain.

Like Asha, the woman had a slender, athletic appearance. Her clothing was also quite similar but less elaborately patterned. At the moment she was the size of a girl around twelve years old. Looking up at Asha and John she smiled and her size slowly increased until she was compatible with their own. The birds didn't seem to notice.

Asha and John sat down carefully at the base of another tree. After a few moments some of the birds came over to Asha and fluttered around. One of the birds settled briefly on John's head before thinking better of it and moving to Asha's shoulder.

The little birds were surprisingly noisy, especially when you were up this close. John watched as some continued to hunt through the leaf-litter on the ground around them, while others fluttered around Asha and the other woman.

Some minutes later the swarm of little birds moved slowly on, and it became quiet in the clearing.

"Hi, Nona," said Asha, "this is John."

"Hello," said Nona.

John recognised the voice, but Asha and Nona had proceeded as if he had not seen Nona on that first night. John supposed it was simpler that way. "Hi," he replied quietly. Not sure of how best to continue he tried, "I guess those birds answer the question of whether other animals can see you."

Nona smiled. "If you thought that was impressive, get Asha to sit still long enough and you won't be able find her for all the creatures attracted to her. She has a natural mothering instinct that they all sense. I think they come to tell her their problems, knowing that she'll try to help them."

Asha looked down, embarrassed, and Nona looked at her affectionately and then back at John. "You seem to be another injured creature she has taken under her wing," she added.

"Nona!" exclaimed Asha.

John laughed. "Is that what it is? I knew it couldn't be my scintillating conversation."

Nona seemed satisfied that she'd made her point and continued, "Not all animals see us, or not well. Most human domesticated animals seem oblivious to our presence. Wild animals are usually aware of us, but I don't think they all see us as we are. Birds are very aware of us, although how we appear to them is anyone's guess. I sometimes wonder if we appear to them to be trees that move, stand still long enough and they try to nest on you."

"Have you ever met another human that can see you?" asked John.

"Asha's right," Nona said, smiling at him kindly, "you are a font of curiosity. No. When Asha said that you had seen her I was very surprised. So was the entire stand."

Asha explained, "Nona and I both belong to the same stand. We've been friends for a long time. Unlike most of our stand we both like the solitude we can get closer to the edge of the forest, although I think Nona frowns on my curiosity for human goings-on."

"Asha is quite young, by aaranya standards," Nona said. "I satisfied most of my curiosity a long time ago, although I never had the same incentive." She gave John a look he did not understand, though he did notice Asha look down, apparently blushing.

"I think that some of my questions arise because ..." John paused looking for words. "I have trouble imagining what your lives must be like. I cannot imagine life without all the human rushing about stuff. To try and imagine a life that is so immersed in nature is difficult."

Asha continued to look down, her expression hidden.

Nona answered, "I think your questions are partly because you are human and partly because you are male." She added with a grin,

"It's a bad combination."

Relaxing a little more John said, "To watch Asha in the forest is to imagine an idyllic life of communing with the trees, but that feels ... incomplete. It seems like there must be more, but I also wonder if I am being offensive just by asking."

Nona chuckled at that. "No, you are not offensive. To anyone not of the aaranya, even another narun, the relationship we have with the trees is difficult to understand. I imagine it could be similar to the relationship of human shepherds to their flocks, but even that analogy has its limits. Our relationship with trees aside, we are still a community of imperfect beings.

"We have arguments and misunderstandings. I sometimes think it is only because there are so few of us that things do not often get out of hand. There is room for people to get away from each other while their differences sort themselves out. No, we are not a perfect people."

Nona looked from Asha to John and then asked, "Have you considered trying to tell others of your kind about us?"

John gave a bitter laugh. "Not seriously. I'm having enough trouble trying to believe it myself."

"Oh." Nona paused, unsure of his response. "Others in the stand have expressed the same concern," Nona answered a look from Asha. To John she continued, "You've become a subject of some importance to our little community. It was different in primitive times when sightings would be assigned to ghosts or spirits or whatever, but in this new age of modern humans we worry what you may make of us."

"I don't think John's like that," said Asha.

"It's not really a matter of what John is like, Asha, if others find out then John may not have any control over what happens."

"Nona's right," John said. "I would have no influence – if it ever came to that." He added silently to himself: in fact they'd probably want to study me too. "But I don't intend to tell anyone," he continued. "I figure that's a decision for your people, though I can't say I'd recommend it."

John was uncomfortable, the subject was too close to his own doubts. Searching for a change of subject he looked at Asha and asked, "I've noticed that your weather predictions seem very accurate, is that something inherent to narun?"

"Not to narun. It mostly comes from our trees. Forests, particularly large ones, are usually aware of what weather is coming several days in advance," said Asha.

Nona asked John more about the town and what he did there, and the conversation wandered on. Sometime later Nona made her excuses and departed into the forest.

Asha and John got up after John had finished eating his lunch, and the birds that had congregated around Asha started to move off. John laughed. "Nona was right. You're like Snow White singing to the birds in the forest."

Periods of sunlight made the afternoon warmer as John and Asha wandered through the trees again, touching and listening to the forest as they walked. John occasionally tried out his ability to sense the life around him, still with varying levels of success.

It was dusk when they arrived back at John's house. Asha came in and settled in the lounge while John made himself a cup of coffee and brought it through.

They chatted about nothing much for a few minutes before Asha said, "You said today that you still have trouble believing." It was apparent that she had spent much of the day brooding on his questions to Nona. "After all you have seen and experienced, do you really doubt your own senses that much?"

John looked across into her eyes, trying to find some appropriate response. He was tired, the week of sleeping badly had crashed in on him. He wanted to hold on to the illusion, to let his imagination keep leading him on. He wanted to lie to her – to tell her that he believed in her and her impossible world, and to avoid saying those things that he knew would hurt her. But there was so much he couldn't rationalise to himself, so much that didn't sit well when – sitting alone at the end of the day – he reflected on the time he'd spent with Asha. She had no reflection. Jason not only couldn't see her, he couldn't hear her either. He remembered and felt the crack in his head and all that that implied. He couldn't keep lying to himself, and he couldn't lie to Asha.

"When I am with you I have no doubts, there is no room in my head for denials. ... But when you are gone and I am left with just my memories of the day ... when I am forced to plan for work the next day, my *real* life ... when I remember the night I first saw you ... then, I can recognise how ... how *impossible* you are.

"I want so much to believe you are real, but how can I? I'm broken. I felt myself break. I feel broken." He tapped the side of his head. "The break is tangible, it is there deep inside as a constant reminder that I am no longer whole. It is there day and night, waking and sleeping. It is there when I am with you, and it is there in my real-world life. And, since I am broken, how can I believe the impossible things that my mind tries to tell me? How can I believe that you are real?"

Asha went over and knelt next to his chair. She leaned forward slowly, reached out and held his face. Tears flooded her eyes. "Can't you feel me? Can't you sense my life? The only thing that broke inside your mind were the barriers that prevented you being aware of me. I am here. I am real. *Please!*" she pleaded with him.

He placed one of his hands over hers, looking back into her eyes. With his other hand he reached forward and wiped tears from her cheek. He was trying desperately to believe, but his life in the modern human world conspired against him.

"There is nothing that I know from my life that makes you possible." He dropped his eyes from hers and finished softly, "I can't believe." He reached up and removed her hands from his face.

Asha fell back from him and dropped her head, tears streaming silently down her cheeks. She looked at her hands, seeming to doubt them herself. How could he reject her very existence? Unable to speak, unable to even think, Asha jumped to her feet and ran out into the hall, through the back door, and hurled herself into the forest.

Inside, John stared at where she had been. He had seen the tears fall from her cheeks to the arm of the chair ... but it was not wet. He had wiped tears from her cheeks and felt them wet against his fingers ... but his fingers were now dry as if the tears had never been. He did not try to follow her, there was no one to follow.

5. Lost

John felt bewildered, devastated, lost. For some hours after Asha had left he had simply sat there ... numb ... blank. Eventually he prepared himself for bed and lay down, but no sleep came. Just thoughts of Asha. Thoughts of what he had said to her. Thoughts of what may happen next.

On Sunday he wandered the house in a daze, doing weekend chores by rote, fulfilling the requirements of this real life. On Monday he went to work and spent much of the morning just staring at his desk not knowing what to do, not knowing how to face the real life he had chosen.

Jason came to his desk at lunchtime. "Are you okay?"

John looked back at him with a blank expression.

"Have you had a chance to find someone that might help you?" Jason asked.

John continued to stare at him for a moment before his mind took him back to their conversation the previous Thursday night. "No ... it's probably too late for that anyway," he answered, not realising how cryptic that must sound.

"Too late?"

John just shook his head.

Stan came to John's desk after lunch, his voice full of care – Jason must have spoken with him. "Go home, John," he said. "Take some days if you need them."

So John left and drove slowly home. On the gravel road to his house he was paying so little attention that he almost ran into another car, a van, coming the other way. Only the fact that he was driving so slowly saved them from a serious accident. John could hear Asha screaming loudly in his mind as if he was somehow hurting her yet again. He stared about him, more panicked by the sound of her screams than by the near accident. The screaming stopped. He had imagined that, just as he had imagined everything else. The man driving the van stared at John through the windscreens, shocked by the near accident, and then turned back to the road and sped quickly away, the van kicking up gravel as it went.

John arrived home and walked around to the back of the house, where he sat staring into the trees. Why was he sitting here? Did he expect Asha to return? Did he want Asha to return? If Asha returned, could he learn to believe in her? Would that be a good thing? Did any of these questions actually matter? Probably not. Some things were simply not amenable to logic.

He had believed, for a while, that if he was strong he could overcome his broken mind, that he could deny the false world that it had offered him. So he had been strong; he had told Asha the truth, and she had gone. But that had solved nothing. It had not healed his mind, he knew that, he could still feel the crack, he was still broken. He had hurt Asha and achieved nothing.

John could not believe that Asha existed, but he could no longer deny how important she had become to him. Despite what he had said to her, he did not want her gone from his life. It did not matter whether she was real or not – he needed her! And yet he had denied her.

He got up from the garden-setting and walked into the trees calling her name. He wandered the trails until dark and then went back to the house. For the rest of the week, and the following weekend, John spent most of the daylight hours wandering the forest near his house.

In the weeks following, John returned to work but continued to spend his time at home walking the forest. Sometimes he pretended his walks were just exploring the forest, but he was not really fooling himself. He missed her. He wanted her to come back. He would learn how to lie to her if that was what it took to keep her near.

But she did not appear. John tried looking for Nona too, but could not even work out where it was that they had met previously.

John's grief for Samantha and Ellie had not left him, it would often catch him by surprise, but his obsession with Asha was growing and taking up more and more of his thoughts. Walking the forests filled much of his time, leaving him hungry, so he was eating better, and tired, so he was sleeping better. With food, sleep and exercise, John had not been this physically fit and healthy for a long time.

At work people commented on how well he was looking. John was amused, when he allowed himself to admit what was happening, wondering if they would still be relieved if they knew his health was based on a search for his imaginary friend.

At first Jason was relieved that John appeared to have pulled back from the brink of some precipice, but the feeling didn't last. John had become absent-minded, remote and inattentive, and the work they did together was no longer going well.

As time passed with no sign of Asha, John began to wonder if his previous madness may have been transient, if his mind really had healed and would no longer show what he so desperately wanted ... but then he would go again into the forest and sense the trees. He would feel the breezes flowing through the crack in his brain. He would touch the trees and sense the life flowing beneath the bark, and he knew there was no change. His mind remained broken. If Asha was there to be seen he knew he would still be able to see her. Had he lost her too?

* * *

On a cold but fine Saturday morning John organised the new camping gear he had purchased through the week. He had told work he may not be in next week. They continued to be understanding and he hoped it would last. Jason in particular had seemed relieved that John was taking time off, obviously hoping things would improve when he returned, perhaps hoping that John was seeking the help that Jason believed he needed.

It was mid-morning by the time he finally set out. He set himself a brisk pace to make up for being so late getting away. By the time he stopped for a late lunch he was no longer so confident of his compass. He was trying to maintain a north-easterly direction, trying to get deeper into this huge forest. That was all. He had no more specific plans, just get deeper and deeper in the hope that eventually Asha would appear. In the back of his mind he knew he was being foolish, but since he had no better ideas he simply refused to think about it further.

The slopes were getting steeper, the trees and undergrowth were getting thicker, and his progress was slow – there was no Asha to show him the easier ways through. He shrugged, he would keep going anyway. He finished his lunch, picked up his things, checked his compass, and headed out once more.

The afternoon sun helped make up for the cool autumn day and he was forced to stop and take off his backpack so he could remove his jacket. As he walked on, he began to enjoy the birds calling around him, to feel something of what he had experienced when walking the forest with Asha. The birds mostly kept out of sight, the forest was very thick through here, but he could tell that they often came close, curious about this stranger passing through their domain. Occasionally he would hear the scuffle of leaves as some creature on the ground hid from his noisy approach. Other than the occasional small cloud of insects, swarming through patches of sunlight, there were few bugs to disturb his peaceful walk.

He descended into a valley as the sun dipped below the western hills, and the shadow brought an extra chill to the air so he stopped and put his jacket back on. A while later he got to the top of the next ridge, this one quite high, and realised that night was almost on him. The hills John had been hiking were getting steadily steeper and higher, and the sun was now disappearing beyond them to the west. In the rapidly fading light he tried to find somewhere good to camp the night.

He found a level place between the roots of a particularly large tree and started rummaging through his backpack. He found the rechargeable lantern he had purchased, the package had guaranteed eight hours of bright fluorescent light. He flicked it on and was relieved that it was working after the day being jostled in his backpack. He pulled out the small packages of his two-person tent and his sleeping bag, and unrolled the groundsheet that he had been told would make sleeping on the ground drier and more comfortable.

He was trying to work out how to make the tent pop-up as advertised when the light went very dim. John fumbled his way to the light, switched it off briefly – the night was suddenly very dark – and then back on. It radiated brightly for a couple of seconds and then went dim again. He shook it, partly in frustration and partly in some vain hope it would help, and tried a third time – this time it simply started out dim.

John had the horrible realisation that he probably should have read the instructions before he threw away the packaging, probably he was supposed to charge the lantern before he used it. It seemed obvious now, but he just hadn't thought about it. Truth be told he hadn't thought about much at all, he probably should have practised with the tent too. "At least I can probably work the sleeping bag," he said and grinned ruefully to himself.

In the dim light of his lantern John found he was able to get his tent to uncoil and his groundsheet and sleeping bag laid out. He did not fancy trying to get his gas cooker assembled and a meal prepared in such dim light so he climbed into his sleeping bag. He used his jacket as a pillow. He'd just have to go hungry tonight and work it all out in the morning. He took a drink from his canteen of water, pulled the almost useless lantern into the tent with him and zipped up the entrance. He switched off the dim light and set about trying to sleep.

He thought he would have trouble sleeping, but the day's exercise caught up with him and he was quickly lost in a deep slumber.

* * *

Sometime later he awoke to noises just outside his tent. Something was rummaging through his things – he realised he probably should have brought his backpack into the tent with him. He heard the rattle of his cooking gear and knew that the backpack must still be open and the animal, whatever it was, was pulling things out. John cleared his throat loudly and thumped the ground inside his tent, and was pleasantly surprised to hear the fading steps of the small creature moving quickly away from his tent. Probably just a possum, he thought, but they could be smelly creatures so he hoped it hadn't left a mess over his things.

He unzipped the flap on his tent and looked out. There was a full moon risen high in the sky, and the forest outside his tent was surprisingly bright. The air was still and very cold, and a faint musky smell lingered from the animal that had been at his backpack. He was wide awake now so he decided to get up and enjoy the moonlight. He moved the backpack into the tent and zipped it up, hoping it would stay safe while he looked around.

He was pleased to have camped on a high ridge, the ground was clearer, making it easier to move around. Just a short distance from his tent was a thinning of the trees that allowed him to look out over the valley to the north. The moon was large and bright, and cast a luminous glow over the forest laid out in the valleys and ridges before him. Dew on the leaves glistened like small stars. Occasional patches of low mist showed among the trees in the lower parts of the valleys. Small clouds dotted the sky so that it was interspersed with bright dots of only the brightest stars and the glowing silver and white of the tufted clouds. The air was crisp and cold and felt pleasantly invigorating. John took a deep breath of the clear air, and stared out over the forest, enraptured by the beauty of the night.

Some immeasurable time later John heard what sounded like music, perhaps a distant voice. Down in the valley before him, John thought he could discern a glow beyond that imparted by the moon.

John was caught up in the almost sensual experience of the night, he gave no thought as to whether it was wise when he started to make his way down into the valley. It was only as he entered some of the darker shadows of the trees and thickening undergrowth that he was reminded of how unfamiliar his surroundings were. He thought he saw a brighter patch in the forest ahead, where the moon was breaking through, so he moved toward it. That brightness faded as he approached so he looked forward and saw another.

In this way John found himself near the bottom of the first valley before he realised that he had lost track of his camp site. He had also wandered into one of those patches of mist he had seen from the ridge. Despite the still night the mist seemed to swirl around him, leaving his jacket damp and chilled. He looked down at the ground hoping that his clumsy movements had left some obvious track, but the mist had quickly obscured anything John may have had the skills to find.

After brief consideration he felt confident that he knew the correct direction for his tent and started walking. He felt the ground rising beneath his feet. His breath sped up with the exertion and the underlying fear that he was walking in the wrong direction. It felt as if the mist were moving with him – surely he should have climbed out of it by now. He looked up at the moon, still beautiful, but so high in the sky that it offered little sense of direction. He noticed too that there was a cloud beginning to encroach, not large but its slow moving shadow would make the forest dark again so he hurried his steps up the ridge.

The top of the ridge came much too soon, narrower and lower than the ridge of his camp. The cloud's shadow passed over him. John slipped and fell over as he was turning to look around. He rolled down a few feet before managing to stop himself. He stood up, dizzy. It was like being the blindfolded "It" in a child's game. John no longer had any idea which way he had come from, even to this ridge, and he was now sure that this was the wrong ridge. He sat down on the damp ground to wait for the cloud's shadow to pass.

He was lost. There was no fudging this one. Samantha would often tease him about being lost and he would always insist that he was not lost, he was just not where he had intended to be. That excuse wasn't going to cut it this time. He had no idea where he was, and he had no idea in which direction lay his tent – with his backpack, his food and his compass.

John took a deep breath and willed himself not to panic. All he had to do was wait. In a few hours the moon would have sunk enough to point the way west, it may even be safer to wait for dawn and the sun to show in the east. Once he found the right ridge it should not take too long to find his tent – and food to satisfy his now rumbling stomach.

He moved to a more comfortable position at the base of a tree, and curled up and tried to relax. The night would pass, the sun would come up and everything would look better in the morning, or so he hoped. He pulled up the collar of his jacket and tried to snuggle deeper into it, out of the chill of the mist and the night.

* * *

When he awoke, John was surprised to find the sun shining brightly. It was still early, the air was still chilled and damp from the night, but he had missed the dawn.

He stretched out his arms and then tried to stand – unsuccess-fully. He slipped back to the ground with a groan. He had pain from a stiff neck, an aching back, and numb, chilled, feet that refused to obey him. Sitting there feeling sorry for himself, it took him a few moments to recognise the sound coming from above him: laughter.

About twenty feet above him, sitting on the branch of a small tree, a youth was chuckling, amused at the sight of John's discomfort. Indignant, John pushed himself roughly to his cold feet muttering, "It's not that funny!" only to almost fall over again in surprise at the boy's response.

"Whah! woohhh!" the boy exclaimed and slipped backwards off the branch.

The expected crashing sound of the boy landing on the ground never came. Instead the boy's surprised expression peered around from behind the trunk of the tree, about a dozen feet from the ground. The combined look of surprise and suspicion, and the disturbed appearance of the boy's hair, was so unexpected that this time it was John's turn to laugh.

"Sorry, sorry," John said. "Let me guess. I'm not supposed to be able to see you. Well, that's what you get for laughing at another's misfortune." The absurdity of his statement, and the relief at finding another of the tree-folk, made him laugh even harder.

The boy looked like he was about to flee, but the laughter made him pause, first in annoyance and then slowly relaxing, grinning at the situation. He climbed back to his branch and sat again, pulling himself upright with such mock severity that they both laughed some more.

"So you are him?" the boy asked eventually.

"If you mean the human that can see you then, yes, I am him," John replied. "Have you spoken with Asha?" he asked, suddenly hopeful.

"No, but news gets around. What are you doing here?"

Not sure how he should respond, John answered lightly, "Getting lost apparently. Is there any chance you can help me find my tent?"

The boy dropped to the ground, landing lightly and soundlessly despite the twenty-foot drop. Apparently he was convinced that John meant no harm. Now he was closer, John could see that the boy was really a young man – just small in the manner of their kind. Dressed in a simple but bright green tunic and breeches, he was slender and youthful in appearance, reminding John of a young Robin Hood, or perhaps a matured Peter Pan. His hair was dark and seemed to flow around his head in waves. There was a cheeky cast to his expression and John suspected that he was not the first human to provide amusement for this man – boy, the grin was still a boy's grin.

"It's this way," the boy said, and almost danced off the small ridge into the southern valley. John followed at a much more sedate pace and eventually the boy slowed down enough that John would not get left behind.

"Do you have a name?" John asked.

"Yes," the boy responded with a cheeky grin, obviously intending no further answer.

"I'm called John."

"Yes, I know." The boy smiled again.

"You know it is considered polite to offer your name when introduced?" John tried again.

"I believe my mother may have said something like that." The boy grinned and began to walk lightly backwards in front of John, just as fast and agile as walking forwards. "I sometimes think I may have been a disappointment to my mother."

"Surprise me," John muttered, gaining an even larger grin from the boy who turned and ran up a nearby tree. He did some sort of flip or somersault – too fast for John to see it clearly – and landed lightly and silently beside John.

"It's a beautiful day, isn't it?" the boy said through a wide smile.

Unable to resist the boy's infectious enthusiasm, John could only laugh and agree.

They climbed the next ridge and John had to spend more time watching where he put his feet on the steep slope, but the boy continued to bounce back and forth between the trees. He flickered in and out of the patches of sun and shadow, disconcertingly casting no shadow of his own and sometimes almost disappearing as John caught glimpses of sunlit forest through his body.

At the top of the ridge it was only a short walk before John saw a large familiar tree and the tent at its base. "Thank you," he called to the boy.

John bent down, unzipped the flap of his tent, and drew out his backpack. As he sat back on his haunches he found the boy leaning over him peering into the tent. "Jeez!" he exclaimed in surprise at finding the boy so close. The boy skipped away, laughing, apparently pleased with the effect.

John had a drink of water from his canteen. "Is there a place near here where I can get more water?" he asked the boy.

"Yes," the boy responded, but said nothing more.

John decided to ignore the lack of useful response, maybe he would have more patience after he had eaten.

The boy watched John clear a space for his gas burner, apparently both nervous and fascinated by the flames that appeared. He passed his hand a few times close to the flame – ignoring John's warning that it was hot – until he finally passed his fingers through the flames. He yelped and pulled them out and peered at them to see what had happened. Not too much apparently, and he skipped off to watch from a distance as John finished boiling water to reconstitute his dehydrated meal.

It was not tasty, it was just a pre-packaged camping meal, some cross between plastic and cardboard. It was not enough, it had been a long time since John's last meal – John was wishing he'd gone for the two-person packs. But the warm food did help. His stomach stopped complaining, he felt calmer, and he felt more capable of thinking about the day to come.

First things first, he'd have to find somewhere to relieve himself. He thought of asking the boy to respect his privacy, but considering the boy's cheeky disposition, that was likely to be counter-productive. He said, "Excuse me," and took his hand-shovel and a roll of toilet paper off to find the most private spot he could.

When he came back the boy was sitting in a lower branch, whistling with ostentatious nonchalance. Embarrassment forgotten, John couldn't help but laugh, and the boy's face cracked into a grin, breaking his whistle into a wheeze and resulting in more laughs from both of them.

"Are you going to hang about all day?" John asked.

The boy just shrugged.

John started packing up his camp. It took a couple of goes but he finally got his tent to fold back into the flat round pillow it had started as. The boy thought it was amazing, asking him to coil and uncoil it again and again. The sleeping bag turned out to be more of a problem and John wondered at his assumptions the previous night. Eventually he got it rolled small enough to fit back into its undersized bag and was finally able to close up his backpack.

With his backpack on he took a drink from his canteen and slung it over his shoulder. He looked around expecting to see the boy's cheeky grin, but he was nowhere to be seen.

"Hello?" John spoke loudly. Nothing. "If you're still around you could help by telling me where to find water," he tried again, but still nothing.

"Damn it," John said to himself and started back down the slope he had walked up with the boy. He'd sort of liked the boy's company and had hoped to have it a bit longer.

He hadn't been walking long when the boy appeared, hanging head down from the branch of a tree not far ahead. The boy grinned, chuckled at the frown he saw on John's face, and flipped off the branch landing silently beneath. "This way," he said, and led off slightly to the left of the direction that John had been walking. He moved lightly over the ground, leaping to touch a trunk here, a branch there, all the time moving, but listening intently too, as if to some music that John could not hear.

Eventually John started to understand, there was adoration in the joyous dance of this young man. The way he touched the trees, the way he laughed at the sunlight through their leaves as though they were somehow talking to him.

"This," John said, gesturing around him, "is your home?" More of a statement than a question.

Turning to walk backwards again, the boy grinned and nodded at him. John was about to warn him that he was going to walk into a tree when the boy did some sort of impossible turn and leap. He landed against the trunk and appeared to melt into the wood, smiling widely as he disappeared.

John stopped, open-mouthed, staring at where the boy had disappeared. He had, of course, seen Asha do much the same thing, but he was not sure he would ever get used to it. And what the boy had done seemed different somehow, more of a game, as if he and the tree were sharing the joke – of course the joke in this case was John.

There was another chuckle and the boy reappeared, peering around from the other side. "Neat huh?" he said, and then leapt forward again, moving lightly onward.

John closed his mouth and walked after the boy. He took it slowly, hoping that the boy would come back and get him if he got too far behind.

An hour or so later they reached a shallow, fast running, stream. "Thank you ... very much," John said to the boy and proceeded to remove his backpack. The boy just grinned at him and skipped into the trees.

A while later John was feeling much refreshed from washing his face and torso in the cold running water. He decided the rest of him would do for now, so he dried off and dressed against the still cool morning. He refilled his canteen and then decided the spot was too lovely to leave, so he pulled out his gas burner and made himself a sweet black coffee. He sat with his back against the base of a tree, in a patch of warm sunlight, and breathed in deeply, feeling that he might finally retrieve some of what he had felt last night before getting so clumsily lost.

He sipped at his coffee and considered what he should be doing next. Whatever else, John still wanted to find Asha. He did not want to think about why. He did not want to think about how unhealthy it was to stalk an imaginary friend. He just wanted to find her. He wondered if the boy could help.

The boy emerged out of the trunk, high in a large tree not far to John's right. He grinned widely and leapt down, he seemed to fall impossibly slowly and landed silently. Soon he was standing close to where John was sitting. It was only now, as the boy stood only a few feet tall, that John realised the boy had spent much of the morning almost as tall as John.

"Are you going to hang about all day?" the boy asked John with a grin.

John gave an exaggerated shrug in response and the boy laughed.

The boy bounced to the stream, merged into the water and then reappeared, dry, a little further down. Grown considerably larger again, he skipped forward to sit cross legged in front of John, now matching John in size. He laughed at the stunned look on John's face and after a moment John joined him.

"I'm looking for Asha," John said.

"Yes." The boy responded as if John had said something obvious.

"Can you help me?"

The boy's face turned serious for the first time since John had met him. "Does she want you to find her?"

John considered this. It was rather more up front and direct than he wanted. He knew he should have asked himself this question, but he was not certain that he would like the answer so he had avoided it.

"I'm ... not certain," John said, equivocating. "I miss her. I want to learn more from her. I want her to feel that she can return to her trees ... but I think I have made things difficult for her."

The boy had retained his serious expression, he did not appear to have made any particular judgement yet, so John pushed on.

"The thing is ..." John hesitated. Was there a way to say this that would not gain the same response from this boy as he had from Asha? He'd gone over their conversations in his head and could find no good way to put it.

"The thing is ... I think I am broken. That my mind is broken. I think that you and Asha are products of my imagination. I don't believe you actually exist, but I don't want you to go away."

The boy stared at him for a moment and then rolled over backwards, laughing loudly. He kept rolling, over and over, his body shrinking as he rolled, until he disappeared – without a splash – into the stream. He stepped out further downstream still laughing. He sat back down in front of John and tried to pull himself together, his body growing again to match John.

"You really know how to flatter a girl," he said, and then burst out laughing again.

John stared at him, not amused. "It's not a laughing matter."

"Yes, it is," the boy choked trying to settle himself back down. "You sit there, in all seriousness, speaking to me – but you don't believe I actually exist – asking me to help you find the girl who also – according to you – doesn't exist. And you seem mystified as to why the girl in question may find your attentions ... undesirable. It is funny, it is!" and he was off again, tears streaming from his eyes.

"At least you've come to the right person. Imagine that!" he spluttered out, enjoying his pun. "Can you do me an imaginary bloodhound too?" he slapped his knees, laughing even louder.

John sat waiting. He supposed he could see what the boy was laughing at, but he was still unable to find it funny. At least the boy was not upset by the idea that John did not think he was real. Eventually the boy quietened down.

"Will you help me?" John asked again.

"Yes," said the boy, serious again, and John breathed a sigh of relief.

"Of course, I am not certain that I should. It seems likely that Asha may not thank me for it, but ..." here he started to choke again, "I absolutely must find out what you plan to do for an encore," and he was off again, his laughter filling the forest.

After a few minutes he settled in front of John again. "So what's the plan, boss?"

John looked at him blankly.

"Plan, you know: step one find another imaginary person; step two ..." he gestured back for John to fill in the blanks.

John looked down, embarrassed, at the empty coffee cup in his hands. "I had not even planned on finding you."

"Oh." The boy grinned. "I guess that fits." He seemed to be having trouble stopping himself from laughing out loud again. After a moment the boy continued, "We should probably visit the Glade. Asha may be there, and if not there may be someone that has spoken with her recently."

"The Glade?" John asked.

"Oh." The boy took a few seconds to think how best to explain it. "The Glade is sort of like the heart of our stand. You know what I mean by stand?" he asked and John nodded. "The Glade is our home, a place where we can raise and protect our children, a place where our people come together to talk, and sometimes to celebrate." Pausing as something else occurred to him the boy said, "Come to think of it, the Glade is a place that you cannot enter. But, since you've found me, I can go in your stead and tell you want I find." He grinned at John.

"Well that sounds like a plan," John said, smiling back at the boy. "When do we start?"

"Now is good," came the enthusiastic reply.

So John got up and started packing up his things ready to travel. He didn't think to ask how far it might be. As John followed the boy deeper into the forest he felt some confidence that he may yet be able to find Asha, but they were walking the wrong way.

6. Betrayal

Asha fled through the trees, tears streaming down her cheeks. "I can't believe," he had told her. After all she had shown him, after all she had revealed of herself, after all he had seen and felt for himself, he still did not believe she was real. She stopped running finally and braced herself, exhausted, against a large tree. She reached into it and felt the life pulsing through the sap and the grain. He had denied life, and he had denied her. She sobbed against the tree, not merging yet, the tree did not deserve to experience such disturbed emotions.

Later, the worst of the hurt cried out, Asha merged into the tree and flowed through to its heart. She took comfort from its strength. This was a large, strong and healthy tree, it had life to share, life it wanted to share – it welcomed her. Flowing up the trunk and into the upper branches and leaves, she could feel the night breeze, very cool up this high. She could feel the tender kiss of moonlight on the leaves. Slowly relaxing, Asha found a quiet eddy in the flow of life and let herself be lulled into a gentle sleep, cradled within.

* * *

The next morning Asha woke with the sensation of dawn sunlight warming the chill that had settled on her leaves. Her roots, far down into the warm soil, stretched their toes in anticipation of a new day. Her trunk, only the layer of bark chilled by the cold night, breathed deep of this new morning.

Realising that her essence had spread through much of the tree during the night, Asha concentrated to draw herself together, separating her essence from that of the tree to reduce the confusion between toes and roots, skin and bark. Asha drew into the warm flows within the centre of the trunk, getting a slight high and feeling greatly revived by the time she withdrew from the tree completely. She gave a silent thank you as she pulled her hand free.

A night's rest and the comfort from such a wonderful old friend as this, she smiled affectionately up into the branches, left her feeling much better. She could still feel the stinging pain of John's rejection, but now she felt better able to cope with it. Somehow she would make him see sense, but first it might help to talk with Nona.

Asha opened her senses and reached out. She could feel the individual trees around her. There were many creatures, the night ones nestling down to sleep, the day ones scuttling about on their early morning errands. She reached out further. Somewhere off to the east she could sense a presence – Nona. She set off at a relaxed pace, enjoying the forest as she passed.

Arriving where she had sensed Nona, Asha sat down to wait. Nona's presence had disappeared, she had probably merged with one of the nearby trees. As she waited the occasional bird would alight nearby, its prana humming loudly to Asha's senses. Ants on the ground moved their paths to go around where she sat, keeping their prana separated from hers so that their paths would remain more clearly defined. Asha closed her eyes and let her senses reach out, feeling the flow of life all around her and beneath her in the soil. The feeling was not peaceful as such, it was early morning and there was a great deal of activity, life at any scale is not necessarily restful. It was a feeling of harmony, that around her life was flowing as it should.

Asha was just becoming aware of a small hitch in the energy flow of a nearby tree when Nona emerged from the base of that tree.

Nona saw Asha and gave a sad smile. "You sensed it too? There is a particularly nasty infection growing in a branch up there, we were just trying to see what we could do about it." To an outsider Nona's use of "we" may have been confusing, but to Asha it was just the aaranya way of including the tree itself. They could do little for the tree without the cooperation of the tree's own prana, its own self.

Asha and Nona merged back into the tree. Asha followed Nona up the trunk and they studied the growth together. Allowing their essences to touch they could communicate while still merged with the tree. They flowed around the growth looking for some way to save the large branch, but it was too late. They began to try and isolate it from the main trunk. Blending themselves into the natural flows of the tree they were able to manipulate the prana, bypassing and closing nadis that fed prana to the branch. Their changes would hasten the death of the branch, but they hoped it might be enough to save the tree.

The day was almost done by the time they emerged, both of them exhausted from the hours of concentration and effort spent inside the tree.

"I think it's enough," said Nona, "but we should keep an eye on it for a few weeks. I was about to head up to spend time at the Glade, catch up with some friends. Are you able to watch this for now?"

"Of course," replied Asha. "I was planning to stay around ... things with John ..." She stopped. The hurt of the night before came back, catching her weakened by the efforts of the day and bringing tears again.

Nona came forward and held her, gently whispering, "It's okay. Take your time."

Slowly Asha told Nona about John's refusal to accept the things he had seen, and his final rejection of Asha herself. "It's just so stupid! Why won't he believe his own senses?"

Nona was silent for a while. Still holding Asha, she finally said, "Have you considered that this may be for the best? That it may be the best thing for you, and for us, that John continues to believe we don't exist. It means he is unlikely to tell anyone about us ... and it would allow you to move on to a more productive relationship." Nona squeezed Asha to quell her objection. "Whatever it is you feel for John, you know that it can't go anywhere. Asha, why not leave him alone? Let him deal with this own problems, they don't have to involve you." Nona felt Asha tense in her arms and let her slowly pull back.

"It's wrong," Asha eventually responded. "This isn't about my feelings. I suppose it was about my feelings last night, being rejected like that hurt ... I wasn't prepared.

"But this is about John. It can't be right, can't be healthy, to deny your own senses like that. It can't be good to believe in your own brokenness the way he does. Since last night I've realised that rejecting me has solved nothing for John. He will still see narun and still believe his mind has broken. He needs help to get through this – and no human can help him."

Asha paused, trying to sort through her emotions. "I want to help him. I'm not sure how to help yet, but I've decided that the first step is to stay near him. If he wants to see me again I want to be there."

Nona looked thoughtfully into Asha's eyes. Reaching forward she grasped one of Asha's hands in both of her own. "Are you sure you are not holding out for more than there can be? I hate to see you torment yourself over something that you cannot control. There may be no good end to this, Asha, for either of you."

Asha smiled back. "I am not very sure of anything, only that I *have* to try."

Nona nodded. "All right, if you have to try, try. When I get back from the Glade I will come and check on you, just to see how it's going and to remind you that you have a stand that would like to see you."

It got dark as they talked, but the forest is never really dark to the aaranya. The life of the trees and the soil remained bright to their senses, so Nona and Asha said their goodbyes and Nona started her journey north. Tired as they both were, Nona would not go far tonight, but she wanted to make a start. Asha found a nearby tree and merged to spend a peaceful night held in its comforting presence.

* * *

In the morning Asha woke much refreshed and feeling happier for having made up her mind what to do. She merged into the tree that Nona and she had tried to help and found that their adjustments were still holding, she should check it again in a few days.

Asha knew it was the first day of John's working week, the last few weeks had reinforced her knowledge of the human world and its emphasis on time. So there was no need for her to hurry, John would be gone for much of the day, but she decided she would spend most of it near the house anyway. Having made up her mind she wanted to act on it.

She arrived at the house in time to see John driving off to work, but not soon enough to sense anything of his mood or equilibrium. Asha began merging with a few of the trees around the house, they never did quite so well as those deeper in the forest so they would benefit from any extra care that Asha could provide.

Not long past midday Asha emerged from a tree, tired from her efforts, thinking she should go further into the forest and find a tree in which she could rest and revive before John got home. About to go, she heard a vehicle coming up the gravel road. She waited in the hope that John may have come home early.

Just a few minutes later a dark blue van came up the driveway. Asha moved around the trees so that she could watch the front of the house. It was certainly not John. A small, balding man got out of the van, went to the front door and knocked loudly. When it was not opened after a couple of minutes the man fiddled with something at the locks and the door swung open. Asha was appalled on John's behalf, she knew that humans were not supposed to do this sort of thing.

He was only inside for a few minutes. He came back out and waved at the van. The side door of the van opened and a burly, dark-haired man stepped out. Asha thought she also saw another figure in the shadows in the back. The dark-haired man carried a large case of equipment to the centre of the cleared area in front of the house. There he assembled a tripod with some elaborate device at the top. He ran a cable down to a large box and then attached a small computer to the device. The device consisted of a shiny black dome on top of a simple matte black cube, there were various controls on one side.

Asha heard the device turn on with a beep and felt a strange sensation pass through her body, a sort of tingling and buzzing unlike anything she had felt before.

The man appeared to wait for his computer to do something and then started fiddling with knobs on the device mounted on the tripod. After a few moments he called to the balding man. When the dark-haired man pointed to something on his computer screen the bald man looked over in Asha's direction, but the other man tapped him on the shoulder and pointed at the screen again. He said something harsh but she could not hear the words.

It occurred to Asha that the men may be here with John's permission or even at his request. Occasionally others showed up: a man to read from the meters on the side of the house, and sometimes parcels were dropped off by men driving vans. Perhaps

John had asked these men to do something for him, that might explain how the balding man had been able to unlock the front door.

But it felt wrong. The men seemed surreptitious and sinister. Not in obvious ways but it was the impression Asha had from their behaviour. She wondered about getting closer to the men and that device to see what she could discover, but the buzzing sensation was still there and it made her nervous.

The balding man went back to the van, reached in and came back with a long piece of metal. It looked sort of like the television antenna on John's roof, a simple rod with several short crosspieces, but this one had something complicated going on at one end, the end the man held in his hand. The antenna was connected to some fine cable on a roll which was in turn connected to the device on the tripod.

Following instructions from the dark-haired man, the balding man began to walk out some sort of grid pattern, pointing the antenna at the ground. Asha was concentrating on what the man was doing, his steady pacing back and forth, and it took a few minutes for her to realise that this pattern was bringing him slowly closer to where she was standing by a tree at the edge of the forest. As the distance closed Asha wondered if she should move away, but she was still curious to find out what they were doing.

There was movement from the van and Asha looked over to see a figure emerging from the side door. The figure was entirely enclosed in a strange silvery suit. The visor was dark so that Asha could not see who was inside. There was something strange about its movement. Asha stepped away from the tree where she had been watching, trying to get a better look.

"Now!" came a yell from the dark-haired man.

Asha looked back to see that the balding man had better than halved the distance, and instead of pointing the antenna to the ground, it was now pointed almost directly at her. In disbelieving panic she froze where she was. The dark-haired man flicked a switch on the device and everything around Asha began to tilt and roll. She found herself on the ground, not knowing how she got there, and still the world was spinning around her. If she were human Asha may have thought she was drunk.

Through the scenes rolling past her eyes she saw the balding man

94

walking carefully in her direction, continuing to point the antenna in front of him. She could hear their voices, but couldn't make sense of the words. The figure in the strange suit was coming more quickly, was walking directly toward her. Asha finally registered the fact that they knew she was here. She tried to reach out to the nearest tree but could not make it. She tried to think of some alternative that could allow her to escape, but while the world continued to reel around her she couldn't think clearly.

The figure in the suit reached her and threw some sort of fine net over her body. Everywhere it touched it burned. Asha screamed. Her body reacted instinctively and contracted, trying to avoid the burning of the net. Soon she had shrunk to the size of a young human child, maybe four years old, and could not contract any further. Still the net touched her skin and still she screamed.

Asha was not aware of it, but now her shape was outlined by the fine net covering her body. The dark-haired man ran to the van, put on protective gloves and pulled out a large flat pack of mesh. He brought it over to where Asha lay, twitching in pain, and quickly assembled the mesh into a cage. The door to the cage was opened and the figure in the silver suit bent down and manipulated the netting over Asha's body so that she could escape it only by moving into the cage. Once Asha was in the cage, the netting was taken away and the door slammed shut.

For several minutes Asha's body continued to twitch, it took even longer for her to realise that the disorientation was fading. Her mind continued to reel as if she were still drunk, she doubted if she could stand even if the cage had been large enough to permit it.

Slowly Asha gathered herself enough to realise that her cage now sat next to the open door of the van. The first two men were packing up the equipment, and she could see that John's house was now closed. The figure in the suit was crouched inside the door of the van, watching her. Asha reached out with one small hand toward the mesh of her cage. As she got close to the wire of the mesh she could feel a strange heat, this mesh would burn her just like the netting had. The base of the cage was some dead metal sheeting, there was no passing through that, but at least it didn't burn.

"You sure it's still in there?" asked the balding man as they brought the equipment back to the van.

"She's there." The figure in the suit nodded at the man. "She's very pretty, it's a shame you can't see her," he continued. His voice seemed to be coming from a distance, perhaps distorted by the suit.

Asha stared at the figure. It couldn't be. The humans wouldn't have heard the words, they could only have seen the nodding of the suit. It was a narun!

With his gloved hand the narun picked up a spray bottle from near the doorway and started to spray something at her. She quickly covered her face with her hands, but it turned out to be just a fine spray of water, the droplets beading on her surface and then rolling off.

"The gods be damned," said the balding man in quiet awe.

Asha looked down at herself, seeing her form outlined in fine water droplets. When the spray stopped she shook herself and the last of the water dropped to the bottom of the cage.

"Who are you?" Asha asked the narun.

He ignored her.

"This turned out a whole lot easier than it could have," said the dark-haired man. "He's going to be pleased to finally get this one after all this time."

"You sure it's the one we want?" asked the balding man.

The dark-haired man shrugged, "I assume so, I don't imagine there can be that many around here."

The narun nodded at them, speaking perhaps for Asha's benefit, "She's the one."

"You told me what to expect, but to see it ..." the balding man was still astounded.

"The first is always a bit of a blow-out," agreed the dark-haired man. "You do get used to it after a while – mostly." He grinned. "Come on, let's get it on board."

Using gloves, the two men carefully moved the cage into the van, latching it to the floor with some specially designed clips. The figure in the suit sat on a bench near the back of the van and the dark-haired man moved down to sit opposite.

The side door was closed – making Asha feel claustrophobic. Only a limited amount of light filtered through a small grill in the barrier between the back of the van and the front. The van started and Asha felt it move slowly down the driveway and turn onto the road. Badly frightened she had no idea what to do or think.

The van suddenly lurched and swerved violently to the side before coming to a halt. Asha was swept against the mesh of her cage and screamed in fright and pain as she struggled to drag herself away from the burning mesh. The narun in the suit and the dark-haired man were thrown forward and fell against her cage. The cage creaked but held.

The man leapt back as soon as the van stopped, swearing. "God that's awful stuff!," he said, shaking his hands, trying to shake off the burning sensation from having laid them on the mesh. "Ian, what the fuck are you doing?" he yelled to the front.

"Some bloody idiot driving on the wrong side of the road," came back the shaky reply. The van sped off with a slipping of the tyres on the gravel. "It was him!" Ian called back in a loud, hoarse whisper, sounding even more frightened. "The guy that owns that bloody house. We only just missed him." A pause and then a nervous chuckle, "In more ways than one."

It took Asha a few moments to register what the driver had said. John! She tried to reach out her senses, trying to find John beyond the van, but something about the mesh cage seemed to get in the way. Asha thought about trying to call out in the hope that he would hear her, but she knew she was too late. The van sped down the road and Asha could feel her world slipping away from her.

* * *

Sometime later, Asha in her misery could not guess at how long, the van entered a city. Even though she didn't need to breathe it the air felt choking and poisonous to her. Her captors had ridden silently, ignoring her and each other.

Later still, the van slowed, turned, went over a distinct bump, and began a series of slow downward turns. The meagre sunlight that had been filtering through the grill was replaced by pale, flickering fluorescent light. The van finally came to a stop and the engine went silent.

The driver's door opened and closed. There were loud footsteps as Ian walked around the van. The sliding door was cast back with a loud thump and fluorescent light flooded the back of the van – pale and false, but a relief from the tomb-like darkness it had been.

"Wake up, everyone," said Ian from the door. "Home, sweet

home."

The dark-haired man mumbled something unintelligible, Asha thought it looked as if he had been asleep. He stumbled out of the van and stretched himself noisily. The narun continued to sit in the back, waiting patiently. Again wearing gloves, the men unclipped the cage and lifted it from the van. The narun stepped out behind and followed them as they carried it to a nearby door.

Asha looked around at the dark lifeless cave that was the underground car park. Concrete, noxious fumes, loud echoes and pale flickering light. She had never seen anything like it, had never dreamt that such an unpleasant and barren place could exist. She shuddered.

Through the door was a hallway that included a human security guard in a small booth. At the end of the hallway was an odd double door arrangement, the inner of the doors was metal and covered in a mesh similar to that of her cage. Through these doors they entered another corridor, this one longer and with very high ceilings. It was narrow where they stood but appeared wider ahead because a ramp doubled back to a door on a level above them to the right. At least the air was better here, stale and bitter with strange chemical smells, but mostly clear of the noxious fumes from the car park. There was also the unexpected scent of eucalyptus and sawn timber.

She was carried up the ramp and onto the higher level, into another, smaller, corridor and eventually to a large sterile room, all white plastic and stainless steel. Her cage was lifted onto a low stainless steel table in the centre of the room. The two men left. The narun stayed by the doorway, still enclosed in his strange suit, waiting for something or someone.

"Where am I?" Asha asked him. No response.

"Who are you?" Still no response.

Frustrated, Asha wanted to hit the side of the cage, but she remembered in time how much it would hurt, and so hit the floor instead. Forced to retain her small size to avoid touching the mesh, she tried stretching each limb in turn in an attempt to reduce her discomfort. She was not used to remaining so cramped and still.

A short time later a man came in. Not old, but no longer young. His once dark hair now heavily streaked with grey, his skin creased and tanned as if he spent considerable time outside. He had a kindly face with large startlingly blue eyes, eyes that were looking right at her.

"Hello," he said. "You are a pretty thing aren't you, very pretty."

She just stared at him.

"Oh yes, I can see you. It's not just kids you know. Well it usually is, but some of us adults can be special too." He paused, looking her over. "So you're Asha, hmm? The special friend of Eloise?"

Asha couldn't respond. Things that, in her despair, she had not thought about, started to crowd in on her. How could they have known where to find her? How would they even know she was there to be found? How could they know about her friendship with Ellie? How did he know her name? There was only one possible answer.

John must have told them. She had been so certain that he would keep their secret. It seemed impossible that he would tell – and yet here she was. She wanted to rail against the injustice of it. She had cared for him. She had trusted him.

"I'm Dr Henry Karlin. You can call me Henry or doctor or just about anything you want." He grinned at her, finding himself amusing. "I know you can understand me. We know quite a lot about you narun, having a few narun friends already with us." He gestured to the figure still standing by the door. "Not one of our most talkative friends is Sando."

Asha could think of no suitable response so she remained silent. For Sando to be working for these humans was such an unthinkable betrayal of his own kind that Asha could scarcely believe it.

"Come on, dear, come on," said the doctor. He was still smiling, but starting to sound impatient. "Haven't you got anything to say to us at all?"

Asha just looked at him. She decided that silence was probably best until she knew more. Despite some strange compulsion to tell her story to this man, the offence she felt at John and Sando's betrayals strengthened her resolve to remain silent.

"Okay, all right. I guess you don't have to talk right now. Let's have a good look at you." From somewhere under the table where Asha's cage sat, the doctor pulled out an odd black device, similar to one that had been used to capture her earlier. The top was shaped differently and the base had more controls but it was recognisably a similar device. She cringed as far back in the cage as she could without getting burned.

"Don't panic, dear. It's just a Karlin-Field generator." He gave her a big grin, "Guess who it's named after?

"It's something we've been working on to let us look at you in more detail. The one that found you today was just a low-powered omnidirectional model that we use as a detector. This little baby is much more sophisticated and gives us something like an x-ray image of a narun, the closest we can get to a photograph of you.

"The other device is the one you need to worry about." He pulled out a smaller version of the antenna that had caused her disorient-ation. "With this we can generate a slightly different effect. It's related to the Karlin-Field, but for some reason it is much more disruptive to prana, to the life energy in all things. I've been tempted to call it a Karlin-Beam or a Karlin-Ray, but that starts to sound a bit egocentric, don't you think? Around here they like to call it the ray-gun, makes everyone feel like they're playing a part in Star Trek." Karlin chuckled at his own joke.

"Today you experienced the low setting, which is very disori-enting unless you're wearing the right protection," he indicated Sando's suit. "On a medium setting it can be very painful and poten-tially quite damaging. These newest models have a high setting that will kill, well, pretty much anything. We're not sure why yet, but it works and that makes it very useful.

"Now, we can't get a good look at you in that cage, that mesh gets in the way. That's another of my inventions. Fascinating stuff, isn't it?"

Asha glared at him.

The doctor ignored her and continued, "I'm going to get Sando to open the door to your cage and get you to stand on the table. Since I will have this little beast nearby," he waved the ray-gun, "I expect you will be cooperative."

Sando came forward, slid the cage to one side of the table and opened the door, swinging it right back out of the way. He then stood back by the door.

Asha hesitated, but finally she crawled out onto the low table. Being able to stand upright and stretch properly was a relief, despite the circumstances.

"Good, good. Now if you don't mind just standing still, dear, looking this way. Smile, dear," said Karlin. "And don't panic, the Karlin-Field is harmless." He turned on the device.

Asha again felt the tingly, buzzing sensation she had felt today – and now wished she had had the sense to run from it. The sensation built further as Karlin adjusted some of the controls on the device.

"Turn to the side please," Karlin asked, making circling motions with this hand. Asha obliged as he captured images from all sides. The doctor pressed a few buttons and the buzzing sensation vanished. On a nearby bench Karlin turned on a computer and played back some images. They made little sense to Asha.

"Just a few more things," he said. For the next half-an-hour or so he proceeded to shine various sorts of lights through her, capturing images with other cameras and devices, but nothing else seemed to have any effect that she could feel.

"Okay, that's it for today, dear. That's it. If you could pop back into your box we will have Ian and Darren take you to your room."

Asha hesitated, reluctant to go near that burning mesh again.

"Please, dear," the doctor pointed meaningfully at the ray-gun.

Asha crawled back in, huddling in the centre, and glared out at the doctor as Sando came forward and closed the door on the cage.

Now that he had what he wanted the doctor appeared to be in a hurry to be off. "See you tomorrow, dear," he called, as if she had a choice, and left the room.

A few minutes later the two men that had captured her returned. With gloved hands they lifted her cage and carried it down more corridors. Sando followed behind. They took her into a room that was divided in half by a wall of glass or clear plastic. The two men attached her cage to a hatch on the bottom left of the clear divide, so that the door of her cage now opened into the other half of the room.

When the others had left, Asha crept out and stretched back to her preferred size. On her side of the sparse cell there was a chair, a bed and some sort of plastic plant. Was that someone's idea of a joke? Through the clear wall Asha could see various equipment. She thought she could feel a very faint tingle from a Karlin-Field and assumed she was being monitored.

She walked around the walls, feeling them with her hands as she went. She could not tell what they were made from. The dividing wall was some sort of plastic, not glass, and it was certain that none of the material of the walls had ever contained life. It all felt wrong, alien, perhaps coated with something. There was a faint, lingering and unfamiliar chemical scent to it all. There was nothing for her there, no comfort and no escape. She tried reaching out with her senses but could not reach beyond the confines of the cell. She lay down on the bed. She tried to think but it was all too much. She closed her eyes to the alien world that had engulfed her.

* * *

Hours later, Asha presumed it must be the next morning, Sando returned for her with two different men. The threat of having to fetch the ray-gun was enough to convince her to comply and crawl back into the cage. They carried her in the cage back to the same examination room and the two men left. Sando took up his usual position by the door. A few minutes later Dr Karlin appeared, smiling brightly.

"Good morning, good morning, my pretty little dryad," he said. "Did you have a good night?"

Asha just glared at him.

"Still not feeling talkative? Never mind, I guess that's okay for now, though we may have to insist later. Now, are you going to make me bring out the big threatening ray-gun or can we get along without it today?"

Sando opened the cage and Asha crawled out and sat cross-legged on the table waiting to see what the doctor wanted.

"We are going to do some materials testing," Karlin explained. "We do this with every new guest that comes to us. It is fascinating to discover the subtle, and many not-so-subtle, variations that exist among your people.

"Today, today I thought we'd start with wood. Something nice and easy for you to settle in with." He gave her a big smile as if this was something she should enjoy. The doctor slid out a large, shallow drawer from a bench at the side of the room. Within it lay dozens of specimens of wood.

The entire morning was spent with the doctor pulling out specimen after specimen, and asking Asha to try and merge her hand with the prana of the timber, then to try and pass her hand through the timber without merging, and then to try and lift the timber. After each sample Karlin would ask a few simple questions and Asha would nod or shake her head.

All the timber was easy enough to lift. Any of the small pieces of timber that had been away from a living tree for more than a few days were effectively dead, the prana mostly dissipated. With such wood Asha could pass her hand through easily, the substance of her being passing through the now empty nadis, the spaces and channels where life had once flowed – just as she had been able to pass through John's door. She could not merge with these dead pieces of timber at all, there was almost no prana left in them to merge with.

Things got distasteful for Asha when she was asked to work with recently cut timber. Ian brought a tray into the room late in the morning, it had been gathered very recently. She could partially merge with the fading prana that remained in the wood, but most of the pieces already felt old and dirty. She imagined it must be much like a human being forced to breathe stale air already overused by other humans. Such prana had no pulse, no flow, no freshness and no sense of vitality. It was dissipating and when her hand was merged it felt as if her essence was dissipating with it.

The most recently cut timber she could not pass her hand through directly at all. The existing prana filled the nadis and prevented her from passing through unless she first merged with the existing prana. Any of the timber that had been cut for a day or more she could pass her hand through as if through a viscous fluid, pushing the old prana aside with the greater strength of her own – and that was something that felt very wrong, it felt bad in some more than physical way.

Asha had no idea of the purpose of all these tests, but she could think of no good reason not to cooperate. None of the results surprised her. She lived in the forest and knew all the subtle variations of the wood. For the most part she could have told Karlin all that he appeared to be learning from these experiments, and a thousand more variations he seemed to have overlooked. It was boring, but so far it had seemed fairly harmless and, as far as Asha could see, pointless.

The afternoon was filled with more experiments, but this time with other types of plant matter. Stalks off various shrubs, leaves of the same. Root vegetables, plants still growing in pots and so on. That night, or what Asha presumed was night, she was returned to her cell.

The rest of the week continued in much the same manner, only the materials varied. On the Saturday morning Karlin put her through the same set of tests as the first day she had arrived. He explained that he was just monitoring how she was managing with no trees to sustain her. The rest of Saturday, and all of Sunday, Asha was left locked alone in her cell.

The next week was the same. By the end of it Asha could feel how much weaker she had become. No sunlight, no life. Her own substance was being drained to sustain her activity. She wondered if Karlin's tests revealed this fact.

On the subsequent Monday Ian and Darren carried her down a ramp to another level. There was a very high corridor. Echoes came at odd intervals and shadows fell in unexpected ways so that it all felt more alien to Asha than even the barren halls of the previous level. The smell of eucalyptus and other timbers was stronger here than where she had been kept until now.

The men placed Asha in a cell much like the one she had just left, but taller like the corridor and wider too. On her side of the clear dividing wall was a tree, whose upper reaches almost filled this side of the large room, growing in a platform of soil. The platform was mounted on sturdy rollers. On each side of the platform a cable braced the top of the tree to keep it steady when it was being moved. Behind the tree was a huge pair of doors through which the tree must be rolled in and out of the cell. The tree was nothing like the tall and healthy growths of her forest, but it was alive. She could feel its life pulsing from where she stood. She leapt onto the platform and ran to the tree, thrusting her arms over it, gently merging them into the bark, pressing her cheek against the trunk.

It took her a few minutes to be convinced this was not some sort of trick, that this was not going to turn into a plastic tree or some similar nonsense. Finally she relaxed and allowed herself to fully merge, flowing into the trunk and feeling her way around the unfamiliar tree.

She could feel the roots hemmed in, growing tightly up against each other and the walls of the platform. There was discomfort in the truncation of the branches where they had been constantly trimmed back to fit the corridors and cells of this dungeon. There was also a distinctly uneasy feeling, like teetering on the edge of a void, because the tree's roots had not been able to drill down and gain a deep hold in the earth. The pores of the leaves felt dirty, which she imagined came from the air of the city. But despite all that, the tree felt healthy, almost happy and content. It took Asha a while to work it out and then, as she spread her own essence through the tree, she could detect where adjustments had been made by previous aaranya. This tree had probably been better attended than most forest trees, and this drove home to Asha that she was not the first, that there may be others imprisoned here just like her.

Asha was left with the tree for an entire day. When they came for her the next morning she was tempted to try and stay with the tree until Sando explained that they could drive her out, but doing so would be likely to damage or even kill the tree. So Asha left the tree and crawled into her cage once more. Sando signalled to the men when she was in the cage and they carried her back up to the previous level where Karlin once again went through a series of tests.

Asha was returned to the cell with the tree after the morning of tests. Later, in what she presumed was the afternoon, she was surprised and disappointed to see Karlin come into her cell. He was pushing a large trolley of equipment in front of him.

"My dear, my dear little dryad. The next series of tests you may find a bit distressing," said Karlin. His tone didn't change much, apparently her distress wasn't going to cause him any discomfort. "We want you to merge with the tree and stay merged regardless of what happens. To encourage you to remain we will be using this," he pulled out the ray-gun antenna, "at a setting that will be quite painful to experience. You only have to stay merged to avoid it."

Asha didn't like the sound of this at all, but she could not think of any alternative to compliance. She merged gently, asking the tree to forgive her weakness – she could guess that this was going to be bad for the tree too.

From inside the tree Asha could not see what they were doing. She could sense where they were, and if Sando wanted to touch the tree they could choose to communicate, but otherwise she was limited to the senses available to the tree itself.

Ian came into the room, Sando stayed at his usual place by the door. Ian was given a second of the ray-gun devices and told how to play it across the branches and trunk of the tree. Karlin kept his own gun available and watched for Asha trying to emerge from the tree.

At first Asha felt the prana of the tree give a jolt. Its flow was suddenly disrupted and she could feel the distress. She reached up to where the problem was coming from and felt a tearing sensation, as if her essence was being ripped violently from her being. She pulled back and could only watch on as the prana in that part of the tree writhed. There was a brief respite during which Asha could feel the tingly sensation, stronger than usual, of the monitoring Karlin-Field. She wondered if Karlin was enjoying the show.

Again and again different branches were hit with the ray and each time Asha could only watch and despair. Then the trunk was hit by the ray where Asha was holding her essence. Asha's entire being flinched and she threw herself involuntarily out of the tree. Karlin pointed his antenna at her and she was enveloped by a spinning disorientation and the agonising tearing that she had felt inside the tree, but even more intense and painful out here in the open. Asha could hear herself screaming with the pain. It kept up for long seconds and then stopped.

"Back into the tree." Karlin said coldly. When Asha did not respond fast enough for him he sent another few seconds of the ray. "Now!"

Barely able to control her body, Asha reached out to the tree and merged back into it. The prana of the trunk was settling again after the previous attack. Apparently the damage caused by the ray was not permanent if the tree was given time to recover. Asha hoped the same was true for herself, she felt badly ravaged.

Asha felt the ray strike again, coming down the branches and into the trunk. She pulled her essence back into the roots. The ray concentrated on the trunk for some time before it moved down over the roots too. Asha tried to escape quickly past the effect of the ray, but she couldn't flow past fast enough. After a few seconds she could take no more and threw herself from the tree.

"Again," said Karlin, hitting her with several seconds of the ray.

"I can't!" Asha screamed back at him through tears of pain and frustration. The first words she had spoken to him. "Please stop," she cried and curled up against the tree sobbing, her body twitching from the effects of the ray.

Karlin smiled in satisfaction, "Well now, since you asked so nicely, that might be enough for today. If you'll just hop back in your box we'll take a few measurements upstairs and then let you rest."

When Asha was slow responding he threatened with the ray-gun again, but must have understood further use would only make it harder for her to move.

It wasn't until after the tests had been completed and she was returned to her cell that Asha's body finally stopped twitching. She went to the tree and slowly merged into it, spreading her essence out to try and determine how much damage had been done. The roots had seen the least of the ray and were all settling down already. The trunk had seen the most concentrated fire and was still a maelstrom of disrupted flows, but Asha thought it would be all right in a day or two, especially if she could find the strength to help.

The reality of what had happened appalled her. They really could drive her from inside a tree – where she had always felt so safe. Karlin had a weapon that could drive her people from their forest, and he was using prisoners like herself to refine it. What was it all for?

Neither she nor the tree had enough strength to offer much help to the other, but Asha stayed merged anyway. Just the presence of its life was a comfort – the only comfort she had.

* * *

The next day Asha was forced to wait in her cage while the tree was rolled out of the cell. There appeared to be a huge open cavern behind the door where the tree was taken out, but she was unable to make out much detail. She was left in her empty cell for the day with no further tests. The tree was returned at the end of the day. Merging with it she could tell that it had spent the day in sunlight, she could only wish that she had been with it.

The day after that Asha went through another set of tests, apparently to see how she had recovered. That afternoon Karlin was back again with his trolley of equipment and the torture was repeated. The intensity levels of the ray had been increased, Asha almost fainted with the pain at the last.

The cycle of increasing torture and time to recover was repeated again and again. Asha didn't even try to keep count of the days. Eventually it became obvious that the tree was dying, and Asha knew she wouldn't be far behind if the torture didn't stop.

Another session of torture, another round of tests. This time, however, when the tests were complete, Karlin settled himself on a stool and looked carefully, almost sympathetically, at Asha's small body sitting huddled and trembling on the cold stainless steel table. Asha glared back at him. Despite the helpless pleading forced out of her in each of the torture sessions, she had still refused to speak at other times.

"My dear little dryad, my dear. I know this has been hard on you," Karlin said. "But it really does help me you know. It will be worth all the effort."

Weak and despairing, Asha pulled herself a bit more upright. "Why?" she asked. "Why are you doing this?"

"For mankind," Karlin replied as if it were obvious. "The things that I have discovered, and I am still discovering, are simply amazing."

"And what's in it for him?" Asha nodded toward Sando at his usual place by the door.

"Oh, he and his friends have some plans apparently. They've been such a help, couldn't have done it without them really."

"And John?" Asha asked, the question slipping out even as she thought it. "Did John know what you would be doing ... to me?" John had never been far from her thoughts but she had always pushed the memories away. She didn't know how to face them, hadn't wanted to face them.

If Asha had not been so weak, almost delirious, she may have noticed Karlin's eyes flicker in surprise at the question. As it was she was looking down, bewildered as to how she had come to this point.

Karlin replied cautiously, "John? I am not certain. Does it matter?"

"He said he would never tell," Asha said quietly, mostly to herself. "He didn't even seem to believe it himself. I can't ... I just can't believe he gave me up ... to this. Human or not he just wasn't like that." Looking up she said more strongly, "You must have lied to him!"

"Tell me, tell me about him, dear. Tell me about John." Karlin asked casually.

Too casually, even in her weak state Asha picked up that something about Karlin had changed. He was leaning forward with a look of avid interest. Asha shook her head, trying to clear her thoughts. She hadn't meant to say anything about John, there was no point.

"No," she said, muttering weakly, looking down again now. She reconsidered, there seemed no reason not to tell him. "There's nothing much to tell. After his wife and daughter died ... I guess he just couldn't cope ... not with seeing me as well ... so he told you ... and ... and you took away his problem."

"Oh, that John." Karlin's eyes were wide with surprise and excitement. "He could see you too! Well, well, this is exciting news."

Asha stared at him, her mind still trying to catch up.

"Look, I don't mean to be rude or anything, I don't mean to be rude, but I've got to go. Got things to think about and to plan. Sando will see you get back. And don't worry, dear, the testing is over for now." Karlin slid the last few things quickly away and then he was gone, the door closing slowly behind him as he rushed out.

Asha was returned to her large cell. A different tree had been rolled in, this one very similar to how the previous had been before the ray testing. She supposed the other had been destroyed or left somewhere to finish dying.

Only when Asha had merged with this new tree and began to draw on its strength was she able to think through what had just happened. Apparently Karlin had not known about John. John had not told them about her. He had not betrayed her ... but now she had betrayed him!

7. Acceptance

They came across another stream and John said he wanted to stop and have some lunch. Lunch consisted of fresh water from the shallow stream and some sticky food bars from his backpack. John imagined they were labelled as food bars so you did not mistake them for something else. And then he thought he was being ungrateful, at least they were easy to carry and suitable rations for a hiker as inexperienced as he.

The previous night, in the disappointment with the lantern and the confusion of getting caught in the dark, John had forgotten all about the food bars that he had placed at the bottom of his backpack. He need not have gone hungry. He didn't feel that he needed to share this embarrassing little fact with the boy, the lad was finding enough to laugh about as it was.

The boy had disappeared while John ate his lunch but reappeared as John finished packing things up and putting his backpack on.

"Do we have far to go?" John asked.

"Yes," said the boy. He wasn't sick of the game yet.

"Will we get there before nightfall?"

"No."

"Will we get there tomorrow?"

"No."

That gave John pause. Just how far was this Glade? "The next day?"

"No."

"The day after?" John was starting to get exasperated.

The boy hesitated. He seemed to be caught, at last, in something that could not be answered with a simple yes or no. "No," he said eventually, and then added, "probably not."

"So the day after that then," John said, and the boy nodded. John stood there contemplating this for a few minutes, and then took off his backpack to take another look at what he had packed in there. From the clothes perspective he would be pretty ripe by the time he got home again, but did he have enough food? He counted out his various food parcels.

"I don't suppose we go past any shops on the way?" he asked.

The boy laughed.

He'd packed eight dehydrated meal packs, thinking that he had to be back by next weekend and if he got back earlier he'd eat them at home. He had eaten one this morning. He had also thrown in a few boxes of the sticky food bars but he was not sure whether they considered one bar to be a meal, they sure didn't feel that way when you ate them. However he looked at it, he was going to be hungry by the time he got back home.

"Can you help me find things to eat out here in the forest?" he asked. "It doesn't have to be much, just enough to make what I have last a bit longer."

The boy considered this for a moment. "You're willing to take dietary advice from an imaginary friend?" he asked John.

Embarrassed, John could only reply with a smile, "I accepted weather predictions from Asha."

The boy grinned. "Okay then."

"Great," said John, hugely relieved that he was not going to be forced to turn around now. There was a slight pang of guilt that he would be days late for work, and he was unable to phone and tell them. He had not bothered to pack his mobile phone, not expecting it to work out here and not wanting its presence anyway. He pushed the guilt away, he would deal with that when the time came. He would tell them that he had been lost in the forest, and it would be the truth. John had no idea where he was now. He'd spent the morning following the boy, not even glancing at his compass. He had an idea that they'd continued mostly north but that still left a lot of forest to be lost in.

"Lead on," John said with a flourish.

The boy made his own flourish and danced forward with John following behind.

The journey became more like climbing than hiking. John was amazed at some of the huge trees that managed to cling to the sides of these mountains. If it weren't for the boy, he probably would have turned back, or found himself walking in circles.

The boy led him on, somehow finding ways forward that John could manage without too much difficulty. Even so John was exhausted by the time they stopped that night. He fumbled his way through heating and eating one of his meals, and even managed to thank the boy for his help before falling into bed and an instant dreamless sleep.

When he woke the next morning the sun had not yet made it over the eastern mountains. Outside his tent he found the boy sitting cross legged grinning at him.

"Good morning," muttered John, still feeling bleary.

"Good morning, John," the boy replied brightly. "I brought a selection for your breakfast." He indicated a large pile of things next to him.

"Nothing wiggling amongst it, is there?" asked John. "Not sure I'm up for witchetty grubs or anything like that."

The boy grinned but shook his head. "I can probably find some if you change your mind."

The boy showed him some fruits that he said John should put in his pack, they would be better in a day or two. There were some berries that should be eaten now, they wouldn't keep, and there were roots of some plant John didn't recognise that the boy suggested he might want to toast over his gas cooker.

"If you don't eat, how can you know all this?" John asked, astounded at the boy's knowledge.

"We learned from the humans that were here before you," he said.

"The Aborigines?"

The boy nodded. "They managed to eat some quite interesting things, but I kept your selection to things that I thought were safest for your uneducated stomach."

"Thanks," John replied with feeling. "I'm really not up for interesting things this early in the morning."

Breakfast turned out to be quite an experience. A wide variety of tastes and textures, some he quite enjoyed and some were too sour or bitter for his taste, but he ate them anyway. He was very pleased that the boy's sense of mischief had not extended to his food selection.

That evening, as John prepared his meal, the boy called some sort of animal down from one of the nearby trees. It bounded lightly down the trunk of the tree and scuttled up onto his shoulder. John peered at it curiously. It looked a little like a possum and a little like a squirrel but larger than either. As far as he knew there was no such thing as an Australian squirrel.

"What is it?" he asked quietly. The creature chirruped nervously and moved to the boy's other shoulder as if it was ready to leap back to the trees.

"You've not seen a spret before?" the boy asked. He rubbed gently at the side of the creature's face, its tail curled itself around behind the boy's neck.

John shook his head slowly so as not to disturb the creature.

"They're like us."

John still looked puzzled.

"How on Earth did Asha manage?" the boy said with a grin. "Humans and animals are much the same sort of creature, yes? Well narun and spret are much the same sort of creature. We are both praanin, both creatures made only of prana."

"So they're like animals, but made like you?" John said quietly. The creature seemed to be gaining some confidence and it sat upright on the boy's shoulder making a chattering noise as if scolding John for taking the boy's attention.

"Yes." The boy grinned, "It's one of these you need to imagine as a bloodhound to help us find Asha."

John winced at this reminder of his lack of belief. According to his own logic he had spent two days following a figment of his imagination deep into the mountains. He wondered just how crazy he might be.

After a while the creature got curious and the boy held out his arm toward John. John reached out and the creature made its way cautiously across and up his arm. It sniffed at his ear and then climbed over his head to his other shoulder. There was no smell that John could detect, its fur was soft and the creature felt very light on his shoulder despite its size.

"There are different sorts of spret just as there are different sorts of animals," the boy explained. "Like the narun they are pretty rare these days, you mostly see them when you get close to a Glade."

"So we're getting close?" said John, the creature chattered loudly in his ear.

"Closer," was the non-committal reply.

John tried to rub the creatures face as the boy had, but it scolded him and leapt lightly to the ground. It paused there for a moment and then ran back up the tree it had come from.

* * *

Six days out from home and John's backpack had considerably more room in it despite the supplements the boy had found for him along the way. It was a cold and foggy morning, but John was lost anyway so the fog didn't really worry him much as he traipsed along behind the boy.

It was mid-morning before the fog finally dissipated and the sun could get through, it was struggling now to add warmth to the ever cooler mornings. The sunlight brought into focus feelings that had been growing on John as they walked. The trees seemed taller here and the greens were clearer and more intense, the bark richer in its textures and colours. His vedana, the life sense that John usually had to stop and concentrate on, was more sensitive here. He could feel every tree around him. Each was clearly defined in his mind, its life pulsing vibrantly just beneath the bark. For the first time he could feel the way it reached up into the leaves and could even sense it disappearing into the depths of the earth below him.

The boy, an apparently unstoppable force for mischief and fun, was more subdued. No, John corrected himself, he was not subdued, just diverted. There was a reverence to the way he touched the trees, a respect. You could still see the joy and love in the way he moved through the forest, but the intensity of the life that surrounded them meant that the intensity of the boy stood out less.

Around midday they met an aaranya couple walking together through the trees, holding hands and spending a lot of time looking into each other's eyes. John started to feel self-conscious. It was almost a week since he had last shaved, his clothes were getting grungy and his last few baths in streams had been quick – the weather was too cold to want to dawdle. He wondered what these people would think of such a rough and dirty figure, but he needn't have worried, they hardly seemed to notice him at all.

"So she got you after all, Barma?" the boy called to them.

The young narun man laughed in response, "It must have been getting away from you that did it. I finally saw sense." He looked down into the young woman's eyes again, "I don't know how it took so long."

"If you're the reason he took so long to come around, why don't you just go away again, Andrei? We don't want your sort around here," the young woman called without looking away from Barma. She reached up to brush his mop-like hair back from his face.

"Ha! Got you now," said John, interrupting whatever cheeky response the boy had lined up. "Pleased to finally make your acquaintance, Andrei."

The boy, Andrei, looked back at John with a grin and bowed. To the couple he said, "Wouldn't you like to meet John before you send me away?"

That finally got their attention, they stared at John.

"John, this is Barma and Tilvy. Barma and Tilvy, this is John. He's human." Andrei added the unnecessary last with a cheeky grin.

"Hello," said John.

"Umm, hello," they replied in unison.

"Well, we'll be off then. Come on, John," said Andrei, and he started walking again, leaving the couple staring after them. "Don't worry," he said quietly to John, "they won't be far behind," and then he laughed loudly.

As the afternoon progressed they met more aaranya and Andrei continued to make overly casual introductions before moving on. "The Glade's gonna be rowdy tonight," he said to John more than once.

It was almost dusk before Andrei finally stopped. "We're here," he said simply.

"Where?" John asked. He looked toward two particularly large trees and thought he could discern a shimmer in the air, like a thin sheet of water held vertically between their trunks. "Through there?" he pointed.

Andrei nodded. "That's *the Way*. It's a path or door between the Glade and this forest."

"You said that I can't enter. What happens if I walk between those trees?"

Andrei looked at him. "Assuming the rules are the same for you as for other material creatures then nothing. You just walk through as if it's not there. Of course the rules don't seem to apply to you, not all of them anyway, so I guess it's possible it might be different for you." He grinned. "Wanna try it?" Then his grin faded. "Better not, not just yet." Such reservation did not seem like the boy John had come to know.

Andrei settled himself at the base of another tree and indicated that John should join him. "We'll wait here for a bit."

John looked a question at him.

"It's a matter of acceptance. Sitting here they sort of have to accept you – well that's the plan. When we find the right someone I'll have them stay with you while I go in."

"Is there danger?" John asked.

"No, not really."

John would have preferred him to sound more definite.

"As much as I enjoy watching the surprise on everyone's face when they realise you can see them, we will be more likely to get the help you want if I don't annoy too many people. I've got a knack."

John laughed, it was not a point he was going to argue. "Is the Glade there and I just can't see it or ... or what?"

"I don't know," Andrei admitted. "I think it's sort of nowhere ... or somewhere else. I think if it was there we would both be able to see it. Since you can't see it, and neither can I, it can't be there, so it must be somewhere else. Is that acceptably human logic?"

John gave Andrei an unhappy look. "I might remind you that not long ago I would not have been able to see you either. By that logic you must have been somewhere else too."

"Oh that's different. You're human, we've got to make allowances." Andrei grinned at him.

"And what's there, in the Glade?"

"It's difficult to describe." Andrei looked wistful for a few moments. "It's like here, but better. None of it is material. There are trees but they are not like these trees, they are larger and even more alive. It is the Glade," Andrei finished with what John was learning to recognise as typically narun logic: it is what it is.

The sun was setting over the hills beyond the Way, its shimmer gave a surreal effect to the oranges and reds of the sunset. They both sat silently watching as night fell. Andrei was uncharacteristically quiet and thoughtful. John wondered if he now regretted offering to help.

John was about to ask him if there was a problem when a voice behind them said, "Okay, I'll bite. Andrei, why would you bring the only human that can see us to the Glade, and then sit him right out front?"

Barma and Tilvy were strolling towards them through the trees.

"No offence, John," Barma said, his friendly smile seemed genuine, "but not too many are going to be well pleased to see you ... I mean, to be seen by you."

"I asked Andrei for help," John said. "I didn't realise it may get him in trouble."

"Trouble is probably the reason he agreed to help you," Tilvy said with an affectionate grin at Andrei.

Andrei pulled a face at her and said, "I like him, he makes me laugh."

"Gee thanks," muttered John.

Andrei grinned at John, pleased with the response, and then continued, speaking more seriously than John had seen before. "It felt like the right thing. I don't really know why. When John explained that he was searching for Asha it seemed important to bring him here. I want to go in and talk with Kaia. Would you two stay with him while I go?"

John was pleased at how enthusiastically they agreed, he had been starting to wonder if he may be a pariah here. Andrei gave him a reassuring grin and a wave and ran lightly to the Way. The watery shimmer glowed slightly as he entered, and then he was gone, a slight ripple rolled across the surface, as from a small pebble dropped in a pond.

"He won't get into too much trouble will he?" asked John.

"Nothing he's not well used to," Barma replied.

"So you're looking for Asha?" asked Tilvy, settling down where Andrei had been. Barma sat next to her. Tilvy was fairly short and thin but well rounded in a contrast to Barma's tall, almost stick-figure appearance, her shoulder length brown hair fell in neat, loose curls.

"Have you seen her?" he asked.

"Not for months. Asha's become a bit of a loner, out there on the edge of the forest. She comes back here for short periods but doesn't stay long. When did you see her last?"

John tried to think it through. "Five ... almost six weeks, I think."

They both looked concerned at that, and for the first time John began to worry that this was something bigger than Asha simply wanting to get away from him for a while.

John continued, "You describe her as a loner. She didn't seem that way too me. She struck me as sort of lonely, and now that I've seen this place I wonder why she spent so much time so far away from it."

Tilvy gave John a look, as though he may be unusually thick. She might not know the full story but she thought she had a good idea about some of it.

Barma asked, "She didn't tell you about her brother?"

John looked surprised, "Not a word. I didn't even know she had a brother."

"Well, he's sort of the reason Asha went into hiding, seclusion, whatever you call it. Why she now spends so much time away from here, we think, or I think anyway."

Tilvy interrupted, "Barma, don't you think we should leave it for Asha to tell John, if she wants too, it's not really our place."

"Oh ... but it's not like it's a secret. Is it?" Tilvy frowned but Barma didn't notice and continued, "Asha has a twin brother. Twins are really really rare among the aaranya so everyone knew them and watched out for them. They're always much talked about, even now. As children they shared a special bond, like most twins I guess, but as they grew up their differences became more apparent. I don't know that Asha ever really saw it, which is why Sarva's departure came as such a surprise to her.

"We were young when all this happened, but everyone was talking about it, which probably didn't help Asha much."

Tilvy took over the explanation, not trusting Barma to get the rest of it right. "Most saw the restlessness growing in Sarva. For some reason a sort of compulsion comes on a few of us to go out and explore the world, even beyond the normal explorations of youth. It was growing very strong in Sarva and so it came as no surprise to most when he announced that he and a few friends were going away for a while. But Asha was devastated. She didn't want to leave here, but I'm guessing Sarva didn't even ask her. I think he should have. It may have helped if Asha had had the chance to decide, to say, that she didn't want to go with him rather than feeling left behind. I think she felt terribly rejected. Deserted."

John felt a pang of guilt, guessing that his own rejection of her would have been like reopening this earlier hurt.

"They left, to the north I think, and Asha just sort of ... moped around, for a long time. Not that Asha was ever the life of the party – like Andrei tries to be – but she had always been a happy person. Sarva leaving like he did seemed to take something from her. For a long time I think she was just waiting, expecting that Sarva would feel the loss too and come back for her, but he never did. It's been years now.

"Finally she said that she was leaving too. She went south and no one heard from her for a while. Then Nona started spending time down that way and found Asha living on the edge of the forest, where your home was eventually built. After that Asha would come back to the Glade for periods of time, perhaps just to check whether Sarva had returned because she would soon go back to the edge of the forest. Occasionally one of us will visit, but most of us get a bit nervous living too close to your lot." Tilvy grinned at John, trying to lighten the mood a bit.

"I think, away from the Glade, it was easier for Asha to ignore the fact that Sarva was missing. When your house was built she was upset for a while but eventually she became intrigued by the humans that lived there. I think watching them became a sort of hobby. When your family moved in Asha was smitten with the baby. She'd baby-sit every chance she could get." Tilvy saw that John's face had gone wooden and finished up quickly, "So that's what I meant by Asha being a bit of a loner."

John nodded. It all fit. "Thanks," he said simply, not sure what else to say.

Night had fallen and John realised that it was not as dark as it should be. It was as though the air was glowing, he couldn't tell if the light came from the trees or the air itself. The shimmer of the Way had taken on a distinctly silvery sheen and John could see movement behind the shimmer, like looking through frosted glass.

"Is it usual for it to be so light here?" asked John.

"I suppose I shouldn't be surprised you can see it," said Barma. "It's always bright for us here, but humans normally don't notice it."

John saw a few tree-folk come through the forest. They gave a wave to Barma and Tilvy and then disappeared into the Glade. A while later Tilvy pointed to the Way and John could see what appeared to be additional activity, more silvery shadows beyond the shimmer.

"It looks like word is spreading, you may have some visitors soon, John."

A few minutes later a few aaranya came out of the Glade and looked over at where John sat with Barma and Tilvy. Moments after that some tiny figures flew out through the Way. To John they looked like fairies, the glowing winged figures of human fairy tales. They darted here and there but generally stayed close to the main group.

John gasped in wonder. "Who?" he managed to whisper.

"Some of our children," said Tilvy, the affection obvious in her voice. "They will be very curious about you."

The group moved slowly toward where John sat and he was able to make out more detail of the small figures in flight. The resemblance to fairies remained, the wings and the subtle glow, but as they got closer he could see the children's faces and the differences in their sizes and maturity. They were beautiful, but beautiful like carefree, happy children rather than something supernatural. They reminded John of human children in a playground, but a playground with a whole other dimension. They chased each other up and down and around, laughing and giggling among themselves. Their voices, reflecting their diminutive size, came only softly to John.

As they got closer a few of the braver children would dart forward to get a closer look at John, hover for a moment and then dart away to one of the adult aaranya that accompanied them. John could not help but smile at these beautiful children – but it was a sad smile, tainted by the memories of his own lost daughter.

"Hello," John said softly.

One particularly small child, a boy, darted in close to his face and stared intently. A tentative hand came forward and touched a tear before he darted away again.

The adults relaxed as they saw John's affection for the children, and the children's lack of fear. A few of the adults settled on the ground nearby, others ascended the trees around the group. The children continued to flit from place to place, and from adult to adult, with the boundless energy of the young.

John looked at Barma and Tilvy in wonder. "I had not expected ... I don't know what I expected ... but ..." he could not finish.

"We are not a prolific people," said Tilvy. "You can understand that our children are very precious to us, for so many reasons."

John nodded as he watched a group of the children chasing each other around the adults. One flew past and hid down behind him for a few moments before thinking better of it and darting up into the tree.

A spret appeared in a nearby tree, much like the creature he'd seen the other night with Andrei. One of the children gave a gleeful yell and flew off after it. Quickly several other children followed him. The spret scuttled up the trunk and disappeared into the branches with the children flying and scampering after him. Some of the adults got up and followed after the children, not able to fly, but making up for it with their agility through the trees.

There was a stirring among the aaranya around John and he looked back toward the Way. It glowed particularly brightly for a moment and a large group emerged from the Glade. John's eyes were immediately drawn to the figure at the front of this group.

Even among a people typically slender in stature this woman was slight. From the lines on her face, and something about the way she held herself, John could see that she must be very old, but she carried herself erect and seemed to tread lightly on the ground. Her hair, a fine cloud swept back from her face, was white with threads of a darker grey streaking through it. Her skin was dark in colour and she had rounded facial features similar to those of an Aboriginal. She had the same large and unusually pale green eyes as Asha. Her small face was bright and friendly, an expression that looked natural to it, although in this moment it may have been aided by some humour from Andrei who John could see walking at her side.

There was an obvious deference to this woman from all that were near her, as though the group was centred on her. Feeling as though he should offer some mark of respect John got to one knee and lowered his head as the group approached.

The old woman laughed, her voice still strong but with a noticeable timbre of age. "We are not so formal here, John, and I am no queen. Please, sit back and be comfortable."

John settled back but left the position closest to the tree for the woman, it seemed the right thing to do. As the woman settled, the others that had acted as a retinue spread out around the pair of them. Andrei sat close beside John.

"I am Kaia," she began as everyone settled. "I am one of the elders of this stand. It is the way of our people that the elders may speak on behalf of the stand when needed."

John nodded his head in acknowledgement. He was surprised by the way things were unfolding. He had expected Andrei to ask around for Asha and to be told whether she would be willing to speak with him. This formality all seemed to be leading to something more, something ominous.

"Of the others here," she gestured to those around them, "some provide assistance and information to the elders, and so are privy to much of what we do. And some are mostly curious ... about you." She smiled as she gestured toward John. "You may be the only human that has ever been brought to this place, certainly the only one that can see it. Not everyone has been happy that Andrei should bring you here. In explanation Andrei has spoken with me and told me of your story, and your search for Asha – eventually," she added with a smile at Andrei who, unusual for him, looked embarrassed.

Kaia seemed uncertain how to continue but eventually said, "Asha is not here and she has not been near here since you last saw her, of that we are quite certain."

John's shoulders slumped. He had been so sure that this was the place to find her. He said, "Asha left the trees around my home for several months, about ten months ago. She was away longer at that time but she did return."

Kaia nodded. "Yes, she visited here fairly often during that period. That was when we first learned of your ability to see our kind. This time is different. ... You've met Nona?" Kaia asked.

John nodded.

"She was here until a few days ago, and while she was here she spoke with me about some of the events before Asha disappeared. She had spoken with Asha the day after your disagreement."

John's spirits bounced back.

"Nona said that Asha was going to return to your house the following day. Apparently Asha was quite definite about staying near you. She wanted to be available to help you with the difficulties you were experiencing."

John looked at Kaia, puzzled. This made no sense. That would have been Monday. He had even come home early that day. If she was there he should have seen her. He had called out for her! "But she wasn't there," he said at last. "I've spent weeks looking for her."

"We know, John, we don't doubt you," said Kaia gently, reassuring. "We fear there is something more behind Asha's disappearance. There have been others in recent times. One or two of our more solitary people have disappeared without trace, and similar has been reported from other stands. Because it has always been the reclusive that have disappeared no one has been certain whether they may have just wandered off – it happens.

"But with Asha ... even if it weren't for what you and Nona told us, Asha was never really a recluse. She still needed people. No one was ever likely to believe she had just wandered off."

"Then what – ?" John started.

Kaia held her hand up. "Please, John, we'll try to explain more later."

John looked doubtful.

"We don't *know* anything, John, we are just concerned," she continued, placating. "I would like to hear the full story from you, from when you first saw Asha." She looked around. "If you would rather do it somewhere more private we can go for a walk."

John was surprised to remember they weren't alone. He hesitated to look around, he didn't really want to see their expressions. He thought about what he had to tell them versus what they already knew, from Nona, from Andrei and just now. If he had abased himself before these people it was already done. Little of the detail would make much difference to their opinion of him. So John began his story, the death of his wife and daughter, the breaking of his mind and then seeing Asha. The months of trying to rebuild his life, and then Asha again, and learning of the narun and the forest ... and then of the night he had denied Asha's existence and her departure in tears.

"And that was the last I saw of her," he finished. Retelling the story reminded John of how convinced he had been that this was all just in his head. Thinking now of all that he had seen, he wondered if he really had enough room in his head to have invented it all.

Everyone was silent for a while, only the distant calls of the children playing in the forest filled the space.

"Thank you, John," said Kaia at last. "I need to go back to the Glade. There are issues that the elders need to discuss."

John looked at her, disturbed that after all he had just told her she was just going to leave him stranded here with nowhere left to turn. "Can't you do anything to help me find Asha?"

"That's part of what the elders need to discuss, John. Whether we can do anything for Asha, and if there is something, whether we can ask it of you."

John reached forward and put his hand on her forearm. Quietly he pleaded, "Whatever it takes, Kaia. Please. I need to see her again."

Kaia patted his hand. She rose gracefully and most of the others rose to follow her back to the Glade. A few steps away, Kaia stopped and turned as if something just occurred to her. "John, you do need to eat. The forest here may make you feel complete, but your body still needs food and water. Eat, sleep and in the morning we will talk again."

As the group walked toward the Way John realised that they had all assumed sizes compatible with his own while they were near him, only as they walked away did they relax and revert to their preferred smaller size. It made it appear that they were walking faster than they were. The group disappeared through the Way with a glow and a large ripple.

"Wow," said Andrei, still seated next to John. "She can really do entrances and exits can't she. It must be a skill that comes with age. And being enigmatic too, that must be another one. You know, I don't think I've got the patience to become an elder. Oh wait, patience is another thing that's supposed to come with time too, that and wisdom. Probably just as well."

John looked across at Andrei, "So you missed what that all meant too?"

"Like I was a seedling in a tall forest, it went way over." There were murmurs of agreement from Barma and Tilvy behind them, so they turned to include them in the conversation. "Most of us leave all the big stuff to the elders and their assistants." Andrei's tone made John think that the assistants got the same sort of respect as student hall monitors at school.

"But you went to Kaia. Why do that if you didn't know about the other disappearances?"

Andrei looked uncomfortable, anything related to his more serious side had that effect on him. "Why do birds land on this branch and not that one? Why do humans rush about in little tin boxes? Why do snowflakes come in such interesting shapes? Who knows? It's a mystery."

"Like why Andrei can't be serious for more than a moment," put in Tilvy.

"Or how Kaia knew I hadn't eaten all day," added John.

"Oh, I can answer that one," said Andrei. "We can see it. It's like your body is calling out *feed me, feed me*, while you stare about open-mouthed waiting for food to fly in."

"What our dear friend really means," corrected Tilvy, "is that Kaia is very sensitive and observant."

Andrei chose to ignore the correction. "So, John, did you want to camp here as entertainment for the people?" He grinned, it was obvious the idea appealed to him. "Or would you prefer somewhere with a bit more privacy?"

"Andrei as an elder," said Barma in wonder. "Now isn't that a scary thought."

"Catch up, Barmy," said Andrei, "we've gone past my elder eligibility, we've mastered mysteries, now we're considering camping."

John got to his feet and shouldered his backpack. "I would like something off the main thoroughfare if we can."

Tilvy showed John to a spot away from the Glade that felt protected, and some bushes gave the location some additional privacy. John eyed the dismal few meals left in his backpack and wondered what the trip home was going to be like.

8. Prisoner

Since revealing John's secret Asha had been left alone in her cell, from the rhythms of the tree she thought it must have been three days.

When Karlin did arrive it was without his trolley of equipment, although he did have a few things under one arm. Asha breathed a sigh of relief. Sando arrived with him and took up his usual place by the door. Asha had been outside the tree, lying in a sort of nest formed at the base of its trunk between some of its cramped roots.

"You look much improved. Feeling better, my little dryad?" asked Karlin.

Asha just stared at him.

"I'm afraid I am going to have to insist that you become a little more responsive," he said. The gentle and friendly tone of his voice was at odds with his words. "Are you feeling better now, my little dryad?" he asked again.

She considered continuing to ignore his questions but memories of the pain made her cringe. "Yes," she said, "some."

"Good, good. That's good my little dryad." Karlin's voice gentle and approving. "I do have some questions for you." He sat back in a chair on his side of the room and crossed his legs, looking through the clear divide at Asha beneath the tree.

One of the things he had brought with him into the room was a large pad. As he lifted it and started flicking through the pages Asha recognised it as John's, and so she knew what Karlin was turning to before he got there.

"This really is a good likeness you know," he said to her. He turned the pad around so that Asha could see the drawing that John had done of her. "I'm thinking of getting this framed, it will be the first good picture we have of one of you." Karlin stared at the picture for a few moments longer before folding the pad and putting it on his knee.

"When did John first begin to see you?" he asked.

Asha looked at him carefully through the clear divide. Despite his usual gentle voice and friendly tones she could tell that there was something upsetting Karlin. In a flash of intuition she guessed that they had not found John yet. She wondered how that could be. John was a man of fixed habits these days, he should not be difficult to find.

Feeling a surge of hope that John may stay free of these people, she tried to work out what questions she could answer and what things she should avoid. She could not think of any reason to lie about the start of things with John.

"It was soon after his daughter died," she finally replied.

Karlin nodded, it was what he expected. "Has he only seen you, or has he met others?"

Asha decided to risk a lie. "Just me," she said, feeling as though the lie was written across her face. She almost blurted out the truth to relieve that feeling.

Karlin seemed not to notice, his mind on other things. "You've obviously spoken with him," he said. "It's been what ... almost a year? How much have you seen of him?"

"I stayed away for a long time. We only just started talking again not long ago." This was close enough to the truth that Asha was able to say it without discomfort.

Karlin nodded his acceptance. "Why? Why did you stay away?"

Asha considered the question and how to answer it. "I didn't know whether I wanted to be seen by a human, and I didn't know how long it might last. When I finally went back he could still see me and so we started to talk."

The questions continued and Asha continued to try and filter her responses. She did not know what may prove dangerous for John, but she tried anyway. The questions turned to how John spent his time, the places that he went, and Asha thought these were the real questions, the things that Karlin really wanted to know. The curious thing was that she felt confident that she could be completely truthful here. John spent almost all his time at home. Aside from work, and the rare work related trip to the city, John had seen very few people and been very few places since his daughter had died.

Karlin was frustrated with her answers. "What about trips into the forest? Did he ever go very far?" he asked.

"No, he always stayed close to home," said Asha. That was mostly true, his walks with her had probably been among his more adventurous excursions and they had never gone far.

There was silence for a few minutes. Finally Karlin asked, "So, if John is not at home, you have no idea where we might find him?"

"No," she responded truthfully.

"We found wrappings off camping gear in his house. If he went camping where do you think he would go?"

"I don't know. He never did any camping while I knew him." Again Asha's response was truthful, but inside she felt a surge of excitement, had he gone looking for her? "Maybe he moved away," she ventured.

Karlin waved his hand in a dismissive gesture. "His car is still there and everything is still in his house – except him."

Abruptly he stood up. "I've no more time for this. You'll have to move to shared quarters for a while, dear, we've other things to do."

Karlin paused as he was going out the door. He looked back. "Don't get too comfortable, I've got a job for you in a few days." Then he smiled. Asha thought it was a smile that might fool many people, friendly and personable in appearance. But it was Karlin at his most selfish, lost in his own plans with no thought or care for how they affected others. As he left Asha felt a cold chill at the thought of what he may have planned for her next.

* * *

A few hours later Sando came back with Ian and Darren. Asha reduced her size and crawled submissively into her cage. At Sando's signal the men closed up the cage and carried her out into the tall corridor. They took a different turn and carried the cage down a passageway and out into the corner of a large dimly lit cavern. She recognised it as much the same as the underground car park where she had been brought in, but much higher, perhaps multiple levels joined. As she looked around Asha realised that the cells and rooms of her confinement were simply part of a two storey building inside the cavern, apparently filling one side of it.

Asha could see large round pillars reaching up to the high ceiling at regular intervals, she shuddered at the thought of the layers above her waiting to crash down. Fluorescent lights flickered around the cavern making most of it visible but still leaving it dim and dismal. Asha could hear what sounded like water lapping somewhere and the air felt very humid. The aroma of eucalyptus and sawn timber was very distinct and underneath it all was an assortment of unpleasant chemical smells. It was surprisingly warm, perhaps heated by the many lights and other electrical equipment. Strange, hollow, echoing sounds came at her from many directions.

The open part of the cavern had two broad aisles down which, she would learn, tree platforms could be rolled from a hydraulic elevator in the centre at the far end. Along one side of the first aisle, the side of the laboratory building, there were a series of large solid doors and she understood these were the doors to the large cells in which she had been tortured, the doors through which the trees had been moved in and out. On the other side of the aisle were a line of mesh cages like tall aviaries. Inside the closest of these were two tree platforms and Asha could make out three aaranya prisoners sitting on one of the platforms, watching her with little apparent interest.

Between the cages and along the walls of the cavern any space had been used as a sort of dumping ground, a place where things were rolled or carried out and forgotten. She was carried past this first aisle, along a narrow pathway between piles of boxes and into the second aisle. This second aisle had mesh cages along both sides – and again the cages had boxes and barrels and other paraphernalia in tall stacks between them.

Asha was distracted as a tree platform outside the cages began to roll, driven by a small electric tractor engine attached to its platform. A human walked near it with some sort of control in his hand. The tree shuddered and wobbled slightly as the platform moved. Asha imagined it was on its way to the surface and sunshine and she wished she could reach out and go with it.

"This place still gives me the creeps," said Ian. Asha was startled by his voice, the men tended not to speak much as they carried her around the corridors. "All these trees and ponds in cages. I know there are supposed to be other things in there, but when you can't see them ... it's like a zoo with all the animals gone." After a moment he shuddered and added, "Never liked zoos much either."

Darren laughed at him, the sound ringing loud and out of place in the cavern. "You watch some of these cages carefully for a while and you can tell there are things in there. That pool in particular, you watch for the splashes and ripples."

"And that's supposed to make me feel better?" said Ian. "That just makes it seem even more like some sort of ghost zoo."

Darren laughed again and then said, "Come on, let's get this one put away before Karlin gets stroppy. You've got places to go."

Sando was standing by a small door into one of the larger cages. This cage was almost in the corner of the cavern, directly across from where they had come in. They carried Asha through that door into a small cage inside the larger one. There was a hatch in the wall of that smaller cage like the ones in the cells. Her cage was quickly attached and Sando indicated that she should move into the larger cage. As soon as she was out Sando signalled to the men and they removed the cage from the hatch. The men and Sando left, the men carrying the now empty carry-cage away with them.

Asha expanded to her preferred size and looked around her new prison. The walls and ceiling were all mesh, even where the cage ran up against the concrete, as though making certain that they would be unable to merge even with the lifeless cement. Asha wasn't certain what the floor was made from but there was certainly no way through it.

There were two tree platforms inside this large cage. Asha could see the large gate at the front where the trees must get rolled in and out. On one of the platforms, beside the tree, were three aaranya: two men standing and a woman seated between them. The other platform appeared to be empty. The three had a faded, haggard look.

Asha walked toward them, not certain how to react. She supposed she had hoped for some greater reaction from fellow prisoners, this blank staring was unnerving. As she got to the platform she jerked to a stop and her hand flew to her mouth to cover a gasp. The woman was sitting because there was very little left of her legs. Both legs stopped about halfway down the thigh, the stumps ending as flat skin, the ends smooth as though they had been cut with a knife. Asha had never seen such a thing with a narun, had never even thought it was possible.

She looked up into their faces. There was a look of annoyance on the face of the man on the left, his stance a protective hover over the woman. The woman and other man just looked back at her blankly as if they had not noticed her shock.

"I'm Asha," she said, not intending to sound so nervous.

The man on the left nodded. Asha thought he looked familiar but it wasn't until he spoke that she recognised him.

"I'm Ceeda, this is Nacee and Briso," he said, indicating the woman and other man.

"Don't you recognise me, Ceeda?" asked Asha.

He looked at her more carefully and then his expression started to soften, and then sadden. "So they got another one from home," he said. "Hello, Asha, I wish it was good to see you. It's been a long time."

Asha gave him a half smile and then indicated the platform, "May I?" He nodded, so Asha climbed onto the platform and sat on the soil not far from the three of them. Ceeda slowly relaxed and he and Briso sat down either side of Nacee against the trunk of the tree. Ceeda pulled Nacee under his arm and she appeared to try and bury herself there.

"How long have you been here?" Asha asked.

"I don't know. Months at least. It could be a year. It feels like years. It's really hard to tell. Nacee was already here but she was ... more talkative then." Asha understood that Ceeda meant that she was still whole then. "She had been here for a few months by the time I arrived. Briso was here before even Nacee arrived, and was already much as you see now. He follows us round, and imitates me, but he has never spoken. I only know his name from what Minzi has said."

"Minzi?" Asha queried.

"You've not met her? Who was the narun with you just now?" asked Ceeda in turn.

"I just assumed it was Sando," said Asha. Nacee shuddered at mention of Sando's name. "He's the only narun I've met up to now. At least ... I had assumed it was always him."

Ceeda nodded. "It's hard to be sure just how many there are, they all look and feel the same in those suits."

"Are there others from home?" Asha asked Ceeda.

"Rizzy was here. She came in ... I think it was a couple of months ago now. She seemed to be holding out really well for a while, but she was taken out a week or more ago and we've seen nothing of her since. She may have been taken to the ruined ones. That's not great but the other possibilities are worse."

Asha looked puzzled, "Ruined ones?"

"You've not met them then, you'd know who I meant if you had. In the lower cells. I can only assume they were once like us. Now they are pale, tiny, fragile things. The few that have any mind at all seem lost and confused. If you let them cling for too long, they all want to cling, they try to drain you. Not that what little they get does them much good. It's distressing to spend time with them, but there are worse things." As Ceeda finished speaking he was looking down with pity at Nacee nestled under his arm.

* * *

Over the next few days Asha learned several things about her prison and her fellow prisoners. In one of the rare moments when Nacee was not beneath the protective wing of Ceeda's arm, she learned that Nacee's disfigurement was the result of some strange experiments with the burning mesh and chainsaws. She had been forced to merge with a dying tree that was then wrapped in the mesh and pieces were cut away. Ceeda had no idea what they had hoped to prove.

"I think the loss of her legs is largely a psychological thing," Ceeda confessed. "I don't think the cut could possibly have been so neat. I am sure there was a loss of her substance, but choosing to show that as a loss of her legs rather than a reduction in her form ... I think it's a sort of protest. Crying out that she has been crippled. In a healthy forest I am sure she would recover, given enough time, but here she is gradually fading."

When Ceeda had first arrived the large corridor, with its enclosed cells large enough to hold the platform trees, had not been completed, so some of the experiments were done in the visible cages. "It was a sort of double torture, for the one undergoing the experiment and also for those that had to watch and listen. Nacee's dismemberment was one of the first experiments done in the relative privacy of the large cells," Ceeda told her. "Whatever they're made of, or painted with, you can't hear or sense what is going on behind those tall doors."

Ceeda also told her of projectile tests, starvation tests and more. Many narun had died in these dungeons and so far no one had any idea what it was all for. Ceeda believed it must have been going on for many years, with Karlin and his assistants gradually refining their tools and knowledge.

The early prison cages, long before Ceeda's time, had just been carefully constructed cement huts with narun guards. What Ceeda had been told was that many of the early prisoners had been captured by being coaxed into traps by the narun helping Karlin. There were some stories of prisoners that found themselves inexplicably cooperative until they found themselves trapped in the huts, but Ceeda had not seen any equipment that had that effect on him.

By the time Ceeda was captured the detector and ray-gun were definitely the weapons of choice, and they were able to disorient him long enough to be placed in a mesh cage, but the gun did not have the power even then that it does now. It was only in the last couple of months they had started testing the ray's ability to drive aaranya from the refuge of a tree. "It's getting progressively stronger," Ceeda said. "The first few times I felt it there was disorientation and pain but if you were prepared for it you could stand it ... for a short time anyway. Now I think he may even be able to kill with it."

Asha confirmed that Karlin claimed that capability.

"Has anyone ever escaped?"

"Not that I know of," Ceeda replied in a flat tone. "Some months ago there was a new-comer in that cage across the aisle. He started calling to us, he wanted to plan something. They took him away and we never saw him again."

"Had they heard him?"

Ceeda shrugged. "Maybe. Or maybe it was just coincidence, it's not uncommon for one to be taken away and never seen again. It's not an experiment I've been tempted to try."

"Who are these narun that are helping Karlin?" Asha asked.

"Have you ever seen them outside those suits?"

"I've seen Minzi a few times and a few others whose names I wasn't told. I've never actually seen Sando, although I think Nacee may have, but I assume he's the same. They're strange. I think they're aaranya, but with murky grey skin and hair. In fact, if I heard correctly, they even call themselves dhumraka: the grey ones.

"They don't talk much in our presence and they don't appreciate questions so you learn quickly not to ask. I've seen them do some really horrible things and heard of worse."

In a cage next to theirs was a large pool, actually several pools placed together. Asha imagined it was so that each part was small enough to be moved, for inside each pool was a collection of water plants that must also need sunlight from time to time. There did seem to be some attempt at special lighting over part of it. Ceeda said the same had been attempted with the trees but it failed to work well enough and produced too much heat for this underground cavern.

In the pools of that cage were two of the jalaja, naiads. Asha's few attempts at speaking with them, having to call loudly to overcome the blocking effect of the mesh, met with silence.

"I think they blame us," Ceeda told her. "The dhumraka feel like they're aaranya of some sort, so I guess that makes all this our fault."

Asha felt that she could hardly blame them. That any narun could be part of all this was incomprehensible to her, but if she could, she would willingly pass the responsibility on to anyone that wasn't aaranya.

"They're not as bad as the samudraka that shared their cage for a while, she had a separate pool for the seawater. When she first arrived she screeched through the mesh at us, so much and so long that we were thankful for the mesh. When the dhumraka came for her she screamed at them, something about her being a princess and they'd be sorry. When they returned her next she was silent. She never spoke again. ... I can't believe that I'd begged for her to be quiet." Ceeda hung his head, embarrassed by his admission.

"What happened to her?" Asha asked.

Ceeda shrugged. "It didn't take long, a few more trips and one day she didn't come back."

On the other side of the naiads was another large cage, but the pile of boxes and crates was too large too see who was in there. Ceeda said there were three or four prisoners in that cage, but they were not much better off than any of the others. None of the other prisoners seemed interested in trying to communicate over the obstruction of the mesh. "They're all beyond it now," said Ceeda. "I think they may all be like Briso, or worse. It seems to be the way we all go near the end." He looked with sadness at the still silent Nacee.

9. Belief

The next morning John woke with a start, there were strange noises outside his tent. He unzipped the flap and looked out to find Andrei leaning against a tree trunk making strange flatulent buzzing noises with his mouth. The sun was not yet up but the forest was light with the approaching dawn, and the air was chill and damp with dew.

"What are you doing?" asked John.

"Just making you feel at home." Andrei grinned and let off another series of blurping sounds. "Isn't that just like the sounds of home? You know, cars going past and all that. Maybe a truck." Andrei let off another string even louder and more flatulent sounding.

"I live down a back road, a long way from the main road. It is very peaceful. I haven't woken up to traffic noises in years ... and when I did they never sounded like a moose with gastric problems," said John. But it was difficult to stay angry with Andrei, even when his humour was off colour. There was something about his exuberance that forced a happy response. "Well, maybe sometimes it did, but that still doesn't make it a good way to wake up."

Barma emerged from the tree beside him. "I thought I'd stay out of the way until you woke up. Didn't want you to think I was responsible for him."

It appeared to be a familiar situation and John guessed that Barma and Andrei had probably once been a regular pairing, with Barma playing straight man to Andrei's fool.

Barma continued, "Tilvy suggested that we wake you early so you had time for breakfast and so on. It sounds like Kaia would like to talk to you not long after sun-up."

The night before swam back into John's mind and he wondered how he had managed to sleep so well and so long. He got up quickly. Andrei led John to a small stream at the bottom of a gully just a few minutes walk away from where he had camped, and politely left him to his morning ablutions, having grown used to John's habits by now. John cleaned himself up as well has he could at the stream and put on the cleanest of his dirty clothes. He wasn't about to win any beauty contests, but it was the best he could do and he felt refreshed – cold, but awake and invigorated.

John packed up his camp quickly, practice had improved his abilities with the tent and sleeping bag. After that John followed Tilvy and the others back to the Way.

They walked around to the front of the Way and John saw that Kaia and several others had already settled at the base of a tree. He tried to smile as he approached but he felt nervous and guessed that it showed. He really had no idea what to expect this morning. A clear space had been left in front of Kaia and the four of them settled on the ground facing her.

Kaia nodded to John and said, "I promised you some explanations and answers to your questions, but before we get to that: from what Andrei told me you have only limited food with you. He said you will have to leave here very soon. Will you be able to make it home?"

John decided that blunt honesty was the best. "I am hoping, presuming really, that Andrei will agree to guide me home. I am totally lost. I have no idea where I am. If Andrei is able to find additional food for me, as he did on the way here, then I imagine I will make it home – hungry but otherwise okay."

Kaia nodded as if this was what she expected. "So we cannot keep you here too long. Andrei also told me that you don't believe that we actually exist, that we are somehow figments of your imagination. Is that still true?"

John felt himself blush, this was something he had still not resolved within himself. Blunt honesty, he reminded himself. "While I am here with you I can only believe you are real, just as I found myself believing in Asha when I was with her. But when I find myself at my work I am going to look back on this time and see that it must have been a dream, my imagination."

"Do you think your work is a dream, now, when you can't see it?" asked Kaia.

John shook his head. "The night that I saw Asha for the first time, I felt my mind break. I felt a crack open, I can still feel it now. My work, my real life, is something that I remember and rely on from before that happened. But all this is new and seems to defy everything that I've ever known." He paused to gather his thoughts. "I have always been a cynic and a sceptic, so it's easier for me to believe that my broken mind is creating illusions than it is to believe ... to believe that all this could possibly be real," he finished quietly, feeling that his explanation was inadequate.

"See what I mean?" said Andrei. "And I thought it was bad when he had two imaginary friends, now he's got all of you too." He grinned across at John.

Kaia waved her hand at Andrei, frowning in deep thought.

Partly in response to Andrei and partly because he felt that his explanation was even more inadequate now than ever, John continued, "With the time I have spent out here this last week it is getting harder to doubt my senses, but I still know that soon I will be back with people that cannot see you or hear you. Back in a world that does not know you exist. Once I am back in that world too ... then all this will seem impossible, unbelievable, fantastical. The delusions of a desperate mind."

"I find it difficult to relate to your situation, John," Kaia responded. "To not believe your own senses is something outside my experience. But, John, it has become very important that you do believe. If what we suspect is true then it is possible that your life is in danger. If you don't believe us in time you may not be able to avoid that danger. And, if you don't believe in us, how can we ask you for help?"

Everyone was silent for a while. Eventually Kaia continued, "Another of the elders may be able to assist you with more technical, or at least philosophical, explanations. He has made a study of such things, he has more curiosity about these sorts of things than most of us. Do you think that may help?"

John considered that, but said, "Maybe later. I am not sure it would really make that much difference. Once you start to doubt your own mind there is really no limit to the layers of illusion and confusion that you can present to yourself. At some point it comes down to the choice between belief and doubt. At some point I will believe in your existence, even when I am not with you, or I will stop seeing you at all and my doubts will have been confirmed."

"Stubborn too," murmured Andrei. He obtained a few chuckles from the group in response.

"So for now you behave as if we exist when you are with us and, presumably, try to behave as if we don't exist at other times." Kaia said.

John nodded.

"Soon you may meet other humans that know we exist." There were gasps from several in the gathering.

"Are they all as bad as him?" Andrei asked and got a few more chuckles.

But Kaia did not smile. "It may be that such humans were responsible for taking Asha.

"John, you are right, I can't make you believe. I can only hope that you will find it in yourself to believe in us before it is too late. If you meet these other humans first, it may be too late. If they are capturing narun then they will also be interested in any human that can see us."

John stared at Kaia. He had not known what to expect, but it certainly wasn't this. If other humans knew about the narun then maybe he would finally be able to convince himself that they were real – or would he convince himself that such humans were imaginary too? There really was no end to such madness once you started. There was nothing else for it, he had to push forward. Whether this was all real or not, he had already committed himself to finding Asha. That's what he would do. Belief would come eventually – or not.

"Go on, Kaia. Please," he said.

Kaia sighed. "For any of my explanations to make sense you will need to know more about our people, to know something of our history. What I tell you now is from the memory of the aaranya, the forest-born. The events I describe involved all the narun, but our tales are not the tales of others. These events separated us. The different kinds of narun no longer mingle and prejudice has only increased with time.

"Also, please, remember that what I tell you now is not represent-ative of our people. If I had the time I would tell you tales of the beauty and gentleness that is more typical of our kind, something to counterbalance this most shameful period of our history. But we have little time. Please don't judge us from what I tell you now." Kaia paused, gathering her resources to tell the tale.

John was surprised to hear the note of apology, of asking for him to think kindly of their people. From what little he knew he felt it was more his own place to be offering apologies.

Kaia straightened her posture and began speaking.

"We are a long-lived people. We exist across the world in many variations, adapting to the forests that are our homes: the pine forests of the colder reaches; the rainforests of the equator; the many broad-leaf forests of more temperate regions; and in recent times some even make tenuous homes in the plantations created by humans. We try to keep in touch but our numbers now are few and our communication is slow. Even so, with our long lives and with elders to pass on stories through the generations, we have accumu-lated a long history. We have tales of our people from around the world, tales spanning many thousands of years. This is the tale of the Aeonian War.

"Long before the time of your Roman Empire, long before the time of your Babylonian, Akkadian or even your Sumerian empires, our people spanned the globe in interconnected communities. We were never an empire. It was not in our nature to form such hierarchies, but we were certainly a civilisation larger than any formed by humans until recent times. There were many Glades, places of great glory and complexity supporting large numbers of our people. The Glades interconnected so that news travelled quickly and our people thrived.

"We had always been a peaceful people. The primitive humans of those times faced many dangers and found it difficult just to survive from one day to the next. But our kind had no such hardships and we found time to develop philosophy and art, and believed ourselves to be a sophisticated people. We watched the struggles of your primitive ancestors and felt superior to them, pitying them for their harsh material existence. Our people believed they had reached their nirvana and they revelled in it.

"But it turned out that we had also been an ignorant people. We thought we were above the ambitions and drives that we so often observe in humans. We thought that our worst problems would only ever be the minor squabbles and jealousies of our past. We thought that nothing would change. We were wrong.

"Where the evil started is gone from our memories, but perhaps that doesn't matter. Our lives had been so easy through this time that we had not developed any wariness. We had not learned to recognise incipient evil, and so it grew without notice or constraint. There rose among us some charismatic narun that claimed that they were special – holy. They called themselves the Jatarupa – the Golden. They claimed that all others should pay respect and tribute to them. Even more, these narun claimed that all the material beings, including humans, should be subservient to them, and to all narun.

"Such ambitions had been foreign to our kind, but by some means these Jatarupa began to draw others to them as followers. Some say that the Jatarupa had ways to force others to do their bidding, others suggest that there is evil within us all and these narun simply released it. However they did it, their influence grew and spread. But some began to resist them.

"Having been peaceful for so long, we had few weapons and little skill at physical conflict. To overcome the stands that resisted them, the Jatarupa turned to those for whom violence came naturally: humans.

"Humans could make tools and weapons, and they could use fire. The Jatarupa found substances in the earth that were inimical to our being. Anything harmful to us must, necessarily, be harmful to all life, but humans are adept at manipulating their environment and were able to make devastating weapons from such things.

"So it was that the Jatarupa began to use force to dominate those stands that resisted them. They gathered to themselves armies of humans and other creatures that they controlled, and fell upon us with weapons and powers that we did not understand. Any stand that would not bow to their rule was obliterated, and those that did bow to them were subjugated in the most brutal manner. When one area was decimated they would move on to another, seeming intent not just on ruling our kind, but on our utter destruction. Our people died by the thousands, by the millions.

"The Jatarupa encouraged humans in their use of fire. They encouraged them to clear huge tracts of land again and again so that the forests could not return, and many Glades faded and ceased to be. The connections between the few remaining Glades were lost and our people became isolated from one another.

"The battles raged again and again, back and forth over this land, and others, for thousands of years. Previously subjugated stands would inevitably rebel against their domination and the armies would return and do it all over again. Our forests shrank, our people died, and the world around us changed forever.

"Eventually the power of the Jatarupa began to fade. The few remaining leaders were killed, and without its leaders the armies turned on themselves and disintegrated. The end, when it finally came, came quickly.

"The war was finally over but the damage was already done. Our land and its population was already changing. Entire species of animals went extinct and even the weather patterns changed. The humans kept up their fire-clearing habits so that forests were unable to grow back even if the weather had permitted.

"Our people are not prolific and our population has never recovered. Even the much reduced forests of today are only sparsely populated by our kind.

"That devastation was long ago, before any of us still living in this stand were born, before any of our parents or their parents were born. Since that time we have tried to be vigilant so that we can prevent such a war from starting again. Over the years we have heard disturbing tales from distant lands, but always they have been comfortably far away, and always the problems have been resolved by others ... until now."

Kaia stopped and looked over the group that watched her, spellbound. The elders had discussed this all night and had finally decided that there was enough evidence, that they should act. Better to act now, and be wrong, than to wait too long. It was possible they were already too late, at least for those, like Asha, that had already been taken.

John watched her carefully. "So you think it may be happening again, that some narun are conspiring with humans? And you think that such a conspiracy may have reason to abduct Asha?"

Kaia nodded. "Here, and at a neighbouring stand, a few of our more reclusive members have gone missing. All stands have some that prefer the solitude of the periphery. There may be many months over which they are never heard from in the Glade. But we couldn't know for certain that any of them had been taken, sometimes people do go their own way.

"Then, a few months ago in a stand to the west, a man saw a small group of humans, or what they originally thought were humans, enter the forest with strange equipment. Later he felt a strange sensation and saw that the group was approaching him, as if the equipment they used had allowed them to find him. Nervous, this man merged with a nearby tree and only partly exposed himself when high above, so that he could watch the group. This witness claims that one of the group was almost certainly a narun covered with some human manufactured material.

"On its own that story is reason enough to worry. If ambitious narun are working with humans with modern technology there is a real concern that they could overrun any stand, that nothing could stop them.

"So we were already worried when you arrived looking for Asha. Your story has convinced us that our growing suspicions are correct. We believe that there must be narun working with humans, and for some reason they are abducting our people.

"But how would they have known where to find Asha?" asked John.

"We don't know. It seems a safe assumption that you told no other humans," said Kaia.

John shook his head.

"Perhaps another of our people told of her or perhaps it is coincidence ... how did they know about any of our people other than searching areas of forest. But that does bring us back to you, John."

John nodded. "I see it. If they are abducting your people for research or interrogation then there is a chance they may want to talk to me too. ... But seeing that doesn't really help me very much. I have to go home, I can't just disappear."

"Trying to disappear may be your safest option," said Kaia.

"You don't seem to have too much trouble getting lost," commented Andrei, earning him a slow smile from John.

"No, it's home from here. I'll just try to deal with whatever comes from there as best I can. Besides, I still want to try and find Asha."

Kaia nodded as if she expected that response. "In that case we would like you to help us, and perhaps we can help you in turn."

John considered this for a few moments. "You really believe that Asha has been abducted?"

Kaia nodded. "We can't be certain, but that is what we think, yes."

"And you think I may be able to help?"

Again Kaia nodded.

"All right then," he said. "How do we start?"

A short time later Kaia returned from the Glade with another elder. This was a tall, thin man with similarly dark skin and rounded features, as if he and Kaia shared a common background. His dark grey hair was liberally salted with silver and his lined face and faded blue eyes looked mostly stern and serious until you caught him in a smile, then it was as if a light had been turned on.

"This is Milla," Kaia said. "He'll walk part of the way back with you."

"Hello, John," Milla said with a deep husky voice.

"Hello, Milla," John returned. "Asha often spoke of you with affection. She seemed to think we would get along very well. Does that mean you ask too many questions too?"

The light turned on, Milla smiled and laughed. "Yes, I am that most atypical creature, a narun with curiosity, an aaranya that asks why."

"And you're coming along to try and convince me you're real," John said.

"If you still need convincing," Milla said, "but I'm also along to offer some education to your companions. We can talk as we walk and you get home sooner and everyone gets to learn what little I can tell them."

Three other figures came up and Kaia introduced them.

Darnu was a slender, rugged looking man with a deep tan. With neat dark hair he had an aura of crisp competence. He nodded to John with a look of reserve, John thought it likely Darnu didn't trust him very much.

At Darnu's shoulder stood a stocky figure introduced as Garjae. The two seemed to be a pair. Similarly aged, mature but not old, similarly tanned, and similarly serious. Garjae was less dark and had an aggressive stance. Another difference was that the look he gave John was even less friendly, there was something about John that offended Garjae to the core.

Trailing behind these two was a small pale figure, he appeared to be not much more than a boy, younger even than Andrei. Beenae was puffed up with self-importance, looking up at Darnu and Garjae with worshipful adoration and obviously pleased to have been picked to go with them.

"Andrei has insisted on accompanying you back," said Kaia.

"What can I say, John?" Andrei said with a grin. "You make me laugh."

"And Barma and Tilvy have decided to go along too," Kaia continued.

"Someone has to keep Andrei in line or who knows where you'll end up," said Tilvy.

Goodbyes were said and the group headed off. Darnu and Garjae tended to walk out to one side, most of the others formed a loose group about Milla and John. Beenae wandered back and forth between the two groups.

"You sure you're up for it, gramps?" asked Andrei from behind.

"I might be an elder but I'm not dead yet," Milla growled. "I can keep pace with you and you can certainly listen while I talk. It's got to be better than listening to you prattle on anyway," he said, and gave a slow swipe behind him. Andrei, who had been attempting some exaggerated imitation, ducked out of the way easily and grinned affectionately at the old man.

While they were close to the Glade they all seemed to be in good spirits and they made good time. It felt to John as if they were always walking downhill. Sometime after a brief lunch-stop the effect began to wear off and the going got harder again.

Milla stayed in a good mood and he continued Kaia's history lesson as they walked.

"It's a fine tale that she tells, as far as it goes, but I feel that it never really makes clear just how close we came to extinction. And not just the aaranya. The Aeonian War affected all the narun, even the samudraka in their oceans were almost wiped out. Of course, they were a mostly coastal people back then so I guess they could not help but be deeply involved.

"One of the reasons why the tale is so spare of detail is that there were so few people left by the end of the war that much of our history from that time, and before, was lost. There were so few left that there were barely enough to form new stands and to continue our kind. The few that survived referred to that time as *kalpaanta*, the end of the world, because they were sure that it was. It is only in more recent generations that we have had the confidence to call it something less."

John asked, "The special talents that Kaia mentioned, was she referring to some kind of magic?"

"That'd about do it for John I reckon," said Andrei. "Tell him we have magic and we won't see him for the dust."

Milla looked at Andrei for a moment. John suspected he was taking Andrei's comment more seriously than Andrei had intended. John wasn't sure exactly how he felt. If this was an imaginary world then what difference would a bit of magic make?

"To listen to some tales of those times is indeed to think of the supernatural. But perhaps the tales are only exaggerating real talents that we know exist."

"Like healers?" asked Barma.

Milla looked across at Barma and nodded. "I met one long ago, far to the east, on the coast. Eenar was very old by the time I met her, but she was still an impressive individual." Milla turned his attention to John. "Some of what I saw her do really did look like magic, but she assured me that it wasn't. We're made of prana and inside our bodies are complicated flows of life-force. She was able to place her hands over areas of the body and influence those flows. It was very similar to what we do for our trees but she was able to do it from the outside and with much greater subtlety.

"Such talents are rare but they do exist and they come in many variations. Eenar was good, but in living memory, ask Kaia, there have been healers with even more dramatic skills.

"It is not a big step to take someone with a healer's talent and twist it so that they can change people for their own purposes. Changing their mood or causing pain or pleasure to force them to be cooperative. Perhaps healing them to be always angry or always devoted or whatever. It is no step at all to imagine a healer capable of killing someone with a touch, they could all do it if they wanted."

"That's ghastly," said Tilvy. "Do you really think that's what happened in the war?"

"I think it fits. We don't seem to be a particularly ambitious or greedy people by nature. Our life has been too easy, compared to that of humans for example, so we never developed the competitive instincts that drive ambition and greed. But imagine an aberration, someone born with both ambition and the talent to manipulate others. Such a person coming into our society would find very little to stand in their way, and after they gained a certain following they would have been almost unstoppable. Once they had changed enough people the whole thing could have taken on a life of its own. They may even have started something they could no longer control.

"But that's all just a guess. I think we have also changed as a people since the war. If the tales I've heard are true then there was a time when someone with my curiosity was not so unusual. There was a time before the war when our people had science and philosophy at least comparable to human achievement in many areas. Their priorities and methods were different, much was purely intellectual and their material sciences were based on natural processes. The buildings and cities of that time were living things, things that didn't leave much residue behind when they died.

"If we really were a different people back then, then our understanding, our guessing, of how the war started and developed could be wrong. If the material sciences were as advanced as some tales suggest then the war may have been more sophisticated than we have imagined – at least in the beginning. It was certainly primitive by the end."

Milla gave a deep sigh. "I sometimes think I was born thirty thousand years too late."

The scale of Milla's regret silenced everyone, even Andrei was unable to find a suitable response.

* * *

That evening they stopped before dusk while there was still enough light for John to assemble his tent and prepare a meal. The others went off with Milla while John ate. When they came back Tilvy was rubbing one arm and looked accusingly at Barma.

"I didn't mean to hit you," he said to her in pleading tones.

"I might have had second thoughts about coming if I'd known you were going to beat me up," she grouched back at him.

"What happened?" John asked, looking up from contemplating his few remaining meals.

"Barma got a bit enthusiastic with his self-defence lessons," laughed Andrei.

Seeing John's questioning look Andrei continued, "Milla explained that we may be attacked and that we should learn how to defend ourselves. Everything was going fine until we armed Barma. Then it was: Lookout! Sir Barma of the Forest Clearing come to save the damsel in distress. Only in this case it turned out to be: Watch out! damsel, when he lost control of his stick and hit her instead of me."

"That's right, it was you he was aiming at," said Tilvy, only just realising that Andrei may have been the true cause of her distress.

Milla arrived and looked unhappily at the three antagonists before going to Tilvy and studying her arm carefully. "That's not too bad," he said and looked up at the other two. "I'm inclined to have you each receive a hit like Tilvy's," he said. "You need to understand just how much difference something as simple as a stick can make."

Milla saw John looking puzzled. "Humans can do a lot of damage to each other with their bare hands, they can even kill each other in various inventive ways. Narun are not really built for such physical violence. We can't be choked and even restraining another can be difficult. We don't have the inertia to make punching more than painful. But arm a narun with a stick or a knife and the rules change. Our bodies are not as strong as yours. By swinging even a simple weapon like a stick it is possible gain the momentum necessary to do real damage, even to kill.

"Tomorrow night, if you feel up to it, I'd like to involve you with our practice. I'd like everyone to see just how much stronger you are, and perhaps show them a few tricks for dealing with humans if necessary."

"That sounds a little ominous," said John.

"We'll take it gently," he reassured. "Tonight I have something else for you."

It was almost completely dark among the trees now, the moon wasn't due up for some hours. John wasn't certain how it was that he was able to see his companions so clearly, more proof that their existence was only in his imagination he supposed. The group settled on the ground in a loose circle near John's tent.

"You heard Kaia suggest that we may be able to help you escape if you get abducted," started Milla.

John nodded.

"Well that would all depend on being able to tell us where you are. To do that you need a way of getting a message to us." Milla held up his arm and started murmuring to it, "Come on Cassey, out you come and say hello. Come on."

A small lump appeared on his forearm and quivered like a nose scenting the air. "Casseta, there's no need to be shy. Come on, out you come." The swelling on his arm grew and slithered forward until it resolved into a tiny furry creature. It looked very much like a small sugar glider except that its colouring was a deep ginger with markings of a darker ginger and white, including stripes that reached down its back to the tip of its tail. The long fluffy tail twitched back and forth until it finally came free. The creature sat there with its large black eyes staring innocently out at John, its nose twitching nervously. After a few moments John realised the creature was glowing slightly.

"Isn't she sweet?" said Tilvy.

Milla reached across and placed the creature on John's shoulder. "There you go, Cassey, meet our friend John."

John heard a quiet, nervous twittering sound.

"Shh, shh, it's fine, dear," reassured Milla quietly, "he's human but he's a friend."

Milla sat back slowly and then said to John, "Just let her sit there for a while and get used to you.

"You've seen spret in the forest?" he asked. John nodded slowly to avoid disturbing the creature. "Well this *isn't* one. This is a brevi. Spret are creatures of the outside world just as we are. Neither spret nor narun can merge with another spret, narun, animal or human, your prana is too dense to let us in. ... The brevi are different. They are creatures of the Glade and, as you saw, they can merge with us. In fact they seem to prefer it that way. A brevi will find some individual they like and may stay with them for years. They come out mostly for attention and to spend time with other brevi. It's a privilege to be chosen. Casseta there came to me a few years ago." Milla smiled with deep affection at Casseta still sitting quietly on John's shoulder.

"They are remarkably intelligent creatures, which will make a change from having Andrei for company." Milla grinned.

Andrei looked back at him as if he had been treated very unfairly.

Milla continued, "I don't think they understand what we say exactly, but they seem to understand our intentions very well. And they also have a little trick that makes them perfect messengers." Milla reached across and Casseta scuttled back up his arm.

Milla lifted the brevi to his lips and whispered something in its ear. He then held out his arm and the brevi ran along it and leapt lightly to John's shoulder. It ran to his ear and he heard Milla's voice say in a whisper, "Tell John that Casseta is a very good brevi and she will stay with him until he is ready to return."

John turned his head to try and look at the creature but it was too close, so he turned instead and looked his surprise at Milla. "Impressive isn't she," said Milla with a smile. "They can repeat quite long messages. Place your hand near her, she needs to get used to you."

Milla looked over to Darnu, "Perhaps if you bring Nuttachen out, he might give her a bit more confidence."

Darnu nodded and muttered to his arm. A few moments later he too had a brevi glowing quietly on his arm. This one was a rich pale cream, its stripes only faintly visible as a darker cream and white. "Nuttachen, you go and tell Casseta that it's all going to be okay," Darnu told his brevi softly.

It leapt down from his arm and bounded up onto Johns knee and then onto his shoulder next to Casseta. John could hear a quiet twittering sound as the two spoke with each other and then they both bounded off his shoulder and disappeared up into a nearby tree, the faint glow of their small bodies quickly disappearing into the night.

"They'll be back after they've stretched their legs for a while," said Milla. "Casseta will stay with you, John, and I'll show you how to talk with her. The important thing will be to only send her off with a message when you're sure she isn't just as trapped as you are."

"What about traffic and other hazards?" John asked.

"It is a risk but they're very quick and very smart, I'm sure she'll be okay. Get her out as much as you can along the way. Get her used to you and used to the changing surroundings, it should all help. Their sense of direction, of place, is phenomenal, as long as she can get out she'll find the others."

It was only a short time later that the two brevis came back. Milla had to persuade Casseta to spend more time with John. He encouraged John to handle her. John lifted her in his hand and she ran up his arm and down into his shirt, tickling him as she made her way down his sleeve and popped back out onto his other hand. How she managed to grip his skin he could not tell. While Casseta continued to explore John, the group continued to chat around him, speaking of people he did not know.

After a while Milla seemed to think that Casseta was ready and he showed John how to place her on the inside of his forearm and encourage her to merge, murmuring nothings quietly until she finally relaxed and seemed to melt into his arm. As she first merged there was an all-over tingling sensation that made John shiver, but once she was inside it felt something like a moving hot-spot. He could tell where she was in his body, the sensation was not unlike the crack in his head except that it was a warm breeze that he felt wherever Casseta chose to settle.

Milla explained, "She's not inside your physical body, she is merged with your prana. There is no physical intrusion, it's not like she's travelling your arteries or anything like that. She is travelling your nadis with your prana. She is temporarily part of the substance of your life."

"That's reassuring ... I think," said John quietly, "it's certainly a strange sensation."

Eventually Casseta seemed to get comfortable above his right shoulder blade and nestled there. She didn't move when John eventually climbed into his tent and settled down to sleep.

* * *

When John woke the next morning Casseta was the first thing he thought of. He thought he could feel her lying still around behind his heart somewhere. He had thought that seeing imaginary people was strange, but feeling a living creature wandering inside your body, even if it was just as part of your prana, went far beyond strange. He thought it should feel bad, wrong, like a parasite or something, and yet if he had to describe the sensation he would have to say that he felt comforted, and that too was strange. He tried to move carefully so as not to disturb her.

There were sounds of activity outside his tent so he made his way out. He was feeling remarkably bright this morning, all things considered. He was hungry and hoped that Andrei had managed to supplement his breakfast again.

He looked down at a small pile of things to one side of his tent. On a piece of bark lay a dozen or more very succulent looking grubs. They were still but John knew just enough about such things to know that they may very well be still alive, ready to wriggle as soon as they were picked up. Next to them stood a clever little cage made of twigs and inside were several large moths that left no doubt as to their status, battering their wings frantically against the bars of their cage.

John looked up and saw Barma looking at him with a bright and expectant expression. "Breakfast," Barma said cheerfully, hopefully.

John looked back down at the grubs and moths and his appetite fled. He looked back at Barma. "Would I be right in guessing that Andrei helped you with the menu?" he asked.

"I wanted to help and he said these were your favourites."

"And you believed him?" queried John. "This is Andrei we're talking about."

Barma's eyes widened and comprehension dawned. He spun around and they both heard Andrei's laughter fading into the trees. "Perhaps you could return these to where you found them?" suggested John. Barma looked down and nodded. As he tried to pick up the moths the clever little cage fell apart and the moths flew off, their wings beating in clumsy stutters. The grubs were not such a challenge so he picked them up and headed off into the trees.

He passed Tilvy as she was coming out carrying various edible items, ones that didn't wriggle. "You could've warned me," he accused her.

"And you could've hit Andrei instead of me yesterday," she responded.

"It was an accident," he grumbled and took the grubs back to where he'd found them.

After breakfast they headed off again. It was a cold morning but the small patches of mist quickly evaporated and it became a bright and pleasant day.

"So what should we talk about today?" asked Milla.

"Well I have been wondering, if it's not too rude, how old you might be?" said John with a note of apology in his voice. "I mean, you're an elder but you don't look that old. If it's rude just ignore me, I know Asha refused to tell me her age."

"Oh, John," laughed Andrei, "and I thought you were brighter than that."

"She didn't seem that upset by it," said John defensively.

"Only because she likes you."

Something about the conversation seemed to offend Garjae, and he and Darnu moved away from the main group again, but Beenae hung around not wanting to miss anything.

Milla interrupted Andrei, "I'm a sprightly four hundred years, well not quite but close enough. But it's not our age that makes us an elder. Elder is sort of like a stage of life except that not everyone experiences it."

"It's like not everyone grows up to become an adult, do they Andrei?" added Tilvy.

"So what does stage of life actually mean? Do you suddenly become wiser or something?" asked John.

Milla laughed loudly. "Oh, I wish! No. This is something that happens between the person and the Glade. There is always a bond between our people and their forest so that they feel uncomfortable being away for too long, but that bond can be broken and replaced with a bond to a different forest, and a different stand or Glade. With elders the bond becomes something stronger. It is very difficult to describe how it feels, but I am now linked with our Glade in some very permanent way. I can only stay away for only a relatively brief amount of time, a few weeks at most, before I must return or I will begin to weaken and fade. If our Glade were to die then

153

myself and Kaia and the other elders would fade with it, whereas these young whipper-snappers could move on."

"So do you choose to become an elder?"

"No, certainly not. It's something that either happens to you or doesn't. It's like the Glade itself chooses. Being an elder does normally extend our lives quite a lot, but if I'd had any choice I'd have stayed as I was. I don't like having my explorations curtailed this way."

This time it was John's turn to raise his eyebrows in question, "What do you mean?"

"I used to be able explore widely, I was often away for months at a time. But not any longer. As it is now there's not a town-library for many miles that has not been severely ravaged by me, but I'd really like to explore bigger libraries in more distant places. I'd even like to explore the cities, but I can't stay away that long."

"Ravaging libraries explains your diverse knowledge of my world, I guess," said John. "Tell me what's currently of interest and I can try to get some books in. Even better, come to my house and I'll show you how to use the computer. You can explore the knowledge of the world from my study."

"Thanks, John, I might take you up on that when this is all over."

That evening they again stopped fairly early for John to make camp. Milla said he had a few things he wanted to go through before it got dark. After John had eaten, Milla had him go through a few things with the others to demonstrate how much stronger and heavier a human was than they. Only when Darnu and Garjae each held an arm did John have much trouble and even then he was confident he could break free if he wasn't concerned about hurting them.

"So everyone can see that wrestling with a human is a no-win situation. Sure we have the advantage that most can't see us, but it is still best to stay out of reach. If you do get caught ..." Milla paused and looked at John. "I want to demonstrate something but I'm not sure how painful it may be to you. I don't think it should be too painful and it does no real damage that I know of, but it may knock you out for a minute or two."

John thought about it for a moment and then shrugged. "We've got to be prepared. Do you want to take Casseta for a moment while

154

we do this?"

"That's a good idea. Darnu why don't you get Nuttachen out and they can exercise while you demonstrate for the others. You know what I want to show everyone?"

Darnu nodded.

The brevis ran off, chasing each other up a tree, and John stood there nervously, not knowing what to expect.

Milla announced, "Okay, everyone watch closely and pay attention to how Darnu does this, we don't what to put John through this too often. John, Darnu is going to slap you on the side of the head, but it's not quite a normal hit. Whatever you feel it probably won't be physical pain. Ready?"

John nodded, he wasn't getting any less nervous by waiting.

Darnu walked up in front of him, his expression carefully neutral. He held his hands either side of John's head, looked around to make sure the others were all paying attention, and then slapped the sides of John's head with both hands. John's world turned white with a loud roar, a brief stab of pain shot through his mind and then everything went blank and silent. When he came to he was on the ground, a rock sticking painfully into his side.

"Sorry, John," said Milla, "I thought Garjae and I would be able to catch you and soften your fall, but you slipped our grip." He gave Garjae an odd look.

"What happened?" John asked. As he looked around, the others had a surprisingly sober look on their faces. He had thought that at least Andrei would have had fun with it.

Milla paused as if considering his words. "Darnu hit you in a way that disrupted the prana in your head. Your system gets shocked into a sort of temporary shut down. It is not something we like to do, or even consider, but it is effective. How do you feel?"

John rubbed at his head. The cold spot was still in there, he thought it had turned hot for a moment when he was hit, but he wasn't sure. "Strange, a bit disoriented, but otherwise okay I think. There wasn't much pain, just a flash. Was I out long?"

Milla looked greatly relieved. "Just a few minutes."

That night John didn't sleep well, he didn't seem able to settle and even Casseta was restless. She ended up emerging and sleeping on his shoulder rather than inside him. John wondered whether the jolt to his system was more disruptive than it had felt at the time.

* * *

The next morning, as they walked, John's lack of sleep had him feeling out of sorts. After a while Milla tried to break the ice, "So how's the belief side of things, John. Any progress?"

When John was slow responding Milla continued, "Kaia tells me you think we don't exist, that's certainly news to me." He made a show of pinching the skin on his arm and tapping himself on the side of the head.

"See, John, I'm not the only one who thinks you're funny," put in Andrei.

John thought back to things that made no sense to him. "The night that Asha and I argued I touched the tears on her cheek. They felt wet to touch but then my fingers were dry."

"They evaporated, John," said Milla patiently.

"Not that quickly," said John. "And anyway, I saw her tears fall but when she was gone the place where they fell was not damp. There were a lot of tears, it should have been still damp!"

"You misunderstand, John. They did evaporate. Our tears are not water. We are made of prana, our tears are prana too. They may feel wet to touch but they're not really. The prana evaporates quite quickly from other surfaces, and left on the skin some may be reabsorbed into the body."

Still not satisfied, John took a deep breath and looked around him. They had come a long way from the Glade, but the forest was still intense with life and his friends showed no sign of the transparency he had noticed at times with Asha. Then he looked at the ground beneath their feet and pointed at Milla's feet. "You could try to explain that?"

The others looked down. "What?" asked Barma, "I don't see anything."

"Exactly! I'm the only one here that casts a shadow. How can that be? If you're real, if you're really there for me to see, where are all your shadows?" John pointed beneath the feet of the others. He was pleased to finally find a tangible way to express his doubts.

Andrei looked down, a puzzled expression on his face, but John couldn't tell whether it was because he didn't know the answer or couldn't understand why John thought it was important.

"I think I see a sort of shadow," said Tilvy.

Andrei walked beside her staring down at where her shadow should be. "Now you're imagining things," he said.

"No, Tilvy's right," said Milla. "You do all have a shadow of sorts. Stop a minute and look carefully."

They did as he said. John stood near Barma and looked down at Barma's feet.

Darnu and Garjae stopped walking and looked back. "Anything wrong?" called Darnu.

Milla waved them on. "We'll catch up in a minute."

"I think I see it ... like it's cooler there," said Barma, pointing to an area near his feet, then he hesitated before adding, "or something."

"Yes, *or something.*" said Milla. "I can't tell you exactly what it is but we definitely shade the ground from the sunlight in some way, just not as much as you do John. The sun is the source of prana, I suspect that what shadow effect we have relates to that fact."

John continued to stare around Barma's feet. "I don't see it."

Andrei looked up. "I really hate to say this, but I'm with John. I don't see it either."

"Never mind," said Milla, "we'd better keep walking."

After a few minutes John said, "It's not just the shadow thing. At times when I've looked at Asha or Andrei it was like I could see through them, or parts of them. As though they were partly transparent. I once looked at Asha in a mirror and it was as if she wasn't there at all. And the one time that I saw and heard Asha in the company of another human it was as though she didn't exist to him. Not only didn't he see her, he didn't hear her either. You simply don't exist for anyone else but me."

"And what, you can't manage to imagine shadows or reflections?" asked Milla with a smile.

John grimaced. "Well ... then there's the whole changing sizes, merging with trees and walking through doors thing. That's not the sort of stuff that normal solid human beings do."

"We're not human, John," said Milla gently.

"You know what I mean!" John said, more vehemently than he had intended. "There is nothing I have ever experienced, before my mind broke, that would help me to accept or explain all this."

Milla nodded slowly to himself as he walked, as if he was starting

157

to understand.

"I felt something in me break and it was only then I started to see things that others don't see, to hear things that others don't hear. Things that I have never seen nor heard before. What am I supposed to think?" said John.

"That is a problem," said Milla mildly. "I finally begin to see your dilemma, John."

They walked in silence for a few more minutes. John was wondering if Milla was ever going to respond more definitively.

"See?" Andrei said, "That's why we have elders, John, instant answers to all life's problems."

The biggest laugh came from Milla. "Thanks, Andrei, it's good to have our worth recognised and appreciated."

Another period of silence and then Milla continued, "John, I doubt if I can say anything that would instantly make you believe in us, but there are a few details that may help when you are ready to believe.

"What do you know about how human eyesight works?"

"Hmm? Not a whole lot. I remember something about the front of the eye acting as a lens and the brain interpreting the light as it falls on the back of the eye. That's about it." said John.

"Eyesight can be a difficult thing to explain," said Milla. "The eye itself is not a perfect instrument. It is in fact quite limited. It has a fairly small point of focus, the rest comes in as blurry peripheral vision. The eye has to move around to fill in details of whatever you happen to be looking at. It is the mind, not the eye, that puts the whole lot together into a single clear image."

"Oh, that's right," said John, remembering. "The image is actually upside down on the back of the eye, the brain sort of turns it up the right way automatically."

"The very least of its tricks," said Milla.

"But what's that got to do with it? I don't think there's anything wrong with my eyes."

"We'll come back to that in a minute, just remember that the mind plays a very large part in what you see."

"What you're really saying is that John has always been imagining things, but it's only recently that he's realised it," said Andrei with a grin.

"I'm not sure that's helpful Andrei," answered Milla, "but less of a joke than you realise." To John he continued, "Our own eyesight is much the same as yours, but more so. Our form is largely a matter of choice and convenience. We use the eyes of our form to help concentrate our visual focus but they don't actually see in the same optical way that yours do. We have no blind spots, our peripheral vision goes right around us." To demonstrate he reached behind, without looking back, and tweaked Barma's nose.

"We narun, all praanin, have no shadows because most light travels through us rather than being blocked and reflected. It is reflected light that the optics of your eyes usually see, but light goes through us, it does not bounce off, so of course you cannot see us in the normal way. We have no reflection in a mirror because no light bounces off our body to appear in the mirror. We wouldn't appear on any normal photograph or video for the same reason.

"The last few nights, John, you had no trouble seeing us after sunset did you?"

"I just thought my eyes had gotten used to the dark," said John.

"No, it really was very dark. I doubt if your eyes are that good. And anyway, the rest of the forest was dark wasn't it?"

John nodded.

"I think that your mind, with its new-found ability to sense life, to sense prana, is detecting our presence so strongly that it is adding us to what you see. Just as it automatically turns the image up the right way, just as it automatically creates a complete focused image, so it also adds in at least some of the details coming from vedana. You really don't see us in any real optical way, you can't, there is no light reflected to be seen, it is your mind adding our presence to the image it constructs of the world around you."

Milla paused for a few moments before continuing, "That's also why closing your eyes can sometimes enhance your ability to sense life in other ways. It stops your mind diverting its attention to the visual centres and encourages you to explore what you are really sensing. You don't actually see us through your eyes, it is the prana in your body responding to our presence."

John considered this, but it was Barma that responded, "So John is actually seeing us in the same way that we see ourselves?"

"Yes," said Milla, pleased that at least someone seemed to be following him. "And he obviously hears us the same way we hear ourselves too."

"Huh?" John looked up, puzzled.

"You said before, John, that your human friend could not hear Asha. I wouldn't have expected him to. We don't speak the same way you do. Just as we use our eyes to focus our sight, so we use our mouth as a way of focusing those thoughts we want to broadcast to others around us. You hear us in the same way that we hear ourselves. It is not sound in the air, it is the thoughts that I want known to others that you pick up from my being." For the last sentence Milla's mouth did not move.

"Telepathy?" asked John, astonished.

"If you like," said Milla, his mouth moving again. "It's not the way we've ever thought about it. It's just the way we speak to each other. There is no sense of ever revealing private thoughts, nor of being able to share more than language. It may be a form of telepathy, but a very limited one."

"And my words to you. Do you receive them the same way too?" John asked.

"Faintly. Mostly we hear the sounds you make, just as we hear the sounds of the forest. We have quite good senses of hearing and smell. Our sense of sight is very much based on our sense of life. We can sense light, to much the same effect as your sight, but that sense is less effective, less detailed and less sensitive, than our sense of life, our vedana."

John was stunned. The idea that he was not seeing exactly what he thought he was seeing was not too much of a surprise, it went along very well with his idea that he was imagining all this. But for some reason the idea that he was not hearing exactly what he thought he had been hearing was a greater shock. It had never occurred to him to question what he had heard. How could he be surprised by this if it was coming from his own imagination?

"Is there a limit to how far away the telepathy works?" he asked.

"Oh yes. By coincidence or not, no one really knows, the ability to hear another's thoughts seems to have much the same range and dispersion limits as your normal human speech. We can shout to be heard further away, or whisper to keep it more private."

John's mind was racing through the last weeks and months trying to see how this new information fitted with his experiences. The partial transparency was explained because he was not seeing them with his eyes. The lack of shadow and reflection seemed to have explanation too. But sound, for some reason that felt important. He went back over his time with Asha and when he had last seen her. All the pieces began to drop into place and each was a perfect fit. He stopped suddenly.

The others went a few steps further before they realised he was no longer with them. They looked back to see him drop to his knees.

"What is it John?" asked Tilvy in fright.

"This ability to hear. You say that it has the same range as normal sound ... but it would not be blocked or muffled in the same way as normal sound. Would it?" He was almost whispering.

"No ... no, I suppose not," answered Milla.

"So if one of you spoke, if you screamed from inside another room, we could hear from the next room as if the walls were not there?" John continued.

Milla knelt in front of John looking into his eyes, watching the emotions swarm. "I believe that is true, John, yes."

"I heard her," John whispered. "She was screaming," he said more loudly. "She was screaming for my help and I didn't think it was real!"

Tilvy knelt beside John and put her arm around him. Milla asked, "When, John, when was this?"

"The Monday after we argued," said John. Seeing the blank looks he explained. "We argued on a Saturday night, the next day is Sunday and I was home all day. On Monday I went to work in town but came home early. I almost ran into a car, a blue van on the gravel road. I was in a daze and I heard Asha screaming. It was so loud that I almost thought she was in the car with me. When I couldn't see her I took it as just another part of my imagination, but she must have been in that van. Screaming for my help in that van. She was so close."

John believed, yes, *now* he believed. "I could have saved her!"

10. Ruined

When they eventually came for Asha there were four of them. Darren, two other humans she had come to know as Barry and Cameron, and a narun in the usual silver suit. Darren was pulling an open tray trolley with several of the small cages folded on it. The small cages were assembled and the prisoners from Asha's large cage were each told to get into one. Asha tried to help Ceeda carry Nacee to a cage but she cringed away from Asha's touch.

Ceeda waved Asha away.

While the four of them were caged, the huge doors were opened and the platform trees slowly rolled out and moved out of the cavern. Eventually fresh trees arrived and were rolled across the cavern and into the cage. With the huge cage doors once more closed the other three prisoners were returned to their prison, but Asha was dismayed to find her cage being carried off by Barry and Cameron. She raised a hand in a brief goodbye, but Ceeda was busy with Nacee and Briso just stared after her.

She was taken up a ramp and into the examination room where her cage was placed on the low table. The others left and the narun took up his usual station by the door.

"Sando?" she asked.

He inclined his head but said nothing. A few minutes later Karlin came into the room.

"Hello, my pretty little dryad," he said loudly as he came in. It seemed to Asha that he had to try harder than usual to maintain his cheerful demeanour. "How are you feeling this morning?"

Asha didn't reply.

Ignoring Asha's silence, Karlin had Sando open the cage and then put Asha through the usual series of tests. At the end of it he seemed quite pleased. "Good, good, very good," he muttered. "It appears that you have been making a good recovery."

When he finished putting everything away he pulled up a stool and sat there looking at Asha as if trying to make up his mind about something.

"Time for you to meet one of our other guests, I think," he said at last. "Your friends downstairs may have mentioned them. These guests are not very well. I am still hoping to find a way to cure them." He smiled as if being a saviour to others was the very least he could do.

"Consider your first visit to be just a chance to get to know them. We have a very specific ... well, we'll get to that. Sando, would you do the honours?" he finished and left the room.

Sando saw that Asha got back in her cage and shortly after Darren, Barry and Cameron arrived. Barry and Cameron were again given the job of carrying her cage. They took her down to a lower level and through a set of doors into another corridor, this one ending in a blank wall. This corridor had small rooms on either side with only clear plastic walls dividing the rooms from the corridor. Most of the rooms were kept quite dark, but in the gloom behind the divide Asha could see strangely distorted figures.

Each figure was small, perhaps the size of a two or three year old human child, but their skin had a pale grey and stretched-thin appearance that made them look like little old men or women. Their head, hands and feet looked disproportionately large on their small withered torso and limbs. The naked bodies were almost transparent with lack of substance. Most were lying on small beds but some wandered aimless and silent about their small cells.

Asha was startled out of her preoccupation by Barry muttering, mostly to himself. "Ian complains about the zoo, but this is the place that really gives me the screamin' heebies. Here I am carrying an empty cage down a hall full of empty rooms and empty beds ... apparently none of them are empty ... but the silence." He couldn't seem to go on and neither Darren nor Cameron offered any disparaging remarks.

Asha realised he was right. To her the rooms weren't empty, she wished they were, but the silence was somehow overwhelming, almost tangible. Watching the pitiful figures she thought it must be the silence that came when even despair had lost its voice.

About halfway along they placed her cage next to one of the plastic walls and worked the hatch to release her from the cage into the cell. Sando motioned for her to get out of the cage and, reluctantly, she did so. The cage was removed and the humans outside made a hurried departure. Sando paused and stared at Asha for a few moments, but finally turned to go. "Enjoy the quiet," he said softly as he walked off.

Asha stood up and enlarged to her preferred size. She looked carefully at the far corner, at the figure on the bed. The figure moved and tilted its head as it became aware of her. The face retained the blank expression of the others she had seen. The deeply sunken eyes aimed in her direction were milky and apparently unseeing. Asha would have assumed the creature, creature was the only word she found, was totally blind except that it kept looking her way as it sat up, stood up and then started walking toward her.

She held herself still as the creature approached. Ceeda had implied there was no real danger here, that it was only unpleasant. It was all she could do to keep from cringing when the small creature spread its arms wide and embraced her legs, its head coming only to her thighs. As it touched she finally recognised it as the praanin being it truly was. A narun, but one ruined beyond any torture or starvation she could conceive. It was totally unrecognisable, she couldn't tell if it had originally been aaranya or jalaja or something else. She couldn't even tell if it had once been male or female, the naked body had no apparent genitalia. And yet ... there was something.

Asha reduced her size and tried to return the creature's embrace, sympathetic now that she recognised it as a fellow narun. After a few minutes the creature still had not relaxed its grip and Asha could feel it trying to drain the prana from her body. It was slow but she could feel the seepage of her substance passing through her skin and into the creature where they made contact. She was in no danger but it was an uncomfortable feeling. Eventually she pulled the creature's arms from around her and led it back to its bed. It offered no resistance, it didn't even seem disappointed.

She encouraged it to lie down again and sat on the end of the bed,

164

back against the wall, hugging her knees. She looked down at the creature, its eyes were still open but it could not be said to be staring. Like the silence of the room, this was beyond blindness.

"Who are you?" Asha whispered. The whisper felt loud and unwelcome against the raw silence of the cell and the hallway.

There was no response. Not a flicker.

Asha tried the same question louder, cringing at the disturbance it made in the silence, but still no flicker. She considered trying to yell but couldn't make herself do it. She thought that to stay here long would be to go mad.

Some unknown time later Asha had closed her eyes and was drifting into an uneasy sleep when she was startled awake again. The creature had woken and was once again trying to embrace her. She held it for a while, her distaste for the creature and its uncomfortable drain on her being was overridden by the pity she felt for its desperate need. After an hour or so Asha detached herself from the creature's embrace again and lay it back down. Ceeda was right, the creature appeared to have gained nothing from what little it had drained from her. Either its need was so great that the small amount of energy taken was insignificant, or the energy it took was lost.

It was only during this second embrace that Asha looked out of the cell and realised that all the creatures she could see were standing as close to her as their cells would permit. She let her senses spread down the hallway and discovered that most of the creatures were doing the same. They appeared to sense her, to sense the sharing of prana that was taking place and wanted to take their own part. When she laid her creature back to bed the others returned to their usual places: most lying down, some pacing silently.

Over the many hours that followed, Asha thought it might have been two days but no longer trusted her sense of time, the creature would sit up at irregular intervals and again try to embrace her. Each time the other creatures would sense the sharing and try to get close. Asha let her creature remain for successively shorter times before putting it back to bed. Feeling tired and weary herself, she was concerned that she did not have the energy to spare; she did not know how long she may be held here.

When they eventually did arrive to take her from the cell she was very ready to go. Whatever pity she felt for the creature there seemed nothing that she could do for it. She felt again that to remain here too long, to believe yourself stranded here, would be to go insane. She wondered if that played some part in what had happened to these creatures.

Returned to Karlin's examination room, Asha was put through the usual series of tests.

Karlin seemed surprised. Concerned about something, he repeated some of the tests. Finally he finished up and sat down, leaning forward to look at her carefully. "You are an unusual little dryad aren't you. Generous, yes, generous to a fault, but most defin-itely unusual. You've given up rather more of yourself than you should have. I'd hoped you'd be ready to start your new job tomorrow but best if we wait a few days I think."

He sat back. "So, what did you think? Did you like Vincent?" he asked.

"What was it?" was all Asha could think to respond.

Karlin tapped the side of his nose and said mysteriously, "Ah ... I don't want to spoil the surprise."

Soon he was gone and Asha was returned to her prison cage.

Ceeda asked, "The ruined ones?"

Asha just nodded, not wanting to talk about it yet. She merged into a tree and tried to lose herself in the flows of its life, wishing she could wash away the memories of that silent hell.

* * *

Some days later the same humans returned for Asha. Asha wanted to ask why it was her turn yet again? What about the other prisoners? But she knew they'd already seen at least as much as she had, and would see more yet. She just didn't want to go.

In the examination room Karlin was not pleased with her progress. "But it will have to do, yes, it will have to do. We can't put this off too much longer or we'll miss the chance. In you hop," he gestured to the cage. Asha climbed in reluctantly.

Barry and Cameron came in and carried her out into the corridor. She was surprised and hopeful when she was taken in a different direction to the last time. She was taken to a cell like the one she'd been locked in when she first arrived, it may have been the same cell, but she wasn't sure. Inside she could see monitoring equipment set up on this side of the divide. The other side was in a gloomy darkness and her hopes fled. There in the darkest corner, on the bed, was another of the creatures. This one appeared to be cringing into the corner of the cell.

Asha's cage was laid by the hatch and she was released into the cell.

Karlin watched, a look of avid curiosity on his face.

The door to the corridor opened abruptly and Darren came in. "It's Ian, possibly trouble," he called to Karlin.

A look of annoyance passed over Karlin's face, then he turned and rechecked the monitoring equipment. "I'll leave you two to get reacquainted," he said. "I hate to miss the big occasion but duty calls."

"Sando, you'd better come too," he finished, and the room quickly emptied.

Asha puzzled over Karlin's words. Reacquainted? The figure in the corner looked even smaller than Vincent had been. She waited where she was for a few minutes, giving the creature time to come to her, but it didn't move.

She walked slowly to the corner. The creature was definitely awake, its head turned as Asha moved. As she got closer she wondered whether the creature had not come toward her because it could no longer walk. It was not only smaller than Vincent, it also looked more transparent and frail. Its milky eyes were so deep they were almost lost. She would not have thought such fragility was possible. She remembered Karlin saying something about missing his chance and wondered if he was referring to this creature. Where Vincent and the others may have been dying only slowly, this one's death could not be far away. She imagined it would be a welcome release.

She thought of Karlin's enthusiasm again – reacquainted. Asha got gently onto the bed and reduced her size as much as she could, trying to appear less intimidating. She reached forward slowly and pulled the small, fragile creature closer to her, eventually nursing it on her lap like a small child. The creature's fragile arms moved weakly at its sides, it may have been trying to embrace her.

She looked at its face and ran her hand across its cheeks and around its skull, so prominent under the thin old-man's skin. There was something. If the eyes were not milky and not so deep? The creature's arms moved again and Asha relented, lifting it and placing its arms about her neck, helping it to embrace her. If it was dying soon then this was the very least she could offer.

There was something under that feeling of old decay, something familiar. Asha used her life sense as she had not dared with Vincent, and she probed into the essence of this creature. She could feel its hunger more pressing than any other need. She pressed further, beyond the naked needs of existence to the being that had lived before need drove all else aside.

"Impossible!" she gasped.

She drew the creature gently back and looked again at its face. She held its tiny hands in one of hers. She ran her hand again over its face and back around over the contours of its skull. "It can't be."

Again she placed the creature's arms about her neck and held it in an encompassing embrace, trying to maximise contact. She rested its head against hers, her arms bracing its back. The creature's arms tried weakly to return her embrace. This time she plunged her senses into it, feeling again for that familiar being. There. Even against all impossibility there was no mistake.

"Oh, my love. My darling. What have they done to you?" her voice soft now, crooning as if to a baby.

Feeling its needs now as if they were her own, she opened herself to it, letting it draw upon her essence as it so desperately needed. Asha felt her substance streaming out from her heart, a golden beam of life that passed through the skin of her breast and into the breast of the creature. The flow was slow at first but building. Prana poured from the centre of her being into the emptiness of the creature in her arms. More! It needed more! She tore at herself, her gift no longer just a beam but a flood of life. She cast her being into the yawning chasm of its need, not caring for herself, only trying against all hope to draw her back from oblivion.

Believing

11. Captive

Ian gave a start – the computer had beeped. The detector, usually rigged on a tripod out in the open, was set up on the passenger seat. Ian looked at the computer screen and saw a couple of weak signals to the north, right on the edge of the range and already fading. Probably just – what was it Karlin had called them? – spret. Whatever they were they didn't like the detector. A couple of times over the last week he'd seen one or two come a little way in, faint smudges on the screen, and then dart off again, disturbed by whatever it was that this device was doing. Karlin said it was harmless. Right. Karlin might be all friendly smiles, but Ian was slowly coming to understand that there was something about the good doctor that wasn't quite right.

He tried to stretch in his seat but ended up having to open the door of the van and get out so he could stretch properly. The joys of being the new man: you got all the crap jobs, like sitting in the forest near this Caldor's house waiting to see if he would finally show up.

He kicked at the ground outside the dirty green van. They'd given him a van that was different to the blue one Caldor had seen before, just in case. But it was still just a van, hardly great luxury. He sighed, and admitted to himself that it was better than working in that creepy ghost zoo in the basement. Upstairs, above ground, was fine. The people there were mostly normal, or as normal as scientists ever got. Sure they treated him like the lackey he supposed he was, fetch this, do that, but you didn't see the silent guys in the silver suits and you didn't have to carry around empty cages that weren't really empty.

It had been explained to him that the company was really two separate operations. There was the public part upstairs that did forestry research, downstairs was something very different, and very private. Whatever the details, Ian was apparently supposed to feel privileged at being part of the private company, someone privy to what went on below ground. The only thing Ian actually felt privileged about was receiving a fat pay-cheque every fortnight, that was the good part. Very good and the only thing that kept Ian at work ... well, the pay-cheque and the feeling he had that leaving may not be quite so simple any more. He didn't know what had happened to the guy he replaced, but he got the impression there was no golden handshake involved.

Ian leaned into the van, pulled out a thermos and poured himself a coffee. Time for his morning break, close enough. Yesterday had been better, no, it had been the day before. At least then he'd gotten to have lunch in the pub so he could set up his casual meeting with Jason Manton. He'd waited until Jason was finished eating, then sat down across from him and introduced himself.

"Hi, Jason? I'm Ian."

Jason looks across and sees the small insignificant man opposite, smiling at him with a bland smile and looking harmless, and all reservation and suspicion drops away.

Ian didn't know whether he had the proverbial honest face, or what it was, but people never felt threatened by him. He put on his best apologetic smile and continued with the cover story he'd been given, "Sorry to disturb your lunch, but I've been looking for John Caldor and was told you might be the man to speak with. I'm from the university where Samantha used to study."

"I thought you guys picked up all her stuff months ago," Jason said. He sounded defensive.

"We did," said Ian, "it's just that there were a few things in amongst it that we will need John's approval to use. Intellectual property rights problems, you know. We can't use some of it without permission from her estate." Another bland smile, and then, "We hate to bother him again but some of it is important."

"He's been away," said Jason. "He was supposed to be back this week but he hasn't shown up." There was a pause and then he opened up a bit more. "Got us all a bit worried actually, it's not like him to miss work without calling in. He's not answering his phone. I dropped over to his house yesterday but he wasn't home. Sorry I can't help you, but I really don't know where he is."

Ian already knew this, he'd watched Jason arrive. Without Ian's skills with locks Jason had been unable to see that Caldor's car was still in the garage.

Keeping it light and innocent sounding, Ian replied, "No problem, Jason, just thought I'd ask while I was in town." Time for a caring and sincere expression now, he continued, "How's John been getting along do you think? Picking up his life again?"

Jason looked down and stared into the bottom of his now empty glass. "If you'd asked me that a few months back I'd have said he was starting to make his way. Slowly and with a lot of trouble, but making it. You know?"

Ian gave a sympathetic smile and nodded, not that Jason noticed this performance.

"But a few months ago something changed ..."

Ian waited while Jason paused, not wanting to push too hard and seem nosy; people remembered nosy. In Ian's experience he just had to give people enough space and they'd eventually tell him almost anything.

"At first it seemed like a good change. He was happier. If I didn't know better I'd have said he'd met a girl. He was distracted and remote, but in a good way. I guess some may have said it wasn't long enough since Samantha had died, but what's long enough?" Jason looked up at Ian, looking for some sort of acknowledgement.

Ian shrugged and tried to look sympathetic.

"Anyway it couldn't have been a girl because he never went anywhere to meet one. Whatever it was it suddenly switched around. Suddenly he was upset and lost again, as he was after Ellie died. He was distracted and remote in a bad way. Short tempered and abrupt. I'd always thought we were friends, but he's never let me get close since they've been gone."

Jason seemed to suddenly remember where he was, and that Ian was really a stranger. "Look at me prattling on. Just been worried about him, that's all."

Ian had the distinct impression that there was more there, that there were things Jason knew and didn't want to share, even with someone as harmless as Ian. But this wasn't the right setting to try and find out more. But, Ian decided, Jason might still be able to help. See an opening and take it, was a motto that had served him pretty well.

"Look, I really don't want to add to John's problems. Rather than me trying to catch him, possibly at a bad time, how about you call me when he turns up. You can tell me how he's doing and when would be the best time to catch up with him." Ian handed Jason a business card. These days no one noticed when a card carried just a mobile number. The wonderfully anonymous mobile telephone: favourite accessory of teenagers and criminals alike.

"That's really considerate of you, thanks." Jason accepted the card and tucked it into his wallet. Pulling out one of his own cards, he said, "Here's my number if you want to call me. I will phone you when I hear from John, but at this stage I've no idea when that might be."

Jason looked at his watch and said it was past time for him to be back at work, and they parted ways.

Ian thought Jason would remember their conversation well enough to phone if he heard from Caldor, but he'd be unlikely to remember Ian's appearance very well. Ian had the experience to know that most people had trouble picking him out of a police line-up.

The bleeping of the computer brought Ian back to the present. He climbed back into the van and looked at the screen. The map on the screen was, to Ian's eyes, just a mass of smudges. Each static smudge represented a tree and there was a sort of background haze that was apparently the soil itself. The only clear space on the map was the house. A single small smudge was moving, coming down from the north.

He watched as the smudge made its way between the trees and eventually made it to the clearing near the back of the house. It paused there for a while and then moved on to the back of the house and finally to the inside.

Ian's instructions had been to verify that Caldor had come home and then call for assistance. He hadn't thought to ask exactly how he was supposed to verify it was Caldor. Hidden in the trees near the road he could not tell just who, or what, that smudge had been. A smudge on the computer had appeared to enter the house, did he assume that was Caldor, or should he do something to check that it wasn't a burglar or something?

Finally he decided to sneak up near the house and see if he could catch a glimpse of Caldor. It was either that or risk bringing his boss all this way on a goose chase. He shut down the computer and switched off the device before getting out and shutting the door softly behind him. He made his way as quietly as he could through the trees to the front of the house.

He watched the windows but could see no movement. Then, to Ian's surprise, the front door opened and there stood Caldor, still in the shadow of the verandah but apparently looking directly at where Ian thought he was hidden in the trees.

"Wow, that was quick! You haven't been waiting for me all this time have you?" Caldor called loudly.

Ian looked around carefully but could see no one else.

"Oh, come on. You don't have to sneak up, I'm here aren't I?"

Ian shrugged, there seemed little point in pretending he wasn't there so he stepped out from the trees.

"That's better. Come on inside while I clean up. You're not in a hurry are you? Only I'd sort of hoped to have time for a shower and shave, maybe pack a bag. Is that okay?"

Now, closer to the verandah, Ian could see Caldor more clearly, standing there bold and friendly, as if Ian was an expected guest. There was a rough beard over his tanned face and his clothes looked worn and dirty. Had Caldor been out in the forest all this time?

"How did you know I was here?" Ian asked.

"My uh ... sight has improved a lot lately," said Caldor with a slightly enigmatic smile. "I'm John Caldor, as I suppose you know. You are?"

"Ian."

"Good to meet you, Ian. Come in. You want a cup of coffee? Only that long-life milk I'm afraid, but I've heard it's usually all right in coffee and tea – I drink 'em black myself."

Caldor walked back into the house and Ian followed, at a loss to work out what he should be doing.

"The kettle's not long boiled so it won't take long to make you something. What's your preference?" Caldor continued to chatter as if this was a normal situation.

Ian agreed to a white coffee and watched Caldor take a small carton of milk from the cupboard, still chatting away. "For a widower like myself this stuff is a real saviour. No rushing down to the shop when you get a visitor that wants milk.

"I'd not even finished my coffee when I saw you'd turned up." Caldor pointed to the half-empty mug on the bench. "I've been dying for a sweet black coffee, I ran out of sugar a few days ago."

Caldor finished making Ian's coffee and handed it to him before he sat at the table with his own mug and took a deep drink. Ian took a seat across from him.

"How long 've you been waiting for me?" Caldor asked.

"Almost two weeks," said Ian. "Can't have missed you by much. You'd been at work the day before we first called." Ian saw a strange look pass over Caldor's face, then the smile returned. They were both wondering just how close that first call had come to finding him home.

"I'm surprised you're alone," said Caldor. "I guess I'm not that scary a person, but I still thought there'd be more than one of you, you know, just in case."

Ian had not thought that John Caldor, graphic artist, was likely to be a scary person either, but this confident, lean and weathered man was not what he had expected. He seemed a very different person to the distressed personality described by Jason. Ian decided to leave the question unanswered.

Caldor tipped back the last of his coffee. "You don't mind if I go upstairs and have a shower etcetera? It's been a while and I really need it." He pegged his fingers over his nose and grinned. "The phone is just there if you need to report in or anything. Mobiles aren't always reliable here."

Caldor disappeared upstairs without waiting for a response. Ian picked up Caldor's phone and called the office number. He got voice-mail and left a message saying only that things had turned out simpler than expected and he'd see them in the city with the package already on-board sometime late this afternoon or evening. Hanging up, Ian thought about the likely responses he would get if they knew he was already talking with Caldor, he was very pleased to have gotten the answering service. To keep things simple he knelt down and pulled the telephone cable out from the wall.

It was more than an hour later when Caldor came back downstairs, looking younger and less wild than he had earlier. He rubbed his face, "Do you know how hard it is to shave when you let it get away that long? Good thing I had a razor in the cupboard, my little electric thing almost had a hernia before I realised it wasn't up to it."

Caldor paused and looked around, and then asked, "How long do you think I might be away?"

"I'm not sure," said Ian.

"Guess these will have to do," Caldor lifted the small carry bag.

Ian walked to the door, Caldor followed and locked up behind them. "I take it you want to go in your car?" he asked. Ian nodded and led the way down the driveway and into the trees where the van was hidden. As he walked he tried to work out how best to handle the situation. Ideally he would like to get Caldor locked in the back of the van so he wouldn't have to worry any more, but he wasn't sure how best to do that. He was concentrating so hard on his own plans that he was surprised when Caldor spoke again.

"What have you got in the back of this thing?" Caldor asked, ignoring him and sliding the back door of the van open.

Was he trying to make it easy for Ian? He seemed supremely confident. Did he know Ian had no gun or hadn't he thought of it? No gun. Now there was a thought, Ian did have a gun of sorts. It may not work as well on humans as it did on those narun things they captured, but it did work. It had been demonstrated on Ian – to prove a point he supposed.

Ian left the driver's side door open and walked around to where Caldor was looking in the back of the van. He opened the passenger side door, trying to be casual, as if he was about to move the equipment from the seat so there was room for a passenger. Under the pretence of disconnecting the computer he plugged in the ray-gun antenna and switched on the device.

"What the ... ? Are you okay?" came Caldor's astonished query from behind Ian.

Ian turned and pointed the antenna toward Caldor's back – Caldor was still peering into the back of the van and hadn't noticed what Ian was doing. Ian could hear the computer bleeping at him, but kept his concentration on Caldor.

Turning to Ian, Caldor started to ask a question but stopped when he saw the antenna in Ian's hand. He paused as if listening to something.

"Is that the detector?" he asked.

"Not exactly," said Ian. "The detector is on but this is more of a persuader. I'd like you to climb into the back of the van. It's all been pleasant so far and I'd really rather not use this," he waved the antenna, "so if you'd just do as I ask I'd be very happy."

Caldor looked at what appeared to be some sort of complicated television antenna in disbelief. "What are you going to do? Hit me with a chat-show?"

"You need some convincing?" asked Ian rhetorically. He pressed a button on the handle of the antenna. Caldor swayed and then stumbled against the van, holding the door frame to try and stop his knees from buckling. Ian released the button and moved another switch. "The next setting is painful. Do you need me to prove it?"

Caldor shook his head trying to clear it and then took a step toward Ian. Ian pressed the button again and Caldor fell to the ground groaning. Ian released the button. "Enough?"

After a minute Caldor got himself together enough to gasp, "Enough." He appeared to reach out to someone and was about to say something, but thought better of it and looked up at Ian. "What is that thing?"

Ian replied, "We call it a ray-gun to keep the inventor happy. You're not the first to make jokes about it looking like a television antenna, but it's definitely Reality-TV, don't you think? Painful for everyone."

"And what, it runs off that device in the front of the car?" asked Caldor.

"That's right. It's not exactly portable but you can't outrun the ray, so up you get."

"And all you have to do is flick the big red switch on that black box there?" Caldor persisted.

"What? Yes. Now get up."

Caldor got up and stepped toward Ian again. Ian pressed the button but nothing happened. Caldor kept coming. Ian looked down to see if he was pressing the right button and Caldor reached forward and snatched it out of his hands.

"Back on," Caldor said loudly and pressed the button, pointing the antenna at Ian.

Ian's world collapsed in pain around him. Worse than the worst alcohol bender he'd ever been on. He had no control of his body. He could hear groans that he supposed came from his own mouth. It felt like someone was running claws through him and scooping pieces out. And then it stopped. It took another minute for his mind to stop spinning. He felt himself being dragged away from the front of the van. Caldor took Ian's place next to the passenger seat and the equipment. Ian looked around to see who was dragging him but saw no one.

"Okay, Darnu, thanks. You can probably switch it off for now, but stay near the switch in case I need it in a hurry. Garjae and Barma that's probably far enough, I don't know what the range on this thing is yet. Keep out from behind him, I don't think it's too picky. You got some of that last blast didn't you, Darnu?

" ... Thought so. Andrei?

"Tilvy, is he all right?

" ... Time, yes. I wonder how much we really have."

Ian listened to what was obviously just half of a conversation and it finally dawned on him that there must be some of those narun here, and that Caldor could talk with them – and presumably see them. Ian supposed he should have seen this coming, but he had hardly believed that the narun were real. He'd only ever seen vague hollows in the air, revealed by water sprayed into the cages. How was anyone supposed to accept the reality of such figures? The hands that dragged him felt a lot larger than what he had seen in the small cages. Anyway, there had been no sign of them when he was monitoring earlier, how was he to know?

"You were heard to say that you would meet someone in the city late this afternoon. Does that mean we have until then before you're missed?" Caldor asked.

"Maybe," said Ian. When Caldor pointed the antenna at him he hastened to add, "I'm pretty new to this job. They may or may not trust me to bring you in alone. You were right, there should have been more than one of us. I was just making sure it was you before I called in the others. They may still come, I don't know."

"Come from where?"

"The city ... probably."

"I want a way to restrain you," Caldor said. "I'd rather not use this thing and I suspect you'd rather that too. Is there anything useful in the van?"

Ian hesitated, he knew what was in there but didn't like the idea of being tied up with them. Caldor waved the antenna. "Your choice."

"In the back on the right, hanging on the wall. They look like big white plastic cable ties. You know what I mean?"

"I think I do," said Caldor. "Barma, can you take a look? They'll look like white straps or belts."

The ties appeared a few seconds later, apparently dangling in mid-air. Caldor took a look at them and nodded. He described what he wanted and how they worked. The straps were attached around Ian's ankles, and then around his wrists behind his back. It took some time, the invisible hands appeared to have trouble manipulating the straps. Caldor relaxed noticeably once Ian was finally restrained. He put down the antenna and came over and checked the straps. He added a second one to each position and pulled them all firm.

"You'll understand if I am less sympathetic about your comfort after the demonstration of that thing, won't you?" Caldor said, pulling the ties another notch tighter.

Caldor walked over to a nearby tree and started calling up into its branches, "Casseta, come on. Come on. It's stopped now. The horrible man isn't going to do it any more." He continued calling for another minute or so before holding out his arm to the tree as if something were climbing onto it. "It's okay my darling girl, it's okay," he continued to murmur for another minute before shivering a little and straightening up. Caldor walked back to the van and Ian just stared at him, he had no idea what to make of what he'd just seen.

"She's fine now I think. She felt it when that thing hit me and got scared," Caldor answered some question that Ian couldn't hear. When Caldor didn't explain himself Ian shrugged and decided to ignore it.

Caldor said, "Darnu, I think we should all get into the van and move. Go somewhere else to talk, in case any of his friends turn up early."

\- \- \-

Not many miles from where they started John pulled over to the side of a different gravel road, again deep within the forest but unlikely to be found if Ian's friends came looking – he hoped. He looked across at Andrei sitting small in the passenger seat. Staying small meant he didn't have to find leg-room amongst the equipment that had been moved to the floor.

"You feeling better?" he asked. Andrei had been caught by the same ray that had hit John.

Andrei nodded, still sombre. "Yeah. Not something I really want to repeat, but I'm okay now."

"Good. I've been worried that thing shot out your funny bone," said John.

Andrei grinned, "Still alive aren't I?"

John smiled back. "Come on, let's talk to the others."

They climbed out and opened up the side door of the van. Their friends climbed out, relieved to be out of the foreign, dead, environment that was the van.

John looked at Ian lying on the floor on the van. "You doing okay?"

"Thought you didn't care?" was Ian's response. John decided that meant he was fine.

John looked across at Darnu. "I think we should try to find out what we can about that stuff," he pointed to the equipment in the front of the van, "so that Beenae can tell the others what they're facing. In case, you know, we're slow getting back."

Darnu nodded. He knew what John actually meant: in case they didn't get back.

Since John's epiphany a week ago he and Darnu had assumed a sort of shared leadership of the small group. Belief in himself, in the narun, and in Asha, had given John a sense of purpose and direction. He had assumed a confidence and self-possession not seen since before he had lost his wife and daughter. Even if Darnu did not fully approve of having to work with a human, he did understand the necessity, and they got along well enough now that John was no longer behaving as a lost and aimless soul.

The original plan, made before Milla had turned back – no one had wanted to risk an elder getting too close to John's house – had been simple enough. John would allow himself to be captured and then try to release the brevi at an appropriate time. Casseta would make her way back to John's home where this group would be waiting and hoping that the brevi could then lead them back to John, and hope they would be able to help when they did find him. A simple plan, but dangerous, there were too many things that could go wrong, too many things they didn't know.

They had stopped early the night before they reached his home, preferring to approach carefully in the full light of morning. When they started the next morning Darnu and Garjae had travelled in front and to the sides as scouts, sensing forward, hoping to be forewarned of any dangers. John was hoping to have time at home to recover from his trip and perhaps even find a human solution to their dilemma. Whoever it was had not come for him in the weeks between Asha's disappearance and his own excursion into the forest, there seemed no reason they should be waiting for him right now.

But it was not to be. Darnu and Garjae returned at approximately the same time to report that they'd experienced some strange buzzing sensation, and sensing forward they'd felt a single human, and no narun, not far from John's house. They had both retreated quickly to stop the group from getting any closer.

John had made a snap decision. If there was only one human then there was a chance he would not be able to see the narun, and that might mean they could overpower him and perhaps use him to gain access to where they held prisoners. Darnu agreed that it was worth trying – John was not the only one worrying about their first plan. They hastily made new plans to try and lure the man away from his equipment, and to trap and overpower him after finding out as much as they could.

It had all gone surprisingly well, right up to the moment Ian had used that ridiculous antenna thing. Darnu was feeling bad, had already apologised for not acting to try and knock out Ian when he first used the antenna, but it had all happened so quickly. None of them had really been prepared for violence, whatever the practice sessions they had held on the journey from the Glade. But they had weathered that, and now they had important information that the Glade should be told.

John rummaged around in the back of the van, there was not much back there that the narun liked to touch. Andrei had earlier discovered the folded cage with its mesh that seemed to burn when you touched it, and John found some netting made from something similar. There were a few pairs of silvery gloves that he found protected his hands from the mesh. The gloves had something like a cotton lining so John got Andrei to try a pair on.

"They feel a bit strange but that lining does help," said Andrei. He noticed Ian watching the gloves from his position on the floor of the van. They must have looked like glove puppets with no hands to hold them up. He prodded him a couple of times, enjoying Ian's bewildered reaction.

"Andrei!" John interrupted sharply. "Try the gloves with the mesh."

Andrei gave Ian a last flick under his nose and then turned his attention to the mesh. He found that he could put his hands on the mesh and even try to lift it without pain. Fascinated, he only reluctantly gave up the gloves for the others to try. Ian watched the gloves move around as though it was some strange conjuring trick.

John found a box containing more pieces of the strange silvery material as the gloves. They turned out to be hoods, jackets, pants and even some odd boots.

"They're the suits that the narun wear. The ones that work with us," explained Ian. "I'd always wondered what they looked like under the suit ... I guess that was the wrong question."

Andrei started to put the various pieces on. Ian watched as a being began to take shape in front of his eyes. Seeing that Ian was watching him, Andrei did a little dance for him wearing just a jacket and pants, then laughed and kept dressing. He looked at the final piece, the hood, dubiously before pulling it over his head.

"Oh, yuck!" he said in disgust, his voice sounding muffled and distant. "This is awful. It's like you've all gone really faint. Well, except for you John, and Ian, you're both still as ugly as ever." He pulled the hood back off. "Wouldn't fancy wearing that for long." He was happy enough to hand the pieces of suit on for others to try.

Each new recipient enjoyed carrying on Andrei's joke, waving or dancing to try and gain some new reaction from Ian. Barma and Tilvy danced together, one wearing the jacket and gloves the other the pants and boots.

It was Garjae who first noted, "From the outside you can't tell who or what is inside the suit at all. I think it would be apparent whether it's a narun or human from the way it moved, but I couldn't tell the difference between Beenae and Tilvy when they were in the suit."

"Garjae! Apologise at once I say. Everyone knows that Beeny is much prettier," said Andrei. Tilvy stuck her tongue out at him but Beenae flushed with embarrassment.

"Just ignore him, Beenae," said Darnu.

The remaining items in the back of the van seemed to be ordinary tools so they left the back and looked over the equipment in the front. John turned on the device and the computer, grateful to discover that the system had been designed to accommodate lack of expertise. They spent a while experimenting with it, trying to work out its range and other details. They were comforted to see that it could not see the aaranya when they were merged with a tree.

"But they can use this to see which tree you enter," John pointed out. "Unless the trees are very close together like they are there," he pointed out a cluster on the screen. "What happens if they chop down a tree while you're inside?" he wondered aloud.

The aaranya all made faces of disgust. Andrei said, "Feeling very human today are you?"

John was about to make an exasperated plea when Darnu interrupted. "It's not a pleasant thought, John, but you're right, we need to consider such things. We would be forced to leave the tree or slowly die with it." He looked at Beenae who was still pulling faces with Andrei at the thought of being inside a dying tree. "Are you paying attention?" Beenae looked embarrassed. "You've got to pass these thoughts on to the others. It's important."

John was looking at the antenna. "Ian? If this thing works on us and the narun ... what's it do to a tree?"

Ian was now sitting on the floor of the van, hands still tied behind him, his feet out the door resting on the ground, also still tied. He'd been watching John, listening to the half of the conversation he could hear. John wondered whether he should have kept their deliberations secret from Ian. He knew that he certainly shouldn't have let Ian see him fetch Casseta, but he had been worried that she would head off back to the Glade if he didn't reassure her quickly.

Ian hesitated, trying to work out how helpful to be. Finally he said, "I don't know what it does to a tree exactly, but I think I have seen it used to drive them," he nodded at where he imagined the narun were standing, "from inside."

They all stared at the antenna with varying mixtures of awe and fear.

Darnu still had the pieces of suit in his hand. "Will these protect us from that?"

John asked Ian. He thought so but didn't know how well. Darnu put the suit back on and had John try the weapon on him, first on low then on the pain setting. They saw there was another setting. Ian said he had never used it and given the skull-and-crossbones marking he would not recommend they tried it either. Darnu observed that the suit did offer protection, although the hood let a small amount of the effect through, making it even more uncomfortable.

The afternoon was well advanced by the time they had explored what they could of the van's contents.

"Any chance we had of surprise is probably gone by now," said John.

"But we've learned a great deal," said Darnu. "Now we have some idea of the sort of things we're up against. I doubt we'd get far without this knowledge. It's been worth the delay."

"Oh, I don't know," said Andrei with a wry grin. "Ignorance is bliss they say, it certainly had a lot going for it over what I know now."

Darnu, always serious, just looked at him and shook his head.

"Beenae, are you going to be okay remembering all this to take back to the Glade?," John asked, then to Darnu, "Perhaps another should go with him?" Part of his reservation was simply that they were obviously headed into danger and he wondered how many they should risk.

Beenae gave Darnu a determined look. "I can do this, but if you send another then let me come with you."

"That would rather defeat the purpose, Beenae. John suggested another, not because he doubts you, but because there is a lot for any one to remember," said Darnu.

John apologised, "I meant no offence."

In the background Tilvy gave Andrei a cuff, cutting short some unnecessary comment.

John asked Ian for the address in the city where he would have been taken and confirmed this was the same as where previous narun were taken. He checked this against what papers he could find in the glove-compartment and it all seemed to be consistent. The building was in one of the industrial estates, warehouses and distributions centres and the like, of one of the suburbs on this side of the city.

He found a street directory and looked up the suburb, noting some choices for motels and also of park-lands where they may find some trees for his friends. He tried to plan out a few different ways they could approach their destination without giving themselves away too quickly if there were detectors turned on. They would take Ian with them, mainly because no one could decide what else to do with him. Andrei had a few suggestions, but none were very helpful.

With their plans made they sent Beenae off on his lonely trip back to the Glade, and the rest of them got into the van. They got Ian settled onto a seat near the back of the van, as a more comfortable alternative to the floor for such a long trip. John reminded Ian that if he opened his mouth uninvited they could probably find something to put in it. Andrei claimed the passenger seat again and John decided not to argue the point.

The sun was setting by the time they drove out of the forest. John chose some back roads to skirt the town in case anyone was watching for them there, and then came back onto the highway – there was paranoid and then there was practical. Even Andrei was unusually sombre and quiet, John supposed they were all wondering whether they would see their home again.

12. Escape

John called through the grill into the back of the van. "I've got to stop for fuel. Find something back there to put in Ian's mouth if he looks like getting noisy."

"Shame you left your camping clothes at home," said Andrei.

John pulled into a self-service petrol station that had no other customers at the moment. He suggested that Andrei stay in the van and got out to fill up.

When the tank was full John went in to pay the clerk. He wondered whether he should be paying cash but decided that was unnecessarily paranoid. As he signed the credit card slip he looked up to see the young clerk staring past him with his mouth open. John looked back to see Andrei with three or four chocolate bars, trying to juggle them.

"Andrei!" he tried to yell in a whisper. All he got was a big grin from Andrei and the bars tumbled to the floor. Andrei picked up the bars and handed them to John, winked and skipped out, making a few more of the confectionery items bounce in their shelves as he passed.

John turned back to the astonished clerk and said the first thing that came into his mind. "Sorry about that. Apprentice magician, you know, still trying to get it right. I'll take these too." He handed across the chocolate bars and dug for some cash out of his wallet. The clerk was now staring out at the van where the passenger door of the van appeared to mysteriously open and close as Andrei got back in.

"Good tricks," said the clerk, handing over change.

Back in the van John threw the offending chocolate bars at

Andrei. "Thanks a bloody lot!"

Andrei laughed. "Just adding some entertainment to what must be a dreary night for the poor boy."

John started the van and drove out. From the back Ian called, "Any chance of some food. We seem to have missed lunch. I'm gettin' a bit peckish back here."

"I'll find a drive-through in the city," came John's curt reply, he didn't fancy trying to get through a busy fast food restaurant with Andrei for company.

True to his word, when they reached the city John picked up a few burgers, chips and drinks from a drive-through takeaway food restaurant. He handed the plastic bag over to Andrei who almost fumbled the strange material. He finally managed to settle the bag on the seat beside him and peered in as John drove off.

With a cautious finger he prodded the cup and wrapped burgers and sniffed the air dubiously. "This is edible?" he asked.

"Sort of," replied John. "It smells better than it tastes."

"Sure smells good to me," came Ian's more enthusiastic reply from the back.

"The food, such as it is, is inside those wrappers," explained John.

"Can I look?"

"Sure," said John, adding loudly with a grin, "if you want to see one, take a look at his."

"Look but don't touch," came Ian's rejoinder from the back.

"His hands are clean," John reassured.

"That's not exactly the point," Ian grumbled.

Andrei unwrapped one of the burgers from the bag. He poked at the bun on top and then picked it off to look at what was underneath, sniffing at the contents. He noticed John looking across at him and, with a grin, prodded the contents with his finger too. John laughed.

"That sounded like touching," came Ian's voice. Both John and Andrei laughed louder.

John caught a glimpse of a fellow van driver looking in from the passenger side, watching a burger move about on its own. "Andrei, you've got an audience."

Andrei looked out and held the bun up, opening and closing it a few times as if it were talking out the window. The lights changed and John had to pay attention to the road again. As they moved off the other driver stalled his van.

"I always like an audience," said Andrei.

"We know," came several voices from the back.

"The question is whether you'll ever get tired of it," said John.

"Thirty-five years and no sign of it yet," came Barma's voice.

John looked across at Andrei with some surprise. He knew the aaranya were often older than they appeared, but it was quite a shock to think that Andrei was older than John was.

Andrei just grinned back at him and shrugged. "No point rushing these things."

John had to pay attention for a while, trying to work his way along unfamiliar routes to a motel he had picked out as far enough away from their destination to be safe, he hoped, but close enough to be convenient.

John checked-in and then reversed the van to its place in front of the room, trying to minimise what outsiders would be able to see when the side door of the van was opened. He walked around the van and opened the motel room door. He dropped the food and key onto a bench inside, and came back out. All seemed quiet.

He opened the door for Andrei. "Straight through," he said quietly. When Andrei was gone he pretended to look for something and then shut the door. Then he slid open the back of the van and waited for his friends to go through into the room. He lent in and grabbed his bag of clothes and said quietly to Ian, "We'll be back for you in a minute." He closed the van door again and went into the motel room, closing the door behind him. He flicked the television on so that no one walking past would notice him apparently talking to himself.

The aaranya were standing around looking uncomfortable, shuffling their feet.

"What is it? What's the problem?" John asked.

"Even the floors are nasty here, John. Don't humans use natural materials for anything?" Tilvy said. When Darnu started to look critical she added, "What? I'm just saying what you're all thinking."

"Here," said Andrei, throwing back the cover on the double bed. "There's a woollen blanket here." He pulled it off the bed and threw

189

it on the floor. They congregated on the blanket, reducing their size and settling down on it.

When they were all settled John sat on the edge of the bed and looked at them. "How did you get by in the van?" he asked

"I sat on some felt I found in the front," said Andrei.

"We turned those pieces of silver suit inside out and sat on those," said Tilvy. "Not great, but better than those vinyl seats."

"Is it going to be much of a problem do you think? Only there's not a lot of all-natural stuff goes on in the city."

Darnu answered, "I think we will gradually get used to it but some material is worse for us than others. This cloth you have on the floor here—"

"It's called carpet, oh-wise-one," interrupted Andrei.

"This carpet you have on the floor here," continued Darnu, not rising to Andrei's bait, "seems particularly offensive. I couldn't really tell you why."

"All right. I guess we'll take it as it comes," said John.

"Look, we can't leave Ian out there in the van all night. It doesn't get as cold here as it does in the forest but it gets cold enough. Darnu, Garjae and Andrei, I'll get you to help me carry him through. Barma and Tilvy, if you can do lookout duty to warn if anyone is looking this way. I'll have to find something to cut those straps so he can—"

"Did you hear that?" asked Andrei.

"What?" John looked over expecting a joke, but Andrei looked serious.

There came the loud roar from the van engine and a small screech from its tyres as it left in a hurry. Its escape was made all the more convenient by John having reversed it into place, so it was already out of sight by the time John got to the door of the room.

"Damn!" swore John, he was selecting a few more choice words when he remembered he had company. He'd taken each step so deliberately, so carefully. He thought he'd been so clever: closing the door and turning on the television to hide their conversation. Instead he'd given Ian the cover he needed to escape. He'd even forgotten that the van keys were still sitting in the ignition. There wasn't much else he could have done to make it easier for Ian.

"Can't help but like the guy a little bit," said Andrei, looking down.

John followed his gaze to the step just outside the door. There was the collection of the plastic straps that had been used to restrain Ian's wrists and ankles. Lying across the straps was the Stanley knife he'd used to cut the straps – the blade considerately retracted now.

"He must have been worried that we'd stay up all night wondering how he got loose, so he left us a hint."

"Some hint," said John. "He probably just wanted to trip us up coming out the door." Then he noticed some blood on a couple of the straps. Feeling vindictive he added, "At least he cut himself, I'd hate to think he'd found it too easy." He kicked the items into the room so they wouldn't attract attention outside and shut the door.

"We're going to have to get out of here. We're not far from Ian's friends – damn! He's got the bloody street directory too." John grabbed his small bag of clothes and took the light jacket from inside, it was the only jacket he had, he hoped they could find some place warm before too long.

John swung his bag onto one shoulder, grabbed the bag of takeaway food – at least he needn't go hungry – and said, "Let's go. Try not to do anything to attract attention. This means you, Andrei."

Andrei gave him a salute and they left the room.

John led the way past reception. He dropped the room key into the night slot, the rest he'd sort out if it ever became important. He hesitated when they got to the street, trying to guess the best way to go. He turned left. He looked behind him to make sure they were all following. They were, sort of, but their eyes appeared to be trying to look all directions at once. The city could be a confusing and overwhelming place, even in daylight. At night the lights of many colours were dazzling, and they hid more than they revealed. The city was a potential death trap to anyone that didn't pay attention. His friends needed a crash-course in walking city streets, pun definitely *not* intended, but they didn't really have time.

"Look here, everyone," he said, and their eyes slowly turned to him. "I need you to pay attention. You need to remember that no one else here can see you – except those we don't want. You can't go out onto the streets without making absolutely certain you can be clear again before any traffic gets to you. And it's not just the street.

See these driveways?" He pointed to a few examples. "Humans are fairly safe on the pavement because drivers will see them and wait for them to pass, but that doesn't apply to you! *You* have to be careful.

"That's all the lesson we've got time for. Stay close to me and pay attention to what I'm doing and saying." And pray I do better than I have so far, he added under his breath.

John took another left, a quieter residential street. He walked as quickly as he could, feeling very conspicuous. He felt like he was walking in a group of six, at least five of whom stood out from your normal city dweller. But in fact to most observers he was just a solitary individual, albeit one that talked to himself, and that was not so unusual in the city.

"What are we going to do if the detector comes past?" John asked. "I'm just another human in a city full of them, but you five are going to stand out."

"Some of these streets have trees growing near them," Garjae said. He was still far from friendly, but since Darnu had started treating John better, Garjae was keeping his feelings more to himself.

"And they can't see or detect you when you're merged. That's a good thought," said John.

"We saw in our tests that you get some warning as the detector approaches. If we stay close to trees we should be able to keep out of their way," added Darnu.

"I'd still like to get further from that motel, which means walking some more. Are your senses working well enough here to guide us along streets with the best trees?" asked John. His own life sense felt muted here in the city, as if overwhelmed by other input.

Darnu and Garjae worked together to lead them along streets with more trees. Barma and Tilvy were given the job of concentrating on feeling for the detector, trying to maximise any warning they might get. Andrei and John concentrated on their immediate surroundings, trying to make sure the group stayed safe from traffic.

While they walked John ate the now mostly cold burgers and chips, hunger compensating for the less than appetising meal.

After about an hour's walking, and having to cross a few quite major roads, the group found themselves in a quiet, leafy suburb.

Judging by the houses and large blocks it was an affluent area. On a particularly quiet street John asked Andrei to take a look at some of the empty houses. "See if you can find one that looks like it might stay empty for the night. I'd like to be able to find somewhere off the street to get some sleep."

Only a few houses later Andrei returned to report a small furnished cottage out the back of an apparently empty house. Andrei passed through the wooden front door and unlocked it. It was ideal. Not only did the house have a very empty feel, but even if they did come home John would be in the granny flat out the back and should have enough warning to get out without being seen. The aaranya organised shifts among themselves to watch out for danger, telling John to get his sleep. He accepted most thankfully, it was late and the day had been exhausting.

- - -

Ian pulled the van to the side of the road. He was only a few miles from the motel, but unlike Caldor he knew this area very well and was pretty certain they could not have followed him even if they wanted. Decision time.

By cooperating placidly with Caldor and his friends Ian had managed to get them to relax their guard and not treat him as a threat. It was pretty much exactly what they'd done to Ian back at the house, except, Ian thought with a grimace, *he* should have known better. Caldor may be some inexperienced country bumpkin but Ian couldn't claim such innocence.

As soon as they left him alone he knew exactly where to put his hands on the knife. It was only a couple of minutes and he was free – mostly. Now he had to decide just how free he wanted to be. The way Ian saw it he had two choices: ditch the van and keep on running, get right away from all this weirdness, or he could call up Darren Davies and fall back into his job – he hoped.

Finding the keys in the ignition had been a real bonus, managing to bring back all the equipment may turn out to be enough to keep Davies and Karlin from losing their cool. Karlin wasn't going to be pleased anyway, but besides being weird, he wasn't Ian's main concern. No, it was Davies. As pleasant as he appeared most of the time, he scared the crap out of Ian. There was a temper there, you didn't need Irish roots and red hair to see that. Added to that, Ian was pretty certain, was training in the military. It was not a good idea to be on the wrong side of Darren Davies. How was Davies going to react?

What finally made up Ian's mind was that he was not sure Davies would let him get away. He suspected Davies to be a man of resources and persistence, a man that may not easily let him go. He pulled his mobile phone from the glove compartment and turned it on. He cringed at the tone of a few of the messages that had been left and then called Davies' number.

He reported what had happened in as few words as he could – if you have bad news get it over with quickly, that was a tactic that had always served him well. Davies told him to report to the office, and that he'd have to wait outside until Davies got back because Ian's pass had been revoked.

Ian did as he was told. It was late now so there was plenty of space on the street. Davies was returning from a speedy trip to Caldor's home, looking for Ian. He was not happy.

Sitting there waiting, Ian thought about Caldor. He wondered what Caldor knew and what his life expectancy was when Karlin got his hands on him. Ian also wondered how he, Ian, felt about helping this to happen. This afternoon's experience had opened Ian's eyes in many ways. So far Ian had simply done what he was told. The occasional demonstration that the cages he helped to carry were not actually empty could have been so much sleight of hand for all that it had really sunk in. He saw nothing, he heard nothing, and this was the literal truth rather than the convenient fiction of his previous jobs.

But this afternoon ... this afternoon he had heard a one-sided conversation that went on for hours. Caldor was either a consummate actor or he was really talking to people that Ian couldn't see and couldn't hear. Nor could he forget the journey in the back of the van. It was dark enough in the van that the bumps and nudges he had received as his travel companions moved around could easily be mistaken for real people in the van with him, but it had been silent and occasional illumination from passing headlights was enough that he could verify that there was no one there, not that he could see. No, this afternoon had shown Ian that he must really have been dealing with real creatures all this time, more than that, real people. Given what Ian had seen of Karlin's zoo, and the silent hall, that was a very disturbing thought.

Too disturbing. He was pleased when Davies' car pulled beside his own with the window down. "Wait here. I'll get the pass sorted and call you," Davies said curtly. Without waiting for a response he disappeared down into the driveway under the building. Not much later Ian received an equally terse call on his mobile, "Come on down, room A."

Ian drove down the ramp and left the van with men assigned to sort through and check the equipment. Meeting room A was warm and quiet after the cold and noisy street. In it were Karlin, Davies and two narun in silver suits – Ian looked at them a bit differently after this afternoon's experience.

Ian repeated his story, trying to ensure it was identical to what he had already told Davies, yet another advantage to brevity.

"So you think Caldor is sitting in a motel room, just a few miles from here, in the company of half-a-dozen narun?" Karlin said, his usual friendly smiles and manner totally missing.

"I doubt if he's still there," replied Ian. "He's inexperienced but he's not a fool. I don't know exactly how many narun were with him … more than four, less than eight is the best I can guess."

"Darren?" Karlin demanded.

"I agree with Ian, Caldor's almost certainly moved on. It's probably worth making a detector run past there, but otherwise I would concentrate near here. It sounds like they're planning on visiting. It's been a long time since we've had any uninvited visitors," responded Davies, he did not sound unhappy at the thought.

"You can do that run tonight?" Karlin asked and Davies nodded.

"Sando?" Karlin asked in quieter tones.

To Ian, and he supposed to Davies, there was silence while the narun spoke to Karlin.

Karlin paused, deep in thought for a while, and then some of his usual cheerful demeanour returned. He said, "Okay. Consider yourself on notice, Ian, on notice. Another mistake like this one and you won't be welcome here. But, all things considered, it could have been worse, quite a lot worse. None of us expected Caldor to be prepared for your arrival, and certainly we didn't expect him to have company.

"For tonight, for tonight I suggest we all get some rest. Ian, I'm having the blue van fitted with a detector unit better suited for mobile use. Starting early tomorrow I want you out on the streets doing some random sweeps. Keep mostly to the streets around this block, but also try a few runs further out. If we get lucky you may find Caldor and his friends, and if nothing else you may scare up one or two strays."

Karlin stood up. "Good night," he said and quickly left the room.

Ian breathed a sigh of relief. Karlin's terse manner revealed how angry he must have been. Ian wondered if Karlin had a boss to pressure him, Davies had hinted as much but Ian hadn't seen one yet.

"I'm pleased you decided to stay with us," was all Davies said before he too left. A less than subtle hint that he knew Ian well enough to know he had considered skipping out.

Ian left the narun involved in their own silent conversation and headed out. Some takeaway, some beer from a drive-through, and then home to a small cold flat. It had been a long day. Ian wished he could sleep in, in the morning, but he would have to tread extra carefully around Karlin and Davies for a while. As he curled up to sleep he wondered where Caldor and his friends had ended up.

- - -

John awoke in the morning to voices from the next room. Andrei, Barma and Tilvy were chatting about the things they'd seen.

"I don't suppose any of you know how to make coffee?" he called out.

"Sorry, John," came Tilvy's voice. She sounded cheerful.

John realised it was much later in the morning than his usual waking time – well, usual for his days of hiking through the forest. He climbed out of bed still mostly clothed, another habit from his days in the forest.

"Good morning, sleepyhead," came Andrei's voice from the door, his usual cheeky smile bright on his face.

"Good morning, Andrei," said John. "I take it everything's okay?"

"Yep. Barmy had a bit of a close call crossing the street earlier, don't think he or the driver were properly awake. But no sign of the bad guys and not a hint of the detector."

"And humans?"

"The houses on either side went through some sort of mad scramble a little while ago and they all left in a hurry. Could it have been something you said?"

"That's usual. It's what I used to do when I lived here. Wake up late, run about getting ready and then drive off in a rush to get to work. Before that it was rushing to school and I guess before that it was pre-school, they like to train us humans early."

"So what's the plan, boss?" asked Andrei. He grinned, remembering the first time he'd asked that question.

"Stage one, I'm going to have a shower," said John.

"Hmm ... not a big plan, but you're getting better."

Waving vaguely to Barma and Tilvy as he came out of the bedroom, John found the bathroom and went in. He was much relieved to discover that they'd left the hot water switched on. From the bathroom accessories John thought that the flat's usual resident was a young male, probably an almost grown son or a lodger of a similar age.

When he came out wearing just a towel the only comment was from Tilvy, "You should be eating better, John."

John gave her a sad smile. "Asha tells me the same thing."

Finding the makings for a sweet black coffee he put the kettle on to boil and then went through to the bedroom and got dressed. He straightened the room as best he could before he left it.

As he sat down to his coffee Darnu and Garjae came in, passing through the wooden front door. "Everything okay?" John asked.

Darnu nodded and then said, "We found signs that other aaranya have been through the trees around here, probably not that long ago."

Garjae nodded his confirmation.

"Is that likely to be a problem?" asked John. "Are stands very territorial?"

"Not in the forest," said Darnu. "It is considered courteous to pass through less populated areas unless you are specifically visiting the stand, but that's rarely a problem anyway."

"But it is difficult to guess whether things may be different here in the city," said Garjae.

"Or whether such folk may be friends of our enemies," added

Andrei.

The others looked at him. It was a thought that had not occurred to them. Darnu reluctantly agreed, "I find that difficult to imagine … but I guess we will have to be wary."

"They've got to come from somewhere," was all Andrei said.

"If they are not friends of Ian's people—" John stopped, frustrated. He'd hoped to have more time to talk with Ian, to try and find out more about the people he was dealing with. "If they are not friends, then this close you would think they would have to be enemies, and if that's the case maybe they would help us."

Darnu nodded. "Given our situation it is probably worth trying to make some cautious contact." He looked at Andrei, and though it obviously pained him to say it, added, "Andrei, I think this is something you may be good at." It was an acknowledgement that people seemed to take a liking to Andrei, even when he was being annoying.

Andrei grinned and gave a deep bow, "At your service, m'Lord."

"There are some things that only I can do," said John. "We need a new street directory and I think we also need transport, we need to be able to get away quickly if they find where we are."

"Horse rustlin' now," said Andrei. "This gets better all the time."

"I wasn't thinking of stealing anything. I thought I'd hire something. I think it's probably safe enough for me to use my credit card, I doubt if these guys have the resources to track us down that way." John thought about his mobile phone, it would probably be safe to use that too. If Ian's people had the sort of resources it took to track him by phone or credit card then it was probably a hopeless situation anyway.

He dug his phone out of his bag and switched it on for the first time in two weeks. The battery wasn't looking good so he plugged in the charger while he used it. First was a backlog of messages, his provider warning him that some of the older ones would shortly be deleted. The first few messages were from Jason, hoping he was having a good time off. Then came the messages from early in this week when Jason and Stan had phoned to see why he was not at work. The messages got progressively more abrupt as the week progressed. The last message had been left just this morning: a stranger's voice, cheerful and charming, that said, "John, my dear friend. We seem to have had some miscommunication. There is nothing to be concerned about. Please, call me on this number and we can chat about it. Ciao."

John looked at his phone and wondered what to do. He did not believe the friendly voice, not for a moment, but there was a definite temptation to call the number. He kept the message but left it unanswered. Until he returned the call they would not know whether he had even received the message. He'd watched enough movies to accept that the bad guys probably had the advantage in this situation. If he spoke with them they could soon blackmail him with threats against Asha, so he was probably better off not speaking with them for the time being at least.

He drew a deep breath and rang Jason's mobile number, hoping that Jason was in a meeting – it was about the right time of morning for one of Stan's irregular meetings. His luck was in, he got voice-mail. He left a message apologising profusely for having missed work. "Things are still in a mess, Jason," he continued, "this is the first time I've had a chance to call you. I'll probably be away for at least another week and the mobile doesn't work well here so you can't call me back." He thought for a moment before adding, "Can you pass this on to Stan for me, I've got to head out again." He hung up and switched the phone off. "Sorry, Jason," he said to himself, feeling bad for lying to his friend but not knowing what other options he really had.

John looked up at his friends. "Time to be moving on, I guess. I suggest you hang around near the end of the street until I come back with a car." To Andrei he said, "If you go wandering off looking for others do be careful. I think it would be best if you stay fairly close, we can look further afield a bit later."

"I was going to come with you," Andrei said with some surprise.

"Best not. Not many trees in shopping centres."

Andrei kept John company for a few blocks, but when the trees got less frequent he fell back and John continued on alone.

- - -

Bored. John had been gone only half-an-hour but Andrei was bored. Darnu and Garjae took themselves much too seriously for his tastes, and Barma and Tilvy had time for no one but each other. He told Darnu that he might look a bit further north, to which the response was simply, "Don't go too far." He had said he wouldn't, but "too far" was such a subjective phrase, wasn't it?

The concrete of the buildings and footpaths, the tar of the roads and the wires stretching everywhere, combined to muffle and distort his life sense. He could sense quite a way up an open street, if there wasn't too much traffic in the way, but he couldn't see much inside or beyond most of the buildings. They had wondered if Ian's detector would suffer similar problems but had no chance to test it.

He hadn't gone all that far when he thought he caught a glimpse of someone – a narun? – darting down a street further ahead. He ran forward to try and get a better view, and almost got hit by a car as he ran across an intersection without thinking. Moving more carefully now, he looked down the crossroad but could see nothing. He ran down far enough to catch another tantalising glimpse of someone moving off from another cross street. Running faster again he caught another glimpse. He was getting closer.

With some surprise Andrei found himself on a busy footpath dodging humans. He stopped himself from trying to match their size, there was no one here to be polite for. It wasn't so crowded as to be difficult to stay out of their way, but it was frustrating to have to remember that they couldn't see him. He was sure he had seen a narun run down this way so he moved further along the footpath trying to reach out with his senses, but he found it all very confusing.

He was walking past a multi-storey car park when he felt the disturbing buzzing sensation of a detector. He looked around and realised there was not a tree in sight. He froze in panic, he couldn't tell which way to run and he could feel the buzzing sensation growing in strength.

He hadn't even seen the figure approach when a hand grabbed his and pulled. "Come on, you idiot, run!" He was pulled up the ramp into the car park and then between parked cars and cars queuing for spaces. Back and forth he ran, pulled this way and that by the figure leading him. Somewhere in the middle of the maze of cars she pulled him to a halt and crouched down behind a concrete barrier, pulling on Andrei's arm until he was crouched beside her.

"What's wrong with you?" she whispered loudly. "Do you want to be caught?" Her tone left no doubt how bad she thought that would be.

Andrei appraised his saviour. Obviously young but also obviously a girl. Somehow she contrived to appear scruffy. Dirt didn't stick to a narun, a fact that Andrei had been known to compare to bears and fur and what, according to human idiom, didn't stick, so there was no reason for her to look dirty. Clothes were entirely optional and essentially part of them so there was no reason to look rough or unkempt. But despite all that this girl managed to look rough, dirty, unkempt and just generally scruffy. But, Andrei grinned, it wasn't as though it didn't look good on her.

"Oh crap, you *are* an idiot," she said, interpreting his grin as something mindless. "I've risked my bleedin' neck to save a bloody witless idiot."

Andrei was, unusually for him, stuck for words. He was still searching for some response to prove that he did indeed have wit when the buzzing sensation came back, stronger this time but also distorted by the concrete and cars.

"Shit!" she said. "They're not giving up." She looked more closely at Andrei. "Are they looking for you?" When he didn't answer straight away she just turned away. "Come on if you're coming," she called back, and began winding her way between the cars. Short as they both were they still ran in a crouch to avoid being visible through windows of cars. They reached the other side of the car park and Andrei could see that she had led him up several levels. There she scrambled onto the concrete wall and leapt into the space beyond. Only when Andrei got to the wall himself could he see the tree below, onto which she had jumped and was now agilely descending.

"Can't be outdone by a girl," he muttered to himself and leapt after her. He felt the buzzing of the detector clarify for a moment but then he reached the tree and was on his way down. He had to run as fast as he could to avoid losing track of her and the detector quickly faded behind.

A few blocks of zigzagging and he saw her jump over a small brick fence and into a front garden. They sat together on the lawn with their backs against the brick fence, facing the front of a suburban house. As far as Andrei could tell there was no one at home.

"Thanks for that," he said at last.

"So you can talk."

"It's amazing what you can teach an idiot to do these days."

"Oh. Sorry about that, but what were you doing just standing there?"

"You know, just enjoying the sunshine, feeling the breeze, passing the time," he smiled at her.

"You know what I mean. Why didn't you run when you felt *them* coming?" she asked.

"As I recall it, I was being led on a merry goose chase at the time, my mind was on other things ... and I'm not from around here, I wasn't sure where to run." The last Andrei admitted rather reluctantly.

"I thought you and your friends looked strange. What are you doing here?"

Andrei looked at her face trying to decide how much to say. It had seemed a strange, oddly distrustful introductory question. "A few of us came here hoping to rescue a friend from those with that detector thing – and perhaps to find out more about them at the same time." He gave her a puzzled look. "How did you know I wasn't with them when you helped me?"

"These days the narun with them are usually in silver suits, and you mostly only see them at night in places that normal humans don't go. But I've seen them, back when it was those narun that lured our people into traps, they were strange grey looking things. I think they're aaranya, but they're not from around here." The girl paused and then, "What do you mean rescue a friend? There's nothing you can do you know. Once someone's been caught by *them* they're lost forever."

Andrei shook his head. "At least one of our group is not likely to accept that, and anyway we still need to find out more about *them*." The girl's expression suggested that she was thinking her original assessment had been correct, Andrei must be an idiot. He continued anyway, "We really are strangers here, we could use help from someone that knows their way around."

She just looked at him.

"That was a hint," he suggested, but she continued to ignore it. "Why were you running from me in the first place?"

"You were a strange group. A few like you and then two that felt much older than they looked. I decided to talk to you but wanted to get you away from your friends first."

Andrei was puzzled by the fact that she seemed to know so much about their group when they hadn't even known she was near. "Well, you're talking to me," he said with a smile. "I'm Andrei."

She stared at him in silence for a few minutes and Andrei wondered if he was going to have his own joke played back on him, but eventually she answered, "I'm Senna."

Andrei gave a nod and a wide smile. "I am very pleased to meet you, Senna." He pondered for a moment. His group really did need some local help, how could he encourage Senna to trust him? "Would you be able to take me to meet others in your stand or perhaps bring others here to meet my friends?" he asked at last.

"You mock me!" she said, offended.

"What? No." His face bewildered.

"You believe that stands and Glades and things still exist?" she asked, surprised.

"I know they do," he said even more surprised. "I belong to a stand and our Glade – What?" he asked again in response to her expression.

"Now I know you lie. If any Glades exist they are hundreds of miles from here."

"I have come a long way, Senna. I don't really know how far. There we belong to a stand and we have the most beautiful Glade in all the world."

She sniffed, not convinced but his sincerity was undeniable.

He looked down at the movement of the shadows and realised how much time had passed. "I really should get back to my friends before they start to worry. Will you come back with me?"

He had another thought, got up and looked around and then sat down again. "More to the point, can you show me how to get back? Please." He gave his best lost puppy dog look.

She laughed. "You are an idiot. Come on then." She was off and over the fence walking quickly down the quiet footpath.

"If you don't have a stand ... well ... what do you have?" Andrei asked, not able to imagine another possibility.

She looked at him, still wondering if he was pulling her leg. "Most of us are loners, couples or very small groups these days. A few years ago there were larger groups but they proved to be too much of a target for *them*. I think the fact that narun are working for *them* has also changed things for us, it's harder to trust one another now."

"But you said their narun were different."

"They are, but not that different. The way they lured so many of us into traps of one sort or another – many taken before they had any idea what was happening – it's changed the way we look at each other."

"But you, you're not like that. I mean you helped me this morning, you're trusting me now."

She grinned at him. "No one but a genuine idiot would try to lure me into a trap with the sort of stories you tell. I'm still not convinced that you're not an idiot, but I'm pretty sure you're not with *them*. If your friends are willing to put up with you they can't be all bad."

A little while later she said, "I think your friends have been looking for you."

Andrei looked at her and she pointed further up the street they were on and also indicated another off that further up. Andrei tried to push his senses that way and thought he could just feel someone. It was apparent that her senses were much better tuned than his to the peculiarities of city life.

Eventually they all gathered beneath a tree and Andrei made introductions. Tilvy smiled to herself at something that none of the others seemed to notice.

"You're all from a stand?" Senna asked, yet again.

"Yes," came several replies, yet again.

"My parents said that all the stands were gone, back in my great-grandparents time."

"Great-grandparents?" said Darnu. "The city hasn't been here that long."

It took a while but they finally learned that most of the aaranya in the city now lived barely as long as most humans. Senna was astonished to learn that Darnu and Garjae, who appeared to be mature but still young men, were over a century old – she had thought that her parents' stories of long-lived older generations were just the exaggerations of the elderly.

"Darnu and Garjae definitely act their age, at the very least," Andrei observed. "I should probably warn you that there is a member of our group still missing. He's a bit strange but he's useful. He can drive a car for a start." Andrei nodded to the large car, a station-wagon, pulling up to the curb not far from them.

Senna looked at the car, the driver appeared to be watching her. She turned and looked at Andrei in surprise.

He answered her unspoken question with a grin. "You guessed it. He can see us and he's human, but please don't hold that against him. He's really not that bad."

It had been a long morning for John.

First there was the dilemma over what sort of vehicle to hire. After much deliberation he'd finally settled on a station-wagon as the best compromise.

Then the shopping. He purchased some thick mats to make it more comfortable for some to travel in the back of the wagon if necessary, he imagined such travel was not legal but the police would never be able to see them. He got some pure woollen blankets to cover the seats and mats to make the floors more acceptable to his friends' sensitive natures. A street directory and some maps leading back to the forests of home that he thought may be useful. Some more clothes and a selection of sunglasses, including a pair of photo-chromatic ones that were almost clear most of the time. A visit to a hairdresser to get his hair restyled and some tinting. Together with the glasses he thought he should be more difficult to recognise now.

The result was a badly battered credit card, but he'd worry about that later.

He looked out the car window at the group sitting beneath the tree. If other humans could see this group they would think they were probably primary school children. It was only when you looked more closely that it became obvious that all these people had the mature builds and expressions of adults – with the possible exception of Andrei who, with a bright cheerful smile on his face, was looking younger than ever today. That's when John noticed the girl sitting near Andrei, a stranger. She was also young in appearance, except for her small size, she looked much like a seventeen or eighteen year old human girl he thought. If he had seen her elsewhere he may have thought her human, her untidy appearance was not something he associated with the aaranya.

He got out of the car and went around to speak with them. When Andrei went to say something he held up his hand to indicate he needed a moment. He opened the passenger door of the car, sat down and pulled out his mobile phone. It was switched off but he placed it to his ear anyway.

"Hello," he said at last.

"Hello, John," said Andrei. "John, this is Senna. Senna, this is John." It was only now that Andrei noticed that Senna was looking worried and seemed to be edging away. "Senna, it's fine. You needn't worry about John, he's really not that scary."

Senna looked around the group and saw that they were all relaxed. "I thought it was only ever young kids," she said. "I've been seen a few times, but only ever by the very young." She looked back at John, still uncertain what to make of him.

"When I first saw one of you it took me by surprise too," said John as gently as he could. "It's been almost a year now." Thinking about how he must look, and feeling self-conscious, he added, "Excuse this," he pointed to the phone, "I don't always hold a phone to my ear for no reason, but I'm trying not to attract attention if other humans are watching."

"You had your hair changed," said Tilvy. "It looks good."

John smiled. "Thanks. I thought it may stop them recognising me too quickly." He pulled the glasses out and put them on too.

Tilvy's mouth turned down, the glasses were not a hit. "Do you think all that will help?"

"Don't you think it changes my appearance?"

She looked at him carefully. "I guess it might help with humans but we see you a bit differently, you'd never fool a narun that way." The others agreed.

"They're coming!" Senna cried suddenly. The other's just looked at her. "The detector, can't you feel it?"

Darnu concentrated for a moment and finally said, "I think you're right. Quick, into the trees. See you in a while, John." They quickly scattered, merging into trees along the street. Senna hesitated, her own inclination was to run, but she ended up following Andrei into a tree.

John walked quickly around the car to the driver's seat and closed the door. He sat there still pretending to talk on his phone. His hand and phone helped to obscure his face so he thought he would be as safe here as anywhere, and he could look out for his friends at the same time. A little while later he felt the buzzing sensation he had felt in the forest at home and he wondered how far away it had been when Senna felt it. He saw a blue van drive past a street further up and thought that was probably the source, it looked familiar. It paid no attention to him and gradually the buzzing sensation disappeared.

A while later his friends began to emerge from the trees, Andrei and Senna were last. John put away his phone and got out of the car to speak with them.

"Your senses are very acute, Senna," said Darnu.

"I thought it was just that Andrei was a bit thick," she said, her smile denying the criticism.

"Oh, he is that," put in John with a grin, pleased to get his own back for a change.

"So they know you're here? They're looking for you?" Senna asked, obviously disturbed by the idea. "It's been a long time since I've seen them out looking much in daylight," she explained.

"Yes," Darnu admitted.

"We sort of borrowed one of their vans to get here," added Andrei, perhaps not realising that this was unlikely to make Senna feel any better.

"It might be safer if we moved," said John.

Senna looked dubiously at the car and said, "You want me to go in that?"

John just looked at her.

"Where are we going to run to if the detector comes past and we're in that?"

"Well ..." John stopped to think about it. "I guess I thought I'd try to drive away from them."

"Not once you get into the thick of traffic," she reminded him.

John nodded, he'd been away from the city too long. "We will need this to get home," he said, "but I am open to suggestions on what we do to get you all around the city in the meantime."

"I'd sort of hoped Senna might show us around," said Andrei.

Senna was about to answer when Darnu interrupted, "You may

want to pull out your phone again, John." He nodded across the road where a woman was pushing a pram, giving strange looks over at John. She looked pleased to be on the other side of the road.

John looked over, gave her a sheepish grin and said loudly, "Just practising my lines." She didn't look convinced or impressed but there wasn't much he could do about that. He went back to the car and sat in the passenger seat again, at least here he was less noticeable. "Senna?"

She looked around the group. "While ever you are staying away from *them* I'm willing to help, but once you start going near *them* again you're on your own."

13. Preta

When Asha became conscious again her first thought was of the creature, and the beautiful young girl that it had been. "Ellie?" she whispered. Her arms contracted but there was nothing in their grasp. Had it been a dream ... a nightmare?

"Asha," a voice prompted softly.

Asha could feel that her back was against a tree. The warm pulse beneath its rough surface was comforting and felt unusually strong.

"Asha," the voice prompted again and large hands grasped her shoulders. "Are you awake, Asha? It's important that you merge. You need to merge, Asha," the familiar voice persisted.

She opened her eyes but her vision was blurred and she could not make out any details. She felt the owner of the voice partially merge into the tree, trying to draw her with them. She resisted at first but did not have the strength to fight for long. Eventually she recognised the need and submitted, merging into the powerful flows near the centre of the trunk. She barely noticed when the other presence touched her briefly and then departed. Had she ever felt such strength in a tree? She drew on that strength as best her weakness could achieve. As the comfort and life of the tree slowly fed her, Asha let her consciousness recede again.

Some unknown time later she became aware. The flow of the tree no longer felt right. While it was strong relative to herself, it felt febrile and uncertain. She withdrew from the trunk and stepped hesitantly onto the platform that held it.

It took a minute or so for her to take in her surroundings, to remember where she was and what had happened.

"Thank goodness," came the voice, heavy with relief. Ceeda. She finally recognised the voice of her fellow prisoner.

Ceeda came across to her platform. "If you had not come out soon I think one of them," he indicated two silver-suited narun standing outside the cage, "may have been going to force you out."

Ceeda seemed unusually large to her, Asha tried to increase her size to match but found it difficult.

"No, don't," Ceeda said with concern. He reduced his size to match hers. "You lost a lot of your prana. I'm surprised you're alive." He took another look at her and then looked at the tree. "I've never seen anything like it before." He shook his head in wonder.

Still feeling incredibly weak, Asha looked back at the tree and was surprised by how sickly it appeared to be. "What's wrong with it?" she asked.

Ceeda gave her a strange look. "Um ... you, I think."

She looked at him.

"It was okay when I encouraged you to enter it yesterday. You were so small and weak, I was sure you were going to die. Accepting strength from the tree was your only chance, but I never expected this. You've improved dramatically since yesterday, Asha, and I think you almost drained the tree to do it. I never knew such transfers were possible."

"Neither did I," answered Asha. She was still weak but now she could stand without assistance and her mind would not leave her central concern. "Ellie?" she whispered.

Ceeda assisted Asha from the wilting tree and over to the platform where Nacee and Briso waited. He encouraged Asha to nestle against the trunk to gain what strength and comfort she could from this healthier tree.

"Who is Ellie?" Ceeda asked. "You've kept repeating the name."

Asha started to try and explain, but could not find the words so she just shook her head.

Nacee paid attention to Asha for the first time, as if Asha's loss of substance made her somehow more accessible. Nacee put a hand over one of Asha's and gave it a light squeeze, offering a small smile as she did so. That was all. Nacee's expression returned to its usual blank state and she nestled up against Ceeda.

Weary from her brief activity, Asha was about to see if Ceeda thought it would be okay for her to merge with this other tree, when the narun from the front called to them. There was a period of activity as the prisoners were caged, the trees were replaced, and then the prisoners restored. Accepting this as encouragement for her to use the trees to regain strength, Asha merged again, but this time spread herself more evenly and tried to draw on the tree's strength more gently.

* * *

When Asha emerged later she was pleased to see that the tree was still healthy. Severely drained and in need of some time in the sun but not badly weakened. Assessing herself she saw that she was still reduced from what she had been but she felt much stronger now. Indeed she felt almost normal. Smaller, but surprisingly well.

She could see Ceeda was watching her from the other platform, not wanting to disturb Nacee from her accustomed place buried beneath the protection of his arm. Asha went over to them and sat with Nacee between them.

Ceeda looked at the tree that Asha had emerged from and then back to Asha. "So the first time was no fluke then. You really can draw on the tree's resources like nothing I've ever seen before."

"It is not something I have ever done before, I don't even know I am doing it ... it just happens."

Ceeda looked at Nacee and started to ask a question, but he was interrupted by a call from the front of the cage.

"The master awaits," observed Ceeda. "I imagine he is going to be very interested in you."

Ceeda was right. Asha was taken to the usual examination room and Karlin was already there. He watched avidly as she was carried in.

"Oh good, good. You're alive," came Karlin's overly jovial voice. "That's another point to you, Sando. I should know better than to bet against your built-in knowledge of the narun. How do you feel now, dear? You certainly look much better than even Sando was expecting, eh Sando?"

The narun, standing at his usual place by the door, made no response.

Asha looked at Karlin, reluctant to speak but needing to know. "Ellie?" she asked.

"The child is remarkably well. Indeed it seems she will live longer than expected thanks to your ... sacrifice. I must say that I am impressed. I'd thought your prior relationship may have made some difference to how things went, but this extremity was quite unexpected. We were delighted, weren't we, Sando?"

Again no response.

"Our unresponsive friend is probably right. Delight wasn't our first reaction. If we hadn't found you when we did, admittedly rather later than we'd intended, it is likely you would have let that thing kill you." Karlin sounded astonished. "None of the children have ever had that effect on a narun. Their effect on humans isn't pretty to watch but narun have not been in danger before. Is it some special talent you have, dear, or does it have something to do with your relationship do you think?"

Asha just looked at him.

"You don't know? Well, we'll find that out in time, that's what I'm here for. Now, just stand still, dear ... looking this way. Smile, dear," said Karlin.

He ran through the usual series of tests and measurements. Approaching the end he began muttering, "Remarkable, remarkable. You are something quite special, dear."

He finished clearing away his instruments and then sat down to look at her. "I am very pleased that you survived, dear, you are definitely something that we've not seen before.

"Obviously you've met Nacee, the other pretty little dryad that shares your accommodation. Two days ago you were closer to death and more greatly reduced than she has ever been, and now look at you. Okay so there is still less of you than there was, but you appear to be quite well nonetheless. And what you have done to those trees is something even Sando cannot explain. Remarkable. We simply must find out more about you." Karlin's enthusiasm was making him even more voluble than usual.

"What did you do to Ellie?" Asha interrupted.

"I thought you were a smart girl from an old stand, surely you've heard the tales? No? These are hungry ghosts, dear. *Preta*, my dear dryad. That's your word for them isn't it, Sando?"

The narun nodded.

"Acintya!" Asha gasped in stunned disbelief, she looked toward Sando in horror.

Karlin laughed. "Oh wonderful, wonderful, my dear girl, just wonderful. Please, don't look at Sando like that. He hasn't deigned to participate in such activity, although some of our other narun friends seem to rather enjoy it. Sando told me that some of you used that term, acintya – unthinkable. But, my dear little dryad, it's hardly unthinkable is it? You have a word for the result, preta, which obviously means your people have thought of it."

Asha glared at Karlin. "Pushing the living prana, the essence of a creature, from their material body ought to be unthinkable!"

She paused, remembering the tales she had heard of the tormented ghosts: ghosts made of prana like the narun, but these were the praanin bodies of the humans or animals that had been violently evicted from their material bodies. According to legend they lived only short and tormented lives once they were forced outside the protected existence of their normal bodies.

But there were still some things she could not understand. "The stories always said that preta looked the same as the material body that they came from?"

"They do, dear, they do, when they are first forced from the body. It can be quite disconcerting to suddenly see two of someone, one material and one praanin," explained Karlin. "But with these children the violence of their expulsion seems to leave them damaged in some way, physically and possibly emotionally too. After a remarkably short time they begin to distort and to shrink and to fade. It's almost as if they are aging before your eyes. It has been fascinating to study."

Asha pushed down the disgust she felt at Karlin's tone of indifference and asked quietly, "But how is it that Ellie and the others are still alive? In the stories it was always how narun like him," she gestured with renewed hatred toward Sando, "killed humans and animals for which they had no more use. In the stories such frail beings have only a short existence outside the body. It is told that they die in great pain and torment."

"Yes, they do die. It is regrettable. But, as you see, we are learning. By careful selection we have been able to extract preta from these specially gifted children and they continue to live. Many still don't live very long, but some live for months, and Eloise is one of the best at almost a year. If only her mother had survived the car

213

crash. With both parents still alive we could have more carefully studied the DNA implications. As it is you tell us John can now see you too, these are indeed exciting times.

"And that's why we need more research and why we need your help. Don't you see? These few sacrifices are needed so that in the future we may be able to extend the lives of great men." From the gleam in his eye it was obvious Karlin included himself under this appellation. "You narun are long-lived. According to your own legends some have lived for thousands of years. By the time my research is complete we humans will be able to share in this bounty. In the distant future I will be famous – I could even be still alive to see it!"

Asha glanced toward Sando. This was not something he could want, even if he was currently helping Karlin, but no expression escaped that anonymous silver suit.

Karlin leaned forward, excited by the thoughts of his eventual success, "I have a theory that some human ghost stories could be based on preta, that there may be circumstances that allow the prana being to escape from the body without the violence you call acintya."

Asha spared Sando another glance, there were some tales he had not bothered to share with Karlin, or perhaps he did not know them. There were indeed stories of humans that had been able to voluntarily withdraw their praanin body from their material body, *and* return to it again. They were tales from ancient history, as close as the narun got to fairy stories, and few took them seriously. Whereas tales of acintya and the preta were something altogether more serious, also from history, but more recent and with an aspect so dark and ugly that they could only be considered horror stories.

Karlin, oblivious, continued, "If I can find those circumstances we may be able to avoid the pain that the children currently experience as a result of their extraction, and if we can achieve that we may not keep losing them."

"Why aren't you keeping them with trees or some other form of life?" Asha asked him. "Surely it is no wonder that they fade and die in those cells."

"We did try, dear, but they are incapable of merging or taking sustenance from the trees or ponds. Indeed, until what you did for

214

Eloise, there has been only one form of sustenance available to them. They can draw life from living humans, but since that tends to be detrimental to the health of the human playing breakfast, you can understand that it gets rather expensive and inconvenient to feed them that way.

"Now you, my dear, now you open up a whole new world of possibilities. Do you suppose your talent could be taught to others of your kind?"

Asha glared at him. "I don't even know what it is that I did, with Ellie or with the trees."

"No, no, I thought that was likely. We'll just have to experiment a little won't we. And no time like the present. Fetch our lackeys please, Sando."

Barry and Cameron were fetched and they carried her cage to the same cell that she had occupied with Ellie. It appeared to be set the same as before, but when Asha crept out of the carry cage and into her half of the cell she could see that it was not Ellie on the bed. Barry and Cameron left the room but Karlin and Sando remained.

"Just be careful, dear," said Karlin. "We don't want a repeat of the other day, but we do need to know whether your talent works with more than just Eloise."

The small grey creature on the bed sat up and turned its pale, blank eyes in her direction. Slowly it rose and came toward her. Asha reduced her size so that the creature's head now came to her waist. As it embraced her she could recognise the essence, this was the creature she had met first, the one that Karlin had called Vincent. She felt its hunger trying to drain her essence but had no difficulty in preventing the loss. Her experience with Ellie had taught her much greater control even at this much finer level, she could now prevent any of her essence draining to Vincent.

"Excellent, excellent," came Karlin's approving tone from the other side of the clear divide as he stared into the apertures of his various equipment.

With no prana coming from Asha to feed his insatiable hunger, Vincent soon released his embrace and wandered slowly back to the bed.

"Good, good," Karlin said, "you have learned a great deal since last you met Vincent. Now, let's see you actually let him feed, dear.

Carefully, very carefully."

Asha looked out at Karlin, reluctant to obey but interested for herself. She needed to know more about this change that had taken place within her, she needed to know she could control it. Karlin had one of his ray-gun devices clearly visible amongst his other equipment, but he made no move to use it or to threaten with it. Finally Asha decided she would proceed, there seemed little to be gained by resisting.

She walked to the bed, sat down on the end, and drew Vincent's frail figure to her. Hugging the creature she felt its arms automatically embrace her and felt its hunger searching for sustenance. Asha pushed her senses into the figure, searching for the being beyond the need. She could feel its hunger dragging at her, but she kept it at bay while she searched for the child that Vincent had been. Slowly her perception pierced deeper and slowly the impression of a young boy, perhaps seven or eight years old, formed within her mind. She could see the slender, fair-haired boy, shy and stuttering among strangers but cheeky and imaginative with his friends. She felt that she could almost see the loving parents beyond the boy and her heart broke.

She opened herself to the boy, stopped fighting off his hunger, and felt him draw upon the essence of her being. It felt like she was being sucked down a vortex of need. The golden beam of her life swirled from her breast to the boy's, and was swallowed up like water on sand. She heard sounds coming at her, "No, no, dear girl. Slowly, slowly," but she no longer recognised it as Karlin. There was only the lovely and loving boy and his desperate need.

But something inside herself did awaken and begin to draw back. Falling into the vortex was no longer a new sensation. Her sense of survival recognised the threat, and this time she had not thrown herself into the need, there was time for her to react to the danger. Slowly the flow was closed, slowly she began to resist Vincent's hunger, and slowly she began to gain control over how much she could afford to give.

"Yes, yes, my pretty dryad, that's it, that's it. You've got it," came the satisfied voice she now recognised again as Karlin.

She was tempted to try and open up again, to completely drain herself, to free herself from Karlin and his plans, but knew she could never complete it before he found some way to intervene. Gradually she closed herself off to Vincent. With his need no longer being fed he was easily detached and she laid him back down on the bed.

She got up from the bed, feeling weak and tired but not dangerously so. Karlin was right, whatever this new skill was, she had already learned some control. She did wonder how much difference this new control really made. What would she do now, if she was faced with Ellie in the same desperate need as before?

She walked to the clear divide and stared hatred at Karlin and the anonymous silver suit of Sando. She had never before felt anything close to the aggression she had seen so regularly in humans, but now? ... Knowing who this boy had been, knowing who Ellie had been, and knowing what these monsters had done to them. ... In her frustration she couldn't complete a coherent thought. Now she was learning anger. Now she was learning hate. Now she was learning what could drive the violence she had seen in others. She wanted to strike out at someone, but there was nothing she could do to release the feelings that were swelling inside her.

Karlin was oblivious. "Wonderful, wonderful. Yes, my dear, wonderful. Come along then, back into the cage. I want to take some measurements and get you back to a tree. Can't stop here, there's so much more to discover."

Powerless to fight back or to defend herself, Asha did as she was bid. Back in the examination room the usual tests were run, and Karlin continued his inane chatter. He didn't notice that Asha made no responses, that she was suffering from a rage and frustration beyond anything that she had ever experienced. In her mind Asha continued to go over and over what these people had done. She didn't know how to express such extreme emotions even had she been free to do so.

Karlin's last words before he sent her back to the prison cage were, "Please use up the tree as much as you can, my dear. We've plenty of trees but not a lot of time. So use it up, dear, get yourself together again. We've lots to discover. There's a good girl."

The examination finished and she was taken to a different, smaller, prison cage. This one held only a single tree platform. Across the concrete cavern she could see Ceeda and other prisoners looking at her, but it was too much effort to try and speak with them, and she had no idea what she would say even if they were closer. She was almost grateful to be alone.

She watched Sando and the humans leave and then she looked around the cavern, but she was no longer paying attention to what was before her eyes. All she could see were the preta and the children they had been, their faces flashed alternately across her mind and mixed in with them was the smiling face of Karlin and the anonymous silver mask of Sando.

Emotions boiled and swirled inside her. Unconsciously her hands clenched into fists and then released, clenched and released. She turned, but still her eyes took in nothing that they saw. Absently she climbed the platform and approached the tree. There was no thought, no sequence of ideas, just this maelstrom of emotions.

She put her hand to the tree to begin merging and the pent-up anger and frustration finally, suddenly, burst loose. She was totally unprepared for the speed at which the unfamiliar emotions overwhelmed her, and there was only the tree in front of her.

She didn't just merge, she tore into it. Inside the tree her frustration found outlet in silent, angry screams that echoed through every part of the tree. Blind and unthinking in her anger, Asha dragged at the tree's essence, ripped at it and tore it free from the timber. Pulling up from the roots and down from the leaves she burned through the trunk and branches like fire. The heat of her rage fed on itself and on the release it found in destruction. Asha's fury grew hotter and larger – the tree stood no chance. Tearing the essence from every part, she consumed its life. Less than an hour later Asha fell from the dead trunk that could no longer support her.

Lying on the musty dirt of the platform Asha stared up into the already browning leaves, some of them looked blackened as if by actual flames. Her anger was now gone, perhaps consumed in the burning heat she had felt inside the tree. She reached her hand out to the now cold, dead trunk. "I am so sorry my friend." Tears came because she knew it was too late, the tree was dead, there was almost nothing left of what made it a living thing. In frustration she had lost control, had lost her mind. In her anger she had killed an innocent. To Karlin it may only be a tree, but to her it was a home, a friend, a life ... and she had taken it for no better reason than it was there when she lost control. She curled up tightly on the ground and cried herself to sleep.

* * *

Asha presumed it was the next day that they came for her again. She was pleased to be taken from the corpse of the tree that she had killed, the proof and reminder of her abject failure. She was surprised to be left alone in the examination room for quite some time. When Karlin arrived he was all cheers and smiles.

"Astounding, simply astounding. My wonderful, wonderful, dryad, will you never cease to amaze us? Sando and I have just been down to look over the tree you had for dinner last night."

Asha cringed at Karlin's cheerful disregard for the life she had taken.

"Amazing. Sando suggests the tree is about as dead as they come. We've sent it next door for them to study. He he! I wonder what they'll come back with. What do you think, Sando, are they likely to make any good guesses?" Karlin didn't wait for a response from Sando, he probably didn't expect one, instead he looked avidly at Asha in her cage.

"Let's get you out of there and take a good look, shall we?"

The tests proceeded as usual with Karlin once again muttering happily to himself. "Imagine if you could all do this, eh? We'd probably run out of trees, he he, but it would be worth it. The study we could get done."

The tests completed and the equipment put away, Karlin rubbed his hands together. "Let's get a bit more adventurous today, shall we? A bit more adventurous?" He looked at his watch. "Darren should be just about ready for us I think. Go and check would you, Sando."

A few minutes later Darren came in with Barry and Cameron. The latter pair carried Asha in her cage, out and down the corridor. Asha was dismayed to recognise that they were heading to the hall lined with the silent children, the preta. Carried through the doors into that corridor she could see that things had changed. The far end had been rearranged into a single larger cell. The clear wall leading into it had a special double-door arrangement, like an airlock. Both doors currently stood open.

As Asha was carried down the corridor she was able to recognise Ellie. The brief glimpse suggested that Ellie was much better than

219

when Asha had seen her last, though still not as mobile as the others. Asha also recognised Vincent in the cell she had first visited, but her cage was carried past them and on and through the double doors at the end. Her cage was set on the floor of this new larger cell.

Already on the floor of this cell there were half-a-dozen other cages, a single preta lay inside each. Also in the cell was another narun in a silver suit. The humans left and the inner door was closed. Barry exited and closed the outer door leaving Cameron inside the lock. The narun still in the cell set about opening the door to each of the cages, opening Asha's cage last. It then moved carefully to the lock and Cameron opened the inner door to let the narun into the lock. He closed the inner door and they both moved to the outside.

Asha climbed from her cage. She was not sure what to expect. The silence of the hall was disturbed today by the breathing and movement of the audience outside the cell. Barry, Cameron and Darren tended to gaze about, looking for any sign that there was something in the cell, but Karlin was intent. He had set up monitoring equipment and kept glancing from it to the cell to make sure he was getting everything he wanted.

Some of the preta began to stir and climb out of their cages. Occasionally one would touch the mesh of the cage as they climbed past the door and would jerk away in response to the burning sensation, but none of them made a sound. Some were stronger than others but all looked very fragile and all had stretched grey skin and milky unseeing eyes. Despite knowing what they were, Asha still had difficulty thinking of these creatures as the children they had been. She knew now that it could be different, that she could look into each and find something of the child locked inside, but she wondered whether she could stand to do so. The two she already knew had broken her heart, could she really stand to add six more?

The first, the largest one whose head still barely reached to the top of her legs, came toward her. She allowed it to embrace her, running her hand around its head in an attempt at affection.

"That's good, that's good, my dear. Slowly does it," came Karlin's voice.

Asha ignored him and watched the next of the preta approach. It hugged her other leg. A third approached and then a fourth. She could feel their hunger dragging at her but she resisted. There were too many, to give at all here would be to give too much.

The fifth and sixth tried to approach, but those already trying to embrace her were in the way. Frustrated they began to try and pull the others away from her. Since they had found no sustenance those closest gave way and let the smaller ones through.

"Good, good. That's good, my little dryad, let them sort themselves out." Karlin continued his approval.

After a while the preta gave up and moved away from Asha. The larger ones moved toward the clear divide, apparently attracted there by their sense of the life that existed on the other side. Asha could see that the preta from most of the other cells were also standing as close to the audience as they could.

"Now pick one out and let it have a little feed," instructed Karlin.

Asha looked at him in frustration. She really didn't want to do this.

"Come on, dear, we have things to learn. Please, don't make me insist."

Reluctantly Asha moved to comply. She reduced her size and picked up one of the smaller preta. She braced herself and then pushed her senses past its hunger. She found him quite quickly, she was getting better at this. A small boy, dark and serious, very young, maybe four years old. She patted the back of his head and felt the sadness swelling inside her, but she pushed the pity down, she needed to stay in control. Slowly she opened herself to his hunger.

"Yes, yes. Well done, dear," came Karlin's voice.

As the energy started to flow between her and the small boy the other preta in this cell and all the other cells turned in perfect synchronisation, they could feel the energy flowing. At once they all moved toward her, those in the other small cells were quickly blocked, but the other five in the cell with her came and tried to embrace her. When they still obtained no sustenance they started to try and climb her and to try and pull away the preta of the young boy receiving the energy.

Asha, concentrating on the young boy and controlling how much she gave to his hunger, was largely oblivious to what the others were doing.

Karlin watched with growing concern as the preta in the cell got more and more desperate. "You'd better get in there, Minzi," he demanded of one of the narun. "She may need some help. Cameron, help Minzi get through."

The preta were no longer just pulling at the young boy receiving the flow, now they were trying to draw directly from him, but without success.

"Stop now, dear, stop. Before things get out of hand," said Karlin.

Asha didn't hear him but was deciding for herself to pull back, to resist the hunger drawing at her while she still had control.

She had barely closed herself off to the boy when she heard Karlin yelling, "No, no. You fool! Get the hell out of there!"

Asha looked over to see that Cameron must have misunderstood Karlin's instructions. Seeing no obvious danger he had followed the silver suited narun into the cell rather than staying in the lock. Now that the flow of energy between Asha and the small boy had stopped, all the preta in the cell had turned and reached toward the other source of life that they sensed close by.

Cameron jerked his hands into the air with a howl of pain when he felt small fingers trying to take hold of him. He swivelled around to try and get back to the door but tangled with and fell over the small creatures that he could not see. As he fell to the floor he landed on one of the preta. The others climbed over him, clawing at whatever part of him they could reach. The buttons tore from his shirt and exposed his chest. When the hand of a preta touched exposed skin it would draw back slowly, and with it draw up Cameron's prana, pulling it beyond the protection of his body. A translucent, fragile, inner skin that their hungry mouths tore at and then drank the glowing liquid prana that spilled from the wound. In their hunger they sucked at the gash they had made, trying to draw on the liquid more quickly.

Asha watched the substance of Cameron's life spilling from the mouths of the preta, a glowing golden fluid that smeared their faces and ran down their necks before dissipating in a faint golden steam. Much more was being lost than they were managing to consume.

Cameron screamed. The touch of the invisible hands seemed to dig deep into his body, the reach of each finger tip like a hot blade tearing through him. He writhed in pain. The preta under his body stopped moving but the others clung on and kept feeding from him. In the extremity of his pain Cameron couldn't think clearly or move coherently, the clumsy flailing of his limbs did little to disturb the determined feeding of the preta.

The suited narun and Asha ran forward and began to try and pull the preta off him. The preta were too weak to resist being pulled away, but as soon as they were released they returned to start drawing from Cameron again and his screaming continued.

"Get them back in their cages, Minzi, then we'll get that fool out," yelled Karlin over the noise.

"Use the ray-gun," said Barry, scrabbling at the equipment near Karlin.

"Get away," Karlin said, and pushed Barry back.

Darren came from behind and restrained Barry while he whispered fiercely into his ear. Slowly Barry stopped struggling.

Karlin continued, "Cameron's a lot easier to replace than the preta. It's his own stupid fault, he's been warned."

Asha tried to help, pulling preta away and handing them to the narun who quickly closed each in a cage. Cameron fell silent as the second last preta was pulled away. Asha thought he had probably fainted. Asha and the suited narun had to work together to roll Cameron off the last of the preta. The small creature from underneath was still alive, but only barely.

"Can you help it?" called Karlin through the divide.

Unable to stand watching it suffer, Asha held it close and reached her senses past its hunger. A young girl, a similar age to Ellie but this one darker, brash and loud. A real little hell-raiser, Asha thought, and smiled to herself as she opened to the girl's hunger, letting her draw slowly at Asha's being.

In the cages in the cell the preta tried to get closer to the energy transfer that they could sense, only to be burnt by the mesh of the cages and jerk back. Again and again they tried.

"Enough, dear, enough. The others may get damaged," called Karlin, but Asha didn't hear.

As the child drew on her essence Asha felt a flutter, an uncertainty in the flow. The strength of its feeding fell away. She followed the energy flows with her senses and found jagged tears in the girl's side from which the energy was dispersing – everything she gave was being lost, along with the essence of the child herself.

Asha sank to the floor and nursed the girl on her lap while she tried to investigate the wound with one hand. When she drew her hand back it was covered with the warm golden fluid of the girl's life. She watched the essence dissipating from her skin, steaming into a light golden mist that quickly faded into nothing. She tried to draw together the tears in the girl's side with her fingers, to seal the wounds closed, but they refused to stay. She tried covering the wounds to block the escape of the girl's prana, but the fluid continued to bleed out past her fingers. She could feel the girl's life ebbing away and her attempts became ever more desperate, but nothing she did made any difference.

Finally, reluctantly, Asha was forced to close herself off. There was nothing she could do and her gift was only prolonging the girl's pain.

Asha cradled the girl in her arms and rocked her back and forth. She could feel the spirit start to fade from the body. The suited narun tried to take the child but Asha clung to her. "In a minute," she whispered, "she'll be gone in a minute."

All too soon the time passed and Asha felt the last faint warmth of life leave the body in her arms. What was left may have been made from the stuff of life but it was no longer alive itself, the spirit had gone. She held the remains out to the narun. "She's gone."

The narun took the remains and placed it in a carry cage. Within hours the remaining prana of the fragile corpse would dissipate leaving nothing left to show that it had ever been. Asha stared down at her hands and studied the golden fluid that still clung to them, it too was almost gone now.

Without looking up Asha called out to Karlin, "What was her name?" For reasons she could not explain it seemed important. She watched the golden steam drift into nothingness as the last of the girl's life evaporated from her skin, the last evidence of Asha's attempts to save her.

"In your cage now, dear, we need to get Cameron out," said Karlin, ignoring the question.

"What was her name?" Asha called more loudly, angry now, not moving.

"Katarina," he replied. "Now, please dear, into your cage."

Asha did as she was asked. She curled up inside her cage remembering the brash little girl whose life she had felt fade. She watched with little interest as Barry and Darren came through the lock, someone had fetched a stretcher. As they loaded Cameron he groaned. Asha saw that one of his hands looked pale and cold as if drained of blood, but she knew it was worse than that, it had been drained of life. She wondered whether he would lose the hand, or more.

A while later she was back in the examination room, Karlin running his usual series of tests.

"Will Cameron be all right?" Asha asked him.

Karlin waved away the enquiry with, "Darren will take care of him."

As he packed up his things Karlin said, "It's always a set back to lose one of the preta, but Katarina was one of our stronger ones and she will be sorely missed. However, as unfortunate as today's events may have been, at least now you have seen some of what we face. Until we found you the only way that the preta could feed was as you saw with Cameron.

"It's a shame you couldn't help Katarina, but now we have learned some of the limits to your talent. You see? Even these little set backs have their bonuses. Now, if only we could work out what it is you share with the preta."

Asha said nothing but her shocked expression must have been clear enough.

"Now, now, dear. Of course you share something with the preta. All other narun are inherently limited in their ability to share or consume prana. To all others it is a slow process. They must merge with their tree or their river and slowly absorb from the life that surrounds them. To you, however, such limits are gone or vastly increased. You can draw on a source incredibly fast and give it away even faster. You've seen the preta, dear, you've felt them feed. Don't you see the similarity? They have no limits either. Well, no obvious limits once they find something compatible."

"Acintya?" Asha questioned.

"Oh no, dear, no, that has nothing to do with this. Pushing the prana of another life from its material body is not absorbing that prana, it is just pushing it out of the way with your superior strength and density, like some strange form of wrestling. No, dear, you saw what you did with that tree last night. You didn't push the prana from the tree, you absorbed it, or a significant part of it. You sit here today almost as large and healthy as you were when you first arrived, despite all that has happened since. That's quite incredible dear. You are a treasure – so much so that you have a special visitor arriving tomorrow."

Asha just stared at him, another human more or less gawking at her in the cells meant very little to her.

"No excitement I see. Dear, dear. My pretty little dryad, this personage is responsible for having set all this up." Karlin waved his arm in an all-encompassing gesture. "So you really must be on your best behaviour."

Asha must have looked surprised because Karlin continued, "Oh no, my dear, I may be the brains behind the research, and so many of our discoveries, but your visitor tomorrow was the one with the vision, the money and the insight to make it possible. As much as it pains me to say it, I would be no one – less – without him."

Returned to her solitary cell, Asha found a fresh tree waiting for her. She approached cautiously, remembering her rage from the night before, but she need not have worried. This night she was sad rather than angry, disturbed rather than frustrated. Sad for the loss of Katarina and for all the preta. Disturbed because she had always assumed Karlin was responsible for all this harm, and that was bad enough, but to find that he worked for another was disquieting to say the least.

Slowly, carefully, she merged into the tree. She needed its comfort if not its sustenance. Spreading herself through the tree she concentrated on what she found there, finding respite from her worries in the familiarity of caring for a tree.

* * *

The next day it was Darren, Ian and, she presumed, Sando that came to fetch her. She was taken directly to the smaller cell, the one in which she had been with Ellie and then Vincent. Released into the enclosed half she saw that it had been divided again, a clear partition separating her from the bed in the corner on which Ellie lay silent and still.

226

"The divide is just a precaution, dear," came Karlin's voice from the door. "We don't want any dramatics today while our visitors are here. Please, excuse us while we go to greet our guests."

Asha, alone in her half cell, looked across at Ellie. She called, but there was no response. She reached out with her senses and could feel her there. She could confirm that Ellie was much stronger than she had been, but still weaker than any of the other preta that Asha had seen. Unable to touch Ellie, there was nothing more Asha could do than wait.

It was not long. The door was opened by Darren and in walked a man with sparse red hair. He was larger and more heavily built even than Darren. He was dressed in a sharply pressed business suit, but had a build and stance more fitted to a weightlifter. Behind him came a small figure. At first Asha thought it was a human teenager, dressed as it was in jeans and a sweatshirt with the hood pulled up over its head. Then her vedana reached past the clothing to the narun underneath. He was a strangely intense figure, a narun like none she had ever met before, or so she thought. There looked to be some sort of music player attached to his belt with leads running up under the hood. The face was mostly obscured inside the hood but what little was visible was oddly distorted to Asha's senses. Behind the visitors came Karlin, beaming with the pleasure of showing off his prize exhibits. Sando entered last and took his usual place near the door.

Darren closed the door and the visitors looked on into the cell. Karlin appeared to be almost bursting with the desire to speak, but must have known from experience when to keep quiet.

"So this is the pair you've been trying to bring together for the past year," said the large man. "This is the dryad you had Jaimee and I go looking for, and all those expense accounts for wasted trips to the forest?"

"Yes, Walt, these are they. It really has proved to be worth all the effort. On the right there you see Eloise Caldor, preta for almost twelve months. She was in the process of dying when we finally reunited her with Asha, the pretty and elusive little dryad on the left. The result was remarkable, well, you saw the reports."

"Yes, Henry, we saw them. You came very close to losing this one after all that effort," Walt responded in a deep voice. "You really should be more careful. Does she speak?"

"She's not been all that talkative." To Asha, Karlin continued, "Good morning, dear, won't you say hello to Mr Waldron Stephenson, my benefactor and your host?"

Asha just glared at them.

The narun dressed as a teenager walked closer to the clear divide and stared intently at Asha. Now that it was closer Asha could see that the face beneath the hood flickered slightly like an improperly tuned television set – it was only the projection of a face. She couldn't see past the projection, which left her wondering what the narun actually looked like. This narun had the human teenager slouch and careless walk almost to perfection, she imagined it must have studied the role for a long time.

"And this dear friend is Jaimee," said Karlin, "or as he prefers to be known, Jamie Stephenson. They find it a convenient fiction for him to act as Walt's son."

Asha glared back at the narun and wondered about the relationship between this traitor to her people and the large human. Who was master and who was slave, and what was it they hoped to gain?

Before this strangely intense narun Asha felt exposed, as if she were naked beyond the protection of mere clothing. There was no buzzing sensation like that from the Karlin-Field, there was not even any evidence that the narun truly watched, since its real face remained hidden behind the mask, but still Asha felt that she was being analysed more deeply than ever before. An involuntary shiver swept through her body.

To her surprise the mask inside the hood took on the appearance of a smile. She noticed that one of its hands was adjusting a control on the device at its belt, the other hand, visible to Stephenson, gave a subtle twitch. Both hands looked to be encased in skin coloured gloves.

Stephenson said to Karlin, "Okay, Henry, let's see what we came to see."

Asha saw the projected smile grow wider before returning to its original blank expression and believed she had just been told something that not even Karlin knew.

Karlin spent a minute checking his monitoring equipment and

then gestured to Darren who came forward to the intersection of the clear walls and pulled a lever. A door that Asha hadn't noticed earlier opened in the clear divide separating her from Ellie.

"There you go, dear. Please go to your friend," said Karlin.

Asha looked at her captors and then across to Ellie. As much as she didn't like cooperating with her captors it was obvious that Ellie needed what only she could provide. She went to Ellie. As she sat on the end of the bed the preta that was Ellie had the strength to sit up and drag itself toward her. Asha leant forward and gently lifted the fragile body into an embrace.

Gently this time, Asha nudged her senses into the creature, exploring its body looking for damage. There were many places that in a human would probably be called bruised, but otherwise there was just the extreme weakness of starvation and the distortions caused by emotional and spiritual torment. There was little that Asha could do for the emotional or spiritual problems, but she could at least ameliorate the starvation.

Asha opened herself slowly to the weak tugging of the creature's hunger. "Yes, my darling," she whispered gently, stroking the creature and remembering the beautiful child she had once been. "Drink, my darling," she murmured and opened herself wider as the thirst drawing at her strengthened. The energy flowed through the skin of her breast to that of the creature, a golden beam from her heart to Ellie's. She felt in control of the flow in a way she had not achieved before. It felt comfortable and right, and somehow satisfying. Gently pushing her senses through the child in her arms she could feel its fragile body absorbing this new energy. There was not enough for growth, but there was enough to add strength and substance to the almost transparent body, there was, perhaps, enough to extend her life.

Unheard by Asha in her devotions, Karlin was enthusing to his guests, "Isn't she something? Every time it happens it's as though she has refined the talent further."

"And she's in no danger?" asked Stephenson's deep voice.

"Oh, I think she was at first, but no longer," Karlin paused and then hurried on, "but given the near tragedy of the first encounter we will be careful just in case."

"Enough, dear, enough," he called into the cell. Even now he seemed unaware of how little Asha knew of what was happening around her, that she was effectively in a trance.

But Jaimee could see, he was paying very careful attention to what happened in the cell. One of his hands gave another subtle twitch.

"Let her go a bit longer," suggested Stephenson, "let's see what she does on her own."

Asha could feel the child growing stronger in her arms and with that strength the hunger drew more fiercely at Asha's being. Slowly, carefully, Asha began to close herself off. "Gently, my darling," she murmured as she felt the hunger trying to tear at her. She pushed her senses deeper, feeling for the child she knew was there. Just for a moment she felt a flash of personality that she recognised as Ellie. "I'm here, my darling," she called as the moment faded.

Feeling weak herself now, Asha closed off completely. The hunger was still tearing at her but was no longer being satisfied. After a few minutes Ellie's embrace slackened and Asha laid her back down on the bed. Getting up from the bed Asha came back to awareness of the cell and herself. She felt weary and, looking down, she could see that she was significantly reduced, but she did not feel the crippling weakness from her first experience with Ellie.

"Wonderful, wonderful," came Karlin's voice. "Now back on your side please, dear."

Asha looked back at the apparently sleeping figure of Ellie on the bed, reluctant to leave.

"Please, dear," said Karlin more firmly.

Asha climbed back into her portion of the cell and the door in the divide was closed.

"So what do you think, Walt?" asked Karlin. "Worth dragging you down here to witness?"

"Yes, Henry, you were right, the reports did not do justice. And she can regain her size and strength in just a few days?" asked Stephenson.

"So it seems, so it seems. She may even be able to recover faster if we had more substantial trees," said Karlin, a hopeful tone to his voice.

"Yes, I think I would like to see her at the Estate too, Henry – although I wouldn't like to see her do to our trees what she did to the one here – they do take time to grow."

"But if we can find out how she does it, if we can get others to do it too, we may at last have what we need to try and recover the preta," said Karlin, enthusiasm filling his voice.

Stephenson looked doubtful. "I agree that more like her would make a useful resource, but I am still not convinced that your preta have any future. To me they look permanently damaged by the process of extraction. I think we have to find another way."

"I am looking, Walt, I am looking."

Both men looked in at Asha, each pondering their own thoughts.

"And what about this John Caldor? When can we expect more news of him?" asked Stephenson.

"Soon, we hope. From what Ian could tell us, Caldor has come to the city looking for this one," said Karlin pointing to Asha. "So we expect him to be around, we're just waiting for him to show himself and then Darren here can pick him up."

Stephenson looked at the brawny figure of Darren Davies. "You will be careful not to damage him?" he said. More of a command than a question.

Darren nodded.

Looking back at Karlin, Stephenson continued, "If Caldor would cooperate he could be very useful."

Asha didn't know whether to be hopeful or to despair. How had John followed her here? How could he hope to help her? What would happen if he was captured? Asha looked across at Ellie. What would he do when he learned about his daughter?

14. Uncle

John put the remains of his tasteless sandwich back in its plastic wrapper. He was eating because it was lunchtime, not because he was hungry. Sitting alone in the car he had finally found a place from which he could look down on the site occupied by the Forest Conservation Research Centre. If you believed the signs around the site, the FCRC was a joint venture between the government and a company called Vanadevatas – which Darnu had interpreted for him as meaning forest-gods. As Andrei had put it, "No inferiority complexes here."

According to Ian this is where John would have been brought, and the company name left little doubt in John's mind that Ian had told him the truth. The research centre occupied all of a very large, level block in the industrial estate. There was only one building, several stories high, at the front and centre of the rectangular block. Around the back and sides of the building, covering the rest of the block, were trees of various sizes and species. Very few were planted directly into the ground. Most were in large pots or huge platforms on rollers that John had watched them move ponderously around. Occasionally specimens were taken into the building itself. There were also a few platforms of water plants, looking like small overgrown swimming pools.

The centre had remained quite busy even over the weekend and today, Monday, had been even busier. John fervently hoped that most of the activity was related to genuine research – the idea that all of those people could be involved in a conspiracy against the aaranya was terrifying. As it was, the amount of money that it must have taken to set up such a place in the city was something else to worry about: people with that much money could buy a lot of influence.

"Why here?" John had asked himself several times, but so far had come up with no answers.

According to the public relations blurb that John had been able to find, it was the huge mobile forest that had made the centre unique. The ability to move and isolate trees for various experiments, and the ability to move trees to equipment permanently set up inside the building, were features that provided new possibilities in forestry research. In addition to research the centre also extracted rare oils from several species of tree and collected unusual timber formations that resulted from some of the experiments, as these were of particular interest to sculptors and furniture makers. Profits from the sale of these helped to offset the cost of running the centre, or so it was reported.

But none of that helped John to find an anonymous way into the building. The only entrances to the centre appeared to be well secured.

Every now and then John would feel the buzzing sensation of the detector going past. He soon correlated these events with a blue van, but it never came close enough for him to identify the driver. A few times he watched it leaving or entering the centre via an entrance to the underground car park, but that had a human guard and a boom gate, so there was no sneaking in that way. This morning he'd watched a posh looking limousine with very dark windows enter the car park and he wondered who their VIP was, and whether he was involved. It didn't occur to John that he may have already met the occupants of the car.

They had discussed trying to get one of his aaranya friends closer, to see if their life sense could detect anything more, but it was going to be dangerous. The centre was full of trees but there were no large trees for a few blocks outside the centre, so there was nowhere to hide quickly if the detector came past. It also had to be presumed that there were narun in the centre, narun who would be able to sense others nearby if they bothered to look.

So John had watched the centre alone. Watched and thought ... and thought and thought, but so far no bright ideas for getting into the building had occurred to him. He was starting to think he would have to let these people take him and see what happened after that.

By the time the sun was setting he was tired and frustrated. He drove back to the building where he had obtained a short term lease on a furnished apartment, it was pretty easy if you had no respect for money. He took the lift to the fourth floor and walked down the oppressive, narrow corridor to his room. A single glance took in the small room, clean and tidy, but sterile and unwelcoming. Exactly how they managed to make these look so attractive in the photos he would never know, but he was hardly ever here so he guessed that it hardly mattered.

He had a long hot shower and then reheated the congealing Chinese takeaway he had brought back with him. He sat down to eat and thought back over the last few days.

Senna had surprised them all by leading them closer to the city centre rather than further away. She explained that the city narun preferred to run from the detector rather than risk hiding in a tree and being trapped. In the complex streets of the older part of the city it was very difficult for anyone in a vehicle to follow you, so difficult that they rarely bothered to try.

During the days, while John was watching the research centre, Senna led the others around the city trying to find others that she knew. So far they had had only limited success. Just as Senna had told them, the city narun were now a suspicious people. They had seen only two of the jalaja, the river-folk, and those had refused to come anywhere near them. The few aaranya they had found had been polite enough, because they knew Senna, but refused outright to come anywhere near John – trusting another of the tree-folk was one thing, but a human was another matter entirely.

His friends spent their nights in some fine old trees in a park across a busy road from John's apartment block. Senna was gradually teaching the others how to get around the city without letting humans run into them by accident. It wasn't easy and the roads could be fatal if they got it wrong. There had been a few embarrassing bumps and, of course, Andrei couldn't resist having a little fun along the way, leaving humans wondering what was happening around them.

Late in the evening, after he had eaten and rested, John would cross the road and wander into the park. The first nights had been

Friday and the weekend which meant that they had to share the park with drunks: the old ones mostly bumbling around, the young ones mostly throwing up. But drunks aren't very attentive so John was able to talk with his friends in the dim light of the park without attracting unwanted attention.

Tonight was Monday night, thought John as he crossed over the busy street and walked into the park. Hopefully that meant the park would be quiet, the drunks might be harmless but they were far from pleasant company. He settled on a park bench and hoped he would not have to wait too long.

A short time later Barma and Tilvy emerged from one of the trees.

"Hi there," called John, surprised to find how relieved he was to be with his friends at last. He hadn't realised how lonely he had been through the day.

Barma and Tilvy settled on the grass across from John's seat, each with an arm around the other. "Did you have a good day?" Tilvy asked.

John pulled a bit of a face. "Nothing new, unless you count some sort of VIP guest this morning. Anything with you guys?"

"We did meet Senna's father this afternoon," said Tilvy.

Her tone made John look carefully at both of their faces. "And?"

"He's weird," said Barma.

"Eccentric," Tilvy corrected, then thought for a moment before saying, "No. He is weird."

"Aren't all the city aaranya a bit strange to you?"

"There's strange," started Tilvy.

"And then there's weird," finished Barma. "And Taiza is definitely weird."

"Taiza is his name?" asked John.

"That's the first thing," said Tilvy. "Taiza is his name now, even Senna uses it, but from what we can gather it's sort of an assumed name."

"A *nom de guerre*, he called it," said Barma.

"Let me tell it," Tilvy admonished. "You know how Milla is unusually curious for an aaranya?"

John nodded.

"Well Taiza is sort of hands-on curious. He lives over near the bay in some of the oldest parts of the city, apparently it's where Senna grew up. He lives near these factories and stuff and spends lots of time in them watching the humans. He plays with the equipment when they're gone."

"He plays with electricity and furnaces and all sorts of stuff," put in Barma, astounded and in awe.

Tilvy slapped his arm lightly. "He seems obsessed by them," she continued. "Unlike Milla, who reads about all sorts of things, and only reads about them, Taiza watches and practices. It's almost like he wished he was human."

"And jumpy," started Barma.

Tilvy hit him harder. "Shush. The whole time we were there he was twitching like he was plugged into an electricity socket," she said. "I think it's probably bad nerves from playing with all that dangerous equipment.

"He was friendly enough, he just couldn't sit still. Senna was a bit defensive of him at the start, perhaps embarrassed by him, but you could tell they are still very close. When Taiza and Andrei got on well she relaxed again."

"I don't know that I'd prescribe Andrei for anyone with a nervous problem," said John.

"I know, I was surprised too. I think Andrei may have some of that curiosity bug too ... and he probably wanted to make a good impression anyway," she finished smugly.

"Is he going to be able to help us?"

"Taiza suggested someone over on the west side, said he probably knew more than anyone else. That's where the others have gone, but it meant they would be late getting back here so they sent Barma and me back to let you know what was happening."

The conversation continued into the dramas of trying to get around the city when its inhabitants couldn't see you. Picking your times and places and learning where to stand and walk.

"The blighters can't even be trusted to obey the street lights," complained Barma who'd almost been knocked over by a car that decided to go through a set of lights while they were still red.

"And rubbish. I can't believe how they just throw rubbish out the window," said Tilvy. She grinned. "We managed to give one or two a surprise when their rubbish magically flew back in."

Laughing, John said, "That sounds like an Andrei trick."

236

Hearing voices, John looked up hoping the others had arrived but instead saw three young men walking into the park. John pulled out his mobile phone so that he could pretend to be talking into it. "Yes, yes," he murmured into the phone as the men got near enough to hear him.

"What'd I tell you?" said one of the young men loudly. "He's gone into the park and must be sitting there alone in the dark, and *here* he is."

John pointed to his phone, trying to indicate that he was in the middle of a conversation.

The young man laughed, "Might help if you'd turn it on." His friends joined in the hilarity.

John cursed under his breath. Just what he needed, an observant mugger. In the dark of the park it was obvious that the phone was not active. Whatever had attracted them, the young men were definitely not minding their own business. John figured that couldn't mean anything good for him. He stood up and put the phone in his pocket. "I was just heading home," he told them.

The men spread across the path blocking the way back out of the park. "I need to make a phone call," the talker said.

"I can give you change for a phone booth," offered John.

"I thought I'd borrow your mobile," was the reply, "and maybe your wallet too?"

"Look guys," placated John, "I really don't want to start anything."

The talker slipped something from his pocket, there was a metallic click and something glinted in the dim light. John couldn't see it clearly but presumed it was a knife.

"Oh shit," said John.

The men all laughed. The talker agreed, "Yes, oh shit. Come on, just pass 'em over." The silvery glint waved in the night.

John tried once more, "I'm in enough trouble already. Any other time I'd be happy to let you have my phone and wallet, but I can't now. Please just leave."

The talker responded with another wave of the blade, "I don't want your life story, mate, just your wallet."

John looked across at Barma and Tilvy, who were standing, watching and wondering what they should do, he continued, "Now if

Andrei were here I'm sure he'd just throw a bit of rubbish and they'd go away." He pointed at the rubbish bin near the park bench.

The three men gave John a strange look, wondering what he was talking about, but they were quickly diverted when a half full can of soft drink hit the talker in the chest.

"Ouch, that would have hurt. Good shot, Barma," said John.

The other two were quickly hit with newspaper and other odds and ends from the rubbish bin. Some of the rubbish, too light to make the full distance, fluttered in the air between them.

The young men hesitated, unable to work out what was happening.

Not wanting to be outdone, Tilvy ran around behind the men and nudged the man with the knife in the ribs with her fingers. The man swung around so quickly that the blade connected with Tilvy's arm and she gave a short squeal.

Barma rushed forward and pushed the man very hard into one of his friends and they both went down in a jumble of arms and legs. Swearing indicated that the blade had connected with someone.

Barma picked up the can he had thrown first and emptied the final dregs over the pair on the ground and then dropped it on them. He went on quickly to Tilvy.

The three young men watched wide-eyed, even in the dim light of the park they could tell that the can had appeared to move on its own.

"Are you all right?" John called to Tilvy.

"I'm fine," she replied, "it's just a scratch. It surprised me more than it hurt."

"You'd better come back out of the way," John said to them as the two men on the ground sorted themselves out and stood up.

The three men looked around wondering who John had been talking to. The talker, the one with the knife, looked like he wanted to come at John again but one of his friends pulled on his arm making him twitch with fright. All three backed away cautiously and then jogged to the street and disappeared.

"Thanks guys and sorry, I didn't mean for you to get hurt," said John. He looked at Tilvy's arm. She was right, it was only a small cut and appeared to be closing even as John looked on. What caught his attention was that it did not bleed red, instead there was a glowing golden steam drifting slowly from the wound and he realised that it must be prana dissipating. As the wound closed over, the steam reduced and then vanished.

"It's okay, John," Tilvy reassured him. "Barma's making an unnecessary fuss," she continued, but looked with love and pride at the young man that had rushed to her aid. His look of concern had her whisper to him, "'I'm fine, Barma, really."

Their conversation was quiet for a while but gradually relaxed. It was more than an hour later that the others finally arrived. It was Andrei's laughter they heard first.

"Nerves of steel these humans," Andrei said loudly.

"You probably just caught him at a bad moment," said Darnu, but there was laughter in his voice too. "Anyway, you're not supposed to be attracting attention, particularly not so close to here."

As they arrived they all had smiles on their faces. Andrei called, "I take back everything bad I've ever said about you, Barmy, compared to these humans you have the courage of a lion."

Tilvy smiled up at Barma. "He's certainly courageous, Andrei, but what brought on your moment of enlightenment?"

Barma was looking a little embarrassed to be the centre of attention.

It was Senna who answered, "Some dork was standing at the corner of the park, fiddling with a knife in full view of the street if you can believe it. Along comes Andrei and tries another of his surprise-the-human-with-levitating-objects tricks—" She looked across at Andrei, "Don't you ever get sick of it?"

Andrei just grinned at her.

Senna continued, "In this case it was an empty soft drink can. The man stares at it like it's some sort of huge horrific monster, then he sort of squeaked and ran off like he thought the can was chasing him."

John laughed and grinned at Barma and Tilvy. "He must have thought that Barma's can-of-death had come to get him again." John went on to explain to the others what had happened earlier. "So thanks, Andrei, your little trick may have saved me a nasty surprise when I went back to the apartment.

"Any news?" he asked them.

Andrei grinned, "We finally found someone that wants to meet you, John. Not sure that that speaks well of his sanity, which is a shame since he also claims to be able to show us a way to avoid being found by the detector. He asked us to meet him tomorrow."

"Wow. That is news. Who is he, Senna?"

"Guyen is an odd-bod from way out on the west side. He's very old," Senna said, then she looked around at Darnu and Garjae and added, "by city standards. Most people think he's strange but he always seems to know everyone and what they're doing. That was true even when there were more of us around to know. Dad suggested him, said that if anything useful about *them* has been learned over the years then Guyen is the one who would know about it. Most of us call him Uncle."

* * *

The next morning John had an early breakfast and met briefly with his friends in the park. They agreed to meet at the address on the west side of the city, John would drive and the others would make their own way. John had suggested they risk the car but Senna was still not comfortable with the idea. The others started out and John went to have a second cup of coffee to give them time to get ahead, it would take them longer to get there.

When John pulled up at the destination he could see no sign yet of his friends. He looked out across what appeared to be part-park and part-children's-playground. John reached out with his life sense but could not detect any narun nearby, he supposed he must be early. There were a couple of children being watched over by a woman, their mother he assumed, as they played in a sandpit. There was also a figure in an overcoat or cloak with its hood up sitting on one of the park benches. It was still a cool morning but not so chilly that the apparel seemed justified. Suspicious, John approached the figure to get a closer look.

As he got close to the bench the hood turned and a rounded face, creased with age, grinned at him from within. "You must be John, the human that can see us." His voice was low and raspy with a suggestion of a chuckle.

"You're narun," John said in surprise. He saw that the man's cloak was a voluminous hooded cape that was pulled around his shoulders and hanging to the ground so that it completely covered his body.

Guyen looked at John with interest. "To properly meet a human at last. All these years living among them and I've never spoken with one. Such a strange way for us to live I've always thought."

John and Guyen chatted easily. There was something open and comforting about Guyen's round face, the deep wrinkles very much the laugh-lines of proverb.

"Here come your friends," Guyen noted, "let's see what they make of my costume."

John looked over the back of the park bench and could see his friends standing at the edge of the park looking across. They were hesitating so he waved to them. As they started forward, John looked across to the woman and two children, she was dusting the sand off the children and getting ready to go. John thought it was probably just as well. He looked around at the houses backing onto the park and he hoped that not too many people were at home looking out their windows right now.

His friends were about halfway to him when Senna called out, "Uncle?" The others looked at her and then looked more carefully at the figure seated next to John.

"Guyen!" said Darnu and Garjae together.

Guyen chuckled quietly next to John and said, "I wonder how close it would have been without young Senna, she's special that one." Guyen pulled back his hood and John was surprised to see that he was totally bald. The smooth shiny pate and his wrinkled face were revealed to be a deep tan colour like a human that had spent years in the sun.

John's aaranya friends gathered around the bench and looked at Guyen with new respect. "That's incredible," said Tilvy, "how do you do it?"

"What she really means," said Darnu with a smile, "is, good morning Guyen, we hope you are well this morning."

Andrei cut in, "Man who seeks to shock his guests should not be surprised with lack of courtesy. If that's not a Confucius saying it ought to be."

"You're probably right, Andrei," laughed Guyen, "but I think I may have proved my point. Before I fill you in on the details I suggest you go back to the edge of the park and take a more careful look." Guyen pulled the hood back over his head and sat there

241

waiting for them.

John sat where he was, he suspected that his senses weren't fine enough for another look to make any difference. A short while later the others returned still excited.

"I see what you mean," said Darnu, "from the edge of the park it is possible to determine that you are narun, but only just. Much further and none of us, with the possible exception of Senna, would have picked you for other than human, even if we were looking for you."

"So it wasn't just me," said John. "Although I should probably point out that I did think you looked suspicious, Uncle. A man in an overcoat sitting near a child's playground would be enough to raise the suspicion of most humans these days." When the others looked puzzled he continued, "I don't really want to go into it, just accept it. This may help you to hide from other narun but humans would look at you twice unless it's cold and wet enough to justify such clothing."

"That's good to know," said Guyen, "I've come to rely on this disguise more and more over the last year or so."

"The effect is from your disguise?" asked Darnu.

"Oh yes, it's simple enough." Guyen closed his eyes and a few moments later his cape and hood blurred and turned into an old-fashioned suit and trilby. The outfit looked well worn, like its wearer. "Try again now."

The effect was obvious to all, even John could feel Guyen's presence more clearly now that the cape and hood had vanished.

"Does it work against the detector?" asked John.

"Yes, or it did the last time I felt it, but that's some months ago now." said Guyen.

"Then why is it that no one else seems to use it?" asked Darnu.

"Simple enough," said Guyen, "everyone else just runs. They are not interested in camouflage. If they feel the detector they run, no awkward clothing need apply. You're the first people I've met that actually wanted to get closer."

"Any chance you guys will take the hint?" asked Senna.

"We're not that good with subtle," came Andrei's response.

Guyen ignored them, continuing, "I use it because I'm old. This will be my seventy-fifth winter. Running is not as easy as it was, so I hide. I hide in plain sight, I look like just another human in the crowd."

"It would not be much use in the forest," pointed out Barma, "not enough humans to get lost in."

"But useful here," said Garjae, "and that's what we need."

"Is it difficult?" asked Darnu.

"I was shown by one not much more than a child, back when the detector was still quite new, but you need a partner to practice with until you get the effect just right."

Guyen paused and looked around the group. "You spoke of the forest, Barma. A real forest, with a stand and a Glade? Things that I have only heard about in tales and yet you all come from such a place … amazing," he spoke with quiet awe.

"I would gladly take you to visit," said John.

"Or to stay," added Tilvy. Guyen had won the approval of at least one of them.

"After we finish our task here," concluded Darnu.

"Yes, your task. A moment." Guyen closed his eyes to concentrate and a few moments later his suit and trilby blurred and once again became a cape with a hood. "Feel this material. Sense it, I don't mind – can't afford to be touchy at my age."

The aaranya, even Senna, crowded around Guyen to study the cape.

"Notice how fine and light the material is. The trick is to generate a covering that is very very light, and it must be almost totally separated. With normal clothing you can cheat but not with this. The best effect is had if there's three or four layers making up the material but it must remain light, with the minimum of substance, and it must cover all of you or be able to be drawn around to cover all of you when the detector draws near." He demonstrated that he could pull the hood across his face, hiding his hand at the same time.

"As far as I can make out it works because only the almost detached garment is found by the detector and the layers somehow hide the body inside. Since the garment *is* detected it must be insubstantial enough to be seen as human."

The aaranya split into pairs and began to practise. Andrei began with a few extravagant concoctions but Senna wasn't in the mood for jokes.

While the others worked, John asked Guyen to tell what he knew of the research centre and its history. "Do you know why they built in the city?" he asked. "It seems such an illogical and expensive place to start."

"I think that we, the city aaranya like Senna and myself, may be the reason they started here," he said. "I heard the first rumours of something happening, hmm, maybe a dozen years ago.

"Back then the place where the centre is built was very much outer suburbia. It's all filled out, there and beyond, since they started. Of course it wasn't the fancy place with its fancy name back at the start, but they haven't moved."

"You've been there?" asked John.

"Hmm? Yes, I've poked my nose around a few times over the years. Nearly had it taken off for my troubles but we had to look. Not that it did us or anyone else very much good. Skaidar got taken on one of those trips, just a few years ago, and there was nothing I could do to save him.

"Nigh on seventy years Skaidar and I had been getting into trouble together. I remember when it was not far even from here to areas of real woodland – this was back when we were not much out of childhood. Not the true forest like where you hail from, but still exciting stuff for two young adventurers like ourselves. Back then some of our other friends kept going, as some young ones are inclined to do, but for some reason Skaidar and I always returned home. For many years we'd talk big about heading north to find the Glades of legend, but eventually we came to admit we were homebodies and happy with it.

"Then home started to go wrong. Rumours from the east of narun disappearing, aaranya and jalaja alike. At that time you'd still see the occasional samudraka in the bay but not since ... but then they've been getting strange and aloof for generations. Skaidar and I were old men already by this time, but we had never totally lost the adventurous spirit so we set ourselves the task of finding out what was happening.

"We may have been adventurous but years had taught us caution. As we travelled east across the city we listened to the tales of others and gained respect for the truth behind the rumours. Strange grey-skinned narun, probably aaranya although no one has ever been certain, were luring some of us away, never to be seen again. People that should have known better would go willingly into obvious traps.

"We eventually traced *them*, as Senna always phrases it, to the block out east that you've been watching. Back then it was just a rough scrub block with a few areas of small trees growing in large pots. There was a small cleared area with a very secure looking building. Skaidar and I tried several times to get close but we were always discovered and chased away by these same grey narun described by the others. I can only imagine that they must have had these narun on watch for people like us.

"But there weren't many people like us. The folk to the east were already becoming suspicious and sullen. We couldn't interest them in attempting a more concerted attempt to penetrate the building. The folk over on this side were content to keep out of the way while ever the troubles were just rumours from the east.

"We left it alone for a long while, there seemed nothing else we could do. Then, maybe four or five years ago, there was an unexpected cessation to the tales that had remained persistent for so long. Naturally Skaidar and I went to investigate. We thought that perhaps the block had closed down, but no such luck.

"In front of the old, small, building was a huge hole in the ground with trucks coming and going as they laid the foundations for a huge new building. We got close enough to see that the same company name was on the signs, Vanadevatas. We got close enough to see that there were still grey-skinned narun around the block keeping watch and chasing us away if we tried to get close to the old building.

"When the rumours started again just eight months later they flew with a vengeance. A detector that moved around the city and easily found groups of narun, and some sort of weapon that would make our people fall over where they stood. And more. The rumours were no longer just from the east. Now people that we knew personally were disappearing, people from the west. Now people we spoke to everywhere talked of the strange buzzing sensation when the detector approached. The small society we had here in the city fell apart and our already small numbers fell even further as more disappeared. The few children were taken by their parents to the ragged remains of woodlands that exist in the farmland in the north and west.

"Still adventurous, but not any younger, Skaidar and I went to investigate again. We found a place that overlooked the centre and could see that it had been transformed. The hole we had witnessed before was no longer there, instead the huge building you've seen was complete. The old building was gone. Most of the block had been cleared and much of the mobile forest you have witnessed was well on its way.

"Perhaps we were over-confident from our previous visits and escapes, perhaps we had not listened carefully enough to the tales of others. Whatever it was, we just assumed we could get away again if we needed. We went down to the block and climbed over the fence. We studied a few of the trees in boxes and could tell that other aaranya had been in them – although we had no idea if they had been friend or foe. We were about to try and get close to the new building when we felt the buzzing of the detector. We quickly scaled the fence and ran up the street, only to discover that all the larger trees in the nearby blocks had died, I suspect now they were killed by *them* for just this reason. Skaidar and I had no option but to keep running.

"But we were no longer young, we didn't run as fast as we once had. We had not the energy to jump fences and run through back yards. The buzzing grew stronger and we knew we could not hide even if we at last found some larger trees, so we kept on running. A gentle hill and Skaidar fell behind. I was almost at the top when I looked back and saw him stumble and fall. I started back down to help him but I suddenly felt dizzy, I could barely walk straight.

"I could see their vehicle coming up the hill behind Skaidar. I tried to call to him but could barely get the words out. In the end I think I was saved because they concentrated their weapon on Skaidar. I got left out of its line of fire and was able to stumble over the crest of that small hill.

"The buzzing faded and I was able to sneak around to peer back down the street. I saw them loading Skaidar back into their vehicle in some sort of cage. He looked to be unconscious but could have been dead for all I could tell from where I was ... for all that I could do either way. For days I tried different ways to get close to the building, they almost caught me several times. Eventually I gave up. It was either that or let *them* take me, and I had not the courage for that.

"And that's it. I've never been back there and I never saw Skaidar again. Nigh on seventy years we'd been together ..." Guyen shook his head, his eyes red. His tale stopped for a minute or so while he drew himself back to the present.

"It was not much more than six months later that I was talking with young Vailan. Barely out of childhood, he and a few mates had returned from woodlands in the north to view the city that their parents had spoken of. They'd been mucking about, experimenting with clothing as youngsters often do, when the detector came past and failed to follow the ones dressed in a certain way. The brave young devils did further experiments, almost taunting the detector and refining what they'd learned. They've gone back north now I think, at least I hope that is where they disappeared to, but they showed me what they'd learned and it has served me well."

The others had all stopped their practise and settled down to listen to Guyen's story.

"I still don't understand why they did this in the city," said John.

"Your friends understand, I think," said Guyen.

Darnu explained, "Even when there were more of you here you were separate groups and individuals. Without a stand, without elders to help you coordinate, you could not act together, you didn't even know who was missing. This would never have been possible in our forest. These grey narun must have understood that. They realised that they could keep picking at the small population of narun here and you would never take concerted action against them. They realised it would probably take a long time to even try to defend yourselves against them."

"And they were right," confirmed Guyen. "More than right. We have never defended ourselves, and now there are too few of us to stand much chance even if we tried."

Darnu continued, "So they've had twelve years or more in which to develop their weapons and expand their power, picking at the local population as they needed. Only in the last few years have they looked further afield."

"I wondered if I was doing the right thing, showing you this trick," said Guyen. "It's why I wanted to wait until today. I wanted time to think. Eventually I understood that you were determined, that you would go ahead whether I showed you or not."

"We thank you, Guyen. Yes, we would have found some way to go ahead regardless. But this disguise will be invaluable." said Darnu, and the others nodded.

"We will look for you, Uncle, when we're done," said John. "Find out if you would still like to see the forest."

"That would be a fine thing indeed," said Guyen, although whether he referred to seeing the forest or the group being able to return was unclear.

The group said their goodbyes and headed back to John's apartment. John felt a sadness as they were leaving, that the seriousness of their task, and John's own insistence on recalling the past, had brought melancholy to a man whose natural expression was so obviously one of laughter and friendship. John looked back and watched Guyen walking slowly away in his old-fashioned suit and trilby. His head was down and, John imagined, his mind once again lost in the past.

15. Spy

Ian grunted as he wrestled yet another of the barrels out of the enclosed cell and back to its usual place between the large cages. So Karlin did have a boss, one that made him nervous. On Sunday, after the news that Stephenson was arriving early the next day, Ian had been called in from his day off and given the job of moving the barrels and cans of hazardous chemicals from the haphazard storage amidst the zoo cages, to be hidden in one of the enclosed cells. Apparently Stephenson didn't approve of Karlin's lack of care and it was decided that out of sight would be out of mind.

It was now early Wednesday morning and Karlin's boss was long gone, so Ian had the job of moving all the stuff back to the usual places. That particular enclosed cell was the one they used for treating the mesh of the cages and painting wall-board with the nasty stuff out of these barrels, it had to be cleared to make room for more work to be done. Lots of the technical work was done upstairs by people who had no idea what the equipment was for, but the application of the nasty and dangerous chemicals was reserved for the privileged few, like Ian.

That thought reminded Ian of ... what was his name? Cameron something. Ian wondered what had happened. Ian had been down here on Sunday when Cameron had apparently been injured. No one gave him any details and it was probably better that he didn't know. There'd been no news since, and Cameron's name had not been mentioned. If Ian read the signs correctly things weren't looking good for poor old Cameron what's-his-name.

One of the barrels almost got away from him and Ian swore loudly, his voice echoing around the cavern. They'd all been warned when they started work: no open flames near any of these chemicals, no sparks and don't drop them. Most of them were at least flammable and some were potentially explosive. No wonder Stephenson thought they should be more carefully stored.

"I hear those dulcet tones," Ian heard Davies say from nearby. He looked up and saw Davies come out of the passage to the labs. "You are being careful aren't you?" Davies asked.

"Some assistance would help you know, some of these are heavy," said Ian, but he tried to keep any annoyance from his voice, there was no point antagonising Davies.

"Sure, in a while," said Davies. "First we've got a tree run."

The tree runs were okay: just a matter of bringing a fresh tree down on the elevator from the yard above, swapping it over with a tree from one of the zoo cages, and then taking the old tree back up again. A daily thing with one of the zoo cages now, but still okay. It was the other bit of the routine that disturbed Ian: carrying the empty-but-not-really-empty cages back and forth between the zoo, Karlin's lab rooms, and that strange silent hall. It had been bad enough before, Ian used to watch the routines played out by the silver-suited narun as if he were watching a mime artist on the street, but now – since his time with Caldor – Ian couldn't help but imagine that there were real figures being moved around in this way. Up in that hall it looked liked some of the figures being moved must be tiny. The money Ian earned was coming to mean less and less.

The last part of the routine was returning the old tree to the yard above. When Ian returned to the cavern Davies was gone. "Sure I'll help," muttered Ian quietly, it didn't pay to complain too loudly. "Yeah, and pigs might fly." Still grumbling he went back to moving barrels and cans out of the enclosed cell.

- - -

Thursday was winding down. John yawned and stretched in the driver's seat of the parked car. It had been a long couple of days. Since finding a way to avoid the detector they'd kept an almost constant watch on the research centre, which meant John had to be there because he was the only one that could drive. He'd managed to get a few hours of sleep, dozing in his seat as they parked, but after two days he was feeling pretty ragged.

Across from him sat Garjae in his cloak with its hood up covering his head, his eyes peering forward through a small space. Such precautions seemed the safest even when they had not felt the detector, since they didn't know what narun in the centre may be watching. It had been a quiet afternoon, as was any time that John spent with Garjae.

John wasn't sure if he was just grumpy from being tired or whether the extended periods alone with the uncommunicative Garjae had finally worn away his patience. Whatever it was he finally asked, "Why don't you like me, Garjae?"

Garjae turned to look at him in surprise.

"Come on, you've been looking at me like you wanted to hit me with something ever since we met," said John. "It's not that I expect everyone to like me, I'm not that likeable, but usually people that hate me this much have some reason. What's yours?"

Garjae stared at him for some moments, trying to gauge whether John really wanted to know. Finally he responded with just one word, "Asha."

John's eyes slowly widened in surprise, he finally understood. Now it was his turn to stare. He'd already admitted his culpability for Asha's capture, as far as John was concerned that was enough reason for any of them to hate him, but only from Garjae had he felt such animosity. There was only one reason that John could see for the difference, "You love her?"

Garjae nodded once and turned back to watch the research centre, his face once again hidden from John by the encompassing hood.

"But ..." John stopped. Back when he didn't really believe in her he thought that his emotions were part of some strange sickness, but since accepting her reality he had not tried to express how he felt for Asha.

There wasn't a whole lot to think about: he did love her, there was no point denying it. Her voice and her large, pale green eyes openly expressed the gentle compassion that was such a large part of what made Asha who she was. He had loved her almost from his first sight of her, and yet it had taken until now for him to recognise his feelings for what they truly were. For a man that didn't really believe in love at first sight it was ironic that this made it twice that it had happened to him. His rational self knew that this didn't mean he loved his dead wife and daughter any less, love for one did not take away the love for another, but the thought was still uncomfortable. It was more than uncomfortable, it was twisted, tragic, foolish and ultimately pointless – his wife and child were dead, and Asha wasn't even human.

He said softly, "Whatever I feel for her, Garjae, it can come to nothing. We're not the same."

Garjae shook his head. "It's not your feelings for her that bother me. I don't hate you for who you are, or even for what you did, although that has at least given me some way to justify my emotions. No," he turned to look at John, "I hate you for existing."

John flinched at the force of the expression glaring at him from Garjae's face.

"I'm sorry," said Garjae more softly. "It's irrational and stupid and it has almost nothing to do with you." He turned forward to watch out the windscreen again, but continued speaking, "I grew to love Asha as she was reaching maturity, but then her brother left the stand and left her devastated. She looked at no one after that. And then she left ... in search of who knows what. When she returned she was still not recovered and she still looked at no one – however much I tried to get her attention.

"And then, out there on the periphery, she finds your family. Humans. She chooses to share your company, she chooses to share your lives. And that was bad enough." He paused again. "But then along you come, not even believing in Asha enough to consider her feelings, and you tell the whole stand of the relationship you two were forming."

John was stunned. Garjae was right, he hadn't considered Asha's feelings as he spoke at the Glade. He hadn't thought. He hadn't believed. "Why did Kaia ask me to talk in front of everyone like that?" he asked.

Garjae looked across at John. "She did offer more privacy you may remember ... anyway she didn't know what you were going to say ... and, if I'm going to be honest, I guess a large part of it is simply that I was much more sensitive to what you had to say than anyone else." He turned back to the front. "To most of the others there I am sure it was just a tragic but romantic tale."

After that they both sat there staring down at the centre, there seemed nothing else to say.

It got dark and they drove back to the park outside John's apartment building. John picked up some takeaway food on the way and ate it in the park while his friends once again practised creating the protective cloaks and spent some time on their self-defence lessons. Darnu and Garjae's greater maturity continued to show in their superior strength and control.

As their practise finished up John was wondering who was going to start the usual night-time discussion. It turned out to be Garjae.

"How long are we going to watch before we do something?" asked Garjae.

"We've been here almost a week," added John.

Darnu said, "We've only been watching for two days."

"I've been watching for longer than that," said John.

They had been surprised that they never saw the grey narun occupying the trees. Everyone had assumed that that must be where they slept, but they were rarely seen among them. For whatever reason the area of mobile forest was mostly unprotected and uninhabited by the grey narun. Other than that surprise they'd learned very little since Darnu and Garjae had joined John's observation of the centre.

"I think we've learned all we can from the outside," said Garjae. "I think it's time one of us went in to find out more. I want to go in with one of those trees that we see taken in each morning."

"What if there's a change in the routine?" asked Darnu. "You could get caught and give away what we're trying to do before we learn anything."

"The routine could change at any time, Darnu," said John. "Even if we watched for months we could be caught by the unexpected."

The others watched the debate in silence, looking back and forth with interest.

"I want to go in tonight and be ready for the morning," said Garjae.

John snapped around to stare at him. "Tonight? Are you sure?"

Garjae nodded. "We don't know what's happening in there, if we leave it too long we may be too late."

John nodded, he'd been feeling the same pressure.

Darnu stared at them both, wondering at their unexpected alliance, and then looked at the others. "Well?" he asked.

Barma and Tilvy looked at each other and shrugged. Tilvy said, "I don't feel ready to start anything ... I wonder if I ever will. I want more practice with the cloak and with our self-defence, but Garjae is already much better at it than the rest of us." Barma nodded his agreement.

Senna stayed silent. Andrei, looking sombre, said, "I need practice too, but Garjae is right, we're not learning anything new just by watching from the outside. If he feels up to playing spy then he might get information we can use when the rest of us are ready."

Darnu sat there and looked around the group trying to work out an appropriate response. "I can't say I like it," he said. "But I can't really argue either. Sitting there all day staring down at the centre and wondering what they are doing to our friends, to our people ..." He looked grimly at Garjae. "Are you sure you're ready?"

- - -

Garjae dropped soundlessly to the ground inside the fence, crouched low and whipped the cloak around him. He pushed his senses out through the darkness ... nothing unexpected, just the trees in their platforms and the human guards at their posts. Discarding further stealth, any presence would be out of place inside the fence, he ran between the platforms until he came to the tree that he and John thought would be the next one to enter the building. He hesitated for a minute, reaching out with his senses, trying to determine if there was any sign that he had been noticed, but there was nothing. He merged quickly, sliding into the warmth at the core of the trunk.

He tried to relax but he was too wound up. Eventually he felt the dawn, late at this time of year, touch the leaves of his tree and felt it react, stretching as it wakened with the day. There would still be a couple of hours before much happened and the warming tree helped Garjae to finally settle down and relax a little.

Eventually Garjae felt the presence of a human approach and he imagined them going through the process of attaching the small tractor to the platform, as he had seen previously. He felt the vibration as the platform rolled over the gravel, the vibration eventually smoothed out as it entered the building. Garjae partly emerged from a branch, mostly hidden among the high leaves. He was in a tiny room, just large enough to contain the tree. The large roller door was still open to the outside and the human was detaching the tractor from the platform. This was his last chance to get out, he took a last look at the bright morning sky and drew back into the tree. A short time later he felt a dip as the room began to descend.

Vertical movement stopped with a slight jerk and shortly afterward he felt the presence of a second man near the platform. Another jerk and the tree swayed slightly as it began moving off the elevator. Garjae pushed his face from an upper branch to look around, but saw a silver suited narun nearby and quickly withdrew back into the tree.

The tree continued to move very slowly, then paused for a while, then moved again. There was a strange muffling sensation and it seemed that the presences around the tree had faded. Garjae decided to be cautious and remain hidden, there were still some shadowy presences not very far away. He felt another tree appear as if through a mist, his senses somehow distorted. He was pleased he had remained hidden when he felt a narun suddenly appear quite close, and another, and another. The three narun got on the other platform and remained next to that tree. Garjae waited. And waited.

Finally he decided that he would have to take his chances and risk partly emerging so he could see where he was. Choosing a high, partly obscured branch he pushed out a bit at a time to look around. His tree and another were inside a large cage. The mesh of the cage, he guessed, was the same as that of the small cage they'd seen in the van. Reaching out with his senses he could tell that it was this mesh that was muffling his life sense, much like being in those odd silver suits.

Garjae moved around inside the tree until he could better see the three narun at the other tree. They were inside this cage and without suits so he guessed they must be prisoners. He stared in horror at the female with her truncated legs, he couldn't imagine what had happened to her. None of them were Asha, which was a disappointment, but none of them looked like the grey narun they'd had described to them either, so he decided to risk getting their attention.

"Hey," he called.

Both of the men snapped their heads around to look at his tree in surprise.

"Hey," he called again to make them look up to where he was only partly emerged.

The expression of the closer of the two men went blank, like a curtain falling, while the other started to get up and then stopped himself and looked around carefully. Eventually he pushed the young woman back against the tree where they had been sitting and came across to Garjae's tree.

Leaning casually against the trunk Ceeda let his hand partly merge and introduced himself, communicating through the tree rather than risk being heard.

"Ceeda! How long have you been here?" exclaimed Garjae.

"Garjae? What the hell ... ?" replied an astonished Ceeda. He looked around hurriedly, hoping that no one was watching. Only Briso seemed to be paying any attention, and that only with his usual vacant stare.

Eventually they managed to swap stories. Ceeda was astounded that anyone would voluntarily enter a place he could only describe as horrifying. Garjae was feeling ashamed that his reclusive friend had disappeared for so long without Garjae's notice.

"You don't need to feel bad," assured Ceeda, "I'm the one that chose life on the outer ... although never in my worst nightmares had I thought it could bring me to a place like this."

"Is Asha still here and still okay?" asked Garjae.

"Something really strange is going on, and I mean strange even for this place," Ceeda answered. "You knew her much better than I, did she always have some special talents?"

"Like what?"

"Like being able to draw strength from a tree at an unbelievable rate. She should have been dead, Garjae, she really should. I can't describe what they did to her, not sure I even know. I've told you about Nacee over there, well Asha was worse, much worse ... then she drew against a tree so heavily that in just one day that she made it sick and saved herself.

"And I've been watching the cage where they have her now. Garjae, she killed a tree in just one night – less! From here I

256

couldn't see much of what happened, but when she emerged afterward it was like she was aglow with life, a bright golden aura that streamed out from her. Everyone felt it, even those like Nacee and Briso. I don't know what she did, or how, and I don't know what they must have done to have driven her to such extremes, but it was incredible to see.

"Each afternoon they bring her in and even through this mesh, just to look at her, you can tell she's not very well, but by morning she looks almost normal again. It's her trees you've seen coming and going from out there so regularly. None of the rest of us go through them so fast, we couldn't even if we wanted to. It was just luck, or lack of it, that you got a tree coming here rather than there."

Garjae pondered this for a while. It was frustrating not to have chosen a tree going into Asha's cage, he was starting to wish that he had put this off for another day.

"I take it there's no easy way out of here," said Garjae. "Do they search the trees when they leave?"

"Not that we've ever seen. They have that ray-gun thing to drive reluctant prisoners from the trees, so most of us know better than to try and hide. They lock us up, change trees and put us back. I don't think anyone's ever considered someone trying to get in here on purpose."

"So if I stay hidden I should be able to leave with the tree."

"I hope so. You don't want to be stuck here, Garjae," said Ceeda with feeling.

"I'd love to be able to speak with Asha," said Garjae.

"I don't think I'd recommend it while she's in that far cage. You'd have to yell very loudly to get past the mesh. If any of those suited narun were nearby they'd hear you."

"How long do you think before they'll swap trees in here again?"

"It varies. Sometimes it's only a few days sometimes it's more than a week. I don't know what drives them, it's certainly not our welfare or the trees," replied Ceeda bitterly.

"Well I need at least a few days. I want to see how this place runs. There has to be a way to get you out of here."

"Nacee will have to be carried," said Ceeda, he wasn't planning to leave her behind.

"We want to get you all out if we can," said Garjae, "but I need to know more. How many of you are there and whether we can get you all out before anyone notices. We don't know how to fight that ray of theirs so we have to avoid confrontation. With John to help us we probably only need to run as far as the nearest street and then we can be driven away."

"Seems strange to be relying on a human after all of this," said Ceeda.

"It's odd, even without having been imprisoned here. ... He tries ..." started Garjae.

"High praise indeed," replied Ceeda to Garjae's reluctant admission. "I've got to get back to Nacee, she gets upset if I'm gone too long."

Garjae watched Ceeda go back and put his arm around the girl, whispering reassurances. Briso's blank stare was going out somewhere past Garjae's tree and he felt a pang of pity that people could be driven to such a state.

That evening he risked emerging completely from the tree so that he could peer around it to get a better view of Asha being returned to her cage. He hoped the mesh of the cage and the bulk of the tree would hide him should the narun decide to look this way. Seeing the narun in its silver suit, and knowing how much the suit obscured the senses, he thought he was probably safe enough.

His heart went out to Asha as he saw how small and downcast she appeared as she climbed the platform to the tree in her cage. Ceeda was right, you could tell that she was in a bad way. She was too small and obviously in considerable discomfort and weakness.

The next morning Garjae was watching again as they came to collect her. But this time he disagreed with Ceeda's assessment. She may be larger and stronger than the night before but she was far from normal. Even from here Garjae thought he could sense the pain coming from her. Not a physical pain, something deeper.

He watched carefully as the tree she had used was removed and a fresh tree was put in its place ready for her return. He watched as the two trees were replaced in the cage across the way, noting carefully how the narun was there mainly to tell the humans when the captives were in the correct places. Whoever these humans were, they had not the extra life sense that John had. Ceeda had told of the doctor that could see them, but he had not seen other humans

258

here that could do it. There had been a recent visitor but he wasn't certain of him.

A short time after the trees had been replaced across the way, two men and a narun came to the cage containing Garjae, Ceeda and the others. The narun ordered Ceeda to guide Briso into a small carry cage. Ceeda urged Briso on and he obeyed in his usual dull trance. Later that evening Briso was returned, he appeared to be unchanged.

Garjae spent his time looking around the dim cavern and trying to take careful note of where everything was: the other cages, the piles of boxes and equipment, and the doors. He questioned Ceeda about the doors he could see, and was told that the series of large doors on the other side, just visible through the line of cages in between, were to allow trees to be placed in what Ceeda called the torture cells. There appeared to be only two ways in or out of the cavern itself: the large elevator at the centre of one end of the cavern, or a small corridor in the opposite corner that led past the torture cells and then up a ramp to the examination rooms and the smaller cells.

When asked about the different smells in the cavern, Ceeda said that he understood from what the humans had said that some processing of trees was done on the level above. There were also the alien smells of chemicals coming from arrays of barrels and cans that Ceeda said they'd been moving back and forth recently for some unfathomable reason.

More days passed and Garjae continued to watch. Every day Asha was taken from her cell and every night she was returned. On another day a prisoner from the cage directly across from them was taken away. Like Briso he was silent and blank in his expression, and dully obedient to the silver suited narun's commands. The following day the prisoner was returned, weaker perhaps but otherwise little different in demeanour – Garjae wondered whether it was too late to save such prisoners, if such damage could ever be cured.

- - -

Andrei watched in fascination as Taiza fiddled with some switches inside a large panel on the wall. It was late Monday night. The huge, echoing interior of the factory floor was lit at intervals by flickering fluorescent lights. They'd explained to the others that

Senna's father wanted to show off some of his toys and he could only do it late at night. So they'd left the others to their night-time routine of waiting for Garjae, and crossed the city to the bay and the factory buildings that Taiza had made his home.

"You got t' turn the cameras 'n' stuff off before you start playing around," he was explaining. "Else all hell breaks loose and you get people swarmin' 'roun' tryin' t' work out what happened. Ha! They really don't like their machines doin' stuff on t' own."

After a few minutes at the switchboard Taiza led them off to a large machine. "'s a lathe," he said. He loaded a small but heavy cylinder of metal between the jaws of the machine. Both Senna and Andrei jumped when he hit a large green button and the machine came to life. "y'd better stand back a bit, 'times bits flick out," he warned absently.

The two of them stepped back and watched as Taiza picked a clear face mask off a hook and increased his size to better fit the machine and the mask. He worked away with various tools at the spinning cylinder of metal for a while, slivers of metal fell about his feet and occasionally flicked further out. Often he'd use pieces of cloth to help him hold the tools more securely, their unnatural surfaces slippery in his hands. Except for an intermittent swearword, and shuffle of his feet as a hot piece of metal touched him, it was the first time Andrei had seen him look calm and settled.

"He's right at home with this stuff," Andrei said to Senna. "Have you seen this before?"

Senna looked the machine over. "Not this particular one, but I've seen Dad work with other lathes. He used to bring me to places like this all the time."

"The love of machines didn't rub off?"

Senna grimaced. "Nope. Not a chance. I've seen him do this sort of thing hundreds of times, more, and I still jump every time he turns one of these things on."

Andrei was very conscious of how close Senna was standing next to him. He wanted to touch her, put his arm around her, but couldn't make himself do it. What if he was wrong? He was pretty sure she liked him, but maybe that was all. Better to enjoy the closeness now than to scare her away by pushing his luck too far.

At least her dad wasn't scary. Strange certainly, but Andrei liked strange, it was much better than boring. Andrei then wondered how Taiza would feel if he saw Andrei put his arm around Senna. He mightn't be scary normally but a man with access to all this human equipment could probably get very scary if he wanted to be protective of his daughter. Probably best to keep his hands to himself, Andrei decided, at least until the machine got turned off.

To take his mind off his proximity to Senna, Andrei looked around at the huge room that was the factory floor. It was a strange mix of openness and clutter, and not a sign of life except the three of them here at this machine. Taiza had apparently grown used to handling the lifeless materials, the metals and plastics. Andrei wondered how long it had taken him to learn his way around this place – and the others like it.

His attention came back with a start as the machine clunked and started to wind down. The machine went silent but Taiza stayed hunched over his work for a while longer, wielding various tools and grunting and swearing. "Jus' a bit longer, kids," he said, and went on working. It took a while but at last he stood up straight and fiddled with the machine. He turned and presented a small piece of metal, delicate in appearance, that shone in the fluorescent light.

Andrei reached forward to pick it out of Taiza's hand.

"Careful," Taiza warned, "'s a bit hot."

It was still hot but it didn't burn. Andrei turned it over in his hand, it looked almost like a flower with intricate layers and folds along an elongated stem. He looked down at the pile of filings on the floor and then back at the small piece of metal in his hand. He handed it reverently to Senna. "That's incredible," he said.

"'s not finished yet. Jus' give me a minute to clean up 'ere." Taiza twitched his way to a brush and shovel and started tidying up around the lathe.

"Can't you just leave that for the humans?" asked Andrei.

"Use' t'," he replied. "But t' bosses started getting funny and you'd have people getting fired from their jobs for mess they didn' make. Same thing goes for that," he waved at the sculpture in Senna's hands. "Use' t' leave 'em lying around when I'd finished. Even found that some o' the 'umans 'd like them enough t' take 'em home. But then some fuddy duddies 'd start t' kick up a fuss about the misuse of the equipment 'n' people 'd get int' trouble again. So, 's the bin for it once we're done."

Andrei stared at the piece in wonder. "So why do you do it?" he asked.

"Fun," came the reply "... 'n' somethin' t' do at night. Not too many of us over this way, even before the strange goin's on with them grey 'ns." Taiza finished sweeping up and they moved over to an area with large cylinders and lengths of hose. "Oxy'," he explained – which was no explanation at all as far as Andrei was concerned.

"It produces a really hot flame used for welding and cutting," Senna elaborated.

"Good t' see you remember somethin' from your upbringin'," Taiza grinned at his daughter. He started turning some taps and fiddled with a device attached to a hose. There was a loud pop and a bright yellow flame sprang from the end of the device. Taiza fiddled with it a bit further and the flame reduced to a small, intense, bright blue spot at the tip of the device.

"Pass 's that thing, Sen'," he asked, holding out his hand. Senna put the metal sculpture into his hand and Taiza bent over a small piece of sheet metal. Andrei lost track of what Taiza was doing, unable to see properly past the glare of the flame. Whatever it was seemed to involve several pieces of wire and metal. A while later Taiza straightened up. "Jus' give it time t' cool down," he said and started tidying up after himself.

Andrei knelt down and peered at the sculpture now mounted on an elaborate stand. "Amazing," he said.

Senna knelt down next to him, Andrei couldn't help noticing how close she was. "He's always been good at making things. All that other people ever see is that Dad spends his time in factories, near humans and machines. The polite ones call him strange, but they never get to see the things he makes. These are what it's all really about. Even Mum never really understood that."

"But he doesn't keep them."

"I don't think it's ever been about the end result," she explained. "He does like someone to see what he's done, that's why he's so happy we came along tonight, but that's not why he does it. He never once tried to show me how he did these things, he'd bring me along just to be an audience. Once he'd shown me 'd lose interest 'n' move on t' somethin' new."

Andrei grinned to himself as he noticed Senna reverted to her father's abbreviated speech. "So he's a frustrated artist," he said.

"That's it exactly. People laugh about how twitchy he seems. They say it's the electricity of the equipment he uses and other, less kind, explanations. But it's not that. It's not a nervous twitch, it's frustration. He's looking for some way to express himself and most of the time he can't find it."

"... until you give him one of these machines," finished Andrei.

Senna looked at him and smiled. "Yes," she said softly and very closely.

"So 'd you like it?" asked Taiza.

Andrei started, he'd almost forgotten there was anyone else there. "Beautiful," he said. Looking down at the sculpture he continued, "I've never seen anything like it."

"Yes, well, 's what I play at. If you've finished gawkin' at it I'd better hide it in the rubbish now." Taiza reached down and lifted the piece, swapping it from hand to hand. "'s bit warm still."

Andrei and Senna stood up. "Could I take it?" asked Andrei.

"You can't go walkin' the streets with somethin' like this," said Taiza. "The 'umans 'll take on badly."

"It's late at night," said Andrei. "No one's likely to notice, and if they do we can leave it on the footpath. It won't get anyone here in trouble."

"'n' what you goin' t' do with it when you get back?" he asked.

"John will take care of it for me."

"Your tame 'uman?"

"He's not exactly tame, but yes, my human friend."

"Well ... why not, I 'spose. Like you say, 's long as 's out of 'ere's the important thing," Taiza concluded. Andrei thought he didn't sound quite as reluctant as his words suggested. "Here you go. Mind now, 's still warm."

Taiza placed the sculpture in Andrei's hand. It was still very warm and the metal felt strange and slippery on his skin. He'd have to carry it carefully.

"Come on you two," said Taiza. "We'd better put things back as we found them." He finished tidying up where they were standing, and then they went back to the switchboard. "'s gettin' harder 'n' harder to get around this stuff these days. Some of the fact'ries have 'puters 'n' stuff controllin' the cameras. You switch 'em off and you still end up with people swarmin' around. May have t' learn how t' program the 'puters eventually, get 'm t' tell the 'umans everthin's okay. Always somethin' t' learn."

"You don't sound upset by that," observed Andrei.

"Not really. Learnin' stuff's 's good a way 's any t' spend your time … 'n' better 'n some."

They waited while Taiza reset the lights and everything back as they should be and then they left the building via a small window and a fire-escape stairway. "You two goin' t' hang around here tonight?" asked Taiza.

"No," replied Andrei. "The others will worry if we don't get back before light. Anyway, I want to get this back while it's still dark," he held up the sculpture.

"How 'd you go wit' Uncle?"

"He showed us how to cloak ourselves against the detector used by *them*," said Senna.

Andrei noticed the inclusive *us*, that was a promising development.

"'s that all?" Taiza seemed surprised.

"It should help us a lot," said Andrei.

"Sure … I jus' thought he might 've gotten more involved. What with 'is history wit' the place 'n' all."

"He did tell us about Skaidar," said Senna.

"And the story did sort of take the fun out of the day," added Andrei.

"Yes, that'll do it," agreed Taiza. Grinning at Andrei he added, "Let 's old codgers start tellin' tragic tales 'n' the fun goes right out o' the day every time."

Taiza walked with them along the quiet footpath for a while. "Must go 'n' speak with Uncle me-self one these days," he continued eventually, mostly to himself it seemed. "Remind 'im o' some o' our mutual friends. Reijo 'd have t' be some help 'n' there's prob'ly others."

Senna and Andrei looked at each other and shrugged, not understanding the direction that Taiza had taken the conversation.

Eventually they came to one of the main roads heading back to the city, the one Senna and Andrei would take through to the other side of the city.

"'ll let you kids go on from 'ere," said Taiza.

"Thanks for tonight, Taiza," said Andrei, and then carefully holding up the sculpture, "and thanks for this. The others are going to be very impressed."

Taiza gave a deprecating wave in acknowledgement.

"Love you, Dad," said Senna and gave Taiza a long hug.

"You too, Sen'," Taiza replied. "Take care o' y'self."

Andrei and Senna had started walking when Taiza called after them, "Andrei! A moment if you will."

Andrei came back, still holding the sculpture carefully, a puzzled look on his face. Taiza leant forward and spoke quietly to him. "Y'r arms 'd be much better placed 'round my daughter than 'round that lump o' scrap metal. In fact, if you don't do somethin' about it soon she's like as not goin' t' hit you over the head with the thing."

Andrei blushed and muttered, "I wasn't sure."

"Be sure, son. You're a nice enough kid, she c'd do worse. Take care of her, 'n' keep her out of trouble." With that Taiza turned and started walking back the way they'd come.

Andrei was stunned. He stared agape after the retreating figure. "Thanks!" he eventually called after Taiza, but he wasn't sure he heard. Then he turned back and looked at Senna who was standing on the pavement waiting for him. He remembered thinking she looked scruffy and unkempt when they first met, and maybe she still did but Andrei couldn't really tell. To him she was simply perfect.

He ran back to her and they started walking.

"What was that about?" Senna asked.

"He was just offering me some good advice," said Andrei.

"Not sure Dad's up for good advice," was the wary reply.

"This was truly excellent advice," said Andrei. He tucked the metal sculpture into the crook of his left arm and then placed his right arm around Senna's waist.

She turned abruptly to look at him.

"Sorry," he said, and removed his arm. "If you'd rather I didn't ..."

"No, that's not it." Senna grabbed his arm and pulled it back around her. "I was just surprised that's all." She snuggled against him as they walked. "I've been waiting for you to touch me all night.

I'd just about given up."

"I didn't know if your father would approve. Never upset a man with an Oxy', I always say."

Senna laughed and Andrei enjoyed the sensation of her moving against him. "Do you mind if I keep my left arm to carry your Dad's sculpture?"

"Huh?"

"Well your Dad seemed to think I might need both arms to hold on to you, but if you don't mind too much I thought perhaps I could still get the sculpture back to show the others."

Senna laughed some more. "Sure. One arm will do – for now."

If any of the humans in the cars driving past noticed the small metal sculpture, apparently waving gently in mid-air along the footpath, none of them slowed to take a better look.

- - -

John sat quietly in the car with Darnu. It was early evening and most of the traffic from the industrial estate had gone. They'd been there for a few hours now, moving positions from time to time to avoid attention and parking tickets, but always trying to keep a view of the back fence of the research centre where they hoped Garjae would eventually appear.

There was some risk of the vehicle standing out in the deserted estate, but both he and Darnu felt that night would be when they were most likely to be wanted. Darnu stayed near the estate all the time, watching it even when John went back to his apartment for food or sleep. John suspected that Guyen's tale of losing Skaidar had gone particularly deep with Darnu.

Time with Darnu was always quiet but it was a more companionable, less antagonistic, silence than time shared with Garjae. To the aaranya Darnu acted, and was treated, as a big brother figure, but his relationship with John was more complex. The initial and fairly obvious disdain he felt for any being that would not believe his own senses had given way to a reluctant respect as John had proven his commitment to trying to rescue Asha. Here in the city Darnu had had to defer to John's greater experience but such a role did not sit all that well.

"Is tonight the night do you think?" asked John.

"I hope so," admitted Darnu. "You and Garjae may have admitted to impatience before, but I really feel it now. To not know whether he has been captured. ... He's been a good friend, I don't want to lose him."

Such a personal admission from Darnu was unusual, almost out of character, John wasn't sure how to respond. "It's hard not knowing," he agreed, keeping it neutral.

A while later John broke the silence with, "It was good to see Andrei and Senna together this morning."

Darnu laughed. "Yes it was. I was a bit disappointed in Senna though." The smile in his voice denied any real criticism.

"What's the problem?"

"I thought she might have curbed his cheekiness, made him start behaving a bit more seriously."

"You're just upset with the dig he got in about you acting your age. No, I think that's one of the things that makes it right. It's still the same Andrei, he's not pretending anything just for her."

"You're probably right. I wonder if she'll come back with us or if Andrei will want to stay here in the city."

"There you go acting your age again," laughed John. "I doubt if they've given such serious considerations much thought."

Darnu started to laugh and then half-shouted, "There!" Before John could respond Darnu had exited the car and quietly closed the door. John peered along the fence line unable to see anything. He watched Darnu run lightly down the street, keeping mostly to the grass next to the footpath, keeping his cape and hood pulled around him. As Darnu approached the fence line John finally saw a figure appear and jump lightly to the top, another light jump and he was down outside. The two caped figures embraced briefly before running back to the car.

As they approached, John started the car. They both climbed quickly into the back and John drove off as quietly and normally as he could. "Asha?" he asked.

"She's okay," responded Garjae.

In the park across from John's apartment, Garjae told the group what he had learned. He told them that Ceeda thought the grey narun called themselves dhumraka. It felt good to have a name for their enemy at last, especially one that seemed to separate them from the aaranya.

He skimmed over most of the tales of torture he had heard from Ceeda, there would be time enough for those if they ever got away. However he was forced to tell them about the state of most of the prisoners.

"I didn't get to speak with Asha," he said, "but Ceeda said she was okay and from what little I could see of her she was better than most in there. Except for Ceeda and Asha, most of the rest are ... it's like they're in a trance almost. Some are better than others but none are well. Most are able to respond to direct instruction, but a few like Nacee are going to need carrying."

"And there's fifteen you think?" said John.

"There was another from our stand, Rizzy, in with Ceeda until some weeks ago. Ceeda had hoped she was going to be returned but he's given up hope now."

"We're going to need bigger transport."

Andrei, his usual spark subdued during Garjae's sombre report, put in, "Maybe not, John. There are a few of the aaranya that we met with Senna that I think we may be able to convince to help. None of them will go into the centre, but if we can get the prisoners out then I think some of them may help us to get them away."

"But we still have to get them away from the centre," objected Darnu.

"I think we should load the incapacitated ones into the wagon and those of us that are mobile should be ready to split up and head in different directions on foot, getting together again later. That way, if there is a pursuit, we don't all get captured together."

Darnu nodded. "You could be right."

"All right," said Barma, "so we've got a plan for getting away, but how do we get them out of there?"

16. Trap

It was more than a week since meeting Stephenson, and Asha's life had taken on a routine. Two humans and a silver suited narun would come for her early in the morning and there would be the regular series of tests with Karlin. The rest of the day would be spent with Vincent or Ellie in a cell with either Karlin or a silver suited narun always watching from the other side of the clear wall.

In the first days she found herself succumbing to a sort of feeding frenzy from the preta that she would have to cut short after a brief period. Weakened by that initial rapid loss she would spend much of the day fending off additional attempts to feed. Asha gradually learned to slow down the feeding process so that it lasted much of the day. This felt less damaging to herself and it allowed her more time to stay in contact with each child, attempting to offer whatever comfort she could.

At the end of the day she would be collected again and subjected to more tests by Karlin before being returned to her solitary confinement in the cage in the cavern. Tired and badly drained by the day's interactions she had no choice but to draw heavily on the fresh tree each night to try and recover herself.

After little more than a week it became obvious to Asha, and she supposed to Karlin, that all her best efforts were not going to be enough. It was as if the preta had some limit beyond which they could not benefit. They were still insatiably hungry, but after reaching some limit, further feeding seemed to have no effect.

Asha thought that both preta had started to show visible echoes of the children they once were, but she couldn't be certain the effect was real. It could just be that both were now so familiar to her that she could see attributes that had not been apparent to her before. She longed to be able to speak with a friend, to gain comfort and understanding of her own. Her new abilities allowed her to sustain herself physically, but she could feel her own emotional state deteriorating rapidly and she didn't know how much longer she could keep going.

But one morning they did not come for her, instead there was unusual activity around the cavern. Half-a-dozen silver suited narun appeared and for the first time she also saw unsuited grey narun, the dhumraka, their dull grey skin and features more distinct than she'd been imagining. There were four of them. Most of the narun went into one of the tall enclosed cells, so aptly called torture cells by Ceeda, these were accompanied by Karlin and Darren. Ian remained out with two others and set about the usual procedure for fetching a fresh tree from the surface.

- - -

Tilvy nestled deeper into the roots, encouraged further by stirrings from Barma above her. Garjae was right, the tree would have been a tight fit for five of them, not that Barma's over-protective urging, pushing her deeper into the roots, was helping much. She could feel a raw patch where one of the cramped roots was rubbing against the wooden wall of the platform and decided to distract herself by concentrating on helping the tree to repair the damage.

She was frightened, she could not pretend otherwise, but she was not going to let Barma face the danger alone and refused to wait to hear how things had gone. Besides, Andrei was much better at interacting with strangers than she was, so it only made sense that he was the one to stay outside. He could help Senna much better than Tilvy could.

Muffled down here in the roots she did not sense the human approaching until Barma warned her. As Garjae had told them, the moving of the platform was a long and slow process. She could feel the tension building in Barma, above her, as the platform progressed.

Their plan was simple enough: Garjae would keep watch and at the right time, when the dhumraka was not watching, he would signal for each to get out of the tree and try to hide amongst the boxes and equipment between the cages. They would rely on the mesh of the cages to help obscure their presence. With the dhumraka's senses muffled by the suit they should be able to hide safely. In the evening when Asha was returned, and her big cage was open, they would emerge and overpower the dhumraka and the humans, pushing them into the cage in her place. Easy.

John had worried that the humans would call for help, but Garjae assured him that he'd seen no sign of radios and they'd be sure to take any mobile phones off them. John had worried that four of them against three, the one dhumraka and two humans expected, was not enough, but Garjae had assured him the unarmed humans who could not see them would not be much of a problem. John had worried ... well let's just say that John had worried. And right now Tilvy was putting a lot more credence on John's worries than she had in the relative safety of the park. Now their plan seemed ludicrously vulnerable. But no one had had any better ideas and none of them wanted to wait any longer.

The platform jolted to a halt at the bottom of the lift. The platform started to move again and word was passed down from Garjae that they were headed in a different direction to what he had expected. They were headed toward the enclosed cells. It was far from comforting that Garjae had let slip that Ceeda called these the torture cells.

Tilvy's nerves were jumping as the platform moved slowly toward its destination ... then it stopped.

"Trap!" screamed Garjae down the tree, obviously in great pain, and then he was gone. She felt Darnu leave to try and help his friend. Tilvy pulled herself quickly toward the trunk to follow them out.

"Hide!" screamed Barma's panic-stricken voice down through the tree. She felt him almost ripped, still screaming, from the tree as he was hit by the ray.

Tilvy retreated back into the roots but could feel the ray tearing at the prana as it made its way down, closer and closer. The ray reached her, and even through the protection of the earthen platform, it felt as if she were being torn apart. Her screams went unheard, merged here deep in the roots of the tree. She wanted to flow past the ray, so she could escape to the outside, but the ray kept

271

pressing her down. She felt the cold, dead wood of the platform wall pressing against the worn root that she had found earlier, it offered sanctuary from the ray, so Tilvy pushed her way through. She emerged through the platform wall and collapsed onto the cold floor outside. She placed her arms over her mouth to stop herself from screaming for all to hear.

"There could be more," she heard a voice call. "Get those others off there and then keep firing. *Kill* the tree if you have to!"

Where Tilvy had dropped from the side of the platform was hidden in shadows, both from the platform and from the nearby pile of crates and boxes. She could see a human standing not far away but he couldn't see her. Now that the ray had stopped hitting her, she found the strength to pull herself between some of the boxes and out of sight. Almost numb with terror, Tilvy kept pulling herself along. To one side of her she saw the burning mesh of a large empty cage. She kept crawling and came to where it joined another cage and looked up into the eyes of Asha, those wide compassionate eyes staring at her with surprise and sympathy.

Asha pointed back into the boxes and called to her in a loud whisper, "There's a box of old silver suits just in through there, try to hide in them." Then Asha turned away to avoid drawing attention to Tilvy's presence.

Tilvy clambered further in among the boxes and found the large box of discarded pieces of silver suit. She tried to cover herself with a blanket of the pieces and then lay back stricken by all that had happened.

- - -

In the open maw of the doorway to the enclosed cell lay the three others. In the brief confusion between when the ray had stopped and when the suited narun had begun to drag them off the platform, Darnu had managed to pull himself together enough to call out his trembling brevi and send it off to warn John and the others, he could only hope that Nuttachen could find a way out. Now he lay with the other two, their bodies still twitching with the effects of the ray. They stared back at the platform, unsure what to make of the fact that Tilvy had failed to appear.

Darnu whispered to the others, "While they're watching the platform get rid of your cape and hood, we don't want to give away that secret." The other two nodded and concentrated as best they could and eventually the capes were gone.

Garjae and Darnu had to restrain Barma from going back to try and find Tilvy.

"What if she escaped?" Garjae whispered to him. "If she got out, or survives all that, then her best chance is if the others don't know there was anyone else in there."

Barma gave Garjae a hurt look that clearly asked, "And if she didn't get out?"

Garjae just shook his head.

It took a long time but eventually the ray had finished its work. The tree was quite dead but there was still no sign of Tilvy. The three friends were dragged the rest of the way into the enclosed cell and the huge doors were closed behind them. They could no longer even see those they had come to save.

- - -

Ian jumped when he first felt the creature climb up his leg, he almost shrieked out loud. Whatever it was, it stopped at his shoulder. He could feel it trembling there, apparently trying to hide behind him. It didn't run away when he put his hand back to take hold of it. He looked in his hand and couldn't see anything, but he could feel its tiny presence shaking in his palm. He released his fingers and felt it run up to his forearm and stop. There was a strange cold sensation and then he shivered all over. He could no longer feel the creature on his arm, but there was a warm sensation moving up inside his arm, it stopped again at his shoulder.

Hearing Karlin call, "Kill the tree if you have to!" Ian looked back up. No one had noticed him, they were all concentrating on the tree. He certainly wasn't going to mention the creature. If he'd imagined it they didn't need to know, and if it'd been real they still didn't need to know; Karlin was just the sort to slice him up in search of it.

Ian glanced to the side and saw some boxes near him move slightly. Again he decided that ignorance was bliss and remained silent.

He watched as suited narun moved things that he couldn't see and then Davies continued to play the ray over the tree, Ian could see it visibly wilting. Eventually Karlin called a halt. Ian stayed where he was, waiting for instructions.

The doors to the large cell were closed and Karlin called to him, "Ian, take this away," pointing to the tree, "we don't need it any more."

When he got the tree out in the open it was obvious that this one should go to the deceased line. He was no horticulturist but there seemed little doubt about it. After disconnecting the platform from the tractor he leaned against it for a few minutes to try and pull himself together. The preparations this morning had smacked of a trap, an ambush, and the little he'd seen and heard just now felt like a massacre. He had no idea how Karlin and Davies had known there were going to be narun in that tree, he didn't want to know, but their solution had a cold efficiency. Ian was starting to regret not running when he had the chance. He hadn't liked his chances then, but he liked them even less now.

He felt the warmth that had settled at his shoulder move back down his arm. There was another cold sensation and then he felt the creature on his forearm again. It paused and then there was a small twitch of pressure as something leapt from his arm. He saw a spurt of dust as something ran across the platform, and then, whatever it had been, was gone.

- - -

Andrei cried in horror, "Nuttachen!" and pointed down the street.

It took John a while longer to see the small figure coming up along the grass between the footpath and the street. "Open your door," he said, and at the same time he started the car and looked around him for danger.

The tiny brevi reached them at last, bounded in the door and up to John's ear. John heard the echo of Darnu's pained voice, "It was a trap. Get out of here!" The brevi pawed at John's shoulder, wanting reassurance and a place of warmth and safety.

John said quickly, "Andrei, Senna. Run to your friends and tell them to scatter. It was a trap. Get them and yourselves out of here. I'll meet you back at the apartment tonight. I'm going to stay a bit longer just in case one of the others manages to get out."

Senna was out the door and running before John finished speaking but Andrei hesitated.

"Go, Andrei! I'm safe enough here, there's still lots of humans about. Help Senna protect your people."

That convinced him and he was gone, his cape streaming from his shoulders, forgotten in his hurry. Looking back to watch them, John saw that Senna had paused waiting for Andrei. She drew his cape back around him and then they both set off again.

The few aaranya they had found to help had not wanted to come too close, they were waiting a few blocks away. They should be safe anyway, John thought to himself, but if Andrei and Senna made a point of warning them they might be more inclined to trust and help again in the future.

John put his hand to his shoulder for Nuttachen to crawl onto, its little body still quivering. Caressing the brevi with his other hand he murmured reassurances, "We'll get him back, we'll get them all back." He just wished he could believe it himself. "Come on, in you go. In and visit with Casseta, she'll want to hear what happened." He murmured further words of reassurance and finally the brevi nuzzled at his wrist and disappeared.

None of the passing traffic of humans appeared to have noticed the mysterious opening and closing of his car doors, nor John's odd behaviour inside the car, but John drove off anyway. He wanted to be closer to the fence in case any of his friends made it out.

A few minutes later he felt the detector and saw the blue van drive past. Face hidden behind his mobile phone, John was fairly confident he would not be noticed. He hoped that Andrei and Senna got everyone away, there should have been enough time.

John alternatively drove and parked around the research centre for the rest of the day. In the evening, as the estate became deserted, he pulled back to the spot where he could watch the block at a distance, hoping against hope that they would appear after all. It was after ten o'clock by the time he gave up, realising that he'd better get back to Andrei and Senna.

He went straight to the park, not stopping to eat, he was not hungry. He walked into the dimly lit park with his heart feeling very heavy. He wondered what they could possibly do now. He was almost knocked off his feet when a figure appeared from out of nowhere and wrapped its arms around him.

"Jeez, John," came Andrei's voice, sounding cracked and rather desperate. "I thought we'd lost you too!"

Further back Senna was standing looking at the ground, her eyes red from crying.

"I'm sorry," said John. "I didn't want to give up on them."

He returned Andrei's embrace for a few moments before Andrei disentangled himself, a little embarrassed.

They sat quietly for a while, each lost in their own thoughts.

Eventually John said, "Andrei, you do know what Darnu would want you to do?"

Andrei nodded. "But I don't care."

"What?" Senna asked of John.

"Darnu would have said that Andrei should return to the forest, that he should go and tell the elders what has been learned here."

Senna looked hopefully at Andrei, but he shook his head. "And what would Darnu have done if he were in my position, John?"

John shook his head too, they both knew Darnu would not have left.

"Darnu said it was a trap, didn't he?" asked Senna cautiously.

John nodded.

"So how did they know we were coming?"

"A new detector?" suggested Andrei.

"No," said Senna, she'd obviously been thinking about this. "If they had a new detector, one we can't feel, then they'd have been using it to find us before now. They'd have found us all waiting near the centre this morning. They'd have found Garjae when he first went in." She paused before concluding, "Andrei, someone must have betrayed us."

"That doesn't make sense either," said John. "If we'd been betrayed they'd have been ready for us outside the centre, we'd have all been caught."

Senna shook her head. "Those that Andrei and I brought along don't know what you or your car looks like. They didn't know where we would be waiting."

"So you're saying that the betrayer was among those you brought to help us?" said John.

"Who else?" Senna asked. "The prisoners are hardly going to give us away."

"They could have been seen before they entered the tree," said Andrei. "If one of the dhumraka were watching from somewhere, wearing one of those suits, Darnu and the others might not see them."

"That'd cover it," said John.

Senna looked doubtful.

There was a period of silence. Eventually John said, "There's nothing more we can do tonight, we'd better get some rest."

"And you need to eat," said Senna.

John looked at her. "What is it with you women? You all insist I should eat."

"They've got a thing against skeletons, John," said Andrei. "Miss too many more meals and you're going to resemble one."

Senna put her hand over Andrei's mouth to stop more smart comments. "It's just obvious that you're running low, John. You're not going to function well if you don't keep your body going."

He reluctantly agreed and went off to try and find a late night takeaway.

- - -

There was no day or night in the cavern. The lights were always on but it was only dimly lit. But it felt like night to Tilvy, she thought it must be getting late. Finally calm again after hours of trembling from the effects of the ray and simple panic, Tilvy pulled herself from under the blanket of silver suit pieces and drew close to Asha's cage.

Asha looked around and decided it was safe. She came down off the platform and sat near the mesh so they could speak quietly.

Keeping it as brief as she could, Tilvy told Asha how she came to be there.

"So John's still out there somewhere?" Asha asked.

"I hope so. I still have no idea how they knew we were coming, so I suppose it's possible they caught him too."

Asha shook her head. "I doubt it. I'm pretty sure Karlin would have been wherever John was, if they'd known. They're very keen to get their hands on him."

"That's something I suppose." Tilvy looked around. "Is there any chance I can open these cages tonight?"

Asha shook her head. "You should leave while you can."

"No," Tilvy said firmly. "If I can't let you out of the cages then perhaps I can look around the place while no one's around. Who knows, maybe someone left the keys lying around somewhere."

Asha explained as much as she knew of the layout of the building and the cavern, but she hadn't really seen that much of it. "Watch out for the dhumraka. I have no idea where they spend the night."

"I'll be careful," said Tilvy. She crept back the way she'd come in, between the boxes and the cage mesh. She emerged and looked at the row of tall doors, behind one set was her Barma. Well, she couldn't get to him from here so she'd have to find some other way.

Off to the left of the row of doors was a lighted corridor that Asha said was where they took her up a ramp and into the laboratory rooms. Closer to Tilvy, on the right side of the building, she could see another passageway between the building and the cavern. Asha didn't know anything about it so Tilvy decided to take a look. It seemed as good a place as any to start her explorations.

This passageway turned out to be just a gap, a narrow unused space between the concrete of the cavern wall and the wall of the laboratory complex. It was uneven and darker than the cavern itself. Tilvy made her way carefully along it. At the other end it opened up into a wide corridor to the left, one half of which went up a ramp to a door into the laboratory and the other half stopped earlier at a solid looking mesh door. Tilvy thought this was probably the entry door that Asha had spoken of, where she had first been carried into this cavern.

The light was better here, it was obviously an area much more frequently used than the dark left-over space she'd just come through. Tilvy went to the mesh door and studied it. The mesh was the same horrible stuff of the cages, but the sturdy latch and lock arrangement was normal metal and inlaid with strips of leather that made it easier for her to grip. She expected the door to be locked but tried the handle anyway. The door opened. Tilvy swung it out of the way and found she had to hold it back to stop it swinging shut automatically.

There was a second door but this one was a normal wood-like panel door. It was not natural enough to pass through so Tilvy turned its handle. It too was unlocked so she pushed it against its closing spring and slipped through into the room beyond, releasing the doors behind her.

The long room was just a closed in part of the corridor that she had come from, forming a sort of controlled entry area. There was a human guard in a glassed-in booth built on one side of this short corridor and next to that was a narrow pair of doors – they looked like the lift doors of John's apartment building.

The human guard looked up from the magazine he was studying. The doors finished closing themselves and the guard shrugged and went back to his magazine. Tilvy guessed he was used to phantom openings and closings.

If this was where Asha had been brought in then straight ahead must be the car park, so Tilvy decided to try the lift. She pressed the call button. Inside the lift Tilvy looked at the sequence of buttons: B2, G, the numbers 1 to 4 and R. With a shrug she pressed the button marked 3.

The lift rose and stopped, but when the door opened she found that the way out was partly blocked by a stack of boxes. Warned by this, Tilvy placed her hand nervously against the lift door to stop it closing. The way it bumped against her hand was a little frightening but it didn't seem to be dangerous. If this stop wasn't used, did that mean it couldn't be used? She looked at the call button on the outside and saw that it had a key-lock next to it. She reached out and pressed the button but nothing happened – so if she had left the lift she would have had no way to get back in.

Out past the boxes Tilvy could see an open-plan office environment. Sparse fluorescent lighting and the low hum of air-conditioning gave the area a cold and desolate feel. She let the door close. The next level up looked like a virtual clone of the previous so she decided to move on to the level marked R.

When the doors opened Tilvy gasped in surprise and stood pinned to the back of the lift. The doors closed but the lift didn't move. Tilvy thought that the R button might have taken her to the top of the building, she'd been hoping to see a starlit sky. Instead what she had seen were tall glass rooms full of water and long, leafy, dark green plants. The light that had filled the lift was tinged green from passing through those pools from a source somewhere above them. The briny smell of the sea and the sweet smell of rotting seaweed still filled the lift. The scent had been there before, faintly, but Tilvy hadn't given it any thought.

Tilvy tried to pull herself together and reason out what to do. They'd all thought the grey narun were aaranya, tree-folk, but maybe they weren't. Maybe they were samudraka, sea-folk, and maybe this is where they spent their time when they weren't helping humans to torture others. If that was the case then to go in there was to walk into a chamber of demons.

But how could she know for certain unless she went in? It was possible these were more prisoners – perhaps they were experimenting with samudraka too. The few pools down below appeared to be all freshwater, perhaps this was where they dealt with seawater.

But the grey ones had to live somewhere. To go in there was foolhardy, all they had to do was reach out their senses to know she was there.

Tilvy shook herself, she was going around in circles. Even just standing here in the lift was dangerous. She pulled her cloak and hood more tightly about herself, the less obvious her presence the more likely they would be to overlook her – she hoped. She'd go through and explore. She had to be bold. Their lives, Barma's life, might depend on what she could discover through here.

Tilvy opened the doors and stepped out. To her left she saw a rack of silver suits and hurried over and dressed in one of them. Their experiments had shown that you could not tell who was inside, so now she hoped to be safe unless one of them actually tried to talk to her.

Feeling a little more secure, Tilvy began to move along the passageways between the glass pools. She saw that the walls of each pool did not extend to the ceiling, and each had a ladder for entry and exit over the top of the wall. Looking further up she realised that the ceiling over this room of pools was glass too, the internal lights were reflecting off it and that made it difficult to see out. There was a low rumble of quiet pumps and the occasional blobbing sound of bubbles rising through the pools.

Tilvy stopped abruptly when she saw a figure in one of the pools. He appeared to be resting along the stem of one of the long, leafy plants, he and the plant were gently undulating in the subtle currents of the pool. The distortion of the green tinged light made it impossible to tell the colour of his skin, but he did feel more like an aaranya than anything else she knew. He appeared to be asleep and Tilvy quickly moved on out of his immediate sight.

She quickly lost count of the pools and the silver suit made it difficult to send out her senses. Whatever, she knew there were a lot. There could certainly be more than ten of these narun up here. Tilvy was convinced these were the grey ones, the dhumraka. The pools had none of the hallmarks of the dreadful prison cells beneath the building.

Tilvy found herself at a low wall, topped with a glass panel, that looked over the side of the building. Down along the side of the building she could see, in the dim city lights, what appeared to be a zigzag stairway leading down to the ground, a fire-escape of some sort. She made her way past the boxes and other paraphernalia stacked along the wall until she was at the head of the stairway. It was open at the top but she thought she could see some sort of gate further down. It didn't look like the sort of thing that was likely to stop a narun. That pretty much confirmed it, these were definitely not prisoners.

Tilvy found a half-hidden place amongst some boxes and settled down to think.

17. Beaten

Back in his apartment room, a rapidly cooling burger sitting on its wrappings on the table before him, John pulled out his mobile telephone again. He turned it over in his hands a few times then got up and got the charger. He plugged it in and set his phone to charge.

He sat down and stared at his phone while he took a mouthful of burger. He chewed without tasting, still staring at the phone.

He turned it on.

After a minute or so he could see that he had messages waiting.

Another bite, another period of staring at the phone.

A deep breath and he started the messages playing.

"John, you can't do that!" came Jason's voice. "You can't ring and then turn your phone off like that. I only missed you by a couple of minutes. ... Need I say it? ... Call me."

John hit the delete button.

"John, me again," came Jason's voice. "Stan's not happy. I think he thinks I'm holding out on him. If you can't call me at least call Stan ... he's really not happy, I mean really."

John hit the delete button.

"John," came Stan's voice. "It's Friday and still no word. I don't know what to make of this but it's really not good enough. If we could talk to you—"

John didn't wait for him to finish, just pressed the delete button. He didn't have room in his head to worry about his old life. He'd try to pick up the pieces later.

"John, my dear friend, it's been a week," came the voice that John remembered well despite having heard it just once before. This new message was almost a week old now. "Come and talk to us, we'll soon sort out this misunderstanding. Call me when you get this, any time. Ciao."

John's thumb hovered over the delete button but didn't press.

"John," came Jason's voice again as the next message started playing.

John hit the delete option without waiting for more.

And again.

The next message was from early this afternoon. "John, my dear, dear, boy," came the now familiar and overly cheerful voice. "It must be getting lonely out there on your own. Call me, we'll work this out."

John snatched at the phone and tried to throw it across the room but it jerked off its charger cord and flicked to the floor instead. He went over and picked it up. He was tempted to stand on it first, to remove the temptation to use it, but instead he just punched at the off button and plugged it back into the charger.

The frustration, the feeling of total helplessness, was boiling away inside him. He had to fight back the urge to get in the car and try to confront them on his own – anything other than sitting here feeling useless while his friends were suffering. He'd been up for hours and hadn't been sleeping well anyway, but he couldn't settle. He grabbed his coat and stormed out of the room, slamming the door, careless of the fact that it was after midnight.

He didn't want the car, the temptation would be too great, so he exited the front of the building onto the footpath. He considered crossing to the park, but why disturb Andrei and Senna with his frustrated restlessness. Picking a direction at random he started walking quickly. He pulled his coat around him against the cold night air.

Blocks passed quickly and without regard as he tried to work out what he could do for his friends. Lost in his own thoughts he didn't notice footsteps getting closer behind him.

The blow to the back of his head seemed to come from nowhere. He stumbled but managed to keep to his feet, his head reeling.

"In there," came a voice.

He was spun by his coat and ended up sprawling on the asphalt of an alleyway, his jeans tearing and skin was lost from his knees and palms as he tried to break his fall. He started to get up but was pushed flat as a pair of knees fell against his back, pushing hard against his ribs. His breath expelled violently leaving him gasping. The smell of asphalt and dirt filled his mouth and nostrils as his face was pressed to the ground.

"Where the fuck's his wallet," came the same voice again, Rough hands felt the pockets of his jeans and coat. "He owes me a fucking wallet – and a phone."

"Hurry up," said another voice from further away.

"I can't find his wallet," said the first voice. The knees, and the hand holding his head, gave another hard push, squashing him again and grinding his face into the ground, as the man stood up. "I'm gonna teach this fuck to have some fuckin' respect! You're into jokes aren't you mate, well try this one: I never hit a man when he's down – I kick him, it's easier."

Pain exploded in John's side as he was kicked in the ribs, and then again. He tried to raise his arms to protect his head but was too late, his head snapped back with the force of the blow. In a daze of stars and pain he was not certain what happened after that. There were more kicks, there was more pain, but he barely registered the individual impacts, it all merged into a red haze.

He vaguely heard the second voice yell, "Someone's coming!" and then he was alone, just the cold night air chilling exposed skin wet with blood.

In the quiet and cold it came to him that his wallet was still on the table in his room, with the remains of his burger. With that thought his stomach gave up on what he had already eaten. His body heaved, the impulse not caring for the pain of the bruises and scratches. He pushed himself to his elbows to keep himself out of the mess and tried to push himself up. The best he could manage was to push himself away, but that was better than nothing.

A cautious voice called from the mouth of the alleyway, "Are you okay in there?"

After a moment John managed to pull himself together enough to answer, "I will be."

"Should I call an ambulance?" the woman asked, obviously reluctant to come any closer, and given the circumstances John could hardly blame her.

"No!" said John more urgently than the question warranted, it was not the sort of attention he wanted. "I'll be okay." He tried again and managed to get to his feet, leaning heavily on the wall.

Standing, he was more visible in the light from the street. The woman, seeing the blood on his face, gasped. "You're bleeding! Are you sure you don't need a hospital – the police?"

In an effort to seem better than he felt John pushed himself closer to the street. "It's okay. It'll wash off. I got off light. I happen to know that one of them owns a knife. He didn't use it. That's got to be a bonus."

John's dazed and gasped effort to lighten the impact of the situation wasn't reassuring the woman very much. He peered at her, one of his eyes already swelling. Girl, he corrected himself, he thought she couldn't be more than twenty. "Things won't look so bad when I get back to my room and clean up," he tried again to reassure her.

She looked doubtful. "Is it far?"

"The Harnell Apartments, just up there," John waved vaguely, hoping he remembered the direction correctly.

"That's two suburbs over!"

"Is it ... oh. Guess I lost track of time."

"You walked?"

John nodded and wished he hadn't.

"I'll give you a lift," she said.

"No, it's fine," he said, his words starting to slur as his lips swelled on one side. "You shouldn't give strange men lifts in your car."

"I don't think you're much of a threat," she said and smiled for the first time. She had a kind face. "Wait here, I'll get my car."

"You don't need to do this," he tried again, but half-heartedly, he was starting to wonder how he would make the distance back to his room on his own.

"Wait," she said and walked off briskly.

Through his dazed senses John felt a strange sensation on his arm where it reached out to the wall trying to steady himself. He looked across to see Casseta partly emerge, her nose twitching nervously. He whispered a few mumbled words of reassurance to her and she drew back in. He could only hope that his own pain and injury had not affected the two brevi too badly.

John wavered where he stood, half leaning against the corner of the alleyway. He was having trouble remembering what he was doing there when a small red car pulled up to the curb.

The girl got out and opened the passenger door for him. He lurched toward her. She ran to steady him. When he got to the car he made a point of looking himself over and dusting himself off. "Don't want to bleed on your car," he explained.

"You're right," she said. "Your back is mostly okay, just don't rub your face on the seat covers," she added with a wry smile.

John tried to return the smile but his face hurt too much.

"I'm Tracey," she introduced herself.

"John," John mumbled.

With a slow painful bend he lowered himself into the small, cramped passenger seat of the car and the girl closed the door behind him. She got in, did an illegal U-turn on the street, quiet at this early hour of the morning, and headed back toward John's apartment.

To John, his mind still in a daze, it felt as though he'd barely sat down when Tracey did another U-turn and pulled up in front of his building. He stared blankly for a moment before reaching for the door handle and turning to his rescuer.

"Thanks," he said. "Really. Thank you very much. I do really appreciate it. ... But promise me you won't make a habit of picking up strange men off the street."

"Yes, Dad, I promise," she said with a smile. "Although I think you'd find it hard to be an axe murderer in your condition."

John tried to smile back at her but thought it probably turned out more of a grimace. He opened the door and said, "Thanks again," before easing himself slowly and painfully out of the car.

As she drove away he patted his pockets and swore to himself. He didn't have the apartment keys. He looked up and saw the red car stopping for a red light at the end of the next block, but there was no way he could run to try and catch her. He looked up at the apartment block and again swore under his breath. He couldn't walk back to where he'd been mugged so he turned and crossed the road into the park.

He stumbled through the dim light to the park bench and sat down with a heavy sigh.

"You were supposed to be sleeping," came Andrei's voice.

286

"So were you," mumbled John.

Andrei was suddenly at John's side, concern in his voice. "What happened?"

"Couldn't settle so went for a walk ... met our friend from the other night," explained John.

"The man with the knife?" asked Senna from behind Andrei, her hand on his shoulder.

John tried to nod then resorted to speech, it was slightly less painful. "Yeah, although he didn't pull his knife tonight." John paused to try and move his tender ribs into a more comfortable position. "I was rescued by a brave or foolish girl that gave me a lift back here. But now it seems I've lost my apartment keys. Could be in for a cold night in the park with you guys – what's left of it."

"Could this be your saviour now?" asked Senna, looking back toward the road.

"John?" Tracey called into the darkness.

"I'm here," he called back and winced with the exertion.

As Tracey approached she said, "I saw you cross the road in the mirror and wondered why, then I looked down and saw these on the seat." She held up his apartment keys.

"That's twice you've saved me tonight," said John. "Thanks." He stood up stiffly and accepted the keys from her.

She looked around. "I thought I heard you talking to someone."

"I often talk to myself," said John, "that way I'm sure of an appreciative audience."

She smiled forgivingly at his attempt at humour, looked around again and then said, "I've got to get home."

"Sure. Thanks. I wasn't looking forward to sleeping out here."

They walked back to her car. There was an awkward silence before Tracey said, "Good night."

"Good night, Tracey, and thanks again," he replied.

"She seemed nice," said Senna from behind him, as Tracey drove off.

"Yeah, really nice. Not real bright to be picking up strange men, but nice ... kind."

"And they don't come much stranger than you, John," said Andrei. "Mind you, it's a wee bit of a stretch for you to question how bright she is when you're the one out walking after midnight and getting mugged."

"Thanks, Andrei, you're always a comfort."

Senna grinned and grabbed at Andrei, "He is, isn't he."

All of them were oblivious to Tracey sitting at lights not far up the road, looking back and watching John in conversation with no one.

John went up to his apartment and was thankful it had a bath. A clean up and long soak did indeed make him look much better, although he suspected the bruises that were still coming out would look pretty impressive.

While he was bathing he got Casseta and Nuttachen out and let them run around the bathroom, telling them not to run off. As Milla had said, they seemed to understand his intention well enough and when he was finished they merged back into his body with no difficulty, in fact they both seemed keen to return, as if to a refuge after a day of disturbing events. John wasn't sure just how good a refuge he was turning out to be.

He fell into bed and was soon asleep.

* * *

The next morning John woke with a loud groan. He was thinking about how badly beaten he felt when an attempt to stretch caused an extra stab of pain and he remembered that was exactly what he was, badly beaten. As the events of the previous day came back to him he hauled himself out of bed, trying to ignore the pain. Eight o'clock. It wasn't as late as he feared, even so he didn't want to lose more time – not that he had any idea what he was going to do with it yet.

A hot shower loosened up his bruised muscles. He looked in the mirror and saw that he was going to have trouble avoiding attention today. His left eye was badly swollen, not completely closed but certainly obvious. The left side of his mouth was also swollen, he could speak clearly enough if he concentrated, but it didn't do much for his appearance.

Dressed in clean clothes he moved around the apartment tidying up. He was at the table putting the burger remains in a bag when his mobile phone rang. He'd picked it up and answered by reflex, before his brain caught up. He mustn't have turned it off properly last night.

"John, my dear friend. I am so pleased you decided to talk to me, so pleased," came the now familiar voice.

John pulled the phone back from his ear putting his thumb over the button to hang up, but he paused, uncertain.

"Come now, John, no need to be shy. We can be friends you know, just give me a chance to explain," continued the voice.

Cursing himself for half-believing the sincere and cheerful voice he responded, "Where are my friends?"

"They're safe, John. They're all safe."

"Then let them go and we'll talk," John said, trying to give his voice the ring of authority.

"First you need to understand what we do here, John. This is important work, this is the stuff of history."

"That doesn't excuse how you've been treating the narun," said John.

"It's just that they don't all understand. We have narun friends here that do understand and are helping us. Your friends ... they're helping us too, they just have to be encouraged."

"You've been torturing them!" John snarled into the phone.

"Yes, the visitor you had in here. Of course he gave you just one side of the story, come to us here, John, and I'll show you the other side. You'll see, it's all going to be worthwhile."

"You're mad!"

There was silence that dragged on, John was wondering if the man was going to hang up.

"That hurts, John, that hurts," came the voice, quieter now. "Of course you are not the first to doubt what we do, not the first. But I'm not alone here, John, another knows the benefit of this work. If you'll just come in and give us a chance."

Trying to calm himself, John said, "Let my friends go and I'll come in."

There was a deep sigh. "John ... John ... I really didn't want it to come to this but you leave me little choice."

There was silence again but John could feel it coming, the threat. It was why he'd stayed off the phone all this time, if they couldn't talk to him they couldn't threaten him.

"We must speak with you in person, John, and if the only way to secure your cooperation is to force it ... well, so be it. Your friends' lives are now in your hands. If you don't turn up here by five o'clock this afternoon the first of your friends will be .... We will leave their body just inside the fence, we can't have the public tripping over it, but you need to be able to see it so that you will not doubt our sincerity."

"You can't do that!"

"We can – and we will – but only reluctantly. And we will repeat the exercise each day until you are convinced."

"I need more time!" said John in desperation.

"For what?" the man laughed. "For last-ditch schemes? John, I presume you realise we are well set here to cope with any nosiness from authorities. We are a legitimate research centre, working in cooperation with the government no less. Should you seek to embarrass us ... well, I hardly need repeat myself, do I?"

In a more conciliatory tone the man continued, "With your friends already here what more time can you need? Come in. Talk to us. You won't regret it."

John couldn't find a response to that.

"Before five," the man said. "Don't be late." The phone disconnected.

John held the phone in both hands, pressed the hang-up button with a thumb and then just stared at it. Last night he'd wondered what would happen if he spoke with them – now he knew. He realised that throughout the conversation the other man had given nothing concrete away, he didn't even know the man's name. Not that it made a lot of difference.

He drew a deep breath. Time to talk to Andrei. There was no choice now, Andrei would have to return to the forest. They would have to be told what had happened and Andrei would have to do it the long way; John wasn't going to be available to drive him.

This time remembering his wallet, he left the apartment and walked out the front. It was getting close to nine o'clock, the few stragglers hurrying to get to work along the footpath took one look at John's bruised face and gave him a wide berth. He couldn't work out why, surely it was obvious that he was the beatee and not the beater.

Forced to use the lights to cross the road, John was getting impatient and jogged into the park ignoring the complaints of pain coming from much of his bruised body. He called out, "Andrei!" He saw Andrei and Senna standing fairly close to a group of people. He didn't think about why such a group would be here in the quiet park at this time on a Friday morning, at this point he didn't care. "Andrei, there's trouble."

"Um, John," said Andrei hesitantly, pointing to the park bench.

Slowing down as he approached, clutching his arms around his painful ribs and lost in his own thoughts, John ignored this and continued, "It's my own damn fault. I must have left the mobile on last night. They rang. Just now."

"John," said Andrei more firmly, "she's here!"

"Huh?" said John.

"What?" said Andrei.

They both finally caught on to what the other was saying. Tracey was sitting on the park bench giving John a strange look.

"What happened?" asked Andrei.

John looked back and forth, decided the damage was done, and answered Andrei. "The worst. Whoever it was threatened to kill the others if I didn't come in. There's no choice now, Andrei, I have to go. I have to be there before five this afternoon or they will kill one of them."

A few feet behind them Senna stood listening, her face aghast.

Seeing this John continued, "They don't seem to know about you, Andrei, or Senna. You have to go back to the forest and tell the others what happened."

"You'd better look to the girl, John," came another familiar voice.

"Uncle?" said John in surprise, finally noticing that the group he'd seen earlier were narun, Guyen and some others.

"The girl, John."

John looked across and saw that Tracey's expression had gone from one of puzzlement to one of fear.

"I'm sorry, Tracey," he said, walking toward her. "I didn't mean to upset you."

"Who were you talking to?" she asked, standing but not moving away.

"I told you I talk to myself a lot," he said, trying to make a joke of it, but he could see by her expression that it was too late for that.

"No one talks to themselves like that."

"Like what."

"It was only half a conversation."

"She's good," said Andrei appreciatively.

"Shut up, Andrei, you're not helping," John tried to whisper, then to Tracey, "Can you accept that I hit my head last night and now I'm hearing voices? But don't worry, I'm sure I'll get over it."

What he thought had been fear seemed to turn to anger. "Bullshit! There's something going on here. When I came back to the park last night I thought I heard you talking and when I was sitting at the lights going away you were talking to someone on the street."

"I don't think she's going for it," said Andrei.

"One of the voices is *really* annoying," said John.

Tracey's anger receded and she gave him a broken laugh.

"Can I sit?" asked John indicating the park bench and then putting his arms back around his chest. "It still hurts."

"Sure," she replied, sitting down too. "After all, that's why I came: to see how you were."

"So why wait over here?" he asked.

"After what I saw last night this seemed like a good place to find you."

"Told you she's good," said Andrei.

John gave him a shut up look and then tried to smile at Tracey, but she was looking out trying to see what John had looked at.

"What'd it say that time?" she asked.

"He said you were good," admitted John.

Tracey looked at John carefully, trying to see if there was a joke or a lie in his expression.

"Why don't you tell her?" said Guyen.

"Because she won't believe me," said John.

Tracey looked askance but John held up a hand while Guyen said, "We could provide proof."

"You'd do that?" asked John.

"She seems okay to me," said Andrei. "I like her."

Senna agreed.

"Want to tell me what the voice said that time?" asked Tracey.

"Voices," corrected John.

"More than one?"

John nodded. "I thought I'd inherited my daughter's imaginary friend."

"You have a daughter?" asked Tracey.

"Had," John answered.

"Oh."

John took a breath and continued, "I discovered that my daughter's imaginary friend was real, and since then I've met lots more of them."

"And they're here?" Tracey asked sceptically, looking around.

John nodded. "But before we go any further ...." He paused trying to work out what he wanted to say. "You need to know that this information may not be safe. It's probably okay, it's not like you can see them, but even so – there are nasty people involved. It might be wiser if you left now, before this goes any further." John waited for some sign that Tracey might accept this advice. Seeing none, he continued, "Or, I can introduce you to my friends."

Tracey looked at John, looked around and then looked back at John. "No candid camera joke?" she asked.

John shook his head.

"Are we talking aliens here?"

"No, this is their home too."

"And you've got bad people after you?" Tracey asked.

"I've got to know, John," said Andrei with a grin. "How did she pick us as the good guys when she's looking at you?"

John looked at Andrei and laughed past his painful ribs, "Good question."

"What?" asked Tracey.

"Andrei wants to know how you guessed that we were the good guys by looking at me."

She smiled. "That'd be the annoying voice you spoke of?"

"So you're not leaving?" John asked Tracey. "It might be wiser."

She shook her head. "Too late now, you've got me curious. Not saying I believe you, but I don't think you're dangerous."

"Let's do this," said John. "Who do you want to meet first?"

Tracey laughed nervously. "How many are there?"

John looked around and counted. Surprised himself, he said, "Twelve. Uncle?"

"We need to talk, John, better wrap up your explanations," said Guyen.

John continued to Tracey, "There are a dozen here but I only know three of them. I suggest Senna first. You and she are both young city girls and she's less likely to cause trouble than Andrei.

"Senna says to say hello and you're not to be scared. Hold out your hand and she'll shake it," instructed John.

Tracey looked around to see if there were any visible people likely to laugh at her and then held out her hand. Senna took it gently. Tracey jumped at the first touch but then accepted it. Tentatively she put her other hand forward. She looked to John who nodded. With her left hand she reached up and touched the back of the hand that held hers. It was warm and feminine. "It feels human," she said with quiet awe.

"They all look human ... Andrei reminds me that the correct phrase is that we look narun." said John.

"Narun?"

"That's what they are. We look much the same, to those that can see them, but narun are made differently to humans," explained John.

Tracey looked at John and then looked back at where she imagined Senna must be crouched in front of her. "Senna? Would it be okay if I touched your face? I don't want to be rude but this is just so hard to accept."

"Senna says that's okay," John passed on.

Tracey's left hand continued to feel its way up Senna's arm, at last finding the side of her head, then her face, her cap and her hair. "You're very pretty," said Tracey.

"Senna just blushed but Andrei is in complete agreement ... oh look, now I've got him blushing too," said John with a laugh.

Guyen caught John's attention so he said to Tracey, "I really don't want to rush you, but I've got to find out why all these others are here. I don't want to keep them all waiting too much longer and I've only got until this afternoon anyway. Do you believe me now?"

Tracey nodded, unable to find the words.

"She's a lot easier to convince than you were, John," observed Andrei. "Smarter do you think?" he asked with a grin.

John nodded, "Probably."

"Did you want to go now?" John asked Tracey, she shook her head.

- - -

Andrei watched as Uncle made brief introductions between John and Taiza and the others that had come to help. Guyen had arrived early with a dozen other aaranya. A few of the group were quickly dispatched to act as sentinels further along the street, just in case the detector came while the group were talking.

Guyen had explained that Taiza had spoken with him and together they agreed that this was their responsibility, that it was wrong to leave to others what the city folk should have faced years ago. Together they had started visiting those few that were left that might agree to help, and they started coming up with ideas about what could be done.

When Andrei had explained what had happened yesterday the whole group was dismayed, but Guyen had rallied quickly, saying that it was more important than ever for the city folk to finally pull together. With the information that Andrei and Senna gave them, the group had started to put together a plan of sorts, but it would need John's cooperation.

Senna had taken Guyen to one side to discuss possible traitors, but Guyen just shook his head and said that they couldn't stop trusting each other now, that was how things had gotten this bad. They should use any of the city folk that were willing to help, he said, it was something that they needed to do if they were to survive. The more they could involve the better.

Then Tracey arrived and then John – with news of time limits. The hopeful feeling that had been building in Andrei's mind suddenly evaporated, they were out of time. He listened as John explained to Uncle and the others the consequences of his morning telephone call.

To everyone's surprise Guyen said, "It's better this way. It'd be too easy to keep putting this off. Now we know what we have to do and when we have to do it."

John looked at him intently. "Uncle, you know I have to go there. I can't let them kill the others if presenting myself can stop it."

Guyen nodded. "I know. But that was part of the plan we'd been talking about before you arrived. Now we don't even have to ask if you will do it."

"Okay, I'm listening. Is this something we can be ready for by this afternoon?"

Guyen nodded. "I think so. Can we talk to Tracey?"

John looked at Tracey sitting and looking rather bewildered on the park bench, and then back to Guyen. "You can't involve her, Uncle."

"Can't involve me in what?" asked Tracey.

John looked at her with concern. "You really don't want to know."

That was the wrong thing to say, Andrei thought to himself.

"Know what?" was Tracey's reply. Andrei was pretty sure he heard warning tones in her voice, he hoped John was listening.

John looked at the ground, trying to frame an appropriate response, then he looked back up at Guyen. "It's right that your people should be in this, Uncle, they are in danger whether they come with us or not. But this is not her fight. She can walk away from here now and be in no danger. She *should* go."

"Go where?" Tracey asked.

"Introduce me," said Guyen, "let me talk with her."

"No," said John. "It's not right. She's not involved."

"John?" Tracey asked. The warning tones were definitely there now, Andrei wondered if he should do or say anything, and whose side he should come in on.

"I think you should go home, Tracey," said John. Too late, thought Andrei. John was saying, "Things are getting involved here and you'd be safer out of it."

"Out of what? You haven't explained what's going on."

"I just thought she may be able to drive a few of us over there," said Guyen, "your car will only fit so many."

John paused, stuck in his turmoil.

"Let me talk with them," said Tracey. She rummaged in her bag for a few moments and drew out a pen and a pad of paper. "Can they write?"

"I can," said Guyen.

"Uncle, no," said John, but Guyen had already sat next to Tracey and taken the pen and pad from her surprised fingers.

"Nothing dangerous," said John. "Promise me, both of you. Nothing dangerous. You've already done more than you should, Tracey."

Tracey just waved at him, she was concentrating on the writing appearing on the pad next to her. "Hello, Uncle," she replied to something on the page. "You have beautiful handwriting."

Guyen paused in his writing. "John, I think you should go around and get to know each of this group. You must be sure to recognise who is who, we don't want any mistakes once we get started. I think Taiza and Reijo may have some questions for you too."

Andrei admired Guyen's less than subtle way of getting John out of the way so he could speak with Tracey privately. He wondered where Guyen had learned to write, it was not something that Andrei had ever considered learning. He'd tried to learn to read but hadn't got far. He leaned over the park bench to look over Guyen's shoulder. He could hear Guyen muttering under his breath as he wrote, "he feels responsible and it makes him over-protective, but we do need your help if you are willing to give it." Guyen looked up and noticed Andrei.

"How about you help John," he said. "You can explain some of what we have in mind as you speak with the others."

"Yes, commander," said Andrei crisply and saluted.

- - -

John was thinking that he'd severely underestimated Guyen. The figure he'd met at the park was a self-deprecating and mild old man, emphasis on old because that was the emphasis Guyen had made himself. Today he was a different man, younger and more positive. There was still that rounded face with its good natured laugh-lines, but now there was an alert decisiveness to his demeanour. Having experienced his own epiphany not that long ago, John thought he could possibly understand the changes he saw in Guyen.

There was a break in proceedings when a council truck turned up to empty the park rubbish bins. Andrei gave them a hand. He wasn't too obvious about it, but enough to get some chuckles out of his audience – those that could see him. While that was happening, John sat on the park bench and spoke with Tracey.

"You don't *have* to do anything," he said. "You know that don't you."

"Sure," she smiled at him. "It's okay, I want to help."

"But *why*? You don't know these people. Hell, you can't even see them, and this really could get dangerous. You really would be better advised to leave here now and forget what you've seen – or haven't seen, as the case may be."

"Fat chance of that. If I walked away now I'd always wonder what it was that I'd missed. I'd always wonder what happened to these people I've met so briefly and strangely. I want to help and Uncle says I can be of use. It is *my* decision."

John sat silent for a while. Now that he had some idea what Guyen and Taiza had come up with, he couldn't deny that a second car and driver would help. It didn't seem like she should be in any danger, as long as she kept away if things started to go wrong. He gave a deep sigh.

She laughed. "You give up?"

John nodded.

"Well let's do something about lunch. If I heard right, you missed breakfast this morning. You should eat more."

"Not you too," he groaned.

"What?"

"Never mind. Come on, I'll buy you lunch."

There was a quiet cafe not far up the street and they sat at one of the tables and ordered.

"I forgot about my face," apologised John, "people are going to wonder about the company you're keeping."

Tracey just shrugged. When the meals arrived, she asked, "Can you give me some background, tell me more of what this is about?"

John considered for a few moments but decided there was no extra danger in telling her the story. "I'll try to keep it short," he said. He surprised himself by being able to give a matter-of-fact recital of the loss of his family and moved on to discovering Asha and then her abduction and his following her to the city.

"So you're in love with Asha," Tracey stated.

John stared at his plate. "Yes," he said, "I am. Not that it really matters." He looked up. "That never really had any chance anyway, but it's all gone beyond that now. It's not just her and I. It's Andrei and Barma and Tilvy and everyone. All these people that I've met. I can't not help them."

Tracey grinned at him.

"What?"

She laughed. "You're the one that was telling me to keep out of it."

John threw his hands in the air. "It's still good advice. Come on, we've got things to do and people to see ... well I do, you just get to drive."

The first couple of hours after their early lunch was spent travelling the suburbs. John drove Andrei and Taiza, Tracey drove Uncle and Senna. Uncle had the pad in his hand so he could tell Tracey where to turn and when to stop. They persuaded as many aaranya as they could to be near the research centre late this afternoon. They needed people ready to help if everything went well and they managed to get the prisoners out.

When they finally got back to the park there was not much time left. John made the necessary phone call and the group split up. John took Andrei, Senna and eight others in the wagon, he dropped his passengers off a few blocks away from the centre before he went on to present himself. Tracey took Guyen and three others in her small car, following a discreet distance behind John.

18. Choice

John drove up to the boom gate. The car park under the building looked dark and forbidding in front of him. The door to the guard booth opened and Ian came out. He gave John a brief wave and then got in on the passenger side.

"The haircut probably would have been enough," Ian said, and peering at the bruising on John's face, he continued, "the makeover on the face is a bit extreme."

"It wasn't intentional," said John, not feeling at all friendly.

"Gods man, you don't have much luck with the people you meet."

"We're holding up traffic," said John impatiently, indicating the car pulling up behind them. He cursed himself silently, he needed to remember to take all this as slowly as he could.

Ian waved to the guard in the booth and the boom gate swung up. "Bottom level, far corner."

John followed the instructions, driving slowly. He parked in a space not far from the corner and remained sitting for a few minutes, making a show of preparing himself to go inside. He could see a dhumraka standing next to the door, the grey skin he'd heard described was obvious even in the fluorescent light. "Is he here to make sure I'm not a fake?" he asked Ian.

"Who?"

"That's right, you've been doing this by Braille." John looked around and could see another dhumraka between cars parked in the row behind them. "Looks like your boss thought I might have had a few friends to spare."

"I prefer it when they wear suits," grumbled Ian. "Come on."

They both got out of the car. John left his keys in the ignition, he was confident that no one would notice. Guyen claimed that one of their group would be able to drive it, if they couldn't get the prisoners moved any other way. John walked slowly to the door. Ian swiped his access card and opened it. As they went through John looked back and saw yet another of the grey narun looking into his car.

Inside the door was a short, brightly lit corridor. On one side was a guard booth and next to that were lift doors. As far as John could see there was only a human guard in attendance. John held the door open for the three dhumraka and waited for them to enter. After a wave to the guard from Ian, they all passed through doors at the end of this short entry hall and into a higher and wider corridor. John made a great show of looking around, walking as slowly as he dared. They followed a ramp up and entered a higher level where John was led into a room – an apparently normal, comfortable, office meeting room. There was a large table in the centre with a number of chairs around it.

Three figures had been already seated, two humans and a narun in a silver suit. All stood and the older of the humans came forward offering his hand. "Hello, John. Good to meet you, good to meet you at last. I'm Doctor Henry Karlin."

John ignored the proffered hand. He recognised this as the cheerful and apparently sincere voice from the telephone messages, the same man that had threatened to kill his friends.

Karlin shrugged and began introductions. "This is Darren," indicating the other human that had been seated, a big man. "You've met Ian before, obviously, and this is Sando," indicating the narun in the silver suit and hood.

"And these?" asked John, pointing to the dhumraka that had followed them in and now stood along the wall.

"Just more of our friends." In a confidential tone Karlin added, "We thought you had more narun friends than just the three that came in yesterday, so we thought we should be prepared to greet them if they came with you."

John was suddenly thankful for his bruised face, it helped hide any reaction he showed to the news that they'd only found three of his friends. He had no idea whether this was good news or bad news. It could even be some sort of verbal trap set by Karlin, so he stayed as neutral as he could and just stared back at the doctor.

Getting no response to his subtle question Karlin asked directly, "Were there more with you, John?"

John looked him in the eye and said, "If I had more such friends, is there any reason I would give them up to you?"

"Well, we can talk about that. Please sit, sit," said Karlin. Ian, Darren, Karlin and Sando all sat along one side of the table, the other narun remained standing against the wall. John looked at the layout of the table and chose the seat opposite Karlin, he appeared to be enemy number one.

"We wanted to meet you, John. To meet you and witness your ability to see the narun, it is extremely rare. You could be a most valuable addition to our team here, most valuable," said Karlin.

John could recognise the start of a sales pitch when he heard one, having given many himself, he let Karlin go on. Karlin's enthusiasm for his own voice promised to make this a long speech.

"As you've already seen for yourself, the narun are special, and there is a lot that we can learn from them. Despite how it may seem, it may seem, we are not that far separated from each other. The narun are made of prana, the breath of life, well, *so are we*. We have a flesh-and-blood support structure, but the real us is not there in the chemical stew of the cells, it's in the prana just like it is with them.

"John. John, this may be the secret to long life. Some of the narun live for thousands of years."

John was barely listening as Karlin continued extolling the virtues of a longer life for humanity, or at least those parts that Karlin thought worthy.

"This is new! John, this is a new science. It's a whole new world that modern man has never even imagined. The ancients had it right. Even many of the words that the narun use have common roots with a language that is thousands of years old. Who taught who that language, eh? You could join us and become part of history."

Karlin was winding down so John interrupted and nodded to Sando, "Will you remove your hood?"

The narun deferred to Karlin who said, "Our friends usually remain fully suited as a courtesy to our less able companions," indicating Darren and Ian. "Why do you want the hood removed?"

"I want to see the face of one that would betray his people," said John, staring directly into the visor of the hooded narun.

"This from a human?" came Sando's response. In distinct contrast to Karlin, John could detect no sign of cheer or friendship in Sando's voice. It was cold, chilly and succinct.

"You measure yourselves by human standards?" asked John. "With *him* as your model?" indicating Karlin with disdain. "Can't you do better than that?"

The narun seemed to stiffen inside the suit.

"Come now," said Karlin. "No need to bicker."

John turned to Karlin and snapped, "You expect me to be happy to be here? You threatened the lives of my friends to get me here, well here I am. Stop pissing around pretending we're all friends!"

Karlin paused, visibly trying to remain calm. "I see no need to ignore the niceties of human society just because we happen to disagree."

"Disagree?" John said loudly. "We don't just disagree, we're on different bloody planets!"

John took a breath and said more quietly, "I don't need you to feed me dog-shit and tell me it's ice-cream. You've spouted a lot of guff about long life and new science, but not once have you mentioned the people you've imprisoned and tortured in your attempts to get there."

"There are always sacrifices to be made in these great leaps forward," placated Karlin.

"Whatever insane universe you inhabit you need some serious help," John said. "Let me spell things out clearly for you. I will not willingly cooperate with you while ever you hold a narun or human against their will. You may force me to do things by threatening myself and my friends, but don't you ever try to call it anything other than coercion!"

Looking down at the table Karlin said softly, "So you refuse to listen to reason?"

"Release the narun and I will listen to whatever you want to tell me ... until then I am only here because you've given me no other option."

"Your wife was a similarly stubborn person," said Karlin, his expression turning sly.

"Samantha?" asked John, perplexed. "What does Samantha have to do with this?"

"You really don't know where she went that day? ... No, I can see that you don't. She said that she hadn't told you, but with all that's happened since, I've wondered."

"What are you on about?"

"It might be easier if I showed you. Watch the screen," said Karlin. He indicated the large, flat television screen mounted on the wall and pressed a button on a remote control from the table.

The screen flickered and then showed a black background with white writing. Karlin's voice came from the speakers reciting what was written. "Video recording of initial interview with human subject one-fifty-three, Eloise Caldor. Also present is her biological mother, Samantha Caldor." The screen flashed bright and was suddenly filled with a view of an office room very similar to this one. John glanced around to see if he could see a camera recording this interview. He couldn't but that probably didn't mean much.

Movement on the screen pulled his attention back. In the office in the video the door opened and in walked Samantha and Ellie. At the bottom of the screen a date was displayed. John's heart leapt, drumming out an uncertain beat in his chest. The date was imprinted deeply in his psyche. The date his life was destroyed. The date that Samantha had died.

On the screen Karlin walked into view and shook Samantha's hand. "So pleased you could make it, Mrs Caldor," came his cheerful voice. Samantha just nodded, obviously not comfortable. "This must be Eloise," he crouched to shake her hand too. "Aren't you just the most beautiful child," he cooed. Ellie looked at him uncertainly.

John wanted to scream at him, "Get your hands off her!" but it was much too late for that.

The on-screen Karlin directed his guests to chairs in line with the camera and walked back to his own which was out of view.

"This place is not what I expected," said Samantha, her voice awakening an agony of memories in John. "I thought we'd be speaking at the university."

"We don't maintain an office there any longer," came Karlin's response. "My boss prefers the security and privacy of these less obvious premises."

John frowned at this reference to Karlin's boss, he had assumed Karlin was in charge here.

On screen Karlin continued, "Believe it or not there is some correlation between the researches of this centre and what you came here to discuss."

"The papers you published suggested some link to life systems such as forests. Is that what you believe may have caused the phenomenon that Ellie is experiencing?" asked Samantha. John recognised the academic tone she always took on when discussing work.

"Her imaginary friend? Yes, in all likelihood her friend is very much tied to the forest."

Finally it was coming clear to John. Samantha had started to take Ellie's imaginary friend more seriously, concerned that there was something more to it. He knew of her concerns, but his own scepticism must have kept her from talking to him about what she was doing. She must have found something at the university that led her to Karlin. She'd arranged this interview without mentioning it to John. She hadn't wanted him teasing her if it turned to nothing.

The discussion on the video got technical for a few minutes and Ellie began to get restless.

"We're boring you aren't we, dear?" came Karlin's friendly voice. "Can we try a brief experiment?" he asked Samantha. She nodded. A few seconds later the door opened and closed as though someone had entered, but no one was visible on the screen. John could see Ellie watching a figure that he couldn't see. "You see her too then Ellie?" said Karlin, the satisfaction obvious in his voice. Ellie nodded.

The video paused, his wife and daughter now still images on the screen. John sat forward, aching to see more, not wanting it to end. While the video was playing he had a family again.

"What follows," Karlin's voice in the here and now interrupted John's reveries, "what follows is a long period in which we finally convince Samantha that the narun are real beings. It was Eloise that finally tipped the balance I think ... in more ways than one."

Karlin took a careful look at John. "We might have eventually convinced Samantha to help us, but Eloise refused to even consider introducing us to her friend."

John nodded, "Ellie was always a perceptive child, I bet she saw through you all right."

Karlin shrugged. "When we got onto the subject of how Eloise would be involved in our studies your wife turned ... defensive."

"You really are a bastard – but then you know that," growled John in a low voice. "What did you do?"

"It really was an accident, John, an accident, please believe me. Samantha and Eloise left here in perfectly good health. I merely asked one of my associates, he's no longer with us, to drive after her and try to convince her to be sensible about it all. Apparently she saw his car following and reacted badly, very badly, speeding up to try and evade him. He should have backed off then but, regrettably, he didn't."

John stared at Karlin in disbelief. This man had destroyed everything that had meant anything in John's life and the best he could call it was regrettable? He felt himself trembling and didn't know if the cause was rage, misery or disbelief. "So after you killed my family you came back for an encore, is that it?" the words leaving his mouth without much thought.

"But, John, we didn't kill your family. Eloise still lives," Karlin spoke softly.

At first John wasn't even sure that he had heard correctly, he looked down as he replayed the words over in his mind to try and understand them. He responded quietly, struggling to stay in control, "You really are a sick man, Karlin. I held my daughter's dead body in my arms ... I buried her next to her mother."

"You only buried her material body, John. We saved the breath of her life, her prana. She lives on here, just a short distance away from where we sit. Her dryad friend, Asha, is helping her to recover." Karlin continued to speak quietly but his confidence was returning. He had John now, he could feel it. Karlin gave his previous words some time to sink in before he continued, "She will only continue to live while our work here continues. Only with the help from narun like your friends can she survive. You have to help us, John. For your daughter's sake."

John's head snapped back up. "Christ! I thought you'd hit bottom already. You want me to sell out my friends for the sake of my daughter?"

"That's a fairly harsh way to phrase it, John," said Karlin softly, a smile creeping back into this voice.

Having just watched her on the screen, John had found it all to easy to believe Karlin's assertion that Ellie was still alive, but where was the proof? "You lie, Karlin! My daughter is dead. I grieved for her for months."

"I don't expect you to take my word for it," Karlin replied easily. "When you are ready I will take you to the dryad and she will confirm what I have said."

"Why not take me directly to Ellie?"

"Regrettably Eloise is a little difficult to recognise in her new form, despite the dryad's best ministrations, and you will be unable to touch her. But the dryad knows her, she will convince you." Karlin's words were confident.

When John didn't respond to that, Karlin continued, "Eloise can only continue to live with the support of this centre." The multiple layers to this lie bothered him not at all. John didn't need to know that she was probably dying slowly, and he certainly didn't need to know that her human body only died because they had turned up at the hospital, lured John away, and forced the prana from her body. "You have no choice, John, if you want your daughter to live you have to help us to continue our studies."

John put his hands to his face and bent down over his knees. His heart and his head were ablaze with conflicting emotions and panic. His daughter alive? Could he allow himself to believe it?

The task he had set himself when he arrived here was to try and distract as many of the people involved in this horror for as long as he could. While he was sitting here, Andrei, Guyen and the others were trying to enter the prison and rescue the prisoners. And more. Guyen said they had to try to destroy this place if they could possibly manage it. If they didn't destroy it then more narun would be captured and the cycle would start again.

So the dilemma that Karlin had presented was both more difficult and more urgent than even Karlin knew. John could give up all his friends, and the city narun that had volunteered to help, in the hope that Karlin had told the truth and that his daughter might still live ... or he could stay quiet and hope that his friends would succeed, that

307

his friends might survive but his daughter would be doomed.

He shook his head and tried to bury his fingers into his skull. He'd gladly die rather than have to make this choice, and he was almost out of time.

Then, through the panic and frustration, John felt things begin to fall into place and realised that the choice was already made.

- - -

Ian was staring at the screen. A child. A beautiful little blond girl. He'd no idea. Now, as he heard Karlin's self-satisfied lies, he was piecing together what he'd seen here in the last few months. Those down in the zoo might be narun, or whatever they were called, but from what Karlin was saying now, those things in the silent hall had been kids. Human children!

Sure he'd heard Karlin call them by human names, but hell, people called their dogs by human names, so that didn't mean much. If that's what Karlin and Davies had been up to then Ian was left with little doubt what had actually happened to his predecessor – and probably what had happened to Cameron what's-his-name too. This was *definitely* something he should have stayed away from. He really didn't want to be here, though he supposed it was better than being down in the zoo with Barry. He wondered if he could sneak away while they were busy with Caldor.

Ian couldn't quite work out whether Karlin was trying to get Caldor to cooperate, or whether he was winding him up to breaking point. He could feel the tension in Davies sitting next to him, waiting for Caldor to crack. Like Ian, Davies had concluded that violence was the most likely outcome from the broken man in front of them.

Ian looked across the table at Caldor. The man was visibly shaking, his head in his hands, staring down at his feet. He was a mess. He'd been gaunt but otherwise healthy looking when Ian had seen him last, but the man across the table was beyond gaunt and had obviously not been sleeping well. The bruises rising from his beating were turning ugly. The city had not been kind to this man.

Something changed. In great surprise Ian watched as the shaking of Caldor's shoulders slowed and then stopped. The man slowly straightened in his chair. Ian felt Davies almost rise from his seat in anticipation of trouble. Caldor ran his hands back through his hair, wiped his face, and then looked across the table at Karlin.

"Would it be all right if we watched the rest of this?" he asked, indicating the screen. His voice was eerily calm. Ian didn't trust this, he looked across at Karlin.

A puzzled expression passed briefly over Karlin's face before his usual self-confidence reasserted itself. "You'll cooperate?" he asked.

"What choice do I have?" Caldor returned calmly.

Karlin seemed satisfied with that and pressed a button on the remote.

On the screen the beautiful woman and her young child came back to life. Ian watched as Caldor turned to face the screen. A tormented expression showed on his face as he watched the video, and the trembling returned to his shoulders. Ian wondered if he was witnessing some sort of self-abuse, watching this video was obviously tearing the man apart.

- - -

John had found his answer in Karlin's admission of Ellie's recalcitrance. Even at five years of age she had that stubborn streak of loyalty and responsibility, a streak that John's friends could have told him was inherited. She wouldn't betray her friends and she wouldn't thank her father for doing it for her. He had to believe she would approve of this decision, it was the only one he could live with … for now. Time would tell whether he could stand to live with this decision either.

- - -

Andrei and his companions were huddled, in their cloaks, out of the way behind some boxes on the ground floor level, waiting for the remaining humans to pack up and go. He hoped that John could keep the people distracted, this was taking longer than they'd hoped. This afternoon the humans in this workshop were showing unexpected dedication.

This level above the prison was a large open workshop where they processed trees that were rolled in from outside. Oil extraction, timber sawing and milling and large covered areas where trees were isolated for various experiments. Scattered around the area were large boxes of sawdust waiting to be taken away, barrels of eucalyptus and other oils and various other paraphernalia. Some of these items were of particular interest to his group.

It was Guyen's idea that they should do whatever they could to destroy the prison as they left, to try and put it out of action if they could. Where they process wood, he had said, there is bound to be flammable material. They had found their flammable materials and Andrei's group of urban guerillas included the closest the aaranya ever came to a pyromaniac, Taiza. Taiza's willingness to work with an open flame, as Andrei had witnessed with the Oxyacetylene system, made him possibly unique among their kind.

Slightly younger than Taiza, and much more reserved, was Reijo. Reijo's particular fascination was vehicles. Not cars so much as utility vehicles like trucks, forklifts, tractors and so on. He spent much of his life near warehouses and small farms on the edge of the city, where the humans would occasionally return to find things not quite where they had left them. There were aspects of Reijo's hobby that definitely appealed to Andrei.

Reijo had already been over to investigate a forklift and returned to report to Andrei that it was familiar to him. This was all done with such an overly serious expression that Andrei had to fight all his instincts and stop himself making fun of Reijo.

The others were not as obviously unusual as Taiza and Reijo, but their very presence here set them apart from most of the city aaranya. Only individuals like Guyen and Taiza could have found such a group and brought them together.

The last human in the workshop finally gathered up his things. As he left he pressed a large button that closed the roller door out into the yard, and then he disappeared through a smaller door into another part of the building.

Next to the roller door that had just been closed a room protruded into the building. It enclosed the elevator used to take trees down below. On the inside of that room was a large door giving access to the elevator from inside the building. It was locked with a couple of large padlocks. Taiza's solution was to go looking for something to cut it with, but Reijo touched his arm, shook his head, and held up one finger. A moment later he returned with the forklift and used the tines to simply break off the metal lugs that held the locks to the door.

With Taiza directing, and Reijo driving, they set about moving things that Taiza said would be useful onto the elevator platform.

They stacked them into a wall around the edges of the elevator to act as a barrier in case there were enemies waiting for them below. Then each of them gathered up lengths of wood and metal they could use as weapons if needed. When everything else was in place Reijo backed the forklift onto the platform, tines facing out.

Everyone was ready so Senna climbed up to a window visible from the road in front and drew her cape aside for a few moments before covering again. After a few moments she repeated the gesture, and then again. It was the best they'd been able to come up with in the way of a signal, they just had to hope none of the dhumraka were watching.

Taiza went to the controls and punched the button to take them down ... nothing happened.

After a few choice swearwords Taiza said, "'s locked."

"Can you unlock it?" asked Andrei, holding back his panic with difficulty.

Taiza didn't answer, just mumbled under his breath and started following the cables.

"Leave him to it," said Senna, "he knows what he's doing." She drew Andrei back out of the way.

Taiza moved a few things out of his way and exposed a metal box. He rummaged around to find the necessary tools and soon had the cover off. He continued to mumble and swear to himself as he pushed wires around inside the box. At one stage there was a stream of sparks and the swearing got louder but then he returned to mumbling.

Andrei was getting nervous, his hands shaking up and down in Senna's. They couldn't expect John to distract these people forever and they couldn't call back the others to wait while they sorted this out.

"Ha!" came Taiza's call of satisfaction. He thrust the screwdriver he was holding into the box, there was a great spark and then the lift began to descend.

- - -

Tracey gave a small yelp in fright when the back door to her car opened and closed. They were parked just up the road from the large building that John had disappeared under more than half an hour ago. Guyen, Uncle, as she had come to know him, had kept her distracted and entertained so their time had passed quickly.

She watched as the pad and pen wobbled in the air above her passenger seat. After a moment it was turned to face her.

"You still want to do this? This is your last chance to back out," asked the elegant script.

"Yes," she said. "I'm ready." She wasn't really certain that she was, but she'd come too far to back out now, even if Guyen thought it was still an option. Why was she here at all? She supposed there was probably something about John that had reminded her of her father, something earnest, loyal and well-meaning. That had started it and then there was the mystery of these invisible people, including Uncle, this sage old man with the beautiful handwriting. She imagined he must have a suave and distinguished appearance – something that would have amused Guyen greatly.

Tracey started the car and drove back to the building. She turned in and stopped at the boom gate. She could hear the guard asking her questions through the speaker in the centre of the driveway, but she hadn't wound down her window. She simply waved across to the guard in his booth at the side. The guard leant forward and gave winding motions with his hand, indicating that she should open her window to better hear his instructions. Tracey just laughed, smiled innocently to him and waved again.

Distracted, the guard didn't notice the back door of her car open briefly, nor did he notice when the door to his booth opened. He was still gesticulating to Tracey when his eyes suddenly went dull and he slowly leaned back into his chair.

The back door to the car opened and closed again and the boom gate raised. The pad came up with the message, "Daina will stay to operate the boom gate. We can go on."

"Okay," replied Tracey and drove into the car park. This was the part of the excursion that they hadn't told John about. He thought Tracey was staying outside the building to help Guyen or others get away if that proved necessary, but Uncle had explained that he wanted her closer. Her presence and her car gave a legitimate excuse for their presence. Apparently the narun in the car would appear almost as humans thanks to some sort of cloaking arrangement that she didn't understand, and humans in a car should not attract attention. That would hopefully get them down below the building to where John had been taken – to see without being seen themselves.

Tracey drove slowly past the few remaining parked cars looking for John's station-wagon. It should stand out, she thought, the park was almost empty now; the Friday night rush to get home was almost done. They were getting close to the end, to the turn that would take them back up, when she felt a tap on her arm at the same time that she saw it with a small group of cars at the end.

The pad came up with the message, "Safe to park," thankfully written in large letters, it was quite dark down here. Tracey pulled in close to the other cars.

The back doors to her car both opened and closed. A few moments later the pad and pen wobbled in the air again. When held up it read, "The door there is locked. Any ideas?"

Looking at the door and its surrounds Tracey thought she could make out a camera and speaker arrangement. "I might be able to get someone to open it," she said, "if you can deal with it from there."

"Okay, let's try that," was the response on the pad.

Tracey got out of the car and saw the passenger door open too. She went to the security door, found what looked like a call button and pressed it. She noticed a light come on under the monitoring camera and then the speaker crackled.

"This is a secure area," said a man's voice. "Please go back to the ground floor and enter via the lobby."

"Hello?" said Tracey loudly. "Hello?" She jabbed at the call button a few times. "Hello?"

"You have to go back to the lobby," came the man's voice again, louder and sounding frustrated.

Pretending that she still couldn't hear she jabbed at the call button several times more. Over the speaker she could clearly hear a loud buzzer sounding in the guard's booth every time she pressed the button. "Hello?" she called loudly and jabbed the button again.

The man's voice came again, loudly and slowly, "Go ... back ... up ... to ... the ... lobby."

Tracey pressed and held down the call button, calling again, "Hello? Hello?"

She heard the frustrated man's voice say something like, "Stupid cow, hang on a minute," and the speaker went quiet.

Tracey stood back a bit and waited. The door opened part way, a middle-aged man with little hair and a paunch leaned through and started to say something. He cut off when the door was abruptly forced the rest of the way open and he started to fall forward. A few moments later his eyes went dull and he collapsed to the ground. She watched as he was dragged back inside. She gave another startled yelp as a hand gently nudged the small of her back indicating that she should come in with them.

She entered the short, well lit corridor and the door closed behind her.

The pad and pen was wobbling beside her. "Thanks," it said. "That was clever."

"Talking to you gave me the idea," Tracey explained, only half in jest.

"Ha, ha," appeared on a fresh page. A few moments later it said, "Straight-ahead, do you think?"

Tracey looked at the guard booth, the guard was being dragged back in and laboriously set back on his chair. They appeared to be trying to make it look like he had gone to sleep, but unlike the car park guard, the proximity here was unlikely to make it convincing. Next to the booth was a typical pair of lift doors. She pressed the call button and the doors opened immediately. Inside showed that the lift was already at its lowest level, B2. Given that they knew they had to stay below ground level then this lift seemed irrelevant. She turned around, saw her pad and spoke toward it. "Yes, straight-ahead. If we can hold this door open you can stop people coming up behind us from here," she indicated the lift.

Eventually they got a few phone books, manuals and even slid out a small cabinet from the guard's booth, and jammed them in the doorway. The vibrations of the lift door made it appear irritated by the obstructions, but did not manage to shake the objects loose.

"There could be an alarm that calls someone to this," said Tracey. After more thought she continued, "but this time on a Friday night it'd have to take time to respond. I guess we're okay for a while."

The pad was held up, "Oinar will have to stay here with the guard. You should go back to the car now. Plessy and I will go on."

Tracey took a deep breath and shook her head, she'd made her choices. "I've come this far."

"It's not safe," came the message on the pad. "We promised John not to put you in danger."

"You may have promised, I just nodded a lot. Come on, before someone finds us." Tracey walked toward the doors at the end. They went through into a high corridor.

"Which way would you pick?" appeared on the pad in front of her.

Tracey pointed to the dark passageway on the other side. "That way. It looks less used, so we can stay out of sight longer."

The passage they were following was rough and uneven, and had a musty, mouldy smell. It was brighter at the other end, and as they approached Tracey could see that it opened out into a large man-made cavern. They reached the end and Tracey stared into the cavern, a mix of cleared aisles between huge aviary-like cages interspersed with a clutter of boxes and barrels and things. Directly in front of her there were some shiny columns, hydraulic rams supporting a large elevator platform currently forming part of the ceiling.

Hands grabbed her shoulders, she had to stop herself calling out in fright. She was pulled back against the wall of the building where it formed one side of the passageway. The pad and pen were thrust into her hand and she was pushed gently deeper back into the passageway. She peered at the pad in the dim light. "There are guards you can't see," read the message. "Stay back!"

A few minutes later hands grabbed at her again and started dragging her quickly back down the passageway, away from the cavern. It was difficult to try and run; it was dark and she was worried about tripping over the one that was pulling at her. A deep humming started and the hands pulling at her let go. She looked back toward the sound, and imagined her companion must be doing the same.

In line with this passageway she could see the elevator platform descending from the ceiling. She felt the person that had been pulling her brush past on his way back to the cavern. Tracey followed more slowly and cautiously, thinking that perhaps staying with the car might have been a good idea after all.

19. Rescue

The platform descended slowly, maddeningly slowly. Andrei could now see that it was open at either end rather than on one side as it had been at the top. The forklift wasn't going to be in position when they reached the bottom, but they'd deal with that then. Word passed along that there was one human and three dhumraka visible below, two of them were not in suits. The narun in the suit was holding a ray-gun, the human was pushing the trolley to which it was wired.

Andrei whispered along the line, "Let's not wait for them to make the first move. Let's go now, before they have a chance to get help." He got a nod of agreement from each. Taiza and Reijo would stay here, the rest would go over their improvised wall. Andrei tried to gauge the progress of the elevator, not quite halfway – good enough. He touched Senna's arm then picked up the lump of wood he'd found above. "Now!" he yelled.

They discarded all pretence at stealth. Thrusting their cloaks behind them they leapt over the wall and down to the floor more than twenty feet below them. Each carried a stick or metal bar and each was ominously quiet. They fell, more slowly than a human would, their cloaks billowing behind them.

The suited narun raised his ray-gun and held down the button. He tried to bring it to bear on as many of the falling figures as he could. One, two, three coiled in pain, but then the weapon was ripped from his hands. Uncle had crept up behind him and jerked violently on the cables. Plessy, coming up beside Uncle, slapped the human on both sides of the head and it collapsed to the ground.

Uncle swung the ray-gun like a club. The protrusions of the device hit the dhumraka on his upraised arms and tore through the suit and his skin – prana oozed from this wounds, and he fell back clutching at his injuries. Behind the dhumraka one of Andrei's group swung a heavy stick against the silver hood. The suited narun fell to the ground and lay still.

Andrei hit the ground running, Senna close behind him. He had his sights set on a dhumraka that was trying to get away, they couldn't afford to have the alarm given yet. The man had seen them leaping from the elevator and turned to run, only the fact that he'd stumbled as he turned meant they had any chance of catching him. Andrei strained to run faster but was quickly overtaken by Senna, she'd dropped her weapon and leaned forward into the sprint. The dhumraka man slowed to turn down the corridor that led up into the laboratories, but Senna didn't slow at all, she scooped her shoulder into his midriff and slammed him into the wall.

Andrei arrived a few steps behind and swung his stick against the man's head. The dhumraka collapsed to the floor. Prana oozed in a golden fluid from the head wound onto the man's grey skin; he didn't move.

"Are you okay?" Andrei asked Senna.

Rubbing her shoulder, she grinned back at him and nodded.

"Remind me to stay on your good side," he said.

"Just remember this the next time you tell a joke at my expense. You can't outrun me, Andrei."

The elevator platform was just over halfway down now. Taiza was looking over the improvised wall and Reijo was already manoeuvring the forklift. It looked like everything had gone their way. Andrei could see Guyen over with Tracey near the other passageway.

"What's she doing in here?"

Senna shrugged.

"I'm glad it's Uncle that'll have to explain it to John."

- - -

Tracey squealed when hands touched hers. The hands loosely held one of hers and patted it in reassurance. They let go and she saw the pad and pen, which she had dropped in fright, picked up and start wobbling. After a minute the message appeared, "It's okay, Tracey, we did it." There was a pause while the pen wobbled a bit more, "For now at least. Wait here. When we've got the prisoners out we'll take them back to John's car."

The pad and pen were pressed back into her hands, she felt a quick pat on her shoulder, and then his presence left her. She stood in the mouth of the passageway and watched the impossible stage of the cavern: the actors were not only mute, they were invisible ... or mostly. A pair of silver gloves rose from the trolley, filled out and wandered off down the aisle.

- - -

Andrei tugged at his silver gloves as he looked around. The human and the three dhumraka, all unconscious at least, were being dragged into an empty cage. The three of his group hit by the ray were doing okay, sore and sorry, but no permanent harm. On one side of this aisle were solid doors that he presumed opened to the torture cells. Along the other side, the tall mesh cages were empty until he got to the end, that cage held three prisoners – they watched Andrei with dull, disinterested eyes. He walked down a narrow pathway to the second broad aisle with its mesh cages on both sides. From the cage against the wall in front of him was the first sign of interest he'd seen.

"Andrei?"

Andrei probably wouldn't have recognised Ceeda except that he knew he was here from what Garjae had told them. "Hi, Ceeda," he said. He went to the cage door and pulled at the lock.

"You'll need a key," said Ceeda.

"I think we may have another solution," said Andrei. He looked along the aisle. "Where are Asha and the others?"

"Asha's in there," said Ceeda, pointing to the laboratory building. "They took her up this morning as usual, but they haven't brought her back yet. The ones that were captured yesterday, I couldn't see who they were, are behind the second pair of those large doors."

"The torture cells," said Andrei.

Ceeda nodded. "Where's Garjae?"

"In there, you tell me," Andrei pointed to the torture cells.

Ceeda grimaced and shook his head in disbelief.

"I'll be back in a minute," said Andrei and ran back to the elevator.

He came back riding on the tines of the forklift with Senna. They jumped off and Andrei flourished at the gate, "Abracadabra!"

Reijo lifted the tines up to the level of the lock and dropped them, neatly snapping off the lock with a minimum of noise or fuss.

"Do them all except the enclosed cells," called Andrei, "we'll be right behind you." Aside to Senna he said, "As much as I hate to leave our friends locked up, those cells look like part of the main building, they'll hear us open those, so we'd better leave them to last."

With his gloved hands he pulled the tall gates open far enough to easily get in and out. "Out you come," he called to Ceeda, but Ceeda had already jumped onto the nearest platform where he had gathered Nacee into his arms. He jumped back down with Briso following closely behind.

The next cage that Reijo had broken open contained the two jalaja, the naiads. They looked suspiciously at Andrei as he pulled open their gate.

"Come on," called Andrei. "Don't hang about. We don't know how long before we're discovered."

The jalaja still hung back.

"Look, you don't have to get close to us, just follow behind. When you see your chance to go just take it. I don't have time for anything more." Andrei moved on past an empty cage to the next cage that Reijo had cracked. In there were four aaranya, they all looked mobile, but they also looked blank and uninterested.

Briso was blankly wandering off in the wrong direction so Senna went and guided him back. Three others from the elevator joined their group and Andrei left them with Senna to start guiding this first batch toward the dark passageway on the right. The jalaja had come out of their cage and followed cautiously behind.

Andrei grabbed a couple more of his group, they had been helping Taiza and Reijo to place flammable material around the cavern. "Let's get the others out," he pointed to the other broken cages.

Taiza called to him as he went past, "We shouldn' have much trouble. Most o' this stuff 's goin' t' burn real good," he grinned and indicated all the boxes and rubbish that were already between the cages.

Andrei acknowledged with a wave but hurried on to the other prisoners. He was thankful this place wasn't full. Five of the six

319

prisoners from the two end cages in between the aisles, were milling about. They had let themselves out when the doors swung open after Reijo had broken the locks, but they had not wandered far. Andrei and his friends herded them in the right direction and then Andrei went back to find the sixth. He was a small man sitting quietly on the platform, staring into space. He didn't seem to be registering anything that went on around him.

Andrei had no option, he bent down and scooped the man into his arms. The man was certainly light enough, it didn't feel like there was enough of him. "What's your name fella?" Andrei asked. There was no response. "Can't remember? Never mind, I've had days like that." Andrei jumped down from the platform and hurried after the others.

They got their group down to the end of the dark passageway and from there to the double doors that were being held open for them by Guyen.

All the prisoners were used to being cooperative, pathetically so, so it did not prove difficult to cram them all into the back, and onto the back seat, of the station-wagon. Tracey was behind the wheel, Senna sat on the seat behind her to make sure she was not disturbed by any of the passengers. Guyen took the front passenger seat so he could pass messages to Tracey.

The jalaja had stayed to one side and refused to come anywhere near the car or the human that was in it.

"Okay," said Andrei. "You don't have to go in the car. When it leaves just follow it up to ground level. From there you're on your own. Be careful, the traffic is very busy out there. Don't get yourselves run over after finally getting out of here."

The two stared at him for a moment and then the man nodded. Andrei figured that was probably as close as he'd get to thanks.

When everyone else was clear Andrei touched the glass briefly where Senna was sitting. "Hurry back," he whispered. She nodded. Andrei tapped the roof to let Tracey know she could go and moved back to the doorway. He watched as Tracey backed out and drove off with their dozen invalid passengers on their way to freedom at last. The two jalaja jogged after the car.

A dozen. He went over it in his head a few times. Shouldn't there have been another? He looked around the car park but couldn't see anyone they'd missed. He shrugged. Time they got back to rescue his friends.

- - -

Tracey drove slowly around the car park. As she reached the exit the boom gate opened automatically and she drove through. She only had time for a brief glance into the guard booth, the guard still sitting in his chair. She had to presume that it was not actually him operating the boom.

The traffic wasn't too bad just here. There was not much through traffic in the estate and most of the workers would have already left for the weekend.

A few minutes later Guyen waved his prepared, "Anywhere here," note in front of her and she found a driveway to pull into. The back door behind her opened and then the tailgate. A minute or so passed then the doors closed again. Another prepared note, "Let's go," waved and she waited for a break in the traffic and backed out. The procedure was repeated another three times at various places, each some blocks out from the research centre. No humans among the Friday traffic, busier out here at the edge of the estate, paid any attention to the doors of Tracey's vehicle opening and closing without human intervention. During the last stop there was an extended delay.

Unseen by Tracey, Ceeda tried to get Nacee to go with one of the aaranya they'd met at this location. "Garjae and the others risked their lives to save us, I've got to go back with you and help," he told Guyen and Senna. "And we've got to look for Briso. I lost track of him when we were coming through those doors. He could be wandering anywhere back there."

But Nacee refused to settle with anyone else, Ceeda had no choice, he had to stay with her.

"We'll look out for Briso as we go back," assured Senna. Ceeda nodded his thanks and then reluctantly departed with Nacee. The aaranya that met them here would take the rescued prisoners off to places of relative safety.

Guyen held a note in front of Tracey, "Back to the centre now, if you're up for it."

- - -

John dragged his attention away from the screen and his

impossibly alive wife and daughter. The others in the room were getting restless, the events on the screen were not so compelling to anyone else. He supposed that it was only Karlin's desire to win his cooperation that had let things drag on this long.

John addressed Ian, "So, Ian, how do you find working for this lot?"

Ian looked at Karlin, who indicated that he should respond. Karlin pressed a button on the remote that paused the figures on the screen. Ian thought for a moment before answering cautiously, "It's okay."

"Wow, that's a glowing recommendation. Come on. Karlin wants me to join your fun here, surely you can do better than that."

Ian looked very uncomfortable. Karlin and Darren looked at him expectantly. Watching his lack of enthusiasm, John realised that Ian probably didn't want to be here any longer. Eventually Ian answered, "The pay's good." Then seeing the unhappy expression from Karlin he added, less convincingly, "the hours are flexible and the work's unusual ... interesting, you know."

Moving his attention to Darren, John asked, "And you?"

Darren grinned back at him. "This is a fun place. I've always found it to be satisfying work, suitable to my skills. And the company's unusual," he added the last with a nod to Sando.

John looked at Karlin. "Your staff are very compelling," he said with deep sarcasm. "Let's cut to the chase. You said that Asha and Ellie were near here?"

Karlin was uncertain how to react to John's inconsistent behaviour. "Yes, John, they're here, they are here. The dryad and your daughter are in a room just down the hall. Would you like to see them now?"

John thought quickly. He'd probably kept everyone here as long as he could, perhaps moving would be a way to keep them together for a bit longer. Anyway, he had to locate Asha if they were going to rescue her too. He nodded to Karlin.

He was led into a room that was divided down the middle by a clear plastic wall. Looking through it he saw a bed in one corner. On it was sitting Asha. She looked drawn and tired and smaller than he remembered, but her face ... those gentle eyes. They stared back at him with a confused mix of hope and despair. He stepped quickly to the divide and placed his hands against it, pushing as if he could make it disappear. "Asha," he called in a plaintive tone.

It was only then that he realised she was holding something and remembered that his daughter was supposed to be here too. He stared at the small, pale being in her arms. Could it be? If he hadn't been warned he would have rejected the possibility outright, but that warning and now the affection with which Asha held the creature stopped him. He looked up into Asha's eyes and they smiled sadly back at him. "Ellie?" he asked in a whisper.

Asha nodded. Carefully she got off the bed, enlarged to human compatible size and carried the being to the divide, holding it up like a mother displaying her baby. John studied the creature. Pale grey skin, thin and stretched like an old man's. The large head, hands and feet, the withered limbs and torso. There seemed nothing that was recognisable as the beautiful child that had been his daughter. He concentrated on its head, the milky, blank and staring eyes that looked his way without recognition. Maybe ... there was no hair but there was something about the shape of the skull that reminded him of Ellie as a newborn ... but he had to admit to himself that that could be his imagination.

He turned back to Karlin, who was watching him avidly, apparently monitoring the events with equipment in the centre of this side of the room. "Let me in there. Let me touch her!" John demanded.

Karlin shook his head. "That's not possible, John, I'm sorry. I'll explain it all later."

John snarled and stepped toward Karlin, but Darren stepped between them.

Karlin called past Darren, "Ask the dryad, she'll confirm it."

John turned to Asha.

The desperation in his eyes broke her heart, but she nodded. "He's telling the truth, John, you can't touch her."

"But you ... why? How can I ...?" he stopped and just stared at the being. Could he believe it? Could it be Ellie?

Asha held the being carefully in one arm, bracing it on her hip, its weak arms trying to embrace her. She placed her other hand against the clear divide. "It is her, John. It is Ellie. You can't touch her because that would hurt you, physically harm you. I've seen it

323

happen."

John placed his hand opposite hers and stared back into her eyes, the same warm compassion in them now as when he'd first seen her. Through the clear plastic divide he could feel Asha's warm and familiar presence and slowly his swirling emotions calmed.

"Are you okay?" he asked softly.

She shrugged. "As you see."

He nodded. "Don't give up," he said and tried to tell her with his eyes what he could not say out loud.

She moved her hand toward his bruised face. "Did they do that to you?"

John shook his head. "No. That was someone else, a misunderstanding."

The door to the corridor burst open and an aaranya appeared.

"Sando! They're letting the prisoners out!" the intruder called from the door.

"Briso!" Asha gasped in surprise.

The narun at the door saw Asha's response and grinned at her. His form wavered, became indistinct, and then clarified again to a grey skinned narun, a dhumraka, like the others in the room.

"Stop showing off, Briso," said Sando sharply. "What's happening?"

"Ten or more aaranya came down on the freight elevator," Briso explained. "They overpowered the others. They're letting prisoners out and leading them out to the car park. They're almost done, I only just managed to sneak back past them to tell you."

Sando turned to face John. "This was an act?" he asked, his voice incredulous.

Flooded with relief that the plan was working, John laughed loudly into the face of the anonymous silver hood. "You have no idea," he replied. "And now they're going to burn this poisoned hell down to a scorched hole in the ground!"

Sando reached up and pulled the silver hood from his head. He stared intently at John.

John looked at the pale but handsome young face in surprise, this wasn't a dhumraka. The youthful face that stared back at him was more like the aaranya in appearance, but pale like a porcelain doll, with white-blond hair, and the palest, ice-blue eyes that John had ever seen.

Excruciating pain flared at John's temples. He lifted his hands to his head and he felt a strange compulsion to hit himself. He fought against it, but the urge was feeding on his desire to put his hands to the pain. Faintly he heard Sando's voice, "*No one* laughs at me." There was another twist in the pain and John only stayed upright because he fell back against the clear wall behind him. "I can kill you like this!" Sando continued, his voice mature, cold and even, at odds with his youthful appearance.

In the background John could hear a confusion of voices. Karlin and the dhumraka were shouting questions at Briso, Darren was shouting about chemicals, but behind them all John picked out and clung to Asha's voice calling to him. He could feel the warm presence of her hand trying to reach him through the clear divide.

"John! What is it? John!"

Clinging to the sound of her voice, he concentrated and pulled his hands away from his temples. With the others distracted, no one stopped him as he managed one step and then another toward Sando. The pale, youthful eyes grew wide in surprise and then Sando's concentration deepened. John felt the pain grow stronger and knew he had only moments of strength left. One more step and he threw his fist as hard has he could at the blond, youthful face.

He connected. There was a brief flash and the pain disappeared but left him dazed. He overbalanced and started to fall forward.

Darren turned from Karlin and saw John falling. He caught him and threw him back, hard, against the clear plastic wall, it cracked as he hit it.

Still dazed John shook his head, trying to clear it.

Darren grabbed him roughly by the front of his jacket and shook him. "Can you stop them?" Darren demanded, there was more than a touch of panic in his voice.

"Stop what?"

"Stop your friends from setting fire out there."

"Why would I want to?" said John.

"Because they'll blow us all up!" Darren yelled. "Karlin's been having us store all sorts of crap down there. It's not just going to burn, it's going to *explode!*"

- - -

The doors to the enclosed cells were pairs of large, solid doors that closed together at the centre. Andrei stood with Taiza and Reijo staring at the broken lock. Reijo had easily scraped the forklift tines past the lock and snapped it off but the doors still wouldn't open. Something must have jammed inside. The doors were tightly fitted, so they couldn't get a grip on them anywhere to pull or lever against whatever obstruction was holding them closed.

"We've got to get them open somehow," said Andrei, "my friends are behind there."

Reijo tapped on his shoulder. Andrei looked at his earnest expression and Reijo indicated that Andrei and Taiza should step back out of the way. Reijo bounded back to the forklift, manoeuvred it in line with the door to the right and pushed the throttle. The forklift jumped forward and then jarred to a halt as it hit the centre of the door. A deep boom filled the cavern.

The tines of the forklift successfully embedded themselves into the door. Reijo adjusted the angle of the tines, so they would not drag out, and then pushed the throttle into reverse. The forklift wheels slipped and whined on the hard floor. Reijo flicked the throttle a few times, and tried lifting the door. The large door rattled against its hinges and then he hit reverse again. There was a metal shrieking noise and then the door suddenly opened, the bottom hinge coming away at the same time.

Andrei ran through the gap to see three of his friends standing against the clear wall on the far side, staring in fear at the opening. He grinned, "Godzilla to the rescue. Come on. Before the door comes the rest of the way down." They stared at him in momentary confusion. "Come on!" he called. He looked around. "Where'd you hide Tilvy?"

That shook Barma out of his stasis. "You've not found her yet?" His expression was desperate.

Andrei took one look at his friend and cringed. If Tilvy wasn't here, where was she? "Come on, Barmy," he called. "We haven't got all these doors open yet. Come out and help instead of hiding in here, loafing."

Reijo didn't need help. Having made so much noise already he discarded any attempt to remain quiet. It took him a few goes to disentangle the forklift from the first door, but eventually he managed it. Darnu, Garjae and Barma exited their cell rapidly to get clear of the ponderous door left swinging by its top hinge. In rapid succession, and with a great deal of noise, Reijo got the other doors open. The other enclosed cells were all empty except for one end, where the cell contained barrels and tins of chemicals, half-finished cages and pieces of mesh – apparently used as a work area rather than a cell. There too Reijo had difficulty with the door, like the first it was left swinging from a torn top hinge and it creaked and swung ominously, so everyone stayed clear.

Barma was looking around the rest of the cavern with growing desperation.

Andrei tried to settle him. "It's okay, Barma, we haven't collected John or Asha yet either. I'm sure we'll find Tilvy inside with them."

Barma looked at Andrei carefully, his eyes anxious. Ever since they'd been locked in the cell Darnu and Garjae had been reassuring him that Tilvy would be in a cell out here in the cavern, and now Andrei was telling him something else. Where was she?

- - -

Ian was decided. It was past time he moved on, not even his fear of Darren Davies was enough to hold him here any longer – this place had gotten too weird. If they were killing kids now he wanted nothing to do with it. As soon as he got the chance, he was leaving.

Karlin had fallen quiet, he was looking down, standing very still and staring at the headless silver suit stretched out on the floor. He was ignoring everyone else as if only he and the suited figure were there. Davies was concentrating on Caldor.

Davies shouted, "It's going to *explode!*"

A dull boom resounded and the room vibrated. Davies was right! Well this mother's son wasn't waiting around to get cooked. Ian sprinted to the door and felt some small person fall back out of his way as he burst through and ran down the corridor. He turned down another corridor and out a door onto the ramp. More booming and metal shrieking noises, louder out here, turned his fear into panic. He jumped to the lower level and scrambled his way through the double doors, hurting his hand on the mesh as he pushed past.

In the short, bright corridor he noted that the lift doors were open and the guard in the booth was slumped to one side. Trouble. He saw the door to the car-park opening and didn't wait around to see if it was friend or foe, or whether he could see whoever it was at all. He leapt for the lift and stabbed at the buttons. He turned and saw the obstructions in the door and started to throw the books and cabinet out of the way. He hoped the flying debris would keep others away. As the doors closed and the lift began to move he sank to the floor in relief. He looked up to see what button he'd hit: 2. Shit! Still, if those bangs were as bad as it was going to get he'd probably have time to get out before the fire took hold. As soon as the door opened he'd be off, whatever the floor.

True to his resolution, as soon as the doors had opened enough, he pushed out past some tall lockers and turned to run past some workbenches scattered with electronic components. He ran up to a solid looking door and twisted at the handle, but nothing happened. He twisted and jerked but it refused to budge. He looked around but there was no other door. His panic was returning. He raced back to the lift but the doors had closed. He stabbed at the button but it didn't light up. He hit it harder to no avail. He pushed at the lift doors but they wouldn't move either.

He forced himself to calm down a bit. He looked around at where he was and the memories slowly came back to him. He'd been shown this place when he'd first joined up. It's where they built Karlin's ray-guns and his other gizmos. It was a secure room. Only authorised people were allowed in here and even those people weren't allowed down into the cavern – so of course lift access was locked out. He slammed his fist against the lift door. "Gods damn it! You idiot, Ian."

He went back to the locked door and pounded on it and called out. Nothing. It was now late Friday afternoon, anyone that might normally be outside would be on their way home. There were supposed to be guards around, but this place could be an inferno, or worse, before one came within hearing distance. He started to experiment with his vocabulary.

A hand touched the back of his arm and he screamed.

- - -

John stared back at Darren in disbelief. Not more! This couldn't be happening. Not another impossible choice, he simply couldn't do it.

"No!" he shouted back at Darren. "Not until you get Asha and Ellie out of there!" He slammed the clear plastic wall with his hand.

There was a dull boom and the room vibrated.

Darren froze for a moment as if expecting the room to burst into flames. Finding himself still breathing, he lifted John and slammed him back against the plastic again; the wall groaned in protest. "Don't you understand? They'll kill us all!"

"Then you'd better hurry."

Darren turned to Karlin, looking for help, support or at least acknowledgement, but Karlin continued to stare down at the unmoving figure of Sando. "Karlin!" he called, but there was no response.

One of the dhumraka knelt down next to Sando and touched his face gently. When she stood up she glared at John. "How dare you strike him!"

Briso came in from the door and touched her shoulder. "Minzi, we don't have time for this. Even if there's no fire, we're outnumbered now and they've captured one of the ray-guns down there. Let's take Sando and get out of here."

She pushed Briso's hand away and glared at him. "Sando will want his revenge on this human."

There were more dull booms and vibrations.

"Let's do it for him and get out of here." Briso was getting impatient.

"He won't be happy with that."

"He'll be less happy if we let him burn. Come on." To the others he called, "You two, take care of the humans."

Together Briso and Minzi lifted the unconscious Sando. "Gently, Briso," Minzi demanded. She cast John a last glare of hate and then the two began to carry the silver suited figure toward the door.

John watched the two other narun coming up behind Darren. "Watch out," he called, trying to get Darren's attention away from Karlin. "They're coming for you."

Darren turned back to John, "Wh—?" His question was truncated when one of the narun slapped his head. His eyes went dull and he slipped to the ground. John had to push him away to stop being dragged to the ground with him. His fall forced the two dhumraka to take a step back.

John tried to keep his eye on both of them at once. He was stronger but they were quicker. They came at him from the sides. He pushed himself away from the wall as hard as he could. He pushed Karlin toward one attacker while he turned, still moving, to face the other. This man had come at him hard, confident of his speed. Instead of trying to dodge, John grabbed the man and held him close, turning as his momentum carried them both across the room. The man's eyes widened in pain and surprise as he was crushed between John and the wall. When John pushed himself away from the wall the dhumraka slipped to the floor and lay still.

John turned and looked at the second narun that had just disentangled himself from Karlin. The dhumraka looked at his collapsed companion behind John and decided he'd had enough. He ran for the door and John let him go.

Karlin was on the floor in front of the clear wall. The jolt appeared to have shaken him free of his previous stasis but it had done little for his comprehension. "My children, Sando, my future. My little ghosts, Sando, what are we going to do?"

John went to the divide, to one side of Karlin. "What's wrong with him?" he asked Asha.

She looked down at Karlin and shook her head. "I'm not sure. He seemed to go blank when you hit Sando. Maybe Sando's been making his decisions for so long he's no longer able to make his own."

John pulled his attention away from the pathetic figure on the floor. "Stand back, Asha."

Holding Ellie protectively, Asha did as she was asked but looked puzzled.

John took a few steps back and then threw himself at the wall. It creaked and groaned. The crack that had started earlier grew a few inches but the wall held. His own bruised ribs protested at what he was doing. He took a few steps back and drew a deep breath, ready to repeat his assault on the wall, but stopped when Asha came to the wall with her hand in the air.

"John, stop! There's a door." She pointed to John's right, there was a clear plastic door set in the clear plastic wall. John just hadn't noticed it.

He gave Asha an embarrassed grin. "I was trying to impress you."

He went to the door and found it locked, but there was a crack around the lock from the flexing of the wall. "Stand back," he said. Asha did so. He kicked the door and the crack widened. On the second kick the door flew open and slammed back again. He pushed it back for Asha to come out.

As Asha stepped through the door she smiled at him. "Karlin probably has the key."

John laughed, "I've got a lot of pent-up frustration, leave me something to do."

He stepped forward but wasn't sure how to greet her. She put her hand on his chest. "Be careful, John. You mustn't let Ellie touch you." With Ellie balanced carefully away from him, Asha leant up and kissed him gently on the lips. "Thank you for coming for me," she said softly.

John stood there for a moment stunned. "Aw, shucks ma'm," he replied at last, "'tweren't nothin'."

Asha smiled at him and placed her hand up to his cheek.

He put his hand over hers, pleased that she seemed to understand his lack of sensible words.

Karlin got to his feet but was still muttering to himself about children, ghosts and Sando.

"What do we—" John broke-off his sentence. "The fire," he said urgently, "we have to warn the others."

Asha held back. "There are other children here, John. We've got to help them if we can."

"We'll come back. Come on, Asha, we may not have much time."

- - -

Tracey caught a glimpse of a small, balding man through the open door. She couldn't tell what scared him. Some loud noises came through the still closing doors to the cavern, maybe it was that. Whatever it was, he scrambled into the lift and a shower of books followed as he cleared the door so it could close. Once he'd gone, Tracey felt Guyen usher her into the corridor.

"I wonder what lit his tail?" appeared on the pad, held before her.

"Maybe I should have done my hair before we came in," she said.

"Ha ha," appeared on the page, and then, "Senna and Oinar will go ahead to see what's happening, make sure it's safe to go through and see what those noises were about."

331

She saw the doors at the end open and close.

"Should we call the lift back, do you think?" she asked.

"We'll wait for the others to return – just in case."

Tracey forced herself not to pace, she was worried that she'd keep running into Guyen.

It was only a short time later that the doors at the end of the corridor opened again. Through it came a silver suit with no hood and no head visible. It appeared to be having trouble walking, perhaps partly supported by hands that she only guessed were there by the indentations in the suit. Guyen pushed her back toward the wall, she could feel his presence standing protectively in front of her.

- - -

Guyen watched as two grey narun entered, supporting between them a young man that was pale in appearance and unfamiliar to his senses. Guyen didn't know what to make of him, but from the protective stance of the dhumraka he presumed that it must be an enemy. The young man was only half-conscious, but recovering.

Guyen pushed Tracey back to the wall. He wished he'd insisted that she remain in the car, she would be helpless if these decided to attack. The trio edged cautiously toward the lift doors.

He heard the dhumraka man answer a whispered question from the other, "I don't know who she is. I saw her in the cavern with the others." Guyen finally recognised the man, it was Briso, the prisoner they were supposed to be looking for. He'd only seen him briefly in the cavern, still disguised as a catatonic aaranya, but it was certainly him. So here was their traitor.

The doors to the cavern opened again and they all turned to see who it was. It was another of the dhumraka. He stopped short, trying to determine what was happening.

"Are the other humans dealt with?" asked Briso.

The newcomer hesitated and then shook his head. "One of them, the other was too strong." Deferring to the narun in the suit he added, "I am sorry, Sando."

Sando lifted his head and stood under his own strength, releasing the others. "Come here, Yudai."

The third dhumraka, Yudai, walked to the trio.

"The doctor?" asked Sando.

"I think the doctor's mind is broken," answered Yudai.

Sando nodded as if expecting that response.

"Your hand, Briso," Sando commanded.

After a moment of hesitation Briso put his left hand forward and Sando clasped it between his own. "After helping Minzi and Yudai here you will return to the prison. If the intruders fail to start their fires you must light them. The fires must be ignited. *All must burn*, Briso."

Briso stared into Sando's eyes with adoration, "All will burn, my Sando."

"Minzi, Yudai, your hands," commanded Sando. Minzi hesitated, her eyes pleading. "Your hand," Sando repeated and Minzi submitted.

Drawing their hands together between his own, Sando intoned, "You will remain here. You will kill these two. You will make certain that none can leave the cavern. *All must burn*, Minzi. *All must burn*, Yudai."

The two joined Briso in staring at Sando with adoration. "All *will* burn, my Sando," they responded, their voices loud in their intensity.

Sando looked at Minzi with a strangely dispassionate affection, touching her shoulder he said, "Take your time, lover, have some fun."

Guyen watched this process in disbelief. When the three dhumraka turned to him he saw that their faces were fixed with an unnervingly zealous expression. Their minds now carried only one imperative, there would be no negotiation. Guyen thought he now understood the catatonia he had seen in many of the prisoners, it was almost certainly one possible result of Sando's power.

He noticed the continuing expression of concentration on Sando's face and it took him a moment to realise that he was being encouraged to remain still. He shook himself free. "I'm too old to be taught new tricks," he said in defiance. He picked up the pad and wrote one short word in large letters, "Run!"

- - -

Tracey looked at the pad. "Run!" it said. Why should I run? she wondered, I'm quite safe here. This is a good place to stand. Somewhere in the back of her head there was another voice telling her to believe the note. It was screaming at her, but so faintly that she scarcely noticed it. She could feel the warm comforting presence of Guyen in front of her, he would protect her.

The pad and pen fell to the floor and she felt Guyen turn and try to push her toward the car park. Why would she want to go out there? In here she was safe with Guyen. She grasped his arms, she didn't want to leave him.

- - -

The lift doors gave a *bing* and opened. His arms held by Tracey, Guyen looked back over his shoulder. Sando walked into the lift and turned, he looked at Guyen with a grin and winked.

The lift doors closed and suddenly Tracey released her hold on his arms. A horrified expression appeared on her face. She couldn't understand what had happened, what she had been doing. There was a moment of indecision and then she started to move toward the door to the car park, but it was too late, Minzi was already there. A deft touch with one foot tripped her up and Tracey fell to the floor.

Guyen moved to help her but was grabbed from behind. He was spun around to find himself facing Yudai. He feinted into Briso and then pulled back and broke free, dodging forward past Yudai. Old he might be, frail he refused to admit. He scooped a heavy book from the floor and swung it back, striking Yudai on the shoulder and forcing him back.

Briso and Yudai came at him from the sides. As he turned toward Yudai, Briso grabbed Guyen by his cloak and swung him back against the wall. The concussion made his head reel and he crumpled to the floor. He looked up in time to see Yudai pull an empty drawer from the small cabinet that they had jammed in the lift doors earlier. It swung down at Guyen's head and he only just managed to roll out of the way.

Guyen got to his feet and backed up behind the small cabinet. As Yudai came at him again he kicked it forward and Yudai overbalanced. Guyen tried to grab at the drawer but Yudai recovered and thrust it forward, hard into Guyen's ribs. He grunted in pain and fell back. Yudai followed up quickly with a hard swing that struck Guyen in the back and he fell to the floor. Another swing and Guyen cried out with pain as the hard wood of the drawer tore into his arm.

He rolled again and was trying to get up when Briso kicked at him from behind. Falling forward he felt the drawer crash again into his back, this time he could feel it tearing through his clothes and skin and into his body. He rolled over and raised his arms but the drawer tore past his injured left arm and into his stomach.

- - -

Tracey had barely registered the pain of her fall when she felt a body fall upon her back – it was feminine. Tracey struggled to get up but the invisible figure slapped her lightly on the side of the head. The effect was out of proportion to the weight of the hit, Tracey's world spun.

The person or thing that lay on her back was embracing her, squeezing her tightly, almost passionately, and then the pain started. At first it was a light burning sensation on the skin, starting at the tips of the fingers and toes, but it quickly spread like flames up her arms and legs, the pain burning deeper as it spread. Tracey screamed and tried again to get up. There was another slap on the side of her head and her world spun again.

Through her dizzy senses Tracey saw the guard standing in the doorway to the booth, staring down at her. She tried to call out, to plead for help, but couldn't tell if any words made it out of her mouth.

The burning eased. "Oh good," a faint feminine voice sounded directly in her head, "there's another one. You don't mind waiting your turn, do you darling?"

There was another hard slap on the side of her head and Tracey's world turned black.

- - -

Guyen was losing, he could feel it. It wasn't surprising. He was old. Another strike into his back and he roared in defiance and pain. He forced himself to roll over. As the drawer struck him in the stomach he embraced it. When Yudai tried to lift it again, Guyen came up with it and pushed straight into the surprised Yudai, slamming him back against the guard booth. Guyen swung the drawer out of Yudai's grasp and struck Briso a glancing blow across the side of the head, the dhumraka fell to the floor.

Yudai pushed himself away from the guard's booth. His eyes were still full of the zealous dedication Guyen had seen before. Yudai came straight at him, a direct rush, and tried to grab the drawer. Guyen spun around to keep it out of reach. He felt Yudai crash into his back. Yudai's hands found and tore at Guyen's wounds. Roaring in pain, Guyen pushed himself back and the pair of them fell backwards over the overturned cabinet.

Guyen kept rolling and gained his feet before Yudai. Yudai was kneeling, trying to push himself upright, when Guyen swung the drawer with every ounce of strength he could find. One corner of the drawer tore through Yudai's forehead and prana gushed from the wound in a bright golden explosion that spattered the drawer and Guyen. The zeal faded from Yudai's eyes, his expression turned to surprise, then to pain and then life left his expression completely and he fell back against the cabinet.

- - -

When consciousness returned, Tracey heard a strange tearing noise but saw only a drawer swinging in the air. A few feet away from her lay the guard, there was a look of terror and pain on his now lifeless face and it spurred Tracey into action. She was halfway to her feet when she was pushed from behind and once again sprawled on the floor.

Again the figure lay along her back and embraced her tightly, and again a faint feminine voice entered her mind directly, "You can't leave yet, darling. I haven't finished having my fun yet, and the fun is mine to have, Sando told me I could."

The burning sensation started again and Tracey tried to scream for help but another slap to her head sent her into a daze. She tried to move but had no control over her body.

Inside her head she heard the voice again, "This is fun, isn't it darling."

"Who are you?" Tracey tried to say, surprised to find any coherence over the burning that had spread through her entire body. She could feel the presence on her back in a way she had never experienced before.

"Oh darling, I'm now closer to you than any lover will ever be. You are mine. I will experience your body for the few moments before it dies and it will be ecstasy. Don't rush now, darling, the longer we can keep this on the edge the better the experience. ... Here, let me hold you a little tighter."

336

- - -

Guyen wavered where he stood. He looked around for Briso. He was having trouble focusing. Finally he saw Briso stumbling out through the doors into the cavern, a short shout of pain came from him as the mesh of the second door pressed against his already injured arm. There was no question of chasing after him, Guyen could barely stand.

He stared down at the corpse of Yudai for a few moments, his thoughts trying to fight through the fog rolling over his mind. There was something else he should be doing. He stumbled a few steps. There was the guard lying on the floor ... twice. One was the physical body, the other was the preta, both were dead. Someone had pushed the prana from his body. Minzi ... Tracey!

He looked to where Tracey had been. His vision was still fading and it took him a moment to see that she was just a short distance further on. She was a blurry figure in his eyes. He finally made out Minzi embracing Tracey's body. Acintya! This is what had happened to the guard. Tracey was a blur because some parts of her prana were already exposed. He had to do something, but he couldn't use the drawer, he might hit Tracey.

Guyen let the drawer slide from his fingers and knelt down behind Minzi. Minzi was already partly submerged into Tracey's body and Guyen had trouble finding a place to take hold. Eventually he managed to slide his fingers around her neck and began to pull. His strength was fading but still he squeezed, still he pulled and twisted at Minzi's head. "Let go of her," he demanded.

"Uncle?" he heard Tracey's voice call to him faintly, sounding directly in his head.

- - -

Tracey heard a different voice in her head. "Let go of her," it demanded. It was not a voice that she'd ever heard before, but for some reason it sounded familiar. It reminded her of the warm and comfortable presence she'd felt next to her for so much of this incredible day.

"Uncle?" she asked quietly, uncertain.

"It's me, Tracey," came the voice again. "*Fight*, Tracey. She's trying to kill you. Fight it with everything you've got!"

"Oh shut up, old man," the woman's voice returned. "You're dying anyway. Why don't you just fuck off and leave me to it?"

Through the strange new awareness of her contact with these beings Tracey could feel the truth of these words, could sense the pain and growing weakness of Guyen's body.

"Not a chance grey-bitch, this is one you're not having," came Guyen's voice.

"Like you can stop me, old man."

The conversation was distracting the woman on her back, she was letting go. Tracey felt the pain diminish, and she regained some control of her body. A burning sensation scraped along her nerves and then both presences were gone, Tracey felt them rolling off to one side.

Remembering Guyen's injuries, that he was probably in a fight he could not win, Tracey tried to crawl along the floor in the direction they had gone. She felt the bodies entwined in front of her, the woman was on top. Tracey grabbed one arm and pulled. Still on her knees, Tracey tried to spin the being and flung it against the wall as hard as she could. At the last moment she lost her grip.

No longer sure where anyone was, Tracey scrambled backwards on her knees and raised her arms to try and protect her head from an attack she would never see.

Fingers dug sharply into her side and then were gone, making her flinch and gasp. Then again on her other side. Again, this time on her back. Tracey turned, sliding on the floor and unable to get up. Again. She was being played with. Tracey tried to swing her fists but hit nothing. There was a sharp jab in the side of her leg, touching a nerve and making her cry out in pain.

On the floor she saw a battered looking drawer slide as if knocked. There was a jab into her other leg. Guided by unfamiliar instincts, Tracey reached out and grabbed in the air. Her hands closed around some fingers and she held on tightly. She raised her other hand and surprised herself by intercepting another arm as it was swinging toward her head. She tightened her grip further as the unseen figure tried to pull away. Tracey knew that she mustn't let go.

Tracey saw the drawer rise and swing in a ponderous circle. She kept herself from flinching away as it flew toward her. The drawer jerked to a stop just a short distance from her, and there was a crunch and a horrible tearing sound. Tracey thought she saw a bright golden flash and then the drawer dropped, clattering to the floor. Something had spattered across her face and arms, Tracey could only imagine that it must be blood.

The hand and arm Tracey was holding went limp, a light body now hung from her outstretched arms. Sure that she must be holding on to a bloody corpse she let go and shuddered as it fell against her legs. She pushed herself back with her knees as quickly as she could.

"Uncle?" she asked into the silence of the room.

The drawer on the floor twitched slightly and then was still. Tracey stared intently, as if by not blinking she might finally see something. Near the wall opposite the guard booth she saw the pad move and then the pen.

"Uncle!" She half crawled to where she could see the pen wobbling over the pad which was still resting on the floor. She made her way around the security guard but found a second, invisible body next to it. Shuddering she moved around it as well, and on toward the wall. When she got there she slowed and felt her way carefully, eventually touching a leg and following it up his body. In places her hand came away wet as if with blood.

"Uncle, I'm so sorry I didn't run when you told me. You should have left me for being such an idiot."

The pen tapped the pad. Tracey looked down but had to wipe away the tears that were forming in her eyes before she could read it. "Tell the others that Sando can influence minds."

"Sando's the one that was in the suit?"

A tick appeared on the page.

"And it was him that stopped me from running?"

Another tick, and then the pen tapped the pad again. The next line said, "You must go now, it's not safe here."

"Are you coming?"

It took a moment and then a cross appeared.

"Are you really dying?" she asked.

A slow tick.

"I'm not leaving you here alone."

A slow, wobbling line drew under, "not safe here."

"You saved my life," she whispered.

The pen wavered, trying to find its place on the paper and then slowly wrote, "did something right." The elegant script she'd come to know was gone now, this was a barely legible scrawl, trailing off noticeably on the last word. The pen slipped and fell, and rolled off the pad onto the floor.

"Uncle!" she called. There was no movement so she felt forward carefully and found his body. She was surprised at how small and light he seemed to be. Surely he hadn't been this small before. She carefully manoeuvred her body so that his head was resting on her lap. She felt his rounded face with its deep lines and ran her hands back over his bald head. Here was the man that had caught her affection within a few minutes with his gentle good humour. This was the first time she'd had any idea what he really looked like, and that was only a best guess from what she could feel with her finger tips. Even so, she thought, "Uncle" did seem very appropriate.

She felt something on her arm, Guyen was touching it, making small swirling motions. After a moment she understood and reached for the pad and pen. She held the pad while he wrote. Slowly four words appeared in large scrawl, "Skaidar would have approved."

Tracey hadn't heard of Skaidar but nodded anyway. "Yes, I'm sure he would," she said.

Guyen held her hand for a few minutes and then his grip slipped. Some indefinite time later Tracey sensed a change in the body she nursed so lightly on her lap. Uncle was gone.

20. Fire

Andrei was turning his head back and forth between the two passageways. The one on the left led into the laboratory building, the one on the right went around behind it to the car park. With all the noise they had been making the enemy had to know they were here now. Where were they?

Taiza called to him. "The fires 's ready t' go 'n' I've turned their sprinklers off. Ain't nothin' goin' t' stop it once we start."

"Fires?" Andrei asked, "We need more than one?"

"'s best. It'll start faster and be harder t' put out." Taiza looked back over the cavern. "I know how to light 'em but it's not like I've got a lot o' experience with burnin' buildin's. There's stuff 'ere that's goin' t' burn in a flash, stuff that's not goin' t' burn at all, 'n' stuff like those trees that'll burn proper." He shrugged his shoulders in resignation. "'s anyone's guess as t' what it'll do all together, but I don' think I'd want t' hang about too long."

They had started walking, making their way to the other side, when a call made Andrei look back. Senna appeared from the passage on the right with Oinar. She ran up and hugged him. "I hurried back," she said.

He grinned at her. "You're just in time, we're about to warm this place up. Where's Uncle?"

"He stayed back with Tracey while we came to see why you were making so much noise."

"I wonder if we should collect them before we start up here," Andrei said.

"We need to find Briso too, one of the prisoners," Senna explained. "Oinar said that he saw him come back through here

341

after we left."

"I wondered if you were one short," said Andrei.

"It looked like he came out of the lift," said Oinar from behind Senna.

Andrei nodded, that would explain how he'd been missed.

"There was a human came rushing through and took the lift just as we arrived. He seemed in a real panic," said Senna. "So the lift is not blocked any more."

Andrei frowned. "Why would they do that? ... Could that be the only other way out?"

Darnu had been listening quietly in the background. "That could make it a dangerous place to be sitting if we start pushing from this side."

"And if we have the fire started on this side we could end up trapped," said Andrei. Turning to Darnu he continued, "Perhaps you and Garjae could—"

"I'm going in there with you," said Garjae firmly, indicating the passage into the laboratory.

Andrei turned to Oinar. "Perhaps you could collect a few people and go through. You don't need to stop anyone from escaping, even *them*, we just want to be sure it stays open for us."

Before Oinar could respond, a metallic screech resonated across the cavern, followed by a huge booming crash and then a series of lesser crashes and bangs. The large door to the end cell, the one used as a workshop, had finally torn off its hinge and crashed down onto the materials below. Toxic smells blew out from the debris, some of the barrels and tins of strange chemicals had been ruptured in the fall.

- - -

John and Asha were just turning down the passageway to the cavern when the noise hit. John thrust himself in front of Asha and they both crouched. John wondered if they were too late, if the fire had already been started. The vibrations subsided and they both stood, Asha holding Ellie protectively.

At the end of the sloped passageway John recognised a couple of aaranya looking off to the side. Nothing seemed to be burning and John breathed a sigh of relief. "Hello," he called. Those waved to others, and by the time John and Asha had reached where the passage opened into the cavern, everyone was waiting there to greet them. Introductions and explanations were necessarily short.

"I worried that you'd started fires already," said John. "Apparently some of the stuff down here may be explosive, you won't want to be near it when it goes up."

Taiza looked shocked. Andrei, pale, said, "We were just about to start them up and come and get you."

Barma was pleading quietly with Asha, "Have you seen Tilvy?"

Asha explained that the last she had seen Tilvy was well, that she'd gone off to explore the building, but Asha hadn't seen her since.

Andrei looked puzzled, "Where is everyone? They didn't just decide to let you go, did they?"

John shook his head and started to explain.

Asha interrupted, "There are more children like Ellie in there. We have to try and do something for them." Seeing puzzled looks Asha continued, "Ellie is a preta, but they were human children, we have to help them."

"How is it they still live?" asked Darnu.

Asha shrugged. "I don't know. They were children specially chosen by the doctor here. Humans can't help them. Even if they could see them, they can't touch them without getting hurt. We can't leave them here."

Behind their conversation started a metallic tapping sound that gradually gained their attention. At the other end of the aisle, amid the debris of the fallen door, just out from the passageway behind the building, knelt an aaranya. He held a short metal bar in his right hand and he was tapping the end of it sharply against the floor.

"Briso!" called Andrei. "We've been looking for you old sod."

John looked at the figure at the other end, appalled and unable to speak for an interminable moment. Briso had reverted to his aaranya prisoner disguise but his eyes had changed. No blank catatonia, no arrogant showing-off, now there was an insane madness in his eyes. Briso stared back at the group, grinning or grimacing manically, and continued to strike the floor with the metal rod. His legs were soaked in whatever fluid it was that pooled on the floor where he knelt. His body appeared to be quivering, almost out of control.

"Briso is a traitor," Asha called to Andrei.

"And he's trying to strike a spark in that fluid," finished John, finally breaking free of his surprise. He started running forward.

Plessy was closer and faster. He leapt at the maniac figure of Briso and tried to grab at the metal bar, but the moment his skin touched the fluid he screamed. It was the paint used to coat the mesh of the cages and it was toxic to all life, and especially to praanin. The manic grin on Briso's face grew wider and wilder, he lifted the bar higher and brought it down harder.

The initial flare forced John to halt and throw his arms up in front of this face. A few steps in front of him he heard Oinar yell in pain, he reached forward and pulled him back, placing his own body between the heat of the flame and Oinar. There was nothing they could do for Plessy, both he and Briso were already dead, their bodies quickly dissipating in the intense heat of the fire.

There was no escape down the passage behind the building, it was now a wall of fire from the burning cell. The freight elevator was engulfed in flames that had blown out from the cell, and rising heat was sucking flames into the workshop above. Flames were already reaching further into the cavern, climbing almost every surface, even the mesh cages – the coating was highly flammable even when dry.

"Run!" John yelled. "Before it all goes up. Back through the building."

Asha tried to wait for John but Garjae scooped her forward, moving her with the others. She cried out, "Wait, we have to get the children!"

Just as the passageway sloped back up to the laboratories there was a corridor that went to the right, along the other side of the enclosed cells. At the other end the fire was already burning fiercely, small explosions sending showers of sparks. "No!" Asha exclaimed, as she saw that the fire was rapidly encroaching further into the building.

They reached the upper level and Darnu pulled on Garjae's shoulder to slow him and Asha down for a moment. "Where are they, Asha?" he called. "We'll get them, you keep going."

"I'll show you," she said, and pulled out of Garjae's grasp. She pushed Ellie into Senna's arms. "Take care of Ellie," she demanded and pushed Senna and Andrei forward. "Take her to safety."

Asha headed to the right, deeper into the laboratories. Garjae, Darnu and some of the others followed close behind. John stood for a moment, torn between following his daughter and following Asha.

Taiza pushed him forward. "Take care o' your daughter, 'n' mine. I'll see t' these." With that he followed Asha deeper into the building.

John ran after Andrei, Senna and his daughter.

As they exited the building onto the ramp they could see heat and flames already lapping from the passage behind the building, the narrow channel formed a natural chimney that drew the fire to hotter and brighter intensity. John followed the lead of the others, leaping directly to the level below rather than going down the ramp toward the hungry flames. Through the doors he came to an abrupt halt with everyone else.

On the floor in front of them sprawled bodies, fading splashes of golden fluid were spattered around the room, faint steam rose from the fluid as it dissipated. To one side sat Tracey, tears streaming down her face, apparently oblivious to the audience that had just intruded. Movement caught his eye and John saw the lift doors closing on Barma, a look of intense concentration on his face.

Andrei touched his arm, "You'd better be the one to approach her, John, any of us would just scare her."

The others stood aside for John and he finally recognised the small figure laying against Tracey. It was Guyen, Uncle, and from the gashes in his body and the pools of golden fluid that still lay steaming around him, there was little doubt that he was dead. Carefully avoiding the bodies on the floor, John stepped close and crouched in front of her. "Tracey?"

Her tear-stained face lifted and stared at him, uncomprehending at first. Recognition slowly dawned. "He saved my life," she said.

"He saved many lives," said John softly. "We have to move now, Tracey, there's a fire. Come on." He reached for her arm.

Tracey leaned away. "I can't leave him."

"You have to, Tracey. We all have to leave. Come on." This time John reached down and gently lifted Guyen away from her. He laid the body carefully to one side. He looked briefly in wonder at the golden fluid on his hands and then reached for Tracey. Holding each

345

arm firmly, he stood and she followed in numb compliance. "Do you think you can drive, Tracey?" he asked. "Please. We need you to take some of our friends."

Tracey stared blankly at his chest for a few moments and then shook her head and looked up. "John?" she said, and then nodded. "Yes, I'll be okay. What did you want me to do?"

"Can you take as many as possible with you now? Take them back to the park where you met us this morning. Just take them and go, I'll stay here for the others that still have to get out."

Tracey nodded, vaguely to start and then more firmly. "Okay." She turned toward the car park door and then looked back. "Now?"

John nodded, and the group followed her out. Senna got into the passenger seat, holding Ellie carefully. Andrei looked at John. "Go on," said John. "Go with them. Tracey's going to need help, so will Senna. Keep Ellie away from Tracey and any other humans."

"I can't write, how can I talk to Tracey?"

"Do the best you can, I'll explain to Tracey," said John. Turning to Tracey, now seated behind the wheel with the door still open. "There's no one travelling with you that can write. You'll have to do the best you can. I imagine that may mean Andrei leading you at times and, I don't know, maybe tapping your arm once for yes and twice for no or something." He looked back at Andrei and added, "Be good."

Andrei squeezed into the front with Senna and five others squeezed into the back seat. Oinar stayed with John, he was feeling slightly singed but otherwise okay.

John watched as the small red car receded up the almost empty car park. He hoped that Tracey really was up to the drive back because no one in the car with her could offer much help. He turned to Oinar and said, "Let's see if the others have made it through yet."

In the short, brightly lit, corridor they were once again confronted with the corpses and the strange debris, including an oddly battered drawer. John shook his head and wondered what had taken place, it didn't seem likely that Tracey would be able to tell them much.

John slipped through the doors into the cavern. The flames coming from the passageway on the other side had increased but things did not look so desperate as he had worried they would. He climbed up onto the ramp and started to walk up toward the door into the laboratory.

A tremendous concussion ripped through the cavern. John was knocked off his feet and almost fell from the ramp. He looked up to see that the door he had been approaching had been ripped from its frame. He stared aghast at the flames that were pouring through the opening. He looked back down the ramp, the flames there were more intense than ever. All ways back into the building were blocked by flame.

Asha was still in there somewhere. If they were still alive they had no way out.

- - -

Asha raced down the corridor. She'd hated to leave Ellie like that, but she knew that no one else was likely to see the preta the way she did. Only her time with them had allowed her to see past their alien and desperate natures to the children they had been. She had to try and save them.

At the end of one of the corridors she could see the glow of the fire already coming through the walls. She saw the door into the silent hall and ran to it, but when she tried to push through, it wouldn't move. She looked through the window in the upper part of the door and saw Karlin walking from cell to cell along the hall, opening the doors as he went. He was muttering to himself as he walked.

Garjae came up beside her. "We've got to hurry, Asha, we don't have long before the fire breaks through."

"I can't open the door. We've got to get them out of there." Asha pushed at the door again, she was starting to feel desperate. She could hear the fire roaring elsewhere in the building.

Taiza came up. "Give me a look," he said. He peered at the lock and tried to look in through the window. Pushing on the door he shook his head. "'s a strange thing, 's not the lock, he's got it bolted on the inside." He peered at the glass on the top of the door. "The glass 's not goin' t' be easy t' break either."

Seeing Asha's growing desperation Garjae looked at the door and tried throwing himself at it. To little effect, their bodies didn't have the momentum required.

"Karlin!" Asha called into the room. He turned and looked vaguely in the direction of the door. "Henry!" she called again.

"Unlock the door, Henry."

Karlin took a vague step toward the door. "Sando?" he called back. "Sando, my children, my ghosts. Sando ... my future?"

"Open the door, Henry," Asha called again. "Open the door and we'll save the children. Henry! You must open the door!"

Karlin took a few steps toward the door and then paused. The preta, attracted by the life they sensed in Karlin's body, turned their heads and wandered blindly toward him. A few stopped at the wall in the corner of their cell, not realising there was an open door nearby. Others found the door and wandered toward him, their arms reaching forward.

"My ghosts, my ghosts," crooned Karlin. He knelt down and stretched out his arms to greet the first that came to him.

"No! Karlin, no!" yelled Asha. She could see that the wall in the silent hall was glowing now, the fire was going to break through at any moment.

Garjae tried to pull her away. "We're too late, Asha. There's nothing we can do."

Asha shook him loose. "Karlin! Henry! Open the door!" she shouted, but the doctor paid no attention. She watched as the first of the preta reached up to his exposed throat.

A scream wrenched from the doctors body and he tried to stand but now two more preta had come to him and reached for him, tugging at his hands. There were more screams.

Asha saw Vincent approaching the doctor. "Vincent!" she screamed, tears streaming down her face. "No! Vincent! Come to *me*. Vincent!"

As Garjae and Darnu grasped her arms, she saw Vincent pull away one of the weaker preta and then he leaned in and embraced Karlin's head. Karlin's screams reached a new crescendo and then abruptly stopped.

Asha let Garjae and Darnu draw her away. In the window in the door she saw a bright flash as the fire broke into the hall. In moments she could see flames licking at the window of the door and she knew that the children were lost. There had been no sound from them, they had remained silent to the end.

She turned and let Garjae lead her away. She heard Taiza swear and then say, "We ain't goin' back that way." She looked up and saw that flames filled the ramp back to the upper level.

A huge blast knocked them into the wall and the fire rushed toward them. They ran back past the silent hall and on into corridors unfamiliar to her. They looked into rooms as they went, hoping desperately for a way out. They retreated into a long narrow room that appeared to have been used as a bedroom or rest area. A couple of stretcher beds and the lack of personal effects suggested a place used only occasionally. There was no way out of here and the way back was blocked by a wall of fire. Taiza closed the door, it would give them a few precious seconds longer.

- - -

John gave a start when a hand touched his shoulder. He looked down, Oinar's face looked up from the level below, concerned that John had been hurt. "I'm okay, but they're not. They've no way out." He had to shout over the growing noise of the fire and the destruction of the cavern. No way out, he repeated to himself.

Quickly he got up and went down the ramp about halfway, unable to get close to the flames coming from the other side. He looked at the wall of the building and thumped it with his hand. This wasn't concrete, it was a wood frame construction covered with some sort of panelling. He tried thumping it harder with his fists, harder and harder, but could not get through.

Oinar came up and grabbed at his shoulders, obviously thinking that John had gone mad. Maybe soon, thought John, but not just yet. "This is thin, it's breakable," he shouted at Oinar. "I just have to find something to break it down."

He jumped back off the ramp and rushed into the small corridor. He ran into the guard booth hoping for something useful like an axe, but there was nothing. He looked around in growing panic. Then he spied the small cabinet, already emptied of its contents and drawer. It looked light enough to carry but solid enough to do some damage. He picked it up and rushed back past the bewildered Oinar, pushing through the doors into the cavern. Every time the door was opened the draft would draw the flames forward.

He threw the cupboard up onto the ramp and jumped up after it. He took a good grip on the top of the small cabinet and braced himself. "Stand back," he called to Oinar. He swung the cabinet back and crashed it into the wall of the building. A shallow dent appeared but nothing more. He bent down to look, he'd hit a stud. Moving a bit further along he swung the cupboard again.

It crashed through, a jagged tear appearing in the wall. It was only small but it was a start. Another two swings and the opening had grown enough that he thought someone might be able to crawl through it. He knelt down and tried to tear the opening wider with his hands.

Through the hole he could see the panel on the other side of the wall, he turned slightly and tried kicking at it. He could feel it begin to give way as the nails that held it pulled out from the studs. Suddenly it was gone and he had to pull himself back out so he could look down through the hole. Staring back at him were the slightly wizened features of Taiza.

"Never thought I'd be so happy t' see a human face." Taiza grinned up at him.

Behind Taiza, John could see Darnu and Garjae dragging back the panel that he'd kicked from the wall. He started to blink, and realised that smoke was being drawn into the room and out through the hole he'd made. The flames couldn't be far behind.

The aaranya came out quickly. Asha saw John and almost collapsed into his arms. As the others came out it was obvious that they'd failed to rescue the other children, John didn't need to ask why Asha was so upset.

Darnu came out last. As he slipped through, John could see that flames were already entering the room behind him.

They rushed through the doors into the short corridor and John felt the air, like a wall of heat, flowing through with them.

John paused at the car park door. He couldn't stay here long, this small corridor would soon be engulfed, but something was bothering him. Finally it came to him. He'd seen Barma enter the lift. He passed Asha to Garjae and ran back into the corridor and over to the lift. He pressed the button but nothing happened. He pressed it a few more times but still there was nothing. Either it had turned itself off after detecting the fire or it was damaged. He looked at it for a long moment but couldn't think of what he could do.

Darnu called from the door, "What is it, John?"

"I saw Barma take the elevator," he said.

"He must have gone looking for Tilvy."

John nodded. The fire was already burning through the walls. He had no choice, he couldn't stay here. He ran to the door to the car park and pulled it closed behind him.

It took only moments for everyone to get in the car and John drove out. The boom gates were fixed open but John stopped momentarily and Daina got into the back seat. The human guard she'd been keeping unconscious was already stumbling to the footpath.

Out on the street John could see a growing audience, some trying to record the disaster with the cameras in their mobile phones. The sun had set almost an hour ago, the street lights were on, and John could see that the fire in the building was already casting a flickering orange glow over its surroundings. He drove out through a confusion of fire engines and police cars. No one stopped him.

John drove up to the place where he knew he could look down on the research centre and parked. The fire was already well established on the ground and first floors and it continued to climb rapidly as they watched.

"Could Barma and Tilvy be still in there?" asked Garjae.

John shook his head. "God, I hope not."

"I might go out and watch for them from the other side," said Darnu. The others agreed that it would be better if they spread out to keep watch.

John was pleased when Asha decided to remain with him, he didn't want to lose track of her again. After the others had gone she climbed through from the back seat to the front. She reached across and held his hand. "You came for me again," she said softly.

"You keep running off. What else am I supposed to do?"

She squeezed his hand and saw him wince. "I'm sorry," looking down at it she asked, "Is it hurt?"

"That last wall was a bit hard."

"You still trying to knock down walls to impress me?" She smiled across at him.

"As many as it takes," he said.

21. Saved

Andrei tapped the back of Tracey's arm twice. No, he could not see through her clothes. Oh, to be able to speak to her, all these chances for humour were going past. Senna grinned at him from her place on the grass in front of them, she knew him well enough now to understand his frustration.

They'd been in the park for a while now. It was obvious that Tracey was feeling lost and depressed, so Andrei was trying to distract her with conversation. Picking up on John's suggestion, they'd started with one-tap for yes and two-taps for no, and gradually expanded the vocabulary from there. Tracey had given Andrei his first foray into writing, a question mark traced on her arm when he wanted her to guess his question.

The other city aaranya that had returned with them had wandered off, but Andrei didn't think they had gone far, they'd want to be nearby when John and the others got back. Senna was sitting across from him studying the small creature in her arms. She was trying to see or feel whatever it was that Asha could, but so far she was not having much success. Andrei continued to try and distract Tracey with a lopsided and distorted version of twenty-questions.

Conversation eventually bogged down over the question of invisible clothing.

"Maybe we should leave that until John gets back," Tracey conceded.

Tap – yes.

"You don't have long to wait," interrupted Senna, "it looks like them now."

Andrei patted Tracey's hand and pointed it in the direction of the street. Down the dark path they could see John's station-wagon pull up to the curb and some of the doors opened. In a hurry to find out what had happened, Andrei pressed down on Tracey's arm and then her shoulder, hoping that she'd understand.

"You want me to stay here?" Tracey asked.

Tap – yes.

"Okay, but please don't be long."

Pat, pat – okay.

Andrei ran to the street and saw that Darnu and Garjae were carrying someone out of the back of the car. He looked hurriedly at the others. There was Tilvy, she was looking with concern at the figure between Darnu and Garjae. He rushed forward in a sudden panic. "Barma?" he called.

"It's okay, Andrei," said Asha climbing out from the back of the car. "He's going to be okay."

Once everyone else was out of the car, John drove off to park beneath the apartment building. The rest of them moved deeper into the park.

"This one," said Asha, indicating one of the larger of the younger trees of the park. Darnu and Garjae held Barma up against the tree. Only as Asha stood next to the semi-conscious Barma did Andrei notice how diminished she appeared. She concentrated and whispered something in Barma's ear, a few moments later they merged together into the tree.

Andrei turned to Tilvy, but before he could express his question she wrapped her arms around him and burst into tears. "Oh, Andrei. I thought I was going to lose him!"

- - -

John hurried up from the apartment car park. He wanted to get back to his friends and see for himself that it was all over, that they were all together again. After checking with Andrei and Senna, and a lingering look at the creature, his daughter in Senna's arms, he went to Tracey and sat next to her.

"Are you okay?" he asked.

"I'm f—" she started and then, looking up at John, her face crumpled and she burst into tears. John held her as she sobbed against his shoulder.

After a while her crying subsided and she began to talk. When she was finished, John shuddered at the thought of what might have happened.

Tracey looked up from his shoulder. "What?"

"Uncle didn't just save your life, Tracey. If you and he had backed down, or been defeated, they would have locked us in that cavern and the rest of us would all be dead now.

"Do you remember if anyone went past you before we arrived?" John asked.

Tracey looked at him blankly for a moment and then shook her head uncertainly.

"Do you care?" Garjae asked John.

John looked back at him for a moment, before responding, "After what they did? No, not really, but it doesn't stop me wondering who else may have survived."

"Do you think Uncle really meant it about Sando influencing minds?" Tracey asked.

Darnu said, "There are ancient tales of narun with such abilities."

John repeated this to Tracey. She nodded. "For me ... it didn't really feel like I was being controlled," she explained. "It was like I was persuading myself to do something when I should have known better. I wanted to stay with Uncle, I wanted him to protect me – and that's true, it is what I really felt and wanted." She shook her head in disbelief. "I can barely imagine what it must be like to have your mind forced to do something it *really* didn't want to do ... like set fire to itself," she finished in a whisper.

There was silence for a while, John was pretty sure that no one's thoughts were very pleasant. Still leaning on his shoulder, Tracey asked, "What that woman was trying to do to me, what was that about? Uncle was appalled by it. I could sense him for a while, it was like we were connected by what was happening, and what that woman was doing to me really affected him, it made him angry despite all his own injuries."

John sat silent. On the drive back he had asked Asha what had happened to Ellie. She and Darnu had tried to explain it to him. They had told him how painful it was supposed to be, and that the victims usually died in great pain and terror. His daughter and other children had somehow survived the appalling process.

Tracey pushed herself away from his shoulder and looked at his face. "John?"

John looked at the young woman. She had made it possible to rescue Asha and his daughter, he owed her everything. He couldn't not answer her questions. "My friends call it acintya," he started, "which means unthinkable." He went on to try and explain what he'd been told.

"And what would have happened to me, my *self*, if I'd been pushed out of my body?"

"Most probably you would have died very quickly, in great pain and emotional distress."

Tracey swallowed and then frowned. "Most probably?"

"We know now that some do survive ... sort of. For some months at least."

Tracey looked at John's face carefully, watching the distress apparent in his expression. "There's something you're not telling me," she said.

John turned from Tracey and looked across at Senna, sitting on the grass holding Ellie. Still staring at the being that was his daughter, he said, "Sitting over there in Senna's arms is my daughter."

Tracey glanced across but could see nothing where John was looking. She turned back and studied his expression. She couldn't understand the tone of his voice, surely he should be happy at finding his daughter still alive.

"At least Asha tells me it is my daughter, that it is Ellie. Of course I believe Asha, but ... you see, I can't tell. It doesn't look like my daughter. It barely looks human. And I can't touch her."

"And she went through ac..."

"Acintya, yes."

"Are there others?"

"There were. ... A dozen or more died in the fire. Asha and others tried to get back to save them, but ...." John shrugged. "According to something I saw there, there may have been more than a hundred and fifty of them over time. I think they were probably all children like my Ellie."

Tracey leant forward on John's shoulder again, this time trying to offer comfort. "Why can't you touch Ellie?"

"I don't know," John replied. "Asha says it would hurt me. I intend to try anyway, but I'll wait until Asha is around to make sure that Ellie will be okay."

"Asha's not here?" Tracey asked in surprise.

"She's in that tree over there," John pointed. "One of us was badly injured and Asha is helping him to recover. It seems she discovered some new talents along the way."

There was a few minutes silence and then Darnu said, "I think you and Tracey need to eat and get some rest."

"Not you too," said John, "I thought only the women hassled me about food."

"Darnu is an old woman," put in Andrei, "and anyway, I thought someone was going to tell me what happened to Barma."

"Darnu's right," said Senna, overruling Andrei. "Even if not for you, John, Tracey's just about done in, I think."

John explained to Tracey what had just been said. "So let me buy you dinner, and if you want I'll drive you home," he concluded.

Tracey thought for a moment before responding. "You're probably right. I'm not sure it's all caught up with me yet, but it probably will soon. But I'll pass on dinner if you don't mind. I'll have something when I get home."

"Are you sure? It's no trouble to me. These lot aren't going to let me get away without eating, even the guys are ganging up on me now."

She smiled. "Thanks, but I think I'd rather go home."

John walked her back to her car. He gave her a hug and kissed the top of her head. "Thank you," he said. "I owe you more than I can say, more than you can know. Thank you."

Tracey returned his hug and just shrugged in response to his thanks. John understood. Most of the usual platitudes were inappropriate in the circumstances. He was about to step away when she reached up and kissed his cheek. "I am glad to have met you," she said.

"I think I've warned you already about picking up strange men off the street," he said.

"You're not so strange, *Dad*," she replied with a smile. She started to get into the car and then paused. "You're not going to disappear are you? I mean, you'll still be here tomorrow?"

John smiled, pleased that she wanted to see them again. "I have to get back home soon. I guess I'll have to start to pull my life back together – not really looking forward to that. But yes, I will be still here tomorrow."

"I'll see you tomorrow then." She got into her car, waved, and drove off.

John stood there and watched until her car disappeared. He shook his head in disbelief. He had known her for less than twenty-four hours but she'd come to mean a lot to him. She called him "Dad" in jest but it felt close, a big brother maybe. He felt protective of her, and responsible. He wondered what her real father would think of him. Not a lot he should think.

He took a detour to pick up a burger, some chips and a drink, and then he hurried back to the park – like Andrei he was impatient to know what had happened to Tilvy and Barma.

As he entered the park he could see that the first of the Friday night drunks had already appeared. Retching noises came from a mostly prostrate figure in one corner. The night was getting on, he supposed. He was tired but he wasn't ready to sleep just yet.

He found Andrei and Senna sitting on the grass not far from the park bench. He knelt down near Senna and peered at his daughter. She turned and reached toward him, but there was no sense of recognition in her blank eyes. It was all he could do not to reach out and touch her. To stop himself, he got up and sat on the park bench and started eating his burger and chips.

Andrei got up from the ground and sat next to John on the bench. "If you want to go and rest, John, we can wait until tomorrow for more tales. I can probably contain myself that long."

John looked at him with mock surprise. Around a mouthful of burger he said, "You? Contain yourself? Since when?"

A laugh came from Senna. Andrei grinned at Senna and then said to John, "Didn't your mother ever tell you not to speak with your mouth full?"

John swallowed and then answered with a glint in his eye, "She may have said something like that ... but then I think I may have been a disappointment to her."

"Hey. No stealing the material, human," said Andrei.

Feeling a twitch in one shoulder, John remembered the brevis. He called them both out. "Darnu," he called, "I've got something that belongs to you." Nuttachen saw Darnu approaching and leapt from John, bounding over the ground and running straight up to nuzzle at Darnu's chin. Casseta stayed with John and she ran busily from place to place around his torso. She seemed particularly curious about the various injuries that he'd sustained. After a few minutes she got restless and John let her go. She and Nuttachen bounded off into one of the trees.

Darnu called after them, "Don't go too far."

John watched Tilvy as she came toward the bench. "I'm not ready to sleep yet. If you're willing to tell us what happened, Tilvy, I would like to hear."

"Sure," she said. "Anything to keep my mind off waiting to see how Barma is doing."

She sat down next to John. Andrei sat back down next to Senna. The others came and settled near the bench, only Asha and Barma were still missing.

Tilvy told them how she'd escaped from the tree and found Asha. That she'd left Asha to explore. That she'd taken the lift, looking out at different floors before reaching the top. She described the strange pools of seawater and plants on the top floor and seeing the figure floating, asleep, in the water.

"So you think they're samudraka?" asked Darnu.

"I don't know. I'm just telling you what I saw."

"I knew there was something fishy about them," interjected Andrei. Senna used her spare arm to elbow him in the ribs.

Tilvy ignored Andrei and continued, "I'd been sitting there for a while, trying to decide what to do next. Finally I decided to head back down to the cavern, at least that way I'd be close to everyone else. I went back to the lift, and removed the silver suit just in case they kept count.

"The lift doors closed and it started to move down. It took a moment before I realised that the B2 light was on before I'd pressed it, and that someone else must have called the lift. I knew I had to get out so I kept jabbing buttons. The lift stopped on level 2 and I jumped out. I assumed it would be like the other floors I'd seen, an open office with many ways out. The lift doors closed and I went to find a way out. There was a door, just one, and it was locked. I'm not sure what it was all made from, but neither the door nor the walls offered any way through.

"The night passed and morning came. Eventually I heard humans in the rooms outside this locked room, but none of them came to the door."

"Why not?" asked Andrei.

Tilvy gave him a pitying look. "As if I'd know."

"More hours passed and I heard the humans outside packing up and leaving again. I started to think I was going to be stuck there for days so I found a spot that seemed to be out of the way and tried to get some rest.

"I was woken by a human stumbling across the room. It was only when I heard the lift doors close that I realised where he'd come from. I got up and watched him. It was Ian, that guy from the van. I stayed out of his way to start with, he was running back and forth in a panic.

"Finally he slowed down. He leaned against the door and started listing all the rude words that he knew – there were a lot – and I decided it was safe to approach him. I touched his arm and he screamed. I almost died of fright, I never expected to have that effect on anyone. The next thing I knew, he was grabbing anything he could lift and throwing it. I think he was trying to hit me, but I just stood back behind a bench until he got it out of his system.

"I didn't dare get close to him again, I kept back and just watched.

"We both heard the lift humming again and he rushed to the lift and started banging on the door. I stayed back and made sure I was cloaked, I didn't think I would like whoever it was that was in there – and I was right.

"The lift went past that first time and Ian slumped to the floor. But it returned just a minute or two later and stopped. When the door opened I thought Ian was going to freak out completely. There was a strange looking man in there, in one of those silver suits, but it had no hood so it must have looked headless to Ian."

"Sando," muttered John in dread.

Tilvy nodded. "Ian suddenly calmed down and stepped quietly into the lift. He stood in one corner with a blank look on his face."

Tilvy paused here. John suspected she was trying to find the courage to repeat what had happened next. She continued, "Tracey's right. It's like you convince yourself of something you've thought about doing or wanting, but wouldn't normally do. I found myself certain that I'd prefer to go with that man, Sando, than stay locked in the room, so I followed Ian calmly into the lift.

"We were taken back to the top floor and there were four dhumraka there. At the time I didn't think there was anything strange or unusual about Sando, even when he pulled off the rest of his suit, but he's definitely strange. He's not grey like the others. He's pale and strong and he feels … wrong. I can't really put it better than that. The dhumraka feel a lot like aaranya, but him? I don't know what he is.

"Sando seemed to be waiting for something. We just stood there near the top of the lift, Sando and the others chatting amongst themselves. And then I smelt it, there was smoke coming up the lift shaft. Sando gave a big grin and began to move very quickly.

"They led us to the fire-escape that I'd seen earlier. I had told myself earlier that I didn't want to go down there, that I wouldn't leave Barma, but of course part of me did want to run and that part dominated me now. That dominant part kept telling me that Barma was probably safe and waiting for me out on the street. I followed the others eagerly down the stairs, I was wishing we'd leave Ian behind so we could move faster.

"We reached street level and crossed the road in front of the centre. I was slowing down, the need to escape was less and it was harder to convince myself that Barma was waiting for me out there when, inside myself, I knew he was still in the building. An explosion came from the building and it must have distracted Sando. His hold over me wavered and I ran, but I only got a few steps.

"I felt pain growing in my head and I couldn't even work out where to place my feet. I fell down and the pain grew. I thought I was going to die. Then, suddenly, it was gone.

"I looked back and saw Barma, he was standing over Sando with this great stick. He was taking a swing back to hit him again but he was knocked aside by one of the dhumraka. Two of them picked up Sando and started carrying him away, the others went for Barma. I scrambled to my feet to try and help, but I didn't have any sort of weapon. As it turned out Barma didn't need my help. The dhumraka didn't have weapons either and after Barma knocked one of them down the other ran for it.

"I ran to him, I almost knocked him down. To find him alive, to have been saved by him, I was just about bursting with relief and joy. I think I said something corny about him being my knight in shining armour." Tears glistened in the corners of her eyes as she remembered.

"But—" started Andrei.

"I haven't finished yet," said Tilvy.

"It was a perfect moment. We were both so happy," she whispered, wanting to dwell on that happy memory. Then she took a breath and continued.

"We looked back at the building and saw flames coming from some of the lower windows. It was all burning so fast. Barma looked appalled and shouted something about having left you all down there and ran back across the road – or started to. He was hit by a police car before he got very far."

"Oh, Barmy," groaned Andrei. "And you'd been doing so well."

Tilvy ignored his interruption, she continued, "I don't think the car even heard or noticed that they'd hit anything. They didn't have their siren going, I'm sure he'd have seen them if they'd just had their siren going.

"I got him off the road before any more cars came and half-carried him off the footpath and into a doorway. There were humans starting to come around to watch the fire and I didn't want them stepping on us. At first he was still conscious, he was muttering something about getting the others out, but he was fading. There was a tear down one side and one leg looked crushed. I could see his life bleeding out of him and there was nothing I could do.

"And then Darnu and Garjae appeared in front of me. At first I thought they were apparitions, I couldn't believe they were real. They carried us both back to the car.

"In the back of the wagon I tried to nurse Barma again, but Asha was there. I wanted to push her out of the way, he was mine! But Darnu held on to me and as I watched I saw the tear in Barma's side begin to close. I thought I must be delirious.

"I don't know what else Asha was doing, but from the outside it looked like she had poured herself into him. I watched as my Barma filled out and Asha seemed to shrink." Tilvy stopped and looked down, confused in her reactions.

"Was somethin' t' see all right," agreed Taiza.

"Milla told of his meeting with a healer," said Darnu, "but this was something more than what even he has seen I think."

John looked at Darnu. "And they're both going to be okay?" he asked.

Darnu shrugged. "Asha sounded confident. What happened to Ian, Tilvy?"

She looked up. "I last saw him when I was getting back to my feet. He'd come back to himself, just as I had. He looked around just once, enough to see Barma's stick I think, and then he ran."

"It's a shame Barma didn't get to finish off Sando," said Oinar. He was still feeling pretty scorched from the first flare that had killed his friend Plessy. "It'd be good to have had some payback for Plessy and Uncle."

"I'd have hit him harder the first time if I knew I wasn't going to get a second go," came Barma's voice from behind the group seated on the lawn.

"Barma!" Tilvy almost flew off the bench and ran to embrace him.

"Ah! ... Not too tight," Barma winced as Tilvy hugged him. "It still hurts."

In the background, John saw that a couple of aaranya were leading another drunk off to a different part of the park. The nice thing about drunks was that they didn't pay much attention to who helped them. The gentle persuasions of the group had kept the area where they were talking nicely secluded.

Tilvy led Barma, he was limping very distinctly, to the park bench and they sat down next to John. To John's unspoken question Barma said, "Asha's still in the tree. She gave a lot of herself to save me, it's going to take her a while to recover. I doubt if she'll come out until morning." He shook himself, as if he was cold, and hugged Tilvy a bit tighter. "I can't remember all that much of what she did to me, but what I do remember was really strange. It was like having bits of me taking on a life of their own."

"So what made you pick a fight with the law?" asked Andrei.

Barma gave him a puzzled look.

"It was a police car that hit you," explained Tilvy. "Leave him alone, Andrei."

"I'll save 'em up for when you're feeling better." Andrei grinned, obviously pleased to see that his friend was recovering.

There was silence for a while. Casseta chose that time to return and quickly nuzzled and merged into John's arm, apparently she'd had enough freedom for the night.

John looked around the group. "I wish that Uncle and Plessy had made it, but it seems now we were lucky not to have lost even more." He looked around at the faces in front and beside him. "I think Uncle would have said we'd done well."

"'s right, I think," agreed Taiza and others murmured their agreement too.

"This old human needs his rest, I'm told, so I'm off to my room," said John.

John gave Tilvy a firm hug and Barma a gentle one. "I'm so glad you're okay," he said.

Kneeling in front of Senna he said, "Good night, and thank you for caring for my daughter." His hand began to reach forward, almost automatically, but he drew it back.

"It's a pleasure, John," Senna said, "she's no trouble."

John stood and approached Andrei. He heard Taiza saying to him, "Today's not what I had in mind when I said t' keep her out o' trouble."

"He's the wrong one to ask to stay out of trouble," said John with a smile.

Taiza grinned back. "Yes, I c'n see that, but I'm pretty sure Sen' c'n cope with Andrei's usual run o' trouble."

"No doubt," agreed John.

"Have you two finished talking about me?" asked Andrei.

"Sure – for now," both John and Taiza agreed.

Andrei accompanied John back to the street. John turned to face him and paused, trying to find the words. "Thanks is not exactly the right sentiment here, it's not big enough. But thank you, Andrei. I couldn't have made it without you."

Andrei looked back at him but seemed unable to find a suitable response. Finally he said with a smile, "What can I say, you make me laugh."

* * *

The next morning John woke to the sensation of a warm hand pushing the hair back from his face. He turned his head with a start.

"I'm sorry," said Asha softly, "I didn't mean to startle you. It was late and I thought I should check on you. ... I guess I just didn't want to wait any longer to see you again."

John looked at the clock and saw that it was after ten o'clock. "Are you okay?" he asked her.

"Not perfect yet, but much better than I was. It's amazing what a difference it makes just to be free."

He pushed himself up a bit straighter.

"You don't have to get up," she said.

"Actually I do," he said, a little embarrassed. "Um, I didn't bring pyjamas, you mind shutting your eyes for a minute or two."

Asha laughed. "If I must."

A few minutes later John returned with jeans on and his shirt buttoned roughly. He boiled the kettle to make himself a coffee. "How'd you get in?" he asked.

Asha pointed to the balcony door, "Andrei told me that door would probably be unlocked and then showed me the best way up the side of the building."

"Yeah, that's the sort of thing he'd notice," said John.

Asha was still sitting on the bed where she had been before, so John took his coffee back and sat on the bed with his back against the headrest. "It sure is good to not be rushing anywhere." He looked up from his coffee and smiled at Asha. "It's even better not panicking about where you are."

"I don't mean to be a worry to you, John."

"That's not something you have any control over." John pulled a face. "That didn't come out right, I sound like a stalker or something."

Asha laughed and then leant in and placed her head against his chest. John placed his coffee aside and put his arms around her, holding her warm presence there against him. He didn't want to spoil the moment but he also knew he needed to say what was on his mind.

"You know that I love you?" he said. He felt her nod against his chest. "Yes, I suppose it's pretty obvious by now – not even I can hide from it. Not that I want to, not now, but for a long time ... I

364

wasn't ready to even think about it. ... Can you understand that?"

"Yes," she said softly.

"But just because I love you ... that doesn't put any obligation on you. I came here to try and help you because I had to. It was partly my fault you were here." John stilled her when she started to object. "It doesn't matter. The important thing is that I did what I had to do, you don't owe me anything."

"John—" Asha started.

"Wait. Sorry, but I need to get this out. I'm human and you're not. It's an impossible situation but I don't really care. I'd do whatever it takes to spend my time with you – but that's all my problem, not yours. If you want to be free of the awkward situation of living next to a human that can see you then you only have to say. If that's what you want I can move into town so that you can have your trees and privacy back. You have friends of your own kind. Without me around making the situation awkward you might find time for Garjae or someone else."

"Garjae?" Asha said in surprise.

"He's in love with you too. He has been for years. ... You didn't know?" John felt her head shake against his chest. "He's not real thrilled with me, or rather, not thrilled with the fact that you seem to like me. And he's right, Asha. I'm not right for you."

"John!" Asha demanded.

"What?"

"Have you finished throwing yourself at walls yet?" she asked. He could hear the smile in her voice.

After a pause he replied, "Yeah, that's probably enough – for now."

"Good. It might help you to know that I love you too." She pushed herself back and looked into his eyes.

"Oh ... well ... that is good." He grinned at her.

"I thought so." She leaned up and kissed him briefly on the lips before continuing, "I think that I've probably loved you since the start. Like you, I haven't been ready to admit it, but it's real and it's been growing the more I get to know you. As for you being human and me being aaranya, I think we should just take that as it comes. If it doesn't work out we can make each other unhappy later, we don't have to start right now. Is that all right with you?"

365

"Sure." He might have said more but Asha leaned forward and covered his lips with hers. Sure, there'd be time to be unhappy later, there certainly wasn't time for it now.

The End of Book One

But the story continues ...

Visit: gmworboys.com to find out more.

Appendix

Glossary

Some of the words and phrases used in this story are my own invention, specifically for this story. Words such as *brevi, narun* and *spret*. Some words are normal English words with some particular emphasis or variation relevant to the story. Words such as *Glade* and *stand*. And many words have been borrowed or adapted from Sanskrit (an ancient language of India). Words such as *prana, preta, aaranya* and more. This glossary provides a reference to explain how these words are used in the story.

I started to use some Sanskrit words when I discovered that *prana* had meaning in Sanskrit very close to what I wanted, and it was a simple word that expressed the concept for which I had found no elegant expression in English. The Internet can be a wonderful place and soon I found the Spoken Sanskrit website that supplied even more beautifully expressive words. The words *aaranya* and *preta* soon found their way into my writing and established a tradition. But, *please*, any misuse or poor interpretation of these words as used here is probably due to my ignorance of languages in general and Sanskrit in particular. This glossary is provided to define the way these words are used in this story. Please *don't* try to use this story or this glossary as a way to learn Sanskrit. Consider the words to be part of a language with common roots to Sanskrit, rather than as Sanskrit itself.

The pronunciations offered here are simply how I hear these words in my head, if you hear them differently that's fine with me.

References used below include:
[s] = Spoken Sanskrit - spokensanskrit.de
[w] = Wikipedia - www.wikipedia.org
[d] = Dictionary.com - dictionary.reference.com

aaranya

[ah-run-ya] – noun, plural aaranya.

From the Sanskrit meaning forest-born[s]. It is the name used by the narun of the forest (the dryads or tree-folk) for their own people. Asha and Andrei are both aaranya.

acintya

[ack-int-yah] – noun / adjective.

From the Sanskrit adjective meaning unthinkable, incomprehensible or beyond thought[s]. Here it is the name used by the narun for the process of creating a *preta* – because the action is considered abhorrent by most narun.

brevi

[bre-vee] noun, plural brevis

A small *praanin* creature (made of *prana*). They have the size and general appearance quite similar to a small sugar glider (Petaurus breviceps[w]), hence the name, but their colouring varies. These creatures are praanin, like *spret,* but are of and from the Glade. They are more intense in their prana and they seem to glow when happy. Unlike spret, or narun, these creatures can merge with animals, with humans, and even with narun. Brevi are as close as the aaranya have to pets. They have a homing instinct and also have greater intelligence than a spret. They can be trained to a certain extent. They can repeat messages given to them to pass on – the message is repeated exactly as it was given by the sender (same voice and tone etc.).

dhumraka

[doom-rah-ka] – noun, plural dhumraka.

Adapted from the Sanskrit for grey (dhuumra[s]). This is the name used by the grey-narun for their own kind. At the time of this book the origin of the dhumraka is not understood by others. Minzi and Yudai are both dhumraka.

Glade

[Glay-d] proper noun, plural Glades

As described by Andrei: "The Glade is the heart of our stand," and "The Glade is our meeting place, a place where we can raise and protect our children, a place where our people come together to talk, sometimes to celebrate." Sometimes also called Aranyavaasa (Forest Residence in Sanskrit[s].) A Glade is a form of *zarana* that is specific to the aaranya.

jalaja

[Jah-lah-jah] noun, plural jalaja

From the Sanskrit meaning born (or living) in water[s]. It is the name used by the narun of freshwater systems (the naiads or river-folk) for their own people.

Jatarupa

[Jat-ah-oo-pa] noun, plural Jatarupa

From the Sanskrit meaning golden[s]. Is the name used by the leaders of the evil narun of ancient times, those that started the Aeonian War – sometimes called kalpaanta for the devastation it caused.

kalpaanta

[Kal-pahn-ta] noun

From the Sanskrit meaning end of the world[s].

nadi

[Nah-dee] noun, plural nadis

From Sanskrit. A channel (tube or pipe) along which vital energies (see prana) flow, connecting at special points of intensity called chakras. The literal meaning of nadi is 'flow'[w] so this word can be used for both the channel and the flow.

narun

[nah-run] – noun, plural narun.

Intelligent beings made of prana (vital energy, see below). We are human (made of flesh-and-blood), they are narun (made of prana). There are different variations (races) of narun, including: aaranya (tree-folk), samudraka (sea-folk), jalaja (lake-folk and river-folk), dhumraka (grey-narun) and yaayaavara (nomads).

prana

[prah-nuh] – noun, plural prana.

From Sanskrit[s][w]. The vital principle. The breath of life. According to ancient belief: prana suffuses all living forms but is not itself the soul or spirit; prana is what gives life to all things; in at least some contexts it is also considered the carrier of thought; the sun is a source of prana.

In this story prana is considered to be the carrier of the true-self and the spirit. Prana suffuses all living things, and this includes the soil and each tree and water system as individual living presences.

In animals, including humans, the prana is more dense than that of trees or rivers etc. The additional density makes it possible for the true-self (and spirit) to pull free of the material body and exist outside it – as a fragile, energy-like entity. The process of forcing this to happen through violence is called *acintya* and such violent expulsion produces *preta*.

Narun, spret, brevi and even preta are all praanin (see below), beings made entirely of prana, beings that have no material body.

There are certain traits peculiar to prana: an attraction and an ability to detect and affect nearby prana. The narun generally explain these traits as simply "life calls to life".

Another trait of prana is its special affinity with water. Asha describes and demonstrates this in the early part of this first book.

This is mostly seen as just another aspect of the close association between life and water.

praanin

[prah-nin] – noun, plural praanin.

Any living creature that consists only of prana: narun, spret, brevi, preta and others. Strictly speaking the Sanskrit definition is just *living creature*[s], but in this story the word describes only living creatures that are made only of prana – those that have no material body.

The prana of praanin (in this story) is sufficiently dense that they can interact well with the material world, the prana-skin acts as a sort of energy force-field. Such creatures, mostly, remain more fragile than their material counterparts but not (necessarily) exceptionally so.

Lack of material existence can make some material interactions difficult. If an object contains life, or once contained life, then the prana or nadis of the object can provide the equivalent of friction and allow fairly normal interactions. If an object was manufactured and carries no life, nor any nadis, then it will feel strange and often very slippery to a praanin.

preta

[preh-tuh] – noun, plural preta.

From the Sanskrit meaning dead, ghost[s] and Hindu mythology for a disturbed ghost[d], often referred to as a hungry ghost[w]. In this story it is defined as "hungry ghost" and used to describe the praanin bodies that were violently pushed from living animals or humans. They look like insubstantial narun and generally don't live very long. (See also *acintya*, *prana*, and *praanin*.)

When first pushed from the material body the preta closely resembles the body that it came from. Usually: if it lives very long (most don't) then the pain, psychological torment and the inability to feed properly all interact to distort the body and it gradually shrinks and fades until the being eventually dies.

samudraka

[sam-oo-drah-ka] noun, plural samudraka

Meaning "of the ocean". (Adapted from the Sanskrit word samudra for ocean or sea[s], I added "ka" to distinguish it with my own meaning for this book.) It is the name used by the narun of the oceans (the nereid or sea-folk) for their own people.

spret

[spret] noun, plural spret

A creature made of prana (see above). Similar in the nature of their existence to narun, but not intelligent. These are effectively the animal version of the narun. Spret is the word used by aaranya, other narun have their own words they use for such creatures in their own environment.

stand

[stand] noun, plural stands

A community of aaranya (tree-folk). (Sometimes also *tarusanda*.)

tarusanda

[tar-oo-san-dah] noun, plural tarusanda

From the Sanskrit for grove, group of trees[s]. A community of aaranya (dryads, tree-folk). (Sometimes also *stand*.)

tiirtha

[ter-tha] noun

From the Sanskrit for sacred place, way, passage, ford, road[s]. This is the door/pathway into a *zarana*: like the *Way* into a *Glade* but describes an entry into a zarana as used by the jalaja and samudraka.

vanadevatas

[vah-nah-dev-ah-tas] noun

Adapted from the Sanskrit "vanadevataa" for silvan deity, wood-nymph[s]. This word is interpreted in the story as meaning forest-gods. This word is used by Waldron Stephenson for the name of his company that manages many forestry related enterprises.

vedana

[veh-dah-na] noun

From the Sanskrit meaning: Perception – also proclaiming, announcing, knowledge[s], traditionally related to "feeling" or "sensation"[w]. This word is used by the narun in this story to describe their life-sense, their ability to feel life (prana) around them, sometimes at great distances. "Life calls to life."

Way

[whey] noun

The gate-way into a *Glade*. This is the aaranya equivalent to the more general word: *tiirtha*.

yaayaavara

[yah-yah-vah-ra] noun, plural yaayaavara

From the Sanskrit meaning nomad[s]. Is the name used by the (land-based) nomadic narun, for their kind.

zarana

[zah-rah-na] noun, plural zarana

From the Sanskrit meaning help, protection, house, dwelling, refuge, shelter, succour[s]. It is the name used by the samudraka for the place of sanctuary that forms in their communities. The aaranya use the word *Glade* for their zarana but it is the same thing, albeit with attributes better suited to the forest than the ocean.

A zarana is a place where life has grown to such strength and power that it extends into its own dimension creating a separate "place" that only praanin, not material beings, may enter.